F
EAS

43,061

W9-AHT-266

DATE			

THE LAST ASSASSIN

THE LAST ASSASSIN

~~~~~~

Daniel Easterman

DOUBLEDAY & COMPANY, INC.
GARDEN CITY, NEW YORK 1985

This is for Beth, whose love
has made so many things possible

Library of Congress Cataloging in Publication Data
Easterman, Daniel.
    The last assassin.
    I. Title.
PS3555.A697L37   1985   813'.54
ISBN 0-385-19794-2
Library of Congress Catalog Card Number 84-18711
Copyright © 1984 by Daniel Easterman
ALL RIGHTS RESERVED
PRINTED IN THE UNITED STATES OF AMERICA
FIRST EDITION IN THE UNITED STATES OF AMERICA

ACKNOWLEDGMENTS

Numerous people have helped improve *The Last Assassin* with their comments, suggestions, and reactions, but there are two individuals without whose help it would never have taken its final shape at all. The first is Jeffrey Simmons, who saw the potential of the original draft and nursemaided it (and me) through its many stages of growth. The other is my wife, Beth, who contributed some of the best ideas and reread every draft often enough to learn it by heart. In return, I can only offer her the love she has always deserved.

D.E.

LIST OF PRINCIPAL CHARACTERS

Tehran
Peter Randall
Masood Heshmat
Husayn Nava'i
Molla Ahmad Rafsanjani
Howard Straker
Brandon F. Stewart
Fujiko Lundkvist
Prof. Iraj Ashrafi
Prof. Jaafar Mo'ini
Nurullah Baqirzadeh
Hajj Reza Turk
Molla Hasan Tabataba'i
Vida Kayvanpur
Rustam Kayvanpur
Sirus Rastgu
Ibrahim Masoodi
Ayatollah Sayyid 'Ali
  Marvdashti
Dr. Felix Rascher
Sohrab Qasemlu

Dhat 'Irq
Muhammad ibn 'Abd Allah al-
  Qahtani

Mecca
Muhammad ibn 'Abd Allah al-
  Qahtani
Juhaiman ibn Saif al-Otaybi

Medina
Muhammad ibn 'Abd Allah al-
  Qahtani
Husayn Nava'i

Washington
Peter Randall
Fatimeh Natsir
Husayn Nava'i
Howard Straker
President James Carter
Arthur Pike

New York City
Husayn Nava'i
Mohammad Ahmadi
Peter Randall
Fereshteh Ahmadi
Nushin Navabpur
Russell Fernwell
Dr. 'Abd al-Latif al-Shidyaq

*Thousand Islands, Lake
  Ontario*
Peter Randall
Fereshteh Ahmadi
Juliusz Rostoworoski
Howard Straker

Kerman
Peter Randall
Sirus Rastgu
Khalil Sohbat
Yitzak Aharoni
Imam Hasan al-Qa'im bi-amr
  Allah

He who arises shall have two occultations. In one of them, he shall be present at the pilgrimage rites. He shall see men, but they shall not see him.

Imam Ja'far al-Sadiq
(Kulayni *Al-usul min al-Kafi* 2:175)

ONE

GHAYBA

PHASE ONE

PROLOGUE

Like a hammer on a red-hot anvil, the noon sun beat down on the bleak expanse of desert sand. Nothing stirred. The air shimmered as waves of heat reflected from baked rock and sand, turning the parched and arid wasteland into a vibrating mirage of living waters. To breathe was a torment, to walk a torture fit for the damned. At the bottom of a dried wadi, a man lay dying of thirst and heatstroke. Two miles to the east, his camel, the soft pads of its feet flayed and scarred by sharp rocks, was already dead. Here, in the deep heart of the Rub' al-Khali, the Empty Quarter of the vast Arabian Peninsula, only the foolhardy or the desperate ever ventured. Few ever walked out alive.

The dying man was an Otaybi Arab, from the west of the peninsula. He had been traveling through the eastern region of Saudi Arabia with a companion from the Iranian Gulf region of Makran, moving among the Bedouin tribes of the Rawashid and Awamir, talking with their leaders and their young men. Two months earlier, the two men had met by arrangement at Kalba, on the eastern coast of the United Arab Emirates. The Iranian had sailed across by night in a small dhow from Jask, avoiding patrol boats from Muscat policing the waters of the Gulf of Oman. Crossing the northern tip of the western Hajar mountains, they had traveled south along the Muscat frontier, slipping two weeks later across the vaguely defined border country between the Emirates and Saudi Arabia.

Once there, they had gone, dressed as Bedouin, around the wells, oases, and temporary camp sites of the desert tribes. It was the summer of 1977, and the efforts of the central government to settle many of the tribespeople had caused considerable disruption in the traditional way of life. But here, on the edges of the kingdom, the harsh realities of the desert preserved and sustained the inborn resistance of the Bedouin to change, and kept alive the spirit of independence and self-reliance that was their greatest inheritance. Like Lawrence, the two men traveled among the shifting population of the sands, preaching, converting. They planned to head across the northern edge of the Rub' al-Khali by slow stages into the heart of the country, through the neck between the Nafud Qunaifida and Nafud ad Dahi deserts, then down through southern Najd to Mecca, in time for the pilgrimage season.

They had been arrested six weeks later, in the small desert settlement of Abu Faris. A local religious leader had complained about their activities and police had been sent from Jabrin Oasis, three hundred kilometers to the northwest. A brief trial had been held in the house of the town's religious judge, the cadi, and on the morning following, they had been taken out to the dusty square.

All the people of the settlement had been there, including women and children. In the center of the square, a black Sudanese policeman was standing, stripped to the waist, his ebony skin glistening in the bright sun. In his hand he held a long, curved sword, a beautiful weapon of Damascus steel that had been in the family of the Shaykh of Abu Faris for generations. It had been lent for the occasion. The two men, hands tied firmly behind their backs, had been led out into the center of the square. The Iranian was made to kneel in the dust at the policeman's feet. Qur'an in hand, the cadi came forward, proclaimed the sentence of death, read from the sacred book, and retired. The executioner, a black shadow against the sun, spread his feet for balance, then with both hands swung the shining blade horizontally behind his back. With a practiced motion, he snapped the sword forward with just the right momentum, cutting cleanly through the upright neck. The head, its eyes still staring, leapt forward and fell face downward onto the dust, showering it with blood. Then the body toppled and fell lifeless, pouring a stream of hot blood over the warm sand, arms and legs twitching in the convulsions of death.

Two policemen took the Arab by the arms and brought him forward to the spot where his friend's body lay, already drawing flies. Even now as he lay in the wadi, he could remember the sight of blood, the stench, the cold, sick feeling in his stomach. The cadi pronounced sentence, read a verse of the Qur'an, and stepped back. The huge Negro stood over him, his shadow falling on him like the wings of Izra'il, the black angel of death. The sword swung back, then came forward with a jerk, stopping short mere centimeters from his neck. He fainted and recovered later to find himself tied astride a camel, headed into the center of the Rub' al-Khali. A guide, sent to ensure that he was taken a satisfactory distance into the desert, explained that the police, small in numbers and isolated, had been uneasy about executing a Bedouin Arab out here in the desert, where the shedding of his blood might cause resentment. Tribal politics were a tricky business and the police left well alone. Instead, they had decided on a token execution and a slow but no less certain death in the sands of the Empty Quarter.

Now, as he lay helpless in the hollow of the wadi, he was delirious with visions of blood and steel. He raved, the single word *al-qiyama* ever on his lips. In Arabic, it meant "resurrection." But what resurrection could he crave now as he lay hours from death in a wasteland where even the vultures never came? The sun slipped in a haze toward the western horizon. As it touched the rim of the desert, he watched it sink, his mind lucid again before the onset of death. A prayer escaped his lips as he followed the path of the dying sun where it fell toward Mecca, far in the west, beyond the numberless sands that stretched across the center of the great peninsula. There, in Mecca, dwelt his resurrection.

Falling unconscious, his hold on life slipping, he did not see the shadow of riders, tall and black as their camels, as they stood at the edge of the wadi, gazing down on him.

TEHRAN
Saturday, 15 October 1977

It was cold. A small group of men, all dressed against the October weather, all wearing black, stood about in the empty street, stamping their feet, blowing on their hands, glancing now and then to left and right. They were waiting for something or someone. It was already midafternoon, and the pale sun would set in half an hour. No one spoke. The street ran in an absolutely straight north-south line through the northern Tehran suburb of Vanak, three blocks from the glass and concrete palace of the Arya-Sheraton Hotel. Beyond, the sprawl of buildings fell away to the underdeveloped northwest of the city, revealing the flanks of the Elburz foothills, covered in ice and snow. There, far from the howling city, all was quiet, all was a shimmer of frost and mountain mist.

The mountains and a distance of barely sixty miles separated the capital from the shores of the Caspian Sea, the Darya-ye Mazandaran. By boat, a few miles farther into that vast expanse of water would bring the traveler across an invisible yet singular barrier, the incessantly patrolled border between Iran and the Soviet Union. To the far northwest lay Russian Azerbaijan, to the northeast, Turkmenistan, with all of Central Asia beyond. Bukhara, Samarkand, Tashkent: names from a golden past of blue domes and slender minarets, of lovely miniatures and even lovelier poetry; today the possessions of a limitless, brooding empire that lay with suffocating weight across the entire northern border of Iran and beyond. Tehran looked north across the most uneasy frontier in the world, the soft underbelly of the Russian giant, a sleeping giant who dreamed always of the warm waters of the south, the oil-rich shores of the Persian Gulf.

A black Mercedes, its dark-tinted windows catching the rays of the sinking sun, entered the street from the direction of the Yusefabad district and glided to a halt beside the waiting group. The door opened and two men stepped out, dressed, like the others, in black. As they left the car, the men on the pavement did not stand to attention or salute, but their bearing changed completely. The first of the car's occupants was Masood Heshmat, special operations chief of Internal Security and Action, the most important of the nine branches of SAVAK, the Sazman-e Etela'at va Amniyat-e Keshvar, Iran's dreaded National Information and Security Organization. Heshmat was directly responsible to SAVAK's deputy director, the head of ISA, Parviz Sabeti, with whom he worked at the organization's headquarters in the notorious Comite building in central Tehran.

A restless man of between thirty-five and forty, Heshmat had a well-deserved reputation for ruthlessness in the interrogation of political suspects. There were two types of pretrial interrogation for such prisoners under the Shah. The first and the more brutal, known as *bazju'i*, was carried out by SAVAK in order to extract the maximum of information before the suspect was handed over to military tribunal officials for further questioning prior to his trial. Masood Heshmat was an expert in extracting information. Behind the walls of the Comite or Evin prisons, his name had come to symbolize pain beyond imagining—and death in a deserted courtyard at midnight.

His companion was an American called Peter Randall, a CIA field agent who had first arrived in Tehran seven years earlier. As he stepped out of the car after Heshmat, Randall shivered momentarily and glanced briefly to the north, at the white specter of Mount Damavand rising through mist into a darkening sky. One day, he knew, fleets of helicopters would rise murmuring over that peak and MiG fighters would thunder down from the steppes of Central Asia. It was a nightmare that haunted him even in daylight. For seven years now, he had lived with Russia as a next-door neighbor, traveling frequently to the border, where he could see it, smell it, all but touch it, a living presence that none of his superiors in Washington could ever hope to understand with such immediacy. He had learned to cope with that presence, to put it in the back of his mind where it could not interfere with his efficiency or freeze his actions. But he could not forget it. It was, after all, why he was here in the first place.

Heshmat waited for Randall to join him on the pavement before turning to the man in charge of the group, all of whom were SAVAK professionals trained in the techniques of urban counterinsurgency.

He knew each of them personally; they had worked together on numerous occasions and he could rely on them.

"Is everything ready?" he asked.

"Yes, sir. Are there any fresh instructions?"

"No; we go in as planned."

Heshmat turned and looked at Randall. His quick, furtive eyes seemed to scrape across the American.

Beside him, Randall seemed tall and lean, his gaunt, lined features a sharp contrast to Heshmat's puffy face and soft, pampered body. Randall's face was thin, almost ascetic, and his light blue eyes held secrets in the gray shadows at their edges. Heshmat had seen eyes like those before, in the faces of men, religious subversives he had interrogated night after night in cold, silent cells. He could never remember the names, only the eyes. They were the eyes of a man who would not part with his secrets even under the severest torture. It seemed wrong, even obscene to Heshmat that an intelligence agent should have such eyes.

He knew the American hated him, despised him for what he was, and for what he did. Randall had once accompanied him to Evin to assist in the interrogation of a Marxist accused of printing anti-American pamphlets, a twenty-year-old girl student from Pahlavi University in Shiraz. The American had never gone there with him again. Randall was good. At thirty-five, some said he was the best American agent in Iran. But he did what he had to do because he saw it as his duty, not because he liked it. There lay the difference between the two men. Heshmat found pleasure, absolute pleasure in his job, and he carried out his tasks in such a way as to obtain the optimum personal satisfaction from them. Randall, on the other hand, would never kill unless absolutely necessary, and even then never in cold blood. Calmly, efficiently, yes, and often, without anger, but not without a certain passion, a sense of pain. He owed that much to someone whose life he was about to take. He avoided the gun as much as possible, and he rejected torture as a method of extracting information. For those, like Heshmat, who carried out such tasks with pleasure, Randall felt only loathing. Heshmat in his turn despised Randall, but he admired his professional skill and he valued him because, in a world made up of deceit and counterdeceit, he thought he could trust him, and he knew that, if need arose, he could betray him.

"Peter," Heshmat asked, "are there any instructions you want to give before we leave?"

Randall looked at him, then shook his head. Heshmat nodded and spoke quietly into a radio set he carried in his hand. A second Mercedes, identical to the first and, like it, carrying no registration plates, glided out of a side street and rolled toward them. The group split, six men climbing into the second car, four joining Heshmat and Randall in the lead vehicle. At a signal from Heshmat, their driver started the engine and they moved off into gathering darkness. The two cars headed north briefly, then turned east toward the line of three main arteries that connect the wealthy northern suburbs of Tehran with the deep, troubled heart of the city center. Using side roads, they moved together rapidly through the Ka'usiyye and Da'udiyye developments into Korush-e Kabir, entering the road just south of Qolhak. Here, they turned north again for about a mile before bearing right down Yakhchal, a country lane that was fast becoming part of the concrete maze of the sprawling city. They passed the German church on their right and the Qolhak German School on their left, outposts of a colonial enterprise that had never got off the ground. Following the bend of the road where it became Amir Hekmat, the cars drew in to the side, their tires crunching the frosted gravel as they slowed and came to a halt.

No one had spoken throughout the short journey. Each man had sat locked in his own world, the coming operation uppermost in every mind. The American had not wanted to come. He was sick of Heshmat and his methods, sick of the sweat-drenched silences that came when he leaned back, his questioning done. But the Iranian had insisted that Randall's presence was necessary on this operation.

He had called early that morning at the American's apartment in Kakh Street, tense and excited, his face unusually drawn and nervous, his eyes gleaming with thoughts that Randall had no wish to penetrate. He hadn't invited him in, hadn't wanted him there at all, but Heshmat had come in anyway and sat down without being asked.

"Peter," he had begun, his familiarity deliberate, intended to grate on the American. Since coming to Iran, Randall had lost his habit of instant first names, and with people like Heshmat he preferred to keep things strictly professional and impersonal; Heshmat knew it, but he went on as he had begun. "Peter, I think we have a lead on the Ibex murders, maybe the Air Force killings of two years ago as well.

It's all come to light in the course of investigations into the attempt on Ashraf in September."

The American nodded, interested in spite of his dislike for Heshmat. He was referring to the shootings in May 1975 of two U.S. Air Force colonels and in August 1976 of three American civilians who had been working on the installation of the secret Ibex electronic intelligence system in Iran. Ibex had been sold to the Shah for over five hundred million dollars by the Rockwell Corporation, in theory to provide border security. But the process of installation had begun to reveal serious problems in the system, and before long, the Shah had started complaining about Pentagon double-dealing. Richard Helms, the U.S. ambassador, washed his hands of the project, so the CIA, which had already been involved in the original deal, found itself trying to sort out the mess. Randall still had unpleasant memories of the string of events that had followed the August 1976 murders. Over a year later, pressure from Washington to find those responsible was still heavy.

"I don't see the connection," he said, still standing, his position an emphasis of his guest's rudeness.

On 13 September that year, gunmen had tried to shoot the Shah's sister, Princess Ashraf, as she was traveling through Juan-les-Pins in the south of France, en route to her villa at Port Gallice. They had killed a woman friend in the car with her and wounded another man, but her driver had rammed their vehicle and enabled the Princess to make an escape.

"We think the same group may have been responsible for all three attacks," replied Heshmat. "Yesterday we received a report about a house in Qolhak that's being used by a small group of men in their late twenties. None of them mix well with their neighbors, they come and go at strange hours, and all the signs are that it's a terrorist cell. The man who gave us the report says he heard two of them talking one day in French."

"Your man knows French?"

"A little. Enough. He followed them to a café where they met a third man. He spoke Persian with them. They talked about America, about Washington—the third man had just come from there. Afterward, this man left and the other two started talking in French again. One asked the other what he thought of Americans; he just said,

'They die badly,' nothing more, just that. Then they talked about other matters, nothing important."

"But they could have been referring to anything. Plenty of Americans have been killed here. Why single out the killings you mention?"

"Conjecture, nothing more. If they made an attempt on Ashraf, they must be Feda'iyan-e Khalq, and I already think the Feda'iyan were responsible for the other murders."

"So why don't you come again when you've got proof of that? I'm sure you'll find a way of obtaining your evidence. Just don't ask me to help, that's all."

"I want you to come with me tonight. We're raiding the house."

"That's a police job."

"Of course. And you know how it will end if I leave it to them."

Randall knew. Police policy was to surround a terrorist hideout, open fire, and shoot it out with those inside. Nine times out of ten, there were no survivors.

"Why bring me in at this stage? Until you get a confession that they actually were involved in the killing of Americans, this remains a purely internal matter. Come again when you've got your evidence."

Randall was being deliberately obtuse. The CIA had been deeply involved with Iranian intelligence since the late 1940s and had been directly concerned, together with the FBI, in setting up SAVAK under Teymour Bakhtiar in 1957, after which they had provided a permanent U.S. intelligence mission in Iran. Involvement in so-called "internal matters" was standard procedure.

"I'm being polite." The sarcasm in Heshmat's tone was not lost on Randall. "American deaths have been mentioned already. They're in the report. I want you to be there, in case something goes wrong, in case mistakes are made. I want you to know I tried to take them alive. You have to be there."

Randall watched his face, saw the excitement, the craving for action bottled up within him, ready to burst forth. He knew it would be released in the fury of the coming raid, to be replaced by a cold, unfeeling calm in the torture rooms of the Comite. But there was more. The American knew from long and bitter experience the complexities of Iran's military-security web, the labyrinth of machinations and countermachinations that reflected and intensified the Machiavellian tangles of Iranian life in general. He knew how everyone involved in security and intelligence watched everyone else, how

SAVAK and Military Intelligence, the Rokn-e Do, were in constant conflict, how officials of the Special Bureau, the Daftar-e Vizhe, kept an eye on SAVAK, and how, at the center of the web, the Shah sat like a spider waiting for prey.

The director of SAVAK, General Nematollah Nasiri, was a former military governor of Tehran who had been official security chief since 1965. The organization's ISA had been headed until 1972 by another general, Naser Moqaddem, now head of Rokn-e Do. Randall knew that Heshmat had been a long-time favorite of Moqaddem and suspected that he wanted him to become head of SAVAK. He also knew that, within the intricacies of this weblike power struggle, he himself was being used as a lever within the all-powerful CIA organization in Tehran.

The door of the Mercedes opened and Heshmat stepped out onto the pavement. Far out in the blackness, a dog began to howl; the packs of stray dogs that prowled by night on the fringes of human habitation were moving once again. In spite of himself, Randall shivered.

2

TEHRAN
Saturday, 15 October 1977

Heshmat walked to the back of the car in which he had come, opened it, and unloaded arms and ammunition, which he proceeded to distribute to his small force. Randall refused the gun that he tried to press into his hands, indicating that he preferred to use his own Browning magnum if it proved necessary for him to open fire at all. He hoped he would not have to—operations like this, he knew, were always messy.

At a signal from Heshmat, the group split into four, each unit heading for a different side road that would bring it to the house independently of the other units. It was already dark, and the black-clad figures moved unseen and unheard toward their destination. No one was about in the streets. They were deserted and silent, like a stage before the play begins. In that strange way no outsider could understand, word had got about that something was about to happen. The silence was immense, consecrated to terror and the night. Wise residents kept behind locked doors. This sort of operation was common enough to be accepted as part of life in Tehran. There would be shooting, perhaps even explosions, during the night, but by morning all traces of the incident would have been removed: doors replaced, windows reglazed, bodies hauled off for burial, blood washed from the walls, and shells and bullets collected from where they had fallen in the streets. Death itself would be unmade. The residents would know what had happened, rumors would spread; but that was all to the good, it encouraged passivity and magnified fear. And there would be no evidence for the foreign press and human rights campaigners, no shrine to serve as a focus for internal critics.

Within five minutes, they were in position. Heshmat whispered instructions into his radio. A man slipped out of the shadows beside him, one of half a dozen he had posted earlier to keep the house and its occupants under surveillance. He told Heshmat that they thought there were six or seven men inside, that no one else had entered or left the house all day, and that they seemed to be unaware that they were being watched. There had been no attempt to make a break. The operations chief nodded and picked up a small megaphone he had brought with him from the car.

"Listen," the thin voice echoed through the darkness. "We know you are in the house. We know you are armed. You are surrounded and outnumbered. Put down your weapons and come to the gate, one at a time. Your lives will be spared. If you do not obey these instructions, we will be forced to shoot."

The echoes faded and a deathlike silence fell on the street. Even the dogs were quiet. In the many years he had come on raids like this, Heshmat had never known the suspects to surrender. All of them knew what to expect in the bare concrete corridors beneath Evin, knew there were simpler paths to the same ultimate destination. The silence would stretch for a minute, two minutes, perhaps three, but in the end it would be broken by the first round of gunfire as desperate men attempted the impossible.

The house was barely visible in the dark, its silhouette merging with the opaque mass of the sky. It was a small, two-story building, flat-roofed, surrounded by a small, unkempt garden and a high wall with a single metal gate—an ordinary north Tehran house. There had been lights in a front room on the upper floor, but these were extinguished as soon as Heshmat began to speak. All was darkness and an eerie silence that stretched and stretched. One minute. Two minutes. Three minutes. What were they waiting for?

Heshmat raised the megaphone and spoke again.

"If you do not surrender yourselves to me within one minute, I will give orders to open fire. Your deaths will be unnecessary. Give yourselves up."

Again the darkness swallowed the echoes and silence enveloped the street once more. Thirty seconds passed and there was no response. Heshmat whispered into his radio, telling his units to stand by to fire. Forty seconds. Nothing moved in the house or garden. Fifty seconds. A dog barked in the distance, its howls terrifying in the tense stillness. Sixty seconds. Heshmat lifted the radio to give the order. Without warning, sudden, sharp, and tremendous, a single shot rang out from the roof of the house. The man standing beside Heshmat erupted backward into the wall behind, his skull shattered by the bullet. The body crashed and slumped to the ground, jerked once, and was still. Heshmat threw himself to the ground, followed by the rest of the group near him. His hand went to the side of his head; it came away sticky and wet, but he knew it was not his own blood that trickled down his cheeks.

Silence descended once more. The dog stopped barking. Heshmat's radio buzzed with the confused staccato whispers of his unit leaders, each trying to understand what was happening. He spoke quickly, his voice still low.

"There's someone on the roof, a sniper. Can you spot him? He's not visible from this side."

There was a pause, then one of the voices answered.

"Yes, I see him."

"Then stop him."

The radio fell silent. Within seconds, a second shot rang out, again from the roof. Heshmat spoke urgently into his handset.

"Firuz. What happened? Can you still see him?"

No answer.

"Firuz," repeated Heshmat, an edge of panic creeping into his voice, "can you see him?"

The handset crackled, then another voice sounded.

"This is Ahmad. He got Firuz. Right through the head. I can't see him. He's . . ."

Another shot exploded into the silence.

"Ahmad, are you all right?" shouted Heshmat.

"Yes, I'm all right. He didn't shoot in this direction."

Another voice broke in.

"He shot Hushang."

Heshmat hesitated, caught in a situation he had never even anticipated. Suddenly, someone was beside him and a hand was reaching for his radio. It was Randall. The American snatched the handset and shouted into it.

"Pull back, for God's sake. He's picking you off. The bastard's got a night sight. Take cover." He turned to Heshmat and rammed the handset back into his shaking hand. "Come on, Heshmat, let's move." They ran, half crouching, to shelter behind a car parked ten yards away.

"What the fuck were you doing?" Randall yelled as soon as they had hunkered down behind the vehicle. "I thought your boys were professionals, I thought they were handpicked. That guy's just taken out three of them as if he was plucking fruit."

"This never happened before."

"It's happening now. Have you got your spotlight?"

"It's with Mehdi."

"Where the hell's he?"

Heshmat called. The man with the spotlight was nearby, behind another car. Randall called him over and he came, a short run through the darkness.

"Here"—the American turned to Heshmat—"give me your rifle. Mehdi, you shine the light on the roof when I say go. Sweep it across, then hold it if you catch him."

Randall crouched at the back end of the car, aiming the rifle in the general direction of the roof. It was not the first time he had been under sniper fire at night. He had been with the 26th Marines at Khe Sanh all through the winter of 1968. Many nights he had lain out on the sandbags to watch the C-47 flareships trying to take out NVA positions with their Mike-Mike guns, their red tracers filling the air; and in the silences between, enemy snipers had returned to shoot and shoot and shoot into the quiet, beleaguered base. Lying here waiting for the next move, unwanted memories of that winter eleven years before came into his mind, and he almost expected to see a C-47 rise above him in the darkness. He steadied the rifle, placed his eye to the sight, and shouted "go!"

A bright beam of white light shot out, wavered momentarily, then found the roof and quickly played over it. There was nothing, no one. Without warning, a shot came from a first-floor window: the searchlight exploded in fragments of flying glass and spun out of the man's hands onto the road, where it rang out briefly like an alarm bell. Its echoes were gathered into the night and hushed.

"Jesus," shouted Randall. "Whoever he is, that guy means business. Get your men into the wall, where he can't target them. Then move in. And do it quickly before the rest of them start firing."

Heshmat hesitated briefly, unwilling at first to take orders from the American. But he knew he had no choice. Randall had had combat experience, he had developed instincts for acting under fire. The Iranian gave the instructions. His men ran in quickly, weaving toward the wall on all four sides of the house. At every moment, they expected another shot, another fatality, but all was silent except for their breathing and the sound in each man's ears of his own heartbeat. On a second order, they lobbed grenades over the wall. Four small explosions rocked the ground floor of the house. Under cover of these, they moved over the wall and began to open fire with submachine guns toward the upper floor. Glass shattered as bullets crashed into the upstairs rooms. Leaving two men to provide covering fire, the remaining agents rushed the house.

Heshmat riddled the front door with bullets before kicking it open, then fired again into the room ahead. They waited until the unit that had entered by the back door made contact, then joined them at the foot of the stairs. The ground floor was clean. The terrorists must all be on the next floor, waiting for them, determined to finish it all in a single moment of violence. Heshmat gave orders to put on masks, then lobbed a tear gas cylinder up to the first landing. They waited for the gas to take effect, but a minute passed without movement. Whoever was up there was going to stay put.

One of the squad fired a short burst up the staircase, then rushed to the landing. He opened fire again, then stopped. The others lined themselves up along the stairs. All were badly unnerved by the deep silence that followed every burst of gunfire, every rush of activity. Randall remembered the silences of Khe Sanh, timeless gulfs that were followed by the howling of death. Ahead of them, at the top of the last short flight of stairs, were three doors. If their opponents did not come out, they would have to go in. At the end of the short landing, another flight of about ten steps led onto the roof. The terrorists might be there by now. Heshmat spoke to the men at the wall outside.

"Rashid, Mahmud! Can you see anyone on the roof?"

Both answered in the negative.

Heshmat, now at the head of the stairs, turned to the men below him.

"That's settled. We go in. Ahmad, Ali, you two take the room on the left, Reza and Jaafar on the right. Randall, come with me and Sadiq; we'll rush the middle room. Check your ammunition. Now, move into position."

The men filed up the stairs onto the landing, ready to move, fingers on triggers, millimeters from firing. At a single word from Heshmat, they opened fire simultaneously, pumping lead into walls and doors, then rushed forward.

Randall and Heshmat crashed through the middle door, lifting their weapons. What they saw stopped them in their tracks: against the back wall the bodies of seven men leaned crazily like bloody dolls, their cut throats like grinning mouths, their eyes staring and lifeless. Blood still flowed from the wounds; a long knife, sticky with the red liquid, lay at the feet of one man, and beside it was a rifle equipped with an image intensifier—he must have been the sniper. After making his token resistance, he must have come down and told the others it was pointless their trying to escape. There were no weapons in evidence, except for the knife and the rifle. Rather than be taken alive, they must have squatted by the wall and allowed the sniper to slit their throats before he took his turn to sit beside them and finish himself off in the same manner.

Randall, inured to scenes of violence though he was, turned away, profoundly shaken by the sight, by the gratuitousness and the excess of it. It was not the blood or the disarray or the obscenely lolling heads that sickened Randall—he had seen as much and far worse in his years as an agent of an organization that dealt daily in violent and pitiless death. What disturbed him, what he knew straight away he would never be able to expunge from his memory however long he lived, were the faces. Seven faces, all wide-eyed, all frozen in death, in the same death, all suffused with the same look of fanatical dedication, almost of exultation, a look that seemed to mock the stillness and pallor of the death that had fallen on them.

Turning away, Randall saw Ahmad and Ali come in from the room to the left. They had found nothing; the room was empty. They looked in horror at what Heshmat and the others had found; Heshmat alone seemed unmoved by the room's ghastly carnage. Then Reza, one of the two men who had stormed the other room, appeared in the doorway. He too stopped dead when he caught sight of the row of bodies. Heshmat turned to him, questioning.

"Sir," he said, "you'd better come in here."

They all followed Heshmat into the room on the right. What they saw there could not equal in horror the scene in the first room, but it highlighted it in a dark and cruel way. The room was a small arsenal. Rifles, submachine guns, pistols, boxes of ammunition, explosives, crates of grenades, enough for fifty or a hundred men, were stacked along three walls. The men in the next room had not been unarmed. Randall's head spun. Why hadn't they fought back, beyond the brief moments of sniping? What had made death by the knife at the hands of one of their companions preferable to death in combat with the enemy, to the chance of inflicting even a small injury on the giant against whom they fought? Or was it simply wounding and capture that they had sought to evade?

They went downstairs. Here another surprise awaited them. In the kitchen, the charcoal stove was still alight, its door swinging open. Inside, they could make out the black remains of books and papers hastily stuffed inside and burned with the help of paraffin. That was the reason for the sniping, to buy time for these papers to be destroyed. As he turned to leave the kitchen, Randall caught sight of Heshmat bending down to pick up something that had fallen under the table. It was a sheet of blue paper, already folded three or four times. The Iranian opened it, glanced at it, frowned, then closed it again and placed it in his pocket. He saw Randall watching him and turned.

"Peter, I'm afraid you'll have to stay on. We'll need you to confirm what happened here. I hope you understand."

Randall did. That was why he had been brought out on this mission. Heshmat had taken independent action, without orders from above, in the hope that he could use the information from interrogating this group for his own purposes and possibly those of Moqaddem. He had wanted Randall along in case anything went wrong. Heshmat could use pretended CIA interests to cover his tracks. Randall could, of course, try to walk out, but he knew he would not even reach the door. The sniper could, after all, have fired four shots before killing himself: four shots and four fatalities. Randall stayed. Something told him not to ask what had been on the paper Heshmat had pocketed.

3

TEHRAN
Friday, 21 October 1977

A group of eight women, all wearing black chadors, the long head-to-foot veil of Islamic Iran, moved with difficulty through the jostling crowds of Buzarjomehri Street, Tehran's busy southern thoroughfare that runs across the northern end of the bazaar district. The streets here are narrow and crowded, the houses old and dingy. This had been the northern fringe of old Tehran, generations ago now, before the city had begun to stretch away from it farther and farther toward the north, spinning its great web of gleaming modern roads filled with shining cars, white concrete buildings faced with green and pink marble, leaving stranded and wasted the fast-decaying congestion of the south. In summer, the very lungs of the old city were burned and scorched by the airless heat that grew there, trapped and magnified. Into these regions, where faith and poverty were crushed together, the tentacles of SAVAK penetrated hardly at all.

It was early morning, but the streets were already filled with people: the women in long black and flower-printed chadors that enveloped them like shrouds from head to foot, concealing the shabbiness of their house garments beneath the veil of drab uniformity; the men in cheap versions of western clothes—jackets, waistcoats, collarless shirts —most with a three- or four-day beard. No one paid any attention to the eight women as they left the main street and entered Naser-e Khosraw, a short street that flanked the old Citadel Square, where the Ministries of Justice, Finance, and Trade were situated, ironic comments each on the poverty surrounding them.

Immediately on the right was a lane leading into a maze of narrow passageways containing small bookshops. The women turned and entered the winding lane, threading their way through the tangle of alleyways until they came to a shop on the right, no different from any of the others, bearing the name Ketabforushi-ye Shiraz. A sign hanging inside the glass door said, "Sorry, closed due to illness," but the first woman knocked and waited. Within seconds, the door was opened and the women stepped inside. No words of greeting passed between them and the man who had opened the door and who now closed and locked it behind them.

Led by the man, the women headed through a small door at the back of the shop, behind which steps led down to a small basement lit only by a single electric bulb. At the foot of the steps, they paused in turn to remove their chadors, folding and rolling them into tiny bundles. The veil can conceal more than mere poverty or ugliness: all eight were now revealed to be men, one in his mid-forties, the rest in their late twenties. The man who had let them into the shop took the bundled chadors from them and motioned them to be seated along the far wall of the room. All but the older man stooped and removed their shoes before walking over the carpet that had been laid down over the concrete. It was an expensive silk Kerman carpet, resplendent with birds and flowers and a rich border of intricate Persian calligraphy—lines from a poem by Rumi. The luxurious colors and soft, inviting texture were in stark contrast to the bareness of the room in which it lay.

"You are to wait," said the older man, who had been the guide of the others. "He will be here presently." He ascended the steps along with the man from the shop and closed the door at the top behind him. In the silence that filled the room, no one spoke. They were tired and bewildered. The seven had traveled long distances to be in Tehran that morning, but as yet none knew the precise reason for which they had been summoned. Each man had been lodged on his arrival at a different hotel, and no one knew where anyone else was staying. Precise instructions had been waiting for them as to when and where to put on the chadors that had been made ready for them in small packages, and they had been given details about meeting the eighth man, their guide. Beyond that, they knew nothing.

Fifteen minutes passed in silence before the door at the head of the stairs opened again. A single figure stood there briefly, then descended the steps. He was dressed in a black aba, the robe of a religious leader, and wore a small black turban wound tightly about his head. His face was that of a man of about forty, thin and bearded, but his eyes seemed much older. Where his right hand should have been, there was a stump dressed in a thin black linen cloth. He stood on the brightly colored carpet, his black clothes and black, weary eyes as much in contrast to it as was the room. The younger men rose to their feet and placed their right hands on their chests in a token of respect. None had ever set eyes on the man before, but the sight of his missing hand told them at once who he was. His name had often been in their ears and on their lips. In the dimly lit silence, each man could hear his heart pounding, hard and distinct.

The older man removed his shoes and sat on the carpet facing the others. He motioned them to be seated.

"You know who and what I am," he said. "It is in your eyes. Do not be afraid. What I have to say to you concerns you deeply, but I have not come here to punish you. On the contrary, I have come to honor you. But first I must tell you of matters of which you know nothing."

He paused for a moment, his eyes passing slowly along the row of faces in front of him, weighing, evaluating, probing. At last he spoke again.

"Last week, seven of your brothers died in a house in the north of this city, in the course of a raid by SAVAK agents. They took their own lives in order to avoid arrest and interrogation, to ensure that no information be passed to the enemy. You will never know their names nor will you hear them spoken of again, but be assured that their names are known to one who is absent from this meeting, one with whom their names will be safe."

The man's eyes flashed as he spoke the last words, catching the reflected glances of his audience. They understood his meaning.

"Those seven," he went on, "had been trained for some time to carry out a series of missions vital to our cause. They had come to Tehran for the final phase of their training, but SAVAK discovered where they were and brought about their deaths. Seven have died. Seven must take their place."

To the young men sitting opposite him, the thin man's words were scarcely comprehensible. But all understood one thing: they were the seven who had been summoned to take the place of the dead. And they knew that only one person could have summoned them. Hushed, they listened as he continued.

"You will learn in time the details of the missions they had been given to perform. I shall tell you only the main purpose of those missions. Each had been assigned a different world leader to study, to watch, and to kill. Seven assassins, seven rulers of men: Mohammad

Reza Shah, King Khalid of Saudi Arabia, President James Carter, Leonid Brezhnev, Prime Minister Rabin, Anwar al-Sadat, and Pope Paul.

"Each of you here today has been chosen for his proven loyalty to our cause and to its master. You have already been under training of a general nature for several years, and all of you have proved yourselves capable in the face of hardship and danger. You have been tested, all of you, often without your knowing, often by men you have neither seen nor heard, and you have given evidence of your abilities and your obedience. Each of you will today be assigned a ruler, whose life will from that moment on be bound inextricably to your own, whose death will be joined inexorably to your death. The day of our victory is very near. It may be this year, it may be several years in the future. And it may be that the death of one or more of these men will become necessary to the achievement of our widest plans. What we hope for here in Iran cannot be divorced from the politics of the world outside. Should such a killing prove necessary, whether before the day of victory or after it, one of you will be called on to carry out his life's mission. You may have to kill in person or by proxy—each of you will know best when the time comes how the death may best be arranged. You may die in carrying out your task, some of you or all of you. But the reward of martyrdom is very great.

"You will be taken tonight to another place in another city, where you will begin your specialized training. You will be trained as a unit for some time, then separated for individual briefing. On occasion, you will be brought together again for special purposes, but eventually some of you will be sent abroad to begin your missions, while others will remain here in Iran to await orders. Those who will teach you will seem cruel at first, more cruel than you can imagine, but you will come in time to understand and appreciate their seeming cruelty. You will be taught not only how to kill, but also instructed in languages, politics, religion, the ways of commerce and finance and the workings of diplomacy. Your minds and bodies will be prepared for all the demands that may be made upon them. You will be given new names and new identities. You will cease to think of yourselves as you have been and will come to think of yourselves as different people. Your lives will have one meaning and one purpose only: the accomplishment of your missions, the deaths of seven men or their successors.

Yours is a heavy responsibility and you will learn how to carry it or die in the attempt."

His eyes that had been moving slowly back and forth across the faces of the men in front of him stopped and focused on one face, held the eyes of one man; the face was narrow and ascetic, the eyes haunted, deep, and green.

"Husayn," said the one-handed man, "you know me. We have met before when I helped train you in the mountains of Kurdistan. You understand me. And you fear me, not out of ignorance like these others, but out of understanding. What have you to say?"

The younger man looked at him, his eyes steady, his face set. He wondered for the thousandth time how the man in black had lost his hand. They all knew the story, that he had cut it off himself as an act of penance for a wrong committed against their master, that he had passed out several times while severing the wrist, that he had almost died from pain and loss of blood. But he did not carry the stump like a sign of penance, he held it like a token of inward victory. And he spoke to no one about it. The young man addressed him, his voice soft.

"Who am I to kill? Who has been chosen for me?"

Reversing the last words, the man in black answered him directly. "You have been chosen to kill Carter, the President of the United States. And I will tell you this now, for I see it written in your eyes: in killing him, you yourself will certainly die. I see blood all around you, in your eyes and your hair and your clothes; I see you drowning in a sea of blood, you are going down in it and it is covering you." He closed his eyes tightly and fell silent.

Seven faces, drained of color, seemed to mimic the seven faces of the dead in a room in Qolhak. But the eyes were alive. In all the eyes, there was fear and dread mixed with confusion and awe. Yet there was something else, something that could not be named, a burning, a light, a smoldering fire. And behind the light, darkness.

4

DHAT 'IRQ
Saturday, 12 November 1977

It was an hour before sunset on the last day of the month of Dhu'l-Qa'da. Tomorrow, the month of the hajj, the annual pilgrimage to Mecca, would begin, and already close on a million pilgrims had converged on the holy city from all corners of the earth. They had come by ship and plane, by motorcar and camel, even by foot, walking for months, even years, to reach a lifetime's goal. Divine blessings were assured for those who chose an arduous journey to the birthplace of the Prophet, and any who might die on the way had the hope of paradise. Now they were here at their journey's end, tens upon tens of thousands crowding into the little town, swelling its population dramatically, a swarm of humanity intent upon a single objective.

And still they came. Even now, the roads into Mecca were packed with jostling crowds, barely distinguishable among which were the separate parties, each led by a *mutawwif*, an official guide responsible for ensuring that the pilgrims under his charge were lodged and fed and able to perform the rites of the hajj correctly. The guides were essential for the smooth running of the vast annual operation. Many of their clients had never been abroad before, many had not even ventured so much as ten miles outside the villages of their birth, and few of them spoke any Arabic. Most could recite some verses or chapters of the Qur'an, but only a handful could actually speak the language.

As they approached the forbidden city of their dreams, the expressions on the faces of the pilgrims changed perceptibly, the bored gazes born of long traveling giving way to looks of intense piety, awe, and introspection. Mecca is ringed, not by any fence or moat, but by pillars that mark the limits of the sacred enclosure, the Haram, beyond which no non-Muslim may pass on pain of death. Before that point is reached, however, there are stations at which the pilgrim, if he has not done so already, must stop to put on the ihram, the white garment of two seamless sheets, that will mark his entry into a state of ritual purity and allow him to take part in the rituals of the lesser and the greater pilgrimages.

Several miles east of Mecca lies the station of Dhat 'Irq, where pilgrims coming from Iraq and further east pass from their everyday state to that of ihram and proceed at last to Mecca itself. Here the crowds were beginning to thin as the bloodred sun moved down toward the western horizon, passing behind Mecca and Jidda to plunge finally into the waters of the Red Sea. Unobserved by the bands of white-clad pilgrims below, four riders appeared from the east, their slow-moving camels cresting a ridge that overlooked the road. Without a word being spoken, all four halted and urged their camels to their knees. The exhausted beasts knelt down awkwardly without uttering the slightest sound, their silence instilled in them by years of harsh training by masters whose lives depended often on stealth and the power of surprise.

All four men were dressed in black, their faces concealed behind the *litham*, the veil of the deep deserts of the south. They dismounted slowly, their limbs stiff and sore from a forced march of many days, their mouths parched, their garments covered with sand and dust. Above the veils, fierce eyes, like the eyes of hawks, gazed down without pity upon the jostling crowd of pilgrims below. In other days, they might have rushed upon them, eager for booty or the simple sport of a raid, but today they had come to Dhat 'Irq for another purpose. Three of them were Bedouin of the Bani Rashid, wolves of the inner desert, men honed and refined from birth by a pitiless environment that allowed only the strongest and most resilient to survive. The fourth stood a little apart from the others, his eyes shadowed and black like theirs, but alive with a different fire.

Months before, he had been found in the desert near Abu Faris, delirious and dying. A band of Rawashid warriors returning from a raid on an encampment of the Bani Saar had come upon him in the gully where he had fallen to die. Normally, they would have left him to his fate: there is no excess in the desert, no margin for compassion or charity, and that had been a year harder than most for the Rawashid of the Empty Quarter. But as they turned to go, one, sharper-eyed than the others, had caught sight of the dying man's shoulder, where it was exposed to the sun. On the back was a circular birthmark, darker than the skin around it, but of the same texture. The Bedouin are not ordinarily religious, but they are superstitious, and this man was now reminded of the "seal of prophethood" which legend recorded as having been placed between the shoulders of Muhammad.

The riders had brought the dying man back to their camp, where their women fed and nursed him. Within three days, he had recovered and was able to talk, and what he had to tell them held their interest, even as his eyes held their hearts. Within a month, the entire group of seventy men had pledged their allegiance to him much as the Prophet's first followers from Medina fourteen centuries earlier had entered into the Pledge of War, swearing to defend him with their lives should the need arise. And before long that need had arisen.

For some weeks, he and a small band of chosen companions had traveled in the Hadhramaut region, visiting camps of the Bait Kathir and Bait Imani, before turning north again into the Empty Quarter. Toward the end of October, they had embarked on an arduous journey through the heart of the desert, across a waterless ocean of burning sand that had brought them at last to Dhat 'Irq and the borders of the sacred territory of Mecca.

Off to their left, a small spring made its way down the ridge toward a runnel beneath, where it was collected for the use of pilgrims. The young Otaybi left his Rashid companions and crossed toward it. Quickly, he removed his travel-stained clothes, revealing a lean, deeply tanned body from which all traces of softness had been long burned away. Using the water sparingly, he washed himself completely, performing the major Islamic ablution known as *ghusl*. He then took a small razor from a bag he had brought with him and proceeded to shave his body, after which he trimmed his beard and nails and perfumed himself. He was ready to don the ihram. One of his companions now came to him carrying two sheets of pure white cloth that he had taken from his saddlebag. These the man put on, the first reaching from his waist to his knees, the second over his left shoulder, back and chest.

When he was dressed as a pilgrim, he faced Mecca and performed the ritual prayer, then pronounced aloud his intention to make both the lesser and the greater pilgrimage, the umra and the hajj. Finally, he rose, donned a pair of simple sandals, and uttered the cry *"Lab-*

baika," "I am here." His voice rang out into the dusk, over rocks and stones and red sand, and was swallowed up again in their silence. He paused, then turned to his companions, who had stood by respectfully while he had entered the state of ihram. One by one, they came to stand before him, their heads bowed.

He spoke quietly to them for some time as the sky above them grew purple and then black. Stars appeared, and from the road beneath, the sound of small bells tinkling rose up from the caravans of late pilgrims. Here and there, men paused for the evening prayer, but up on the ridge, time was forgotten as the young man spoke to his companions in earnest, ringing tones, expressing his gratitude and offering encouragement for the days that lay ahead. At last, he finished and took a bundle of letters from the bag at his feet.

"Ibn Ghabaisha," he said, "you are to take these to distribute among the Awamir, the Banu Yas, and the Manasir. You, Salim, are to carry these to the Al bu Shams, the Banu Riyam, and the Habus. And you, my dear friend Mabkhaut of the sharp eyes, must take these to the Mahra and the Qarra. I know what I ask of you and I do not think it is a small thing. But these letters must be taken. I shall pray while I am in Mecca that we shall meet again. If not in this world, we shall surely meet in the next, by the waters of Kawthar, beside the Sidra Tree."

He fell silent, then came to his friends and clasped their hands one by one, gazing into their tear-filled eyes without words. And then he was gone, the white radiance of his ihram swallowed up by the inky darkness as he descended the ridge to join the other pilgrims on the road.

MECCA
Sunday, 13 November 1977

He slept that night in a small tent shared with four Indonesians and their *mutawwif,* but he rose before dawn and continued on his way, walking rapidly toward his goal, his excitement mounting with every step that brought him nearer to the city. It was noon when he arrived, exhausted but in a state of exaltation. Ignoring the crowds that pressed around him on all sides, without waiting to rest, he headed directly for the Great Mosque in the heart of which stands the Ka'ba, the focus of the prayers of the entire world of Islam. Entering the mosque by the huge Da'udiyya Gate, he stepped into a sea of living faith, wave upon wave of white-garbed men and shrouded women turning slowly about the great cube of the Ka'ba, draped in its gold-embroidered *kiswa* of heavy black cloth, its shape unchanged since it was built by Abraham endless ages ago. His naked feet burning on the white, marble-clad ground, he plunged into the moving mass of pilgrims and soon made his way to the side of the building, to start the compulsory seven-time circumambulation, beginning and ending at the Black Stone set in the Ka'ba's side, enclosed in its setting of bright silver, like a precious gem set in a ring.

When he had kissed the Black Stone for the last time, he left the mosque by the Safa Gate and performed the ceremony of running seven times between Safa and Marwa. The lesser pilgrimage completed, he returned to the mosque and made his way once more to the Ka'ba. A mobile stair had been set against the northwest wall, in which a small door is positioned seven feet above the ground. The stair had been placed there for the use of some dignitaries who were yet to arrive, and several *mutawa'in,* or religious police, stood guarding it against the press of ordinary pilgrims.

Suddenly, there was a commotion as a group of Moroccan pilgrims began to argue with the policemen, demanding entry to the interior of the shrine. They claimed that they had a right to do so, that they were citizens of Fez, the holiest city of North Africa, the site of the sanctuary of Moulay Idris. A group of Saudis, stern Wahhabis for whom the existence of any shrine but the Ka'ba itself was a blasphemy, accosted the North Africans. While the argument raged and gathered strength as more pilgrims joined in, the young Otaybi slipped behind the guards and ascended the stairs quickly and silently. In seconds, he had passed through the door and entered the shrine, the holy of holies, the innermost tabernacle.

His heart pounding, he stood within the small chamber, empty but for three pillars supporting the roof and gold and silver lamps hanging from the ancient ceiling. Inscriptions in Arabic covered the walls. He closed his eyes and tried to visualize the moment, so many centuries before, when the Prophet, having returned to Mecca as a conqueror, had come into this very room, the heart of Arab idolatry, and had proceeded to smash the myriad idols of the Ka'ba with his staff, crying out in a loud voice, "Truth is come, falsehood is vanquished."

He opened his eyes and looked about him once more. Truth had come and falsehood would again be vanquished. He had found resurrection, and yet another resurrection was to come. But first, there must be a time of concealment, of *ghayba*. He turned and went back out into the bright sunlight.

PHASE TWO

TEHRAN
21 December 1978

The American Embassy on Tehran's smart Takht-e Jamshid Avenue housed the Middle East headquarters of the CIA. A complex intelligence network throughout the region was linked by a range of carefully protected communications systems to the reception and analysis room that formed the heart of the web. Here, coded reports received from the Gulf States, Saudi Arabia, Iraq, Turkey, Afghanistan, and cities throughout Iran itself was decoded, sifted, and categorized. During 1978, the attention of the department was directed increasingly toward reports from local agents.

Since January, the country had been convulsed by revolutionary upheaval. From out of some medieval darkness, men dressed in white shrouds and women in long black veils had appeared on the streets of the major cities, weeping, chanting, defying the bullets of the Shah's troops. Thousands had been killed and buried and thousands more had risen up to take their place. The mass opposition that threatened to tear down the palace of dreams and nightmares that was the Pahlavi régime had started during the holy month of Muharram, the time of mourning for the death of Imam Husayn, when religious feelings are raised to fever pitch. It was now Muharram again and the end could not be far away. Two weekends ago, on 8 and 9 December, two thousand Americans had fled the country before the closure of Mehrabad Airport. On Sunday the tenth, over one million demonstrators had marched for six hours through the streets of Tehran. On the following day, two million had defied the Shah's tanks, their hands clutching rough, homemade flags of green, red, and black: green for Islam, red for martyrdom, and black for Shi'ism, the form of Islam that had predominated in Iran since the sixteenth century.

Outside the embassy, extra Marine guards had been posted; part of the British Embassy had been attacked in November, and violence constantly threatened to turn once more against the identifiable targets of imperialism. That morning, the Shah had asked Gholam-Husayn Sadeghi to form a civilian government, a move that was likely to lead to a further deterioration of conditions in the country. Inside the main embassy building, in a room situated two stories underground, three men sat around a small wooden table, their faces shadowed by dim lighting. Peter Randall and his immediate superior, Howard Straker, the CIA station chief in Tehran, had been summoned at short notice to a meeting with Brandon F. Stewart, chief of CIA operations, Middle East division.

Stewart had moved to Tehran direct from Langley, Virginia, when CIA Middle East HQ had been transferred there from Nicosia in 1973. His appointment had been part of a complex shift in U.S.-Iranian relations at that period, following Nixon's visit to Tehran in May 1972, when a secret agreement had been reached to sell Iran any conventional weapons it needed, including F-14 and F-15 fighters. The OPEC oil-price increase of 1973 had boosted Iran's revenues by a massive amount and given the Shah the spending power to initiate the biggest arms-sale boom of all time. The CIA had come to Tehran in force, and Richard Helms, director of the Agency until that year, had been appointed U.S. ambassador, a post he had held until 1976. Now everything seemed about to collapse, destroying years of work in a few months. Stewart was a worried man. His strained face and dark, hollow eyes betrayed anxiety, an anxiety that overlaid and for the time being concealed the cancer that he knew would kill him before very long. He spoke quietly, but in the semidarkened room, his tones carried authority.

"First of all," he began, "I want to make it clear that this meeting is strictly off the record. This room was cleared for security ten minutes ago; it's completely sterile. No notes are to be kept, and I shall not be informing Mr. Sullivan that we have spoken together. As ambassador, he has a right to know of any discussions involving internal security matters, but my orders from Langley override that. Iranian affairs have acquired too many direct international ramifications to be treated on a purely internal level.

"I have another reason for wanting to keep this meeting quiet. There is serious policy disagreement in Washington about the situation here. As you both know, the President's human rights policy was partly responsible for the demands for liberalization that started here last year. He's still pushing the Shah to use kid gloves, but frankly, things have gone too far for that. Brzezinski and the National Security Council are pushing against Carter and the State Department on this. Zbigniew wants stability in the region and he doesn't care how he gets it. The Pentagon's getting into the act as well. I've been reliably informed that they plan on flying out a man called Huyser, an Air Force general; his official orders will be to make sure the military stays with the government, but unofficially he's been authorized to organize a coup if that's necessary to regain control of the situation.

"The position at Langley is that the Agency's willing to support a coup if it'll work. But, as you both know, we've been building up contacts with the antileftist section of the Khomeini opposition, and my own feeling is that it's the religious leadership who'll carry the day. The Shah's on his way out, that's certain, and whoever takes over has to win popularity, otherwise we're back to square one. If the Commies take control, we may as well kiss this place goodbye, not to mention the rest of the region. The problem is that the opposition's too damned confused at the moment. As soon as they get into power, these guys are going to be clawing one another's eyes out. So who do we back? If we choose the wrong group, we could be out in the cold for years, maybe for good. On the other hand, if we can find a small group with potential leverage inside the wider opposition movement and give them the right kind of support, we may be able to keep control.

"As you're both well aware, the biggest problem as of now is intelligence gathering. Up to January, we were getting reliable reports on the main opposition groups, sometimes from their own members. But the religious cadres are much harder to penetrate. Our standard sources, like consuls, Peace Corps officials, academics, and so on, just have no way to make useful contact with them. Most of our people don't even speak good Persian, goddammit. A lot of our Iranian agents have links with the straightforward political opposition, but their reports are useless for details about what goes on behind the scenes in the mosques, and it's too late to start recruiting new people. I'm not blaming you, I'm just saying how it seems at Mideast level and back home in Langley."

He paused briefly, letting the implications of his last remark sink in, drawing out the discomfort felt by the other two men. He had never been a field agent, but he knew how to control and manipulate them.

"Now, Howard," he went on, "a couple of days ago you sent me a report on SAVAK that got me thinking. It looks to me as if it just might have the lead we've been looking for. I'd like you to go over the material on Heshmat, just to get it clear in our minds and to let Peter into the picture. Peter, I don't have to tell you this is pretty confidential stuff."

Straker nodded, suppressing his impatience with Stewart. The man was a desk agent, a civil servant who knew nothing of the real problems of intelligence gathering in the field. His résumé of the difficulties of obtaining information on current opposition groups had omitted to mention the ten men killed in undercover operations in Tehran, Shiraz, Babulsar, and Nayriz since the beginning of the year, not to mention several others who had disappeared while trying to infiltrate extremist religious organizations in Yazd, Mashhad, and Qum. Before this convulsion ended, more lives would be lost, more minds laid waste, and no one here or in Washington would take responsibility or even express more than token regret. He had known each of those men personally. Four of them had been married, with wives back home, widows he would have to meet face-to-face one day. Nothing said he had to meet them; there was no regulation that asked it of him or anyone else. But he knew he would have to face them. With his left hand, he drew toward him a large thin buff file.

"Several days ago," he began, "I was contacted by Ben Gershevitz, the chief MOSSAD agent working out of the Israeli mission here. Over the years, Ben has been involved with the selection of SAVAK agents for advanced training in Israel, and he's kept us informed of aspects of their internal operations—giving us a kind of double-check on things. During our meeting, he confirmed something we'd known for weeks through other sources: people are leaving SAVAK like rats who've noticed the water level rising. The civilian attack on SAVAK HQ here in Tehran a couple of weeks back frightened even some of the tough guys, and when the cuffs went on Naseri in November it didn't reassure anybody.

"One of the top men who's gone into hiding is Masood Heshmat, a man we've all had our eyes on for some time. Before he ducked out, Heshmat destroyed all his interrogation files so nobody could subsequently provide links between him and his victims—though if they

catch him, I don't think the absence of a few files will stop the bullet
he has coming his way. But he didn't waste time getting rid of his
other material, mostly a lot of files on other people in SAVAK, as well
as MOSSAD and CIA agents—the sort of garbage he collected as a
kind of insurance. Ben was able to get his hands on this stuff, and
after clearing out the files on his boys, he passed the rest over to me.
By now, most of it's gone into the incinerator, and I only wish
Heshmat had gone in with it. But there was one file I kept. This is it
here." He patted the buff file twice, then opened it. Inside, a handful
of papers lay clipped together.

"The tag reads 'Goruh-e Qaf, Q-Group.' I couldn't make much
sense of the name at first, but when I read on a bit, I realized that the
letter 'Q' stood for Qolhak." He looked across the table at Randall.
"The group in question is the one Heshmat found at Qolhak October
before last, during the raid on which you accompanied him."

Stewart's eyebrows lifted slightly and he glanced sideways at Randall.

"It's all right, sir," Straker said quickly, "Peter made out a full
report on the incident. I based my summary for you on it. Anyway, it
seems that Heshmat had become obsessed with this group. He didn't
have any hard information, but he did manage to piece together some
very interesting conjectures and one or two scraps of documentation.

"There's a complete report on the Qolhak raid, including photographs of the seven dead men, together with detailed autopsies and
fingerprints, information on the house itself, and the deposition made
out by Heshmat's original informant, who's only identified as
'Muhammad.' But some of the other papers are interesting. The one
that worries me most is this." He produced a map from the file and
unfolded it on the table.

"This is a map of Iran showing details of all major U.S. military
and intelligence installations in the country. Most of the information
on it is highly classified. It's unheard of for a terrorist group to have
access to this kind of material."

Straker lifted another piece of paper from the file. "This is a sheet
which, according to Heshmat's note, was passed to him by his informant, Muhammad. It's a list of arms' shipments supplied to the
group through Chilivand on the Gilan coast of the Caspian; some of
the items are pretty heavy and aren't included in the list of weapons
found at the house after the raid. Another sheet just has a list of

names. Not all of them mean anything to me, but those that do make me sweat. The first is Faisal, followed by the year 1975, the year he was assassinated by his nephew in Riyadh. After that comes Khalid and the Arabic words *min qarib*, 'soon.' Then Mohammad Reza and Anwar, which must be the Shah and Sadat; they've also got *min qarib* written after them. After that there's nothing that makes sense to me except one entry. It has the Persian words *boz-e kuhi* followed by the year 1976. I passed it over at first, then I realized there was one translation of the phrase that made sense. Peter, does it suggest anything to you?"

Randall sat with his eyes closed, but he was paying close attention to all Straker was saying. Without opening his eyes, he said a single word.

"Ibex."

Straker nodded and went on.

"There's another sheet which starts with a list of names, but the rest is made up of symbols of some sort: strings of letters joined together that don't separate into recognizable words, then meaningless shapes, like a talisman or something. I've seen things like it in the bazaar, but I can't make any sense of it. Does it mean anything to you, Peter? You're the Persian expert."

Straker was only half joking. Randall had, in fact, developed a serious interest in Persian studies during his seven years in Tehran; he spoke and read the language fluently and had made a study of the literature and general culture that few Westerners took the trouble to attempt. He took the paper from Straker. It was a large blue sheet covered with intricate writing in red and black ink and he recognized it immediately as the paper Heshmat had picked up in the kitchen of the house at Qolhak. At the top, four names were written in a legible hand, all of them names of Arabs: Asma bint Marwan, Abu Afak, Ka'b ibn al-Ashraf, and Abu 'l-Huqayq. They meant nothing immediately to Randall, but they seemed somehow old-fashioned, and he was convinced that he had heard or read of them somewhere before. The talisman underneath was incomprehensible to him, as was the text itself; it was meaningless, a piece of gibberish. Or, perhaps, code.

"It means nothing to me, sir. But I think I know someone who may have an idea. With permission, I'd like to show this to him, if you think it would help. I mean Professor Ashrafi."

Straker nodded. "Yes, of course. Ashrafi has been very helpful to us

in the past; he can be trusted, even under present conditions. I'm
sorry—you know that better than I do, Peter. By all means, let him
see it, but don't tell him anything he doesn't need to know."

Stewart interrupted, annoyed that the conversation was passing out
of his control, becoming esoteric and specialized. "Howard, don't you
have any idea who these people are? It all seems extremely vague to
me. And I don't understand the Arab connections."

"Yes, sir, it is a little vague. At first I thought they might be a
branch of the Muslim Brothers. The use of assassination would fit in
well enough. But I found a note at the back of the file in Heshmat's
own handwriting. It gives the names of several important Shi'i clergy
and various mosques and theological colleges in Qum and Mashhad.
According to Heshmat's notes, this group's got links with all of them.
That's what made me think they could be the ones we've been looking for, the lever we need when the time comes. The Brothers are
solidly Sunni, so we have to rule them out—it'd be a bit like the
Jesuits forming links with the Methodists. No, these are Shi'i terrorists, and for all we know they could even be the real force behind
the religious opposition. Whoever they are, they sure as hell scared
the shit out of our little friend Heshmat."

"What makes you think that?"

"His note at the front of the file, sir: 'Contact considered too
dangerous at this stage. Further investigation inadvisable. Close file.' I
think he was frightened, sir."

"So, what makes you think we can make successful contact?"

"It's quite likely we can't. But we have to try. Heshmat was
SAVAK; he may have had particular reasons for being frightened of
this group. After all, he had been responsible for the deaths of seven
of them not long before. Maybe his reasons won't apply to us. If we
can identify them and make contact through the right channels, we
may be able to give them assistance, put them in power once the
revolution really gets under way, then start to infiltrate some of our
own people or buy some of them. I want Peter to reopen Heshmat's
investigation. If he's willing, that is." Straker glanced at Randall,
knowing he would say yes.

"Sure, I'd like to try," said Randall. He was intrigued. And he'd
already become involved a year ago in Qolhak. He'd known then that
it had only been a beginning. Those seven dead faces still haunted
him. They were bound together, all of them, in a single spiral of fate.

If he had known then the end of that beginning, known all that would lie between, he would have stood up and walked out of the room, out of the building, out of Iran.

"I take it we have your go-ahead, sir?" Straker asked his boss. Strictly speaking, he did not need Stewart's permission for an internal operation. But there seemed to be Arab links somewhere, and he wanted to be covered in case the investigation had to move outside the country.

Stewart stared for a moment at the two men opposite him. He knew they both thought of him as a desk man, a tool of silk-suited men at the White House. But in the war he had worked in the field with the OSS, the CIA's predecessor. Very few people knew that, and he never talked about his experiences. And in those years, he had developed instincts, instincts that had never left him. Now, as he looked across the table, he could smell death. Weary with instinct, he nodded and rose to his feet.

The others also stood. Straker picked up the buff file and passed it to Randall. "You'll need this, Peter."

"Thank you." They started to leave. Randall stopped as they reached the door. "Sir, I've just remembered what those names mean, those Arabic names."

Straker and Stewart both turned to him, enquiry on their faces.

"They're the names of four people who were assassinated on the orders of the Prophet Muhammad when he was in Medina. Their crime was insulting him, writing scurrilous verses, spreading discontent."

Straker shook his head, puzzled. "I don't understand. Why are their names on this sheet?"

"I think . . . I think it's a kind of justification." But in his own mind the word he used was not "justification," it was "invocation."

All three men were silent. Stewart led the way out, his instinct for death sharper now, and much deeper.

6

Peter Randall woke to a sound like gunfire. Still half asleep, he rolled from bed, crouching on the floor, his left hand reaching for the Browning clipped under the bed frame. The room was silent, the pale early morning light of winter filtering through the slatted blinds. Then more shots rang out, five in quick succession, coming from the street below. Randall rolled to the window, raised himself to the level of the ledge, and glanced cautiously through the edge of the blind. As he did so, an old Peykan on the other side of the street backfired again as its driver tried in vain to start it. Randall released his breath slowly and dropped the blind back against the window. It was cold outside.

He had been dreaming about Vietnam again: the same dream, the same face, the same screams. The dream never changed. How could it change? For Randall, that day was Vietnam, the rest was before or after. He would always dream that day, and Riley's face, contorted in gruesome pain, would always rise up out of the purple darkness, the eyes staring, and the mouth wide open in speechless terror.

The bed was empty. Surely Fujiko couldn't have gone so early. He glanced at his watch: it was ten past seven, and she would not have to be at the embassy on Takht-e Jamshid until after nine. He called her name and she answered with a shout.

"I'm in here getting breakfast. It's way past seven. Aren't you up yet?"

Fujiko was a second secretary at the U.S. Embassy, and Randall had been living with her for almost a year. She was half Japanese and half Swedish. Her mother's parents had arrived in San Francisco from Yokohama, after the earthquake there in 1923; her father was a third-generation American whose grandparents had come from Malmö in the 1890s. During the war, her maternal grandparents had been interned and had lost the fruit farm in Southern California that they had bought ten years previously and that had just started to break even in 1941. They had been given derisory compensation after the war and had seen a large Chicago-based combine turn their land into a dust bowl after realizing enormous profits. As a result, both had lost any confidence they might have had in "the American Way of Life." Until their deaths in the early sixties, they had lived with Fujiko's parents, bringing to their house a sense of permanent loss—the loss of traditional values, of identity and honor. When the Americans dropped atomic bombs on Hiroshima and Nagasaki in 1945, they shed all vestiges of their Buddhist faith. Fujiko had been brought up in an atmosphere of deep ambivalence, never certain of her identity, unable to be either Japanese or Swedish, and yet discouraged from feeling American. Peter sensed that that was why she had chosen a career in the diplomatic service: it was a means of finding herself by finding her country, something she had to go abroad to do. Here in Tehran, she could be an American in spite of her almond-shaped eyes and her honey-colored skin.

Randall grabbed his robe and made for the bathroom. Fujiko's voice came from the kitchen again, warning him that his coffee would be cold.

"Be there in two minutes," he shouted.

When he entered the kitchen six minutes later, Fujiko was already at the table drinking coffee and eating eggs Benedict on waffles.

"Too late," she said with a smile. "I've had your eggs, they were getting cold. Better get some more out of the fridge if you want any."

It was the second time she'd had his eggs that week. He decided he didn't feel hungry, sat down, and poured himself a cup of coffee. The coffee smelt good: fresh roasted beans, straight out of the embassy commissariat. Iranians, unlike the Turks and eastern Arabs, were tea drinkers, and good coffee was almost impossible to come by in Tehran.

They ate and drank in silence, pleased to be together, and to be starting another day in each other's company. Initially, theirs had been a slow relationship to develop. Peter had met Fujiko at the embassy, liked her, and taken her on dates a few times. Strictly speaking, embassy staff were off-limits to field agents. That worked well enough in Europe or some parts of Asia, but here in what was still a traditional Muslim society, it was far from easy to meet local women.

The ones Randall had wanted had been unavailable, and the ones who had been available he had not wanted.

He and Fujiko had stopped seeing one another after she discovered what he did. But a few weeks after that, she had sought him out. She apologized; she should not have judged him by his profession, but should have waited and given him a chance to reveal himself to her as he was. It was the first time in several years that someone had come in search of his identity beyond the mask of his official self, and Randall had not found it easy at first to take away that mask.

He had never found relationships with women simple or fortuitous. After Vietnam, he had been unable to share himself with others. He had guarded his emotions, become miserly with feelings he feared might not be replenished if they were squandered. His life as an agent had set him further apart, left him closed and, he thought, empty.

But Fujiko had found ways past his barriers, the gross and the subtle both. He could not resist her slow and undemanding approaches, and in the end, in spite of official disapproval, they had decided to live together. His strange life, with its curious demands, its constant uncertainties of mood and time and place, often kept them apart for days, even weeks at a time. But she remained. She never probed, never questioned, though she tried to share and, in sharing, mitigate the pain he carried home with him after every mission.

She was the most alive person he had ever known, alive and very much herself, her independence as basic to her as her femininity. She would never make a success of diplomacy; no one with laughing eyes and spontaneous tongue could hope to rise in diplomatic circles. The practiced smile, the phony handshake, the easy falsehood—these were the passports to success in that world. And he knew that he himself was an even darker part of that sordid universe of deals and double deals.

Randall thought of himself as a more or less unremarkable product of American civilization. Born in 1942 in Chicago, he had lost his father two years later in the Battle of the Bulge, one of the seventy-one American prisoners shot in cold blood in a field near Malmédy, on 17 December 1944. Captain Randall had left his son a uniform, some photographs, a few medals, and a sense of pride that was mixed with an anger born of futility—the latter his wife's share of his inheritance. Peter had excelled at sports and most academic subjects, and had gone on to major in political science at Yale. On finishing his master's, he had worked for several years on a doctoral thesis dealing with U.S. foreign policy in the Persian Gulf, but before completing it, he had volunteered for military service in Vietnam. He had seen action at Hue and Khe Sanh in 1968, killed and wounded numerous Vietcong and been wounded twice himself, spent three months seconded to Psyops in Saigon during 1969, and returned late that spring to the States, sickened by the war, the army, and the futility.

There had been many incidents in Vietnam, many deaths, many faces, many names. But two incidents had stood out above the rest, and the second of these, though not for Randall the worst, had eventually been responsible for his decision to leave. Some months after the Tet offensive in the summer of 1968, Randall had been put in charge of a unit whose task was to capture Vietcong suspects in a group of villages between Da Nang and the Laos border. They had taken a week to move through the area, engaging sniper fire on three occasions, killing ten VC, and taking forty-five prisoners—men, women, and their children. Randall's orders were to take the prisoners back to Da Nang for questioning. Silent and sullen, their faces resigned and passive, they sat in lines in the backs of the open trucks.

Ten miles outside Da Nang, they were stopped by a South Vietnamese Army corps on its way north to Hue. The ARVN colonel in command approached Randall and asked the nature of his mission. He was a small, well-fed man, unsmiling, his eyes unsearchable behind dark glasses, and he carried a thin riding crop in a gloved hand. Randall had seen him before in every major town he had visited and he had learned to keep his distance.

Without asking to do so, the little colonel walked deliberately along the row of three trucks carrying Randall's prisoners, ignoring the American escort, his unseen eyes fixed on the silent rows of villagers. He then walked back to the front of the column, barked out orders to some of his own men, and watched impassively as they marched to the trucks and ordered the prisoners out onto the ground. When Randall protested, the colonel simply ignored him.

With mounting horror and a dizzy sensation of helplessness, the American realized what was about to happen. But he knew it would be futile, even suicidal, to try to stop it with only twenty men. The prisoners were pushed against the sides of the trucks, and the soldiers of the ARVN corps lined the road like spectators at a sports event while their comrades raised their guns and fired. It was over in less than a minute, but Randall would never forget the coldness with which it was done, the careless manner of the executioners, or the pitifulness of the corpses they left behind them on the bloodstained road.

"You may take them to Da Nang now, Lieutenant," said the colonel as he strutted back to his jeep. The column of South Vietnamese moved on and was lost in the distance, swallowed up once more in the green distances of the trail to Hue. Randall ordered the bodies buried where they were, beside the road, and returned to base without his prisoners. It seemed a little thing in the midst of such universal carnage, but for Randall and the men with him, it encapsulated the waste of years in as many minutes.

Randall had lodged a formal protest about the incident. Two days later, he had been summoned to meet his commanding officer, Colonel T. R. Brady. Brady had smiled and welcomed him affably, then turned to business.

"Lieutenant Randall, I know how you feel about this incident. God knows, I'd feel the same way myself. There are rules of war that have to be obeyed, just like the rules in baseball, y'understand. But you found yourself a mean one this time, son. The boy you ran into, his name's Colonel Ky, and I don't mind telling you he's got a hell of a lot of clout in these parts. He's a killer, never takes prisoners, never even asks their names. A mean bastard. Hates the VC like Hitler hated the Jews, only he enjoys taking a personal hand in everything.

"But we daren't stop him, daren't even tell him to hold off. If we did, I swear there'd be bad blood all the way down to Saigon, and you and I, we'd be out of this here army and this here country so fast we wouldn't see ourselves go. This is his country and his war, and there's a lot we don't understand about what goes on between these people. In any case, the gooks he had shot were VC, you said so yourself in your report."

Randall interrupted. "He didn't kill 'gooks,' sir, he killed men, women, and children. In cold blood. And they weren't VC, sir, they were VC suspects. Probably half of them were innocent, but there's no way now of knowing."

The colonel's eyes narrowed. His equanimity had gone.

"I don't need some smart-ass lieutenant out of college to tell me what is and what isn't a gook. If old Ky had shot some of our boys, you can bet I'd be after his skin, see to it he was court-martialed. But this is gooks against gooks, and what they do with each other doesn't concern us. It doesn't concern me, and it sure as hell doesn't concern you. There are things you have to understand about this war, boy, and you'd better shape up quick before you get in a lot of trouble."

Randall had left the colonel's room seething with an anger he had never known before, an anger which soon gave way to a deep depression. In succeeding weeks, he had lodged protests with several other senior officers, but the Tet offensive was claiming lives everywhere, and no one had time or inclination to interest himself in the fate of a few more Vietnamese villagers. When he asked for a fresh posting that autumn, Randall was sent to Khe Sanh. All the winter of 1968 he was there, right through the worst time, the very worst. It helped him forget the road and the bodies and the flies that had gathered almost before they were still.

After leaving Khe Sanh, he was sent to Saigon, where he worked for Psyops. It was there that he first heard rumors of the massacre at My Lai back in March of the previous year, just a few months before the incident on the road to Da Nang. Shortly after that, he received confirmation through a friend in military intelligence that the people in one of the villages he had raided had not been VC, that there had been an error in the intelligence report with which Randall had been briefed. It was enough. He had already served longer than the minimum tour of duty. After three refusals, he finally succeeded in resigning his commission, gave his medals to a friend, and left Vietnam.

But Vietnam did not leave him. It came to him secretively by night in dreams. Sometimes he dreamed of the bodies by the roadside, sometimes he dreamed of Colonel Ky and wondered what his eyes looked like behind those black opaque glasses, but dreaded his removing them. Other times, he dreamed of Khe Sanh, of the incessant shelling, night after night. But those were not the worst dreams. The worst was the dream he had had that morning. Vietnam had held worse for him before he had ever come to the road to Da Nang or the long nights under cover in Khe Sanh.

Two months after his return to the States, he had been approached by men in gray suits and dark neckties, men whose close-cropped hair and smooth voices had betrayed their nonacademic affiliation, and who had proposed an alternative way of life to the young scholar about to resume work on his thesis. Randall had not been impressed at first: the war had jaded him. But they knew about him, knew the right things to say, and the right things not to say. They had told him about intelligence work, the serious gathering of crucial information, how it could be used to avoid violence, to preempt the errors and the misjudgments that led to war and death. They played on his fears and his doubts, contrasted the work of the mind with the rages of the body, strung him out until he wanted to believe them, until he needed to accept that what they said was true or could be made true.

The optimism of the sixties, the rhetoric of international peace and cooperation, still meant something to him then, and he badly needed a means of restoring his faith in himself. Under Allen Dulles, the Bay of Pigs had been forgotten and the CIA had become a force in the world. The Pentagon Papers and other revelations of the seventies were still in the future. In the end, the nameless men had succeeded in persuading Randall that a new role was waiting for him, that his need to justify his father could find expression in another field of service, that his anger at his death and his mother's wasted years could be directed against another, more powerful enemy, and that his despair at the violence and waste of war could be channeled into the work of preventing its outbreak. That was what they told him, and he had believed them.

Now, nine years later, both the need for justification and the anger had gone, to be replaced by something less than cynicism but greater than indifference. He still believed in the ideals of democracy, but in his years in Tehran, he had seen things done in its name that had sickened and, he felt, cheapened him. He himself had committed acts that would have outraged the young liberal he had once been, and had connived at others that outraged the harder man he had become. A conscience is a bad companion for an intelligence agent. It may bring a weakening of resolve that can result in death, not only to the agent himself, but to others to whom he has responsibilities. Randall still controlled his conscience and strengthened his resolve by concentrating on images—the faces of the seven dead men he had found in Qolhak for instance. But images could be offset by others, and his mind was too full of more faces, more deaths, when his own hand had held the knife or wielded the gun.

Then Fujiko's soft voice brought him out of his reverie.

"Do you have to go out today? I'm due at the embassy at nine as usual, but I've arranged to finish at noon so I can read up on a report for a meeting tomorrow. If you're going to be around, maybe I could come back here and fix you some lunch. We could spend the afternoon here while I read the report, then maybe we could go see the new English movie at the Atlantic."

"Sure, I'd like that. What's showing?"

"It's Peckinpah's *Straw Dogs*. Blood and guts, I guess. But show me a movie in Tehran that isn't."

"Dubbed?"

"No, tonight's Tuesday—original version night, when all the Tehran trendies can show their friends how good their English is. Or isn't."

"OK," he said, "I don't know what I'm doing this afternoon, but I should be back sometime, maybe even for lunch."

He reached for the pot to pour another two cups of coffee. As he did so, he looked at Fujiko, thinking again of the changes she had brought to his life. During the past few months, he had become more and more confused by their relationship. He felt that very soon he would have to make a choice, a choice between her and the Agency, between his old life and the possibility of a new one. And he was increasingly certain that he would choose her. He was disillusioned and troubled by memories that kept him awake at nights. With Fujiko, he could return to the States and start the process of forgetting all the empty, bitter years, and could rediscover the future he had once thought lost for ever.

Suddenly, the telephone rang.

"Who can that be? I'm not expecting any calls. Pour some coffee, I'll be right back."

Unexpected calls always meant trouble. He had learned that long ago. The phone was checked daily for bugs, and CIA headquarters often rang with messages. Going into the living room, he picked up the receiver and spoke in Persian.

"*Baleh. Manzel-e Randall. Befarma'id.*"

"Peter? How are you? It's Iraj."

"Iraj? Hi! I didn't expect to hear from you so soon."

Iraj Ashrafi was professor of Persian studies at Tehran University; he had taught Peter Farsi when he first arrived in Tehran and had helped him more than anyone to settle into the life of the city. Ashrafi knew who Randall was and what he did, and from time to time he helped him with information or translations of difficult documents. The professor was politically uninvolved, but at the same time was a keen advocate of liberalization and intelligent Westernization. Now in his late sixties, the professor had been born at the time of the Constitutional Revolution and had been in his early twenties when Reza Khan deposed the last ruler of the Qajar dynasty and made himself Reza Shah. He was a member of an old aristocratic family from Kashan, educated in the traditional manner, a liberal conservative of the old school, polite, cultured, and, Peter thought, very wise. He and Randall had become good friends, largely because of the latter's genuine interest in Persian language and culture, an interest that Ashrafi himself had done more than anyone to inspire and foster. Randall sometimes thought of resigning from the Agency so that he could combine his earlier work in political science with his knowledge of Persian language and society and lecture as an area studies expert at Georgetown or some other university. He saw a lot of Ashrafi and still learned from him.

"Listen, Peter. I've been able to decipher your paper. It does mean something to me, something serious. It's important that I meet you, that we talk. I don't know where you found it, but I have to be told. Can I see you this morning?"

"Can't you tell me now, Iraj? What does the paper say?"

"I'm sorry, but I'd rather not tell you over the telephone. Can you meet me in my office after ten? The university's officially closed at the moment because of the riots, but this happens so often that they usually let staff use their offices and the library. I've a number of things I want to look up before I see you, but if you call at ten, I should be ready to tell you what I know."

"Ten o'clock? I'll be there. And Iraj—you haven't shown the paper to anyone else, have you? Or talked about it?"

"No, you said it was classified. I showed a couple of symbols to a colleague, but they won't mean anything much on their own. I can't talk further now, my secretary has some work for me. See you at ten."

Randall stood thinking for a moment, then replaced the receiver. He shrugged and went back to the kitchen. Fujiko was no longer there; she had returned to the bedroom to dress. He drank his coffee quickly and followed her.

As he came through the door, he caught sight of her standing at the mirror doing her makeup. She saw him reflected, standing behind her, watching her. His face seemed so familiar to her now, like something she had always known: the fair hair swept back from his forehead, the lips that smiled too seldom, the pointed chin that he had yet to shave. But his eyes remained mysterious to her, sad and impenetrable. To Fujiko, it was wrong that a man with such eyes should live the life of an intelligence agent. She never spoke to him about his work, as she preferred that it should not impinge on their life together. But she knew that one day she would have to speak about it. She turned gracefully and smiled at him.

"I must go," she said, "or I'll be late. I'll see you at lunch. Don't get held up." She knew the phone call had summoned him somewhere. He did not have to tell her that.

He returned the smile and kissed her gently on the cheek. She seemed so small, so vulnerable. He could not control the anxiety he felt at such moments for her.

"Off you go, then," he said, his voice light. "Take care."

7

TEHRAN
27 December 1978

The long lines of worshipers straightened, turned to one another with the traditional salutation, "Peace be upon you," and broke up, some heading for home, others staying behind in the mosque to listen to the lesson of the old molla, who took up his favorite position in a deserted corner to the left of the mihrab. The black-clad man and the younger man who had stood by his side for the morning prayer left the mosque together, neither speaking, neither showing recognition of the other. Outside, they retrieved their shoes from the rack before setting off together into the frost-white morning. They walked together, waiting for the crowds to thin out. At last the man in black spoke, his handless arm on the other's shoulder, a horror to him.

"Do you remember, Husayn, when we were together in Kurdistan, how you promised obedience to me, obedience even beyond death?"

The young man's face was pale. The cold air gnawed at him, seeking his bones, exposing him. He nodded.

"Today you will begin to redeem that promise. It will not mean your death, not unless you are foolish—your mission is too important for unnecessary risks. But you must continue to be tested, tried with death in one or another form. Today there are things you must do, matters that call for blood. There is blood, Husayn. Will you shed it for me?"

There was nothing to be said, neither rebuke nor acquiescence. All were superfluous. Blood and its shedding, death and not-death, life and not-life, all lay in hands other than his. He was an angel of death, but his was merely the hand that laid waste, not the hand that set him winging, not the hand that called him home again. Husayn looked again at the man beside him, at the black-wrapped stump, seeing the hand, detached, invisible, inescapable. He nodded and walked on.

Randall's flat was situated toward the bottom end of Kakh Street, not far from the complex of buildings that housed the Ministry of the Court, the Prime Minister's Office, the Senate, and the Pahlavi Museum. It was a short walk to Tehran University, and on a crisp December morning, Peter enjoyed taking an indirect route through the tree-lined side streets of what was one of the few pleasant areas of this brash new city. Thoughts of Fujiko and the enchantment he found in her were still uppermost in his mind, and he wanted to take his time, mentally savoring the sense of her nearness, before his meeting with Professor Ashrafi forced him to return to another, sordid reality.

His thoughts were scattered as he came out of Fakhr-e Razi onto the pulsing boulevard of Shah Reza, named after the father of the present king. Weaving his way expertly through the rushing, jangling chaos of midmorning traffic, he crossed directly to the university gates opposite and made himself known to the police guard on duty. Behind him, small children were shouting as they played along the frozen channel of the *jub,* the tree-bordered water conduit that runs the length of most larger Iranian streets. In the summer, he and Ashrafi used to come here to sit in the shade of a large sycamore, listening to the sound of running water, talking about the poems of Rumi and Hafez and Saadi, or about the works of modern writers like Hedayat, Buzurg-Alavi, or Chubak. It all seemed so alien to his real task here, to the things he was called on to witness and to do in the defense of a freedom that looked more and more to him like the very repression his masters feared. But he knew the poetry and the art were necessary, that without them he would buckle and break, that it was for the sake of Ashrafi, for the sake of the culture he represented, that he fought his lonely battles.

The rather ugly custom-built campus, more desolate than ever in its winter stoniness, depressed him as he headed for Ashrafi's office in the main Arts Faculty Building. Founded in 1935, the university had frequently been the scene of political disturbances since the 1960s, and the police and SAVAK kept a close watch on the activities of students in and around the campus. Following riots there in 1962, SAVAK and police agents had taken up residence in two houses in flanking streets, 21 Adhar and Anatole France, in order to be on hand in the event of disturbances. Randall himself had more than once come here to make contact with Iranian and visiting foreign students, reporting back to CIA headquarters on information received about campus activism. It was one of the jobs he least liked.

As he came into the corridor leading to Ashrafi's office on the third floor, Randall became aware of an unusual level of activity, even of excitement. Normally, secretarial and other clerical staff went about their business in the time-accustomed Persian manner: no rush, no hurry, there is always tomorrow. And today the university was officially closed. But people were moving hurriedly along the corridor and in and out of doors. He sensed that something was wrong. At the end of the corridor, he knocked on Ashrafi's secretary's door and went in. The room was crowded with people: other secretaries and several members of the academic staff whom he recognized. The professor's secretary, a capable gray-haired woman in her forties called Laila Rasekh, was seated in a chair sobbing, a handkerchief clutched to her mouth. Randall noticed that the other women were also weeping, though less fiercely than Laila. A young lecturer called Farid Arasteh, who had been at Ashrafi's apartment several times when Randall had visited, turned and recognized him.

"*Aqa-ye Randall! Khabar-ra shenidid?*"

"News? What news?"

"You mean you haven't heard? Professor Ashrafi was killed this morning on his way to the library about nine o'clock. He was knocked down by a truck in the university grounds, on the drive just outside the library building."

Randall gasped in shock. How could it be possible? He had spoken to him just before eight; it seemed incredible that his friend could be dead just one hour later.

"What happened?" he asked Arasteh. "Did anyone see the accident?"

"None of us was there. But some library staff who were outside at the time have told the police that a small truck, a Volex, accelerated as the professor was crossing. The driver swerved to avoid a cat or something in the road and hit him. But he didn't stop. He just went on, they say, even though they shouted after him. By the time the police came, the truck was gone. I can't get over it: I was talking to him just before he left the building. He seemed preoccupied, worried about something. He must have stepped out without thinking. Such a terrible thing to happen." Arasteh was visibly upset; he had been a close friend of the older man and his wife.

Several thoughts rushed through Randall's mind almost simultaneously. A Volex was a Volkswagen, a popular make of vehicle in Iran—popular and hard to trace. Iranian drivers swerve a great deal, but only to miss pedestrians who have come too close, never for cats, dogs, or other minor obstacles. Ashrafi had not been young, but he had been agile and careful and he had always taken his time to cross Tehran's notoriously dangerous streets; for him to be run over on Pahlavi Avenue would have been unlikely, in the grounds of the university it was unbelievable. It seemed obvious to Randall that Ashrafi's death had not been accidental, but he could not conceive of a motive. He knew only too well the professor's political neutrality. Could it have had anything to do with his visit? Surely not. Who but Ashrafi himself could possibly have known that he was due to visit him that morning? He turned to Laila Rasekh and, after expressing his sympathy on the death of the professor, asked if she had known of his visit.

"Yes, Mr. Randall. Professor Ashrafi left a message on my desk as he went out, saying that, if you arrived before him, I should show you into his office to wait. I had not arrived at work when he left for the library."

"Did you leave your office at all later in the morning?"

"Yes, several times. Once to go to the bathroom, twice to make some photocopies, once to deliver a file to Professor Mo'ini."

Arasteh looked at Randall, a frown of perplexity on his face.

"Peter, what has all this to do with Iraj's death? What possible connection can it have with your visit?"

"I don't know. There can't possibly be any connection," he replied prudently, knowing instinctively that there must be a connection of some kind.

At that moment, the door opened and two policemen entered, one of them carrying a small packet. They asked to speak to Professor Mo'ini, head of the Persian studies department. The packet contained Ashrafi's personal effects, taken from his body at the police morgue.

With the arrival of the police, the small group in the outer office began to disperse. Randall saw that Laila Rasekh was about to leave with them, evidently to go home for the rest of the day. He stopped her, speaking in a low voice.

"Khanum-e Rasekh. Professor Ashrafi had some important documents belonging to me. I was coming to pick them up this morning. I know this is a difficult time to ask, and I hate doing it, but it's vital I find them. Would you allow me to look in his office in case they're there?"

Not for the first time, he wondered how much this woman knew or guessed of his real identity, of the true nature of his relationship with the professor. She looked at him oddly, as if she did know, as if she too suspected that Ashrafi's death had not been an accident.

"Yes, of course," she said. "He did not tell me he had such documents, but if they're private, he would not have done so. Come, his door is open."

Together, they entered the small, cluttered room where the scholar had created for himself a sanctuary from the political disturbances outside his windows. Three walls were lined with books from floor to ceiling, most of them in Persian and Arabic, and here and there, Ashrafi had hung pieces of calligraphy that he had collected over the years. The graceful, curving work of masters such as Mir Imad brought a life of its own to the dusty, ill-lit room.

Stepping toward the main desk, Randall flicked systematically, but not without emotion, through the papers that lay on it. The photocopy he had sent the professor was not there. Nor was it on either of the other desks. With Mrs. Rasekh's permission, he opened the large filing cabinet by the window and glanced through its contents. In the second drawer, he found a file bearing his name. Inside were various letters and notes that he had sent to Ashrafi over the years, all of them innocuous. At the back, he found the envelope in which he had sent the Xerox with an accompanying letter—it was empty.

While he was looking, the secretary had gone into the outer office and spoken briefly to Professor Mo'ini and the policeman. She now returned, carrying the packet that contained Ashrafi's effects.

"Perhaps what you are looking for will be among these, Mr. Randall," she said.

He knew it would not be, but he looked all the same. There was very little: a wallet containing some money, a few photographs (including one of them together taken three years previously during a trip to the tomb of Hafez in Shiraz), his identity card, and other papers; lecture notes; a packet of Winston cigarettes, Ashrafi's great weakness; a watch; two fountain pens; and a reed pen with which the old man had practiced his calligraphy every day. But not a trace of the enigmatic document from Qolhak. It might still turn up somewhere, but Randall held out little hope.

Saying goodbye to Laila Rasekh and Professor Mo'ini, whom he knew only slightly, Randall headed for the stairs. He would learn nothing more here. Perhaps the police would discover something about the Volkswagen van, but he doubted it. What had his old friend found in the strange paper that had necessitated his death? For Peter was certain that that had been its true cause. He left the university by a rear entrance onto Danesh Street, where the Elizabeth Hotel was situated. Here he could sit for a while with a malt whiskey, to think and recover from the shock of his friend's death.

Seated in the hotel's small bar, he thought over the events of the morning. He would have to comb the files for information on Ashrafi's colleagues. Even a symbol, however out of context, might after all have meant something to the colleague to whom the old professor had shown it. The next step would be to find someone else who could decipher the document; if Ashrafi had been able to do so, someone else must be capable of making sense of it. Now that Ashrafi's copy had been stolen, however, the only remaining document was the original in his apartment; he would have to make an extra copy for security. Finishing his second whiskey, he left the bar and made for a telephone booth in the hotel foyer. He wanted to let Fujiko know that he would be back early so that she need not bother bringing anything for lunch. When he got through to her office at the embassy, however, he was told that she had left around ten: there had been extra material to prepare for tomorrow's conference and she had preferred to work on it in comfort. He assumed she would have gone straight to his flat and decided to head there himself for an early lunch before starting work on the central computer. Above all, he wanted to be with her, to tell her about Ashrafi and seek comfort in her presence.

As he walked back along 21 Adhar and Farvardin, he kept his eyes open for the Volkswagen van that he knew might be trailing him. Whoever had arranged for Ashrafi to be killed would know that Randall had been expected at the university at ten and would have someone watching. Once or twice, he thought he saw eyes focused on him, but when he turned, there was no one obviously looking in his direction. He reached the downstairs door of his apartment block, inserted the large outside key in the lock, and went inside. His flat was on the second floor, one of two that faced each other across a short landing.

He rang the bell and waited for Fujiko to answer. There was no reply, so he decided that she must have gone back to her own place first. He found his key and turned it in the lock. Inside, lights were on; perhaps she was back and had not heard his ring. She often listened to his classical records, using headphones. He went into the living room, but she was not there. The flat was unnaturally silent. Something was wrong. His skin prickled; he could feel the wrongness, but he could not pinpoint it. Treading softly, his right hand reaching inside his jacket for the pistol he always carried, he made his way toward the bedroom. The silence seemed to press about him and his breathing became long and shallow.

The constriction in his chest became tighter as he swung open the door of the bedroom, his gun held high, pressing himself against the wall. He heard silence, then the dull sounds of the street. A pale light filtered through the curtains, still drawn. He switched off the hall light and glanced into the room. It was empty, but someone had been there. Sheets, clothes, and papers lay strewn everywhere. As his eyes adjusted to the diffused lighting, he saw blotches, dark stains on the floor, bed, and walls. His heart stopped. The room was awash with blood, fresh and still wet in places.

She lay underneath a crumpled heap of sheets on the bed. He saw immediately what had been done to her and had difficulty in forcing down the wave of nausea that rushed over him. Again and again, he could feel himself retching silently as he viewed the shattered remains of her body. She had been blasted with a submachine gun, torn and scattered by it across the room, a cavity where her stomach had been, her flesh in shreds, all but her face. Her lovely face was untouched, but her eyes stared in agony and astonishment at the ceiling. He closed them, his hands trembling with emotions he could not distinguish—pain, terror, and anger, all mixed, all clamoring for his attention. Pale and voiceless, he covered her again with the bloodstained sheet, and as he did so, his eyes caught sight of a single word written on the wall above the bed in blood: *fahisha*. He recognized it and felt his stomach turn with grief. It was the Arabic word for "harlot." The room spun about him and he stumbled from it, mindless and bereaved.

8

TEHRAN
27–28 December 1978

That afternoon, after men had come to his flat and done everything that had to be done, Randall roused himself from the deep lassitude that had enveloped him after his discovery of Fujiko's body. He had sat for hours, unmoving, fixed in upon himself, wrapped in thoughts and half thoughts, waiting for them to finish. Now he was sick of thoughts, sick of memories that hovered about him hungrily, like vultures at a grave. Steeling himself, he went into the bedroom, cleaned and reordered it as if nothing had happened. The bed was remade as if she had never lain upon it.

Fifteen minutes spent sorting through his papers had been enough to confirm that the Qolhak Group file was missing. That morning, two people very dear to him had died so that someone could retrieve the only extant copies of the blue paper. What had been in it that was important enough to justify the deaths of innocent people? He picked up the telephone, dialed a short number that put him through to a secret exchange in the basement of the U.S. Embassy, and asked for a sterile line through to Harold Straker. A line was made available straightaway.

"Harold? This is Peter. Something's happened."

"I know. I've already been notified. I'm sorry about what happened, Peter, about Fujiko. Jesus, they told me . . . No matter; you know. And I'm sorry as hell about Ashrafi. Have you any idea what he'd discovered?"

"I don't know. He was killed before he could tell me. But I do know he was onto something, and whatever it was, it had him worried; it was in his voice. His copy of the blue paper's missing. And the file was stolen from my flat. I still don't understand how they knew."

"What else have you been doing, apart from deciphering the paper?"

"I've been trying to put names to the photographs of the dead men. I've had six men working on it, but so far they've come up with nothing. No one has any identification for the faces and none of the fingerprints are registered. By now, we should have had at least one, maybe two out of the seven. For Christ's sake, everyone in this country's registered for an ID card. My guess is that none of them will be on record."

"Where have your men been looking?"

"Our files, SAVAK, city police, Imperial Gendarmerie, Military Intelligence, Imperial Inspectorate. That about covers everything."

"Is anyone holding back?"

"I don't think so. Why should they? The clearance Stewart gave me was pretty heavy stuff. And I don't think anyone would have had time to remove all the relevant files, even if they'd known what we were looking for."

"OK. So what are you going to do now?"

"Go after Heshmat. I've had one man making inquiries, but so far nothing. If anything, word of the inquiries has probably got to him by now and pushed him even deeper into hiding. But I plan to start looking for him myself; he's our only sure key to this whole business. I think I know an easy way to flush him out—but I need you to authorize an informal exit visa, using any of our normal escape routes. I'll need it as bait."

"For Heshmat?"

"No, for the man who's going to lead me to him. Heshmat won't leave the country. Not yet, anyway. At the moment, he's safer here, where he has contacts and access to money. Outside, contacts and funds are at a premium, and he'd be in greater danger from any number of opposition groups in Europe or the States. For Heshmat, I want a new identity. By the time I finish with him, it won't matter where; he'll go anywhere I suggest. How long will that take?"

"Give me twenty-four hours for the identity. I can arrange the escape route right away. We've been getting people out through Maku into northern Turkey for the past three weeks. Will that do?"

"That's fine. Has the Maku routine changed?"

"No. Just send him to the usual address. I'll see to the rest. But frankly, Peter, I want to take you off this case. They're on to you by now and they'll try to put you away in case Ashrafi told you whatever it was he knew. I want you out of the country, Peter, tonight. Give me the name of your contact for Heshmat and where I can find him, and I'll put someone onto him."

"Sorry, Howard, but no way. I've some scores to settle. I just want to get out of this apartment without being seen. Will you arrange that? I'll go to the safe house on Jordan."

"Peter, I'm sorry about Fujiko, I know how you must feel. Hell, maybe I don't know. But you can't get personally involved. That way you'll make mistakes, bad mistakes, misjudge situations, get yourself killed."

"Five days, that's all I want; maybe less. But I want to finish this. It started with me and Heshmat back in Qolhak. I'm going to finish it with him. He knows more than he wrote in his file, we both know that. You put me onto this Howard, so you owe me. Help me find him."

"OK, Peter. I'm giving you forty-eight hours. But I'm also briefing Bruce Foster so he can move in. I'll send a laundry van around in half an hour; they'll take you out."

The man Randall sought was an ex-SAVAK agent called Nurullah Baqirzadeh. He had originally worked at the Iranian Embassy in Geneva, the headquarters of SAVAK in Europe, engaged in coordinating surveillance of dissidents in France, West Germany, and the U.K. In August 1976, he had been expelled from Switzerland along with Ahmad Malek Mahdavi, a first secretary at the embassy who had held overall responsibility for SAVAK operations in Western Europe. Back in Iran, he had been employed by the Special Bureau to spy on senior SAVAK officials in Tehran while working under Heshmat as an interrogator at the Comite. Randall had often obtained useful information from him, always at high prices. Since the summer, he had been in hiding, mostly at locations in Tehran. He had approached Randall three times through intermediaries, asking for help in escaping the country. Randall knew he was desperate: Special Bureau files had been leaked to members of SAVAK, and Baqirzadeh was in greater danger from his own former colleagues than from the opposition. He was willing to take his chances with dissident groups in the United States or South America. Randall had put him off until now, in case he needed something in return for his services more valuable than the money Baqirzadeh had offered him. The money, after all, had mostly come from Randall in the first place, and nobody wanted it back very much.

It took Randall until noon of the following day to track down Baqirzadeh to his latest funk-hole. The fugitive had always had close connections with organized crime in the city, and the American was not surprised to learn that he was living near Rayy, in south Tehran, at an illegal gambling and boozing den run by Hajj Reza Turk. Hajj Reza had made a fortune after World War II, mostly through property investment but also by running a sizable part of Tehran's vice market. His gambling den was a dangerous place to go. Hajj Reza's thugs, his *chaqukashan*, were noted for their reluctance to ask questions before stabbing strangers and throwing their bodies in the *jub*. The *jubs* of south Tehran needed frequent clearing. That was why Baqirzadeh had gone there, no doubt in return for useful information and a promise of more to follow. Hajj Reza could turn information into cash as quickly as his accountants could make the cash disappear from human ken. Times like these were good for men like him.

South of Tehran's railway station is terra incognita. Even maps of the city stop dead at the station, as if this marked the edge of the world, where the overeager voyager in search of distant shores might teeter and fall into a bottomless abyss. And an abyss of sorts it is, and in its way bottomless. Tehran falls sharply away from the Elburz Mountains in the north; the temperature becomes progressively hotter and the air fouler as one descends southward, until one reaches Rayy, the ancient Rhages, much fallen from its grandeur. As the rich have built their villas in the cool, spacious expanses of the north, the poor have been pushed in their teeming multitudes and in ever increasing density into the baking slums of the south. Here, poverty, piety, and vice jostle together in a world as alien to the middle-class Tehrani as to the foreigner, and as dangerous to both. Randall was no fool. He had seldom ventured into this region, and never alone. To go direct to Baqirzadeh's hideout would be to ask someone to cut his throat. He went instead to Hajj Reza Turk's villa in the far north, at Shemiran. Hajj Reza lived on squalor, not in it.

They had met before on two occasions, both times to their mutual benefit. Randall was shown into the living room, a grandiose monstrosity like those in most of north Tehran's villas, decorated with a love for the ornate and the garish. Before very long, Hajj Reza came into the room, smiling, his well-oiled skin gleaming, his eyes frosty behind the smile. He was growing fat, thought Randall, the personal embodiment of all his riches.

"*Aqa-ye Randall, khayli khushhal-am. Befarma'id.*" He gestured with a hand heavy with flashing rings toward a red chaise longue. One of the rings, Randall had once heard, was said to be worth more than one million dollars. It was a measure of Hajj Reza's power that, where other people could not venture into the darker regions of south Tehran with even a few tumans about their person, he could walk there unharmed wearing jewelry that would keep a dozen families comfortably for many years.

The American sat down and the small talk, so essential to all enterprises in this country, began. Tea was brought and sweetmeats were served. At last Hajj Reza ended the trivialities.

"Well, Jenab-e Randall, these must be busy times for you. This has been a crazy year. But profitable. You have no time to waste in petty matters, I am sure. What can I do for you?"

"A very small thing, Jenab-e Hajj. I want to visit an old friend of mine, Nurullah Baqirzadeh. I believe he's staying at one of your establishments. Would you be able to arrange a visit? Safely?"

Hajj Reza seemed unsurprised. He smiled.

"Of course, I had forgotten. You are in a similar line of work, are you not? That will not be difficult to arrange. I am going there myself late this afternoon. Why not accompany me? I would be pleased to take you. Stay here until then, make yourself at home. Perhaps you have not eaten lunch? I will have my cook prepare something for you. No, no, it is not *ta'arof,* I mean it. We shall leave at five. Until then, I apologize, but I have important business."

Hajj Reza lifted his huge body from the ample chair in which he had been seated, smiled, placed his hand on his chest politely, and bowed slightly before exiting. Randall stood as well, resigned to spending the rest of the afternoon there. Hajj Reza would not want him to leave now that he had tacitly confirmed Baqirzadeh's presence at the gambling den. Ten minutes later, food was brought, good food, but he did not eat. There were two funerals today, and he would be at neither. Revenge for their deaths took precedence over tears at their graves. He waited patiently in silence.

The jostling crowds made way for Hajj Reza much as the Red Sea had parted for Moses. He was known here and much feared. Behind him,

Randall, flanked by two of his henchmen, moved through the dark untended streets. One of the men carried Randall's Browning, which was to be returned to him when he left. Hajj Reza's car had been left several blocks away; these narrow streets, unsurfaced and filled with rubble and ill-smelling refuse, or choked with shabbily dressed men and heavily veiled women, were only negotiable by foot or motorcycle. But even the ubiquitous Hondas that normally blared and swerved their way past or through every obstacle, human or inanimate, slowed down as they came within sight of Hajj Reza.

They stopped at a dimly lit doorway in a small cul-de-sac, off a street occupied exclusively by printing shops. Hajj Reza knocked three times, then again, and the door was opened immediately from within. Not even Randall guessed that the knock was as much a blind as anything, that a hidden camera watched everyone who came to the door, and that no one was admitted without first having been checked out by one of Hajj Reza's men upstairs. Inside, a dim hallway led directly to a wooden staircase. With surprising agility, Hajj Reza led the way up. They entered a smoke-filled room lit with pale blue fluorescent light. At low tables, small groups of silent men played backgammon or *takhte*, cards, or dice, the silence broken occasionally by a cry of glee or despondency. They seemed poor to the unpracticed eye, but Randall knew that most were wealthy bazaar merchants, that the stakes were enormous, and that the house took a heavy cut.

Around the edges of the room other men sat, some smoking the *qalyun*, the traditional water pipe, the burning charcoal at the top pulsing as they puffed in and out. Others were smoking opium, using long-stemmed pipes, each of which ended in a bulbous porcelain sphere in which a small hole was pierced; they held tablets of raw brown opium to the hole, melting them with small charcoal pieces held in tongs, and pressing the gummy substance down into the hole with a long metal pin. The opium addict, the *taryaqi*, was still a common sight in modern Iran, in spite of several attempts to stamp out the cultivation and import of the drug. There were currently over half a million registered addicts in the country, and probably as many more unknown to the authorities. Opium coupons for addicts over sixty accounted for a section of the legal trade, but Randall knew that Hajj Reza was one of several crime bosses who made much of their money by buying and selling coupons and by importing illegal shipments of the drug from Turkey and Afghanistan.

He was shown into a small room at the back and told to wait. The room was lit by a single electric bulb and contained only a few hard-backed wooden chairs. Two minutes later, one of the *chaqukashan* returned, bringing Baqirzadeh with him. The man looked rough, older than his forty years, much older. He was dressed badly, hadn't shaved for at least three days, and was obviously sleeping badly, but Randall felt no sympathy for him whatsoever. Baqirzadeh attempted a feeble smile, then sat abruptly on the nearest chair. The *chaqukash* left, closing the door carefully behind him.

"It's been a long time, Ruhi," said Randall. "You don't look too well. Not sick, I hope."

"Where have you been, Randall? I tried to get in touch with you, three times. You owe me, Randall."

"Times change, Ruhi, debts get reversed. But don't worry, I've come to help you. You want to leave the country, right? Do what I ask, tell me what I want to know, and by tomorrow you could be on your way. Alternatively, by tomorrow you could be dead. Or worse."

The Iranian's eyes betrayed fear, a rancid animal fear. He breathed heavily.

"What do you want?"

"Nothing much. Just a little information. I want to know where Masood Heshmat is."

Baqirzadeh's face froze. His eyes seemed to grow smaller, to recede.

"You're wasting your time. He's dead."

"He isn't dead, Ruhi, you know that. If he were dead, I would've been told; that sort of information's easy to come by. Where is he?"

"I can't tell you. I swore."

Randall knew that Baqirzadeh was afraid; if Heshmat ever learned that he had revealed his whereabouts to the Americans, death would be swift in coming and slow in taking him.

"You never kept a promise in your life, Ruhi. But Masood won't know you told me. And you'll be long gone if he ever finds out. It's your only chance; I wouldn't blow it if I were you."

Baqirzadeh buckled. The words came in a rush, in a whisper.

"He's living in the bazaar area, I don't know exactly where. But tonight you'll find him in the Shahr-e No. He goes there sometimes to a house on Mortezavi, toward Sina. Number 49. He'll be there tonight."

Randall nodded. The Shahr-e No was the red-light district of west

Tehran, beyond the Darvaze-ye Qazvin. Like the south, it was a dangerous area. Foreigners only went as far as the Shokufe-ye No, a nightclub where they could listen to hit parade singers like Gugush and pick up the better prostitutes. Beyond it was a sort of no-man's land where even he had never been.

He gave Baqirzadeh the address he would need for his escape route and told him when to go. Standing, he went to the door and opened it. The *chaqukash* stood outside.

"I'm leaving. Please tell Hajj Reza."

The *chaqukash* turned and shook his head.

"He wants to see you first. Come with me."

Leaving Baqirzadeh in the back room, Randall followed the *chaqukash* up another flight of stairs to Hajj Reza's apartment. Inside, it was brightly lit, in contrast to the carefully maintained gloom downstairs. Hajj Reza sat on a large divan with a young woman, drinking whiskey. He smiled and beckoned to Randall.

"You have found what you came for?"

"Yes."

"Good. Excellent. I will not detain you. There is just one thing: I hope you will remember this small assistance. Perhaps some time you will be able to repay me."

Randall understood Hajj Reza perfectly. One day, perhaps quite soon, he himself might have to leave the country. Unlike Baqirzadeh, he had the necessary money and connections to do so without much trouble, but there always remained unseen eventualities. In case any should arise, a little help from his friends would not go amiss. Randall nodded.

Hajj Reza smiled and said, "Jaafar will go with you as far as the railway station. There you can find a taxi to wherever you want to go. He will return your gun to you there. This is not a safe place for you, American. Please be careful."

Accompanied by the stony-faced guard, Randall descended the stairs and went out again into the freezing night. In the sky above him, pale stars signaled to one another, indifferent to the squalor that surrounded him on all sides.

9

TEHRAN
28 December 1978

Randall took a taxi to Nawwab and walked the rest of the way. He had difficulty in finding the house, as the streets here were poorly lit and even more poorly paved, and twice he almost slipped into a deep hole left uncovered and unfenced ages ago by workmen. He was stopped four times by women in chadors, shrouded, shivering creatures who offered to share his bed for five tumans, the price of a cheap meal. One of them could not have been more than thirteen. Each time, as he shook his head and walked on, the word *fahisha* echoed like a drumbeat in his mind. He did not feel the cold as he walked.

The brothel was a large, surprisingly opulent apartment in a four-story block built ten years earlier. It was dimly lit and full of discreet shadows that concealed much of the garish decoration, a fearful miscegenation of fake European baroque with debased Persian, not unlike Hajj Reza's house in Shemiran. Randall had no difficulty entering —his American accent sounded like money to whoever controlled the door—but he met a blank when he asked about Heshmat. The madame was a fat Bakhtiari woman who had been in the business of servicing the sexual needs and whims of the powerful and the wealthy of Tehran for the past forty years or so, first in the most direct way possible, then as a procuress. She would tell Randall nothing. No, she knew no one called Heshmat, she had never heard of him, he was certainly not there that night. And Randall knew just as certainly that she was lying. Impatient now, he pushed past the woman and made for the first door on his right. He flung it open and glanced in. Inside, a tall man and two girls were engaged in what seemed to be an acrobatic display. The girls were naked except for tall black boots, but the man wore full military uniform. The doorkeeper and the madame shouted and rushed to pull him away.

"Out! Out! You have to leave! Get out of here," shouted the madame, her puffy face flushed, her jowls shaking with rage and fear. "You have no right to disturb my guests! No right!"

Randall was not interested in "rights," least of all the rights of this woman or her customers. Reaching inside his jacket, he drew out the SAVAK identification card he carried for such occasions. Its effect on the two women was dramatic and instantaneous.

"He is in the second room down this corridor, sir," the fat woman stammered, her hands clutched weakly against her ample bosom.

Randall strode to the door and banged his fist on it.

"Heshmat! It's Randall, I'm coming in."

He opened the door and entered the dimly lit room. Heshmat stood facing him. He was naked and held a gun in both hands leveled at Randall's head. In the corner, a naked boy stood trembling, his eyes filled with tears and, Randall thought, with shame; thin, with pretty, girlish features, the boy could scarcely be more than eleven or twelve. The American felt his loathing for Heshmat increase to a surging hatred. He wanted to kill him, and he knew that was the one thing he must not do. He gestured to the boy, telling him to leave. He scrambled across the bed and edged around him, large-eyed and frightened.

"Put down the gun, Heshmat, I'm not here to harm you," Randall said, arms lifted, indicating that he intended no threat.

Heshmat's anger and fright were evident and he continued to point the gun at the American. Randall sat slowly on the edge of the bed.

"If you want to stand there like that, I won't stop you. But we're going to talk. Now."

The SAVAK agent gently lowered the gun, then reached for his trousers on a chair to his left and stepped into them awkwardly, using only one hand. Fear and caution in his eyes and the gun still in his hand, he sat on the chair across which he had tossed his clothes.

"What do you want to talk about? What is so fucking important that you have to come here? I was just getting the boy loosened up when you came barging in. I could kill you for that alone."

"You know what I want to talk about."

"I don't. Tell me. All I know is that some woman was killed in your apartment yesterday. I don't know why and I don't care. It doesn't concern me. It had nothing to do with me; I'm not even working for SAVAK any longer, or didn't they tell you that?"

Heshmat was obviously still well informed about what went on in Tehran.

"She was the second. Iraj Ashrafi was killed earlier that morning. Two people I cared for were killed because of you. Don't fool yourself, Masood, you're involved."

"Because of me? What do you mean? How can I be involved?" Heshmat's eyes bulged with fear and he raised the gun, his finger tense on the trigger. Randall watched his knuckles whiten, knew that Heshmat teetered on a knife-edge and that the slightest false move would cause him to fire the gun in panic.

"You had a file containing papers concerning the group we raided in Qolhak last year. You code-named them Goruh-e Qaf. That file came into our possession recently. Ashrafi and Fujiko were killed by somebody who wanted it back. Whoever it was has the file now."

Heshmat looked bewildered. "I never tried to get it back. I didn't even know it was gone. It was closed, a closed file, finished. No one else knew it was there. I never mentioned it to anyone."

"I'm not suggesting you had anything to do with the murders. If you had, I wouldn't be talking to you and you wouldn't be alive to know it. But I want to know who was responsible. I want to know all you learned about the group, who they are, what their plans are. If you cooperate, I can arrange for a new identity for you outside Iran— it's already being set up. All you have to do is tell me what you know."

"I know nothing. The file contained everything. You know as much as I do."

"No, Masood, you know more, much more. You closed the file because of what you knew, what you still know."

"I tell you, I know nothing. I don't know who they were, anything about them. We couldn't identify any of the bodies. Faces, fingerprints, teeth, nothing was registered with us or the police or anybody else. That's the truth, you have to believe me. They were faces, just faces."

"Why did you mount a raid like that against them? Why didn't you use the police at the house?"

Heshmat's eyes shifted from Randall to the door and back again.

"I wanted them alive. I wanted them to talk. Information. They had information."

"How did you know? What sort of information?"

"About the assassination attempt, the attempt on Ashraf."

"These weren't the same people; the people behind that were still in France. What information did the group at Qolhak have? Who were they?"

"I don't know. Except . . . We had to know. They were fanatics, you saw what they did to themselves. Fanatics."

"What sort of fanatics? Political? Religious?"

"Both. The mollas are becoming powerful again. In a month, two months, they'll be in power. It's too late to try to stop them."

"What else?" Randall kept on at the Iranian, knowing there was more. Heshmat's eyes betrayed him, told Randall he was still holding back.

"Nothing. They are Feda'iyan, Mujahidin. I don't know."

"You're lying. These are something else. Who are they?"

The Iranian was frightened, but not of Randall. Randall could see his fear, smell it. There was something else, something that terrified even this master of the torture chamber.

"I will kill you, Heshmat, I swear. I don't care what happens, I intend to find these people. Who are they?"

"You don't understand. They . . . no one could believe that they would return, no one. You cannot stop them. Listen, Randall, get me out, otherwise they'll kill me. They've eyes everywhere, nothing and no one escapes them. And they kill anyone who stands in their way, anyone. Get me out of here, then find them. Use your influence to stop them. Find the German. Find him and stop him." Sweat had broken out on Heshmat's face and was running down his neck. Stripped to the waist, his feet bare, he looked pathetic, a broken-down underling of forces he could not control. Randall stepped toward him. He felt no pity, only shame—that he was here, that he was forced to play this game with Heshmat, that revenge drove him to do so.

"Who is the German? How can I find him?"

The screams in the hallway came only seconds before the door of the room burst open. Along the corridor, other doors crashed. Men shouted and women and girls screamed. Randall twisted and caught a glimpse of a man dressed in black standing in the doorway, a sub-machine gun held level at his waist. He tried to turn, to draw his pistol and aim it at the intruder, but the first burst of bullets caught him as he pivoted, throwing him backward across the bed. In the instant before he lost consciousness, fighting his agony, he rolled himself across the bed and fell onto the floor, out of reach of the bullets.

The same burst smashed Heshmat against the wall, pinning him there for agonizing seconds as his limbs jerked and bullets ripped him to shreds. The sound of firing came from other rooms, mingled with half-choked screams and the pummeling of running naked feet. A final burst of firing rang out, followed by an eerie silence. The man in the doorway glanced at Heshmat, saw that he was dead beyond question, checked that Randall too lay still, turned the safety catch on his gun, and stepped back into the hallway.

PHASE THREE

10

MECCA
1 April 1979

There is a small ramshackle house of three stories in the Shi'b al-Mawlid quarter in the northeastern sector of Mecca, a mere fifty yards from the tiny modern library that stands on the site of the dwelling in which Muhammad was born. This is old Mecca, pinched and crowded on the lower slopes of Abu Qubais, the houses tall and narrow, built of rough bricks and mortar, with windows of latticed brick or wooden shutters, from behind which eyes peer, seeing but unseen. Narrow, dirt-paved alleyways thread their uncertain way between the tottering piles of houses, past shadowed doorways and mysterious openings, losing themselves in their own intricacy. Everywhere, there are wild cats roaming in search of food, oblivious of the human life that surrounds them.

It was long past midnight, and the Shi'b al-Mawlid was dark and silent. In a room on the third floor of the house, twelve men slept while a thirteenth kept watch. The sound of regular breathing filled the room, its rising and falling punctuated from time to time by the sound of a dog barking outside. In the silence, the sound of muffled knocking on the door below seemed to echo alarmingly in the room. In an instant, all twelve men were awake, while the guard opened the door and descended the stairs. Whoever was outside did not knock again. He knew that two taps, furtive and pregnant with alarm, were enough to rouse the inhabitants of the house without alerting the neighborhood. Upstairs in the darkness, guns were passed from hand to hand.

The guard opened the door onto the street, one hand free to fire if danger threatened. A single word was uttered and a muffled figure slipped inside, closing the heavy wooden door behind him. He turned to the guard and spoke in an urgent whisper.

"Huwa hadir?" (Is he here?)

"Yes, upstairs. Follow me."

Together, the two men climbed the ancient wooden stairs. When they reached the door of the sleeping chamber, the guard called out, reassuring those inside that all was well. An armed man stepped out of the room, checked that it was so, and motioned the new arrival inside. Someone lit an oil lamp, and the room was filled with a pale yellow light that cast weird shadows across the faces of all present. The twelve men who had been sleeping were already dressed in black robes, awake and ready for action.

The man who had knocked at the door below was dressed in National Guard uniform. He was sweating and his eyes betrayed his fear. Motioned to sit, he lowered himself to the ground and, without waiting for permission, spoke in a hurried, anxious voice.

"Forgive me for this disturbance, but I had to come. Orders have been given to prepare for a raid on this house. They know we are here and they plan to move in an hour's time. I was able to slip out without being seen, but if they discover I am missing, they may realize what has happened and come here at once. You must leave tonight. It is no longer safe for you in Mecca."

Seated facing him was the pilgrim who had arrived in the city by way of the desert over a year ago. His name was Muhammad ibn 'Abd Allah al-Qahtani, a former student at the Faculty of Islamic Law in Mecca. Like many of those who followed him, he was a member of the Otayba, a Bedouin tribe who grazed their sheep and camels in the region between Mecca and Riyadh, the Saudi capital. Two centuries before, the Otayba had ruled in Qatar on the Gulf, but their period of ascendancy had been brief. More recently, they had been used by King 'Abd al-Aziz in the task of pacifying the vast Arabian Peninsula, but their influence had again declined after the defeat of a rebellion launched within the tribe. Now the ambitions of many young Otaybi men were centered in this one man, Muhammad ibn 'Abd Allah.

He was in his mid-twenties, lean-bodied, narrow-faced, with a heavy black beard and piercing gray eyes. He carried a presence, that indefinable thing known as charisma. Sociologists say that charisma is not possessed, only brought to someone by his followers; but there are some people who, by their very appearance and manner, seem to disprove this theory. Muhammad ibn 'Abd Allah was just such a man. When he spoke, his every word and gesture compelled and impressed. He spoke now.

"Do they know of me? Have they heard that I am here?"

The soldier shook his head.

"No, they know only of your brother-in-law. Since his arrest last year, their spies have been eager for news of him. But they know nothing of you, my lord; of that I am certain."

A grim smile crossed the lips of a man by Muhammad ibn 'Abd Allah's side. This was his brother-in-law, Juhaiman ibn Saif al-Otaybi, a man of about thirty-nine, who acted as the outward leader of the group. He had been born around 1940 in the Otaybi settlement of Sajir in Qasim, to the northwest of Riyadh, about ten years after the defeat of the puritanical Ikhwan led by Ibn Humaid. The memory of that defeat still lingered in the region, and Juhaiman had grown up in an atmosphere of rebellion against the House of Saud. In his late teens, he had joined the National Guard, in which he became a corporal in a platoon of Otaybi levies stationed at a base in Qasim. Before long, however, he had rejected life in the army as un-Islamic and gone to Medina to study the religious sciences. In 1976 he had gone to Riyadh as the leader of a small band of zealots and had begun to write fundamentalist pamphlets attacking the Saudi clergy and the Royal Family. His activities had attracted the attention of Prince Na'if's intelligence service, the *mubahith*, and in the summer of 1978, he and ninety-eight of his followers were arrested and imprisoned in Riyadh. Since no clear charges could be brought against them, they had been released after six weeks on the condition that they cease their preaching activities.

What no one outside the group knew or suspected was that Juhaiman was not their true leader, that he himself had given his allegiance several years before to his brother-in-law Muhammad, in whom he recognized the Mahdi, the promised Messiah of Islam, who would proclaim his appearance on earth at the beginning of the fifteenth Islamic century. The time set for that appearance was now only months away.

Muhammad ibn 'Abd Allah nodded and turned toward Juhaiman.

"It is as we feared. You must leave immediately for al-Hasa as planned. It is a long journey, but there is much for you to do there, and you must return by the autumn. Take Musallim, Hamad, and the son of Sulayman. The rest go with me to Medina. It is time for me to make a hijra, to abandon my home, just as the Prophet was forced to do in his day. Let us not waste time in farewells. We shall meet again when the summer is past."

Without pausing, Muhammad ibn 'Abd Allah rose to his feet. The others rose after him, holding back deferentially until he had reached the door and gone out of the room. Arrangements had already been made in anticipation of such a crisis, and now everyone moved quickly. There was no time to lose. Above all else, Muhammad ibn 'Abd Allah must not fall into the hands of the enemy.

In complete darkness and total silence, the door of the house opened and one by one the group of black-cloaked men slipped into the narrow street. Barefooted, they moved soundlessly westward through twisting lanes until they reached the large street that runs from Safa to the north of the city. Here, Juhaiman ibn Saif and his three companions came one at a time to embrace Muhammad ibn 'Abd Allah before vanishing toward the road that would take them north, then east to Arafat, to begin their long journey to the Gulf. The others turned south to skirt the Great Mosque before taking the road to the west of the city that leads north to Medina. Like the Prophet, Muhammad ibn 'Abd Allah would find sanctuary in Medina from those who hunted him. And, like him, he would return before long in triumph.

11

TEHRAN
10 April 1979

The voice of the muezzin calling worshipers to the evening prayer faded with the light. Overhead, the contrail of a northbound 707 turned lazily about Mount Damavand and passed over the Elburz range, and below, the lights of Tehran began to twinkle on against the falling dusk. On the streets, headlights flashed and the ubiquitous taxis of the city, little orange and white Peykans, lit their fairy-light arrangements at back and front as they darted at full speed in and out of the jostling streams of traffic. The roar of engines and horns and people calling out directions to passing cabs blotted out every other sound, including the gentle chanting of the call to prayer.

A casual visitor returning to the city after perhaps a year or two might have noticed little difference simply by glancing over one of the crowded main streets in its heart. He might have been puzzled at the vagueness with which people called at taxis, as if they were no longer sure of the street names. Otherwise, all seemed normal. Boulevard Elizabeth, Ferdowsi, Hafez, and Takht-e Jamshid were all filled with cars, buses, people, and petrol fumes just as they had always been. The traffic was as chaotic as ever, the pedestrians as heedless as always of life and limb. But on closer inspection, significant changes became apparent. There were fewer neon lights, many of the smarter shops and restaurants had closed, old night haunts of the nouveaux riches had disappeared, and shop windows carried few of the imported luxury goods of a year before. On the pavements, there were virtually no European or American faces and none of the smartly dressed young Iranian men and women who had aped the styles of Paris and New York not long before. Such women as were about were accompanied by men, and almost all wore the chador, or at least a dark-colored head scarf. If the visitor had glanced inside the shops and government buildings, he would have seen to his surprise that photographs of Mohammad Reza Shah or the Empress Farah no longer graced the walls. In their place were prints of an old man wearing the turban and beard of a molla.

This was Tehran 1979, the Tehran of Khomeini and his Revolutionary Guards, the Tehran of the Islamic Revolution. In Tajrish and Shemiran, the villas of the wealthy lay stripped and empty. Many had been turned into offices for the committees responsible for the nation's teeming poor and homes for the reformation of prostitutes.

The revolution had brought fewer changes in the bazaars and alleyways of impoverished south Tehran. There had been no smart shops to smash, no flaunting of luxury, no villas or small palaces, no women in jeans, skirts, or with modern hairstyles. Life continued as before, only perhaps more intense, more open and more hopeful. In the main bazaar, no thunder of traffic drowned the wailing chant of the muezzin calling believers to the Shah Mosque. *"Ashhadu anna la ilaha illa 'llah . . . ,"* (I bear witness that there is no god but God . . .) The muezzin's liquid Persian accent softened and made musical the harsh Arabic words, turned them mellow and pleasing.

Already, men were making their way through the great wooden gate that divides the Shah Mosque precincts from the bazaar. At the gate, as always, were the stalls selling tablets and ring stones of agate, inscribed with verses from the Qur'an and the Traditions, and the men who will make for you a seal carved out of solid brass, writing backward with a sharp blade, digging into the soft metal, producing an elegant cartouche of your name in a matter of minutes.

As the light faded and electric bulbs flickered into life throughout the maze of alleyways that makes up the vast bazaar, one of the seal carvers—a young man of about twenty-five—put down his tools and set off into the mosque, as if to join the evening prayer there. Once inside the outer gate, however, he turned right and exited lower down through a smaller gate, opening into a region deeper inside the bazaar. Moving quickly now, he threaded his way through the *bazaar-chehs*, the small secondary streets of the bazaar, passing with evident familiarity by brightly lit stalls selling bales of cloth. Darker shades and heavier stuffs were more in prominence now as the light, gaily patterned chadors gave way to somber grays, browns, and, above all, blacks. Moving without hesitation in the direction of the street he sought, the young man turned right again into Naw Ruz Lane, then made a sharp left turn into Chehel Tan; several hundred meters farther, he veered right once more into a dead end that took him down toward Ghariban Alley. He came out into a maze of residential streets, narrow passageways of mud-brick walls and dark wooden doors, walking steadily until he came at last to a doorway set at the foot of three steep steps. Glancing left and right, he raised his hand and knocked once, paused, twice, paused, once. The door opened, he went in, and it shut again. No one heard the greeting exchanged between him and the doorkeeper as he entered.

Passing along a short vestibule in total darkness, the young man came out into a small courtyard across which he could make out a faintly illuminated opening leading to a flight of worn stone stairs. The house dated from the mid-nineteenth century, little newer than the city itself. The stairs bent sharply three times, ending on a short landing giving onto an open door outside where earlier arrivals had left their shoes neatly arranged in two rows. From inside came the yellow glow of an oil lamp; like many older houses in the bazaar district, this one had not been wired for electricity. Voices could be heard speaking softly. The new arrival bent to unlace and remove his shoes, ducked as he passed through the low doorway, and squinted as his eyes tried to adjust to the light.

On the carpeted floor around the small room were seated seven men, six of them of about his own age, the seventh much older. The young men were all dressed alike in a simple white cotton garment, a *kafan*, or shroud, the symbol of martyrdom that had been worn during the days of the revolution by rows of men and boys that had walked at the head of demonstrating crowds, their lives and their imminent deaths alike dedicated to God.

The older man, with a gray beard and a full mustache, was also dressed entirely in white, in the long robes of a molla; on his head was wound a small green *amameh*, the turban that the clergy of Iran had worn for centuries and that had so recently become a symbol of revolution around the world. The color green indicated his descent from the Prophet.

The new arrival placed his right hand across his breast, bowed, and greeted the old man formally. The latter responded in the traditional manner and motioned him to sit on the floor in front of the door, facing him. Silence fell on the group; they sat, heads bowed, eyes respectfully lowered to the carpet, waiting. Sitting erect, his back against a white bolster at the far wall, his wrinkled, arthritic hands resting on his knees, the old man drew the hush of the room into himself. Age and rank have lost little of their authority in modern Iran. Without moving his head, the molla quietly scanned the men grouped around him. One by one, he looked into their faces, and they responded without the embarrassment or nervousness so many of us in the West experience when gazed at so directly. Theirs was a look of love and total discipline.

The oil lamp cast strange shadows on the cool whitewashed walls of the room; outside in the courtyard, a cricket began to chirrup as the warm April night settled. Beyond, the last phrases of the call to prayer floated into the darkness from a nearby minaret.

The old molla stood and turned to face the southwest corner of the room. His seven companions rose and formed a slightly curving line behind him, all facing Mecca. As they bent in the traditional postures of the prayer, their soft flowing movements were echoed and anticipated across the city in thousands of mosques and private homes and in the heart of emptying streets. The prayer ended and the eight men resumed their former places in silence. The old man leaned gently back against the bolster, his thin scholar's hands resting on his lap; on the right hand, a ring of engraved agate set in Isfahani silver caught the light like a tiny lost star. He inclined himself slightly toward the man seated second from his left and addressed him gently, at the same time passing a small book to him. The young man took the book, opened it, and leafed through it until he came to the page he sought, then cleared his throat and began to chant. It was a prayer designed to be read at the grave of Fatima, the daughter of the Prophet and wife of the first Imam, Ali. Tonight was the anniversary of her death more than thirteen hundred years before. The singer's voice rose and fell, now drawn out on a long note, now catching in his throat, filling the room with a pleasing sadness that brought tears to the eyes of all who sat there.

When the chanting was ended, the young man bowed and passed the book back to the molla, who received it gravely and thanked him. The old man waited for the silence to dissipate, then began to speak, his voice soft, almost indolent, the cultured tones of a well-educated Shirazi. Unlike so many mollas of his generation, he did not try to dignify his speech with affected Arabic words and phrases. He spoke simple but good Persian, soft and sibilant, and used the Persian plural with naturalized Arabic nouns. In Arabic, even words of love sound harsh; in Persian, even a death sentence is like the whisper of your beloved before she comes to you, naked for your embrace.

"Over a year ago," he began, "you were brought to Tehran to be informed of your selection for a series of important missions. Since then, you have undergone the most arduous training, and all of you have demonstrated the qualities we expected to find in you. During the past six months, you have been living under assumed names here in the capital, learning how to hide within a crowd. Again, you have all done well. But tonight a new phase of your training will begin, the most important and the most difficult.

"You have been trained to kill. You know countless ways to inflict death, instantaneously or slowly, but always unfailingly. You have become weapons for the Imam to wield in his struggle, swords sharpened and ready to strike. Some of you have already killed in his name, killed and purified. But now you must begin a new training. Now you must be trained to die. Only when death is easy for you to endure will it be proper for you to inflict it on those for whom you have been chosen as executioners. You must all become more than messengers of death—you must become its embodiment."

He turned to the first man in the row on his right.

"I know that you are ready to kill, that you have already done so more than once. But are you ready to die? Would you die here, tonight?"

The young man fixed his eyes to the ground, then raised them to return the gaze of the old molla. It is impossible to say what passed between them while they held each other's eyes.

"Yes, excellency," replied the man in the shroud, "I am ready."

The old man's eyes were sad. He asked the same question of each of them in turn and each gave the same reply. It was as if it had been a liturgy, yet each spoke for himself, prompted only by inner convictions.

Softly, the molla addressed the man who had chanted the prayer several minutes earlier.

"Morteza, you chanted beautifully this evening. Your voice is truly like that of a nightingale, it is a gift from God. I thank Him that I heard you chant for us tonight."

He paused, seeking the young man's eyes, and holding them as a falcon holds its prey as it flies deadly above. Reaching beneath a folded cloth that lay by his side, he drew out a small, thin-bladed knife. Sweat broke out on Morteza's forehead as the old man lifted the knife and held it out to him. The blade was sharp and polished and it shone like silver in the light of the lamp.

"With a single cut of this knife," the old man went on, "you can sever the strip of flesh that joins your tongue to the floor of your mouth. To do so will render you dumb; it will be a small death for you and, in a way, for all of us who have listened to your voice with such pleasure. You have told me that you are willing to die. You are wearing a shroud. Take the knife."

Pale, his face strained, Morteza took the knife with a hand that he stopped from shaking only by the greatest effort. All his life, he had chanted poetry and prayers, his voice had been a treasure to him, a bond between him and God. With his thumb, he tested the blade: it was razor sharp, perfect. All around him, his companions sat frozen into silence, none daring to look at him. He opened his mouth and placed the tip of the knife to his lips; with a supreme effort, he pushed it farther, feeling the cold steel like ice as it touched his tongue. He closed his eyes, called on Ali for strength and on Fatima, tonight of all nights, for succor. His hand moved obliquely, it was done, and he choked on the warm blood that flooded into his throat.

When he opened his eyes, the old man had taken the knife away and was holding him. Blood escaped from his mouth, a constant stream, crimson staining the white *kafan*.

"Go downstairs," the molla said. "A doctor is waiting to tend to you. You need not return tonight. May Fatima watch over you; you have done well."

With the older man's assistance, Morteza walked to the door and went to the head of the stairs; a servant was waiting to help him down. The molla returned to the place he had occupied before and sat down again.

"Each of you will be called upon to die small deaths like this, to sacrifice those things that are dearest to you. No sword is tempered until it has passed through the fire and been quenched in water. Once you have been tempered, it will be time to teach you how to die. I shall not teach you that. There is another, one whom you know already. He has died many times and will teach you all he knows."

As the molla spoke, a shadow fell across the room and the eyes of the six remaining men turned toward the door. There, framed in the opening, stood the one-handed man, still dressed in black, his eyes blazing. All was silence. Outside, the night grew darker and owls in their multitudes left their nests to hunt for living prey.

12

TEHRAN
Late April/Early May 1979

Pale sunlight filtered into the stark white room and fell gently across the foot of Randall's bed. He had lain immobile for nearly four months, eyes fixed on the ceiling, their infrequent blinking alone an indicator that he was still alive. The room was on the third floor of the Khomeini Hospital—formerly Pahlavi Hospital—off Parkway, ten minutes by ambulance from the scene of the December shooting. Randall had been rushed there, bleeding badly and in desperate need of transfusions, after being found among the corpses in the charnel house that had been a brothel. They had thought him dead at first, so extensive were his injuries, but one of the policemen carrying the bodies down to the waiting vans outside had noticed that his wounds were still bleeding. It had taken five operations and the assistance of staff sent over from the American Hospital at Tajrish to save his life. He had again almost died on the tenth day after a transfusion of contaminated blood, obtained from a center that sometimes used heroin addicts as cheap donors.

Eventually, his body had almost healed, but his mind was still scarred. Only now, in late April, had he started to respond to things around him, but he still woke at night screaming. Nightmares of Vietnam mixed in a complex pattern with dreams of Tehran, visions of the dead on the Da Nang road blurred and crossed with images of Fujiko, mutilated and torn on the crimson bedsheets. The landscape of his dreams was composite, the jungles of Indochina casting their green tendrils out into the streets of Iran. But one dream refused to change. It would always stay the same, no matter what else shifted in the madhouse of his mind.

There are depths in a man that he does not know until external events force him to plunge inside himself, to probe the limits of his mind and soul. During the weeks he lay immobile on the hospital bed, hovering between life and death, Peter Randall discovered within himself strengths and weaknesses whose very existence he had not before suspected. In those long months of inner turmoil, he had held on to life by grappling with images of death, by bringing Fujiko's face again and again before his inner eyes, holding on grimly to the one solid thing in his dissolving universe: the need to find and, if possible, destroy whoever had been responsible for her death. He could not let her be put to rest within himself before that, for the moment he did, he knew he would die with her. In his own cheating of death, and in that alone, could he hope to come to terms with the calculated violence that had ripped them apart so brutally. He was refashioned as men are refashioned in war or prison, and as he moved down through the thoughts and dreams and nightmares of so many arid years, he found numerous facets of himself that were repellent to him now. Yet deeper still, buried by lies and half-truths and violence, he discovered a certain wisdom and a forgotten strength of purpose. In the mad world into which he was about to be reborn, he would need both in abundance.

A nurse, her face shaded by a *chaharqad*, the large head scarf worn by revolutionary women, watched him constantly. During the days, he lay in his bed, staring endlessly through the window that allowed him an almost uninterrupted view of the mountains to the north. But he could walk again, and three times a day was taken for physiotherapy and a short stroll along a corridor on the ground floor.

In the past two weeks, he had started to respond to conversation in English, even to give short replies to questions. The psychiatrist in charge of his treatment was optimistic about his recovery, and privately very frightened about what might happen to Randall once he was fit enough for interrogation. So far, he had resisted pressures from the Revolutionary Committee to allow interviews, but today an order had been received from Husayn Fardust himself, head of the new security organization that had replaced SAVAK—SAVAMA—demanding access. Dr. Quchani knew only too well when to resist and when to give in to pressure. How else had he survived until now?

The door opened quietly and two men stepped into the room, the first wearing the white jacket of a hospital doctor, the second in the gray robes and black turban of a molla. The molla paused to address a few words to the Revolutionary Guard posted at the door of Randall's room. There had been a guard there since February, when the hospi-

tal had come under the control of the Revolutionary Committee and
while it had still been too dangerous for the American Embassy to try
to move Randall. The doctor spoke briefly to the nurse, who had been
sitting on a chair in the shadows of the room's far corner. She crossed
to the bed, lifted Randall with one arm, helped him move up a little,
and propped him against a firm backrest of pillows. This done, she
went out of the room with the doctor, leaving the bearded cleric
alone with her patient. The molla was tall for an Iranian, with a
gaunt, narrow face and hollow eyes; behind the thick beard—a deep
black flecked here and there with gray—thin, bloodless lips were set
in a permanent gesture of determination. He had lived his life in
Qur'an schools and theological colleges, reading the endless volumes
of Shi'i tradition and commentary, mastering the shelves of works on
jurisprudence, writing his own commentaries on the commentaries.
In Qum, he had been involved in demonstrations against the Shah,
and had seen friends beaten by the police, or shot down by the Army.
He had been imprisoned, twice in Evin, once in the Comite, and he
had been subjected to torture by SAVAK officials. But now his time
had come. Some sort of millennium was at hand, and he was here to
feed the great beast with blood. He walked to the corner of the room,
stood for a moment gazing out of the window, then picked up the
chair, brought it over beside the bed, and sat on it.

"Good morning, Mr. Randall. My name is Hasan Tabataba'i. I am
an interrogator attached to the national security division of SAVAMA,
the new Iranian intelligence organization. You do not know me yet,
but I hope that we shall become better acquainted with time. I do not
wish to tire you today, but am here merely to inform you of what is
going to happen to you.

"Since you came here last December, there has been a successful
revolution in this country. In spite of the efforts of the Great Satan
and its allies, we chased the Pahlavi devil and his brood from our soil
and founded an Islamic Republic under the guidance of Imam
Khomeini. I shall not trouble you with details; you do not require
them. Following the change of government, the central Revolutionary
Committee was established at the Comite, and we took control of all
surviving papers belonging to SAVAK. We also arrested large numbers
of former SAVAK officials and agents. From these papers and from
confessions extracted by our interrogators, we have built up a detailed
picture of the activities of your agency in our country. That picture

contains many details of your own work here during the past eight years. You have been a very successful agent, Mr. Randall, very successful and extremely dangerous to the interests of my people. In due course, you will be tried and executed as an enemy agent, but before that there is much that I want to learn from you. You are weak now, but the doctors tell me you can talk and that by next week you can be moved from the hospital. In one week, therefore, we shall move you to the Comite, where your full interrogation will begin. Do you understand what I am saying, Mr. Randall?"

The American lay unspeaking, his eyes open and fixed ahead. He gave no flicker of awareness, no sign that he understood or even heard.

"Mr. Randall, we have to talk a little today. There are things I must know about you before you are moved to the Comite. The doctors tell me you must not be pressured, but I really care very little what effect my questioning will have on you. Much more important issues are at stake. You will tell me what I want to know. Otherwise you may not reach the Comite alive. Do you understand?"

An appalling silence fell. The high white room, its windows double-glazed to filter out all sound from the traffic below, its thick walls designed to exclude noise from inside the building, seemed to embrace and magnify the molla's threats and Randall's failure to respond. One minute, two minutes passed, during which the American did not even blink his eyes. Then, at last, his lips began to move. In a whisper, he said, *"Chera . . . chera bi-Farsi harf nazanim?"*

Bent close to listen, Tabataba'i seemed to grate his teeth as he replied.

"No, Mr. Randall, we shall not speak in Persian. It would offend me. Your interrogation will take place in English."

Randall's eyes flashed for the first time since the molla had entered the room.

"That . . ." he said, "would offend me."

"Do not be a fool, Mr. Randall. If you will not speak to me, you will at least listen. You were brought here from a brothel in west Tehran, following a massacre in which twenty-six people were killed. You were one of six survivors. We have information that you had gone there to interview a notorious SAVAK agent called Heshmat. His body was found in the same room as yours. We believe that the

purpose of the massacre was to kill you and Heshmat. Do you know
who was responsible for the killings?"

Randall remained silent. He shook his head.

"You must have some idea. Who knew you had gone there?"

The American whispered the name that had been on his lips ever
since he had recovered consciousness.

"Hajj Reza Turk."

Tabataba'i frowned.

"No, Hajj Reza had nothing to do with it. He and his *chaqukashan*
were killed later that evening while leaving their gambling den.
Nurullah Baqirzadeh was with them; he was killed as well. We think
the same group was responsible, the group you were investigating, the
group who killed the American woman you were living with. We have
found additional documents in the house in the bazaar where
Heshmat was hiding, but it is not enough. We need more information. You are the only person left alive who knows about this group.
You will tell me what you know."

"I know nothing."

"What did Heshmat tell you?"

"Nothing . . . He told me nothing . . . He was about to tell me
. . . when . . . when they shot us . . . You know more than I do
. . . They're your people . . . religious terrorists . . . You know
who they are."

The Iranian shook his head wearily.

"No, I do not know. That is why I have come to speak with you.
We do not know who they are, but they may endanger the revolution.
We have to identify them, root them out before it is too late."

Randall sensed the fear in Tabataba'i's voice, a fear verging on
panic. Speaking in Persian, he whispered gently.

"You started this fucking mess, you and your lunatic friends. It's
not my business any longer. What the hell do I care if you shoot each
other's brains out?"

A wave of nausea swept over him and he closed his eyes, fighting
the giddiness, struggling to hold on to consciousness. Through the
blackness, he heard Tabataba'i rise and go to the door, heard it open,
heard the footsteps of the nurse in the corridor, then in the room, her
hands holding him, supporting him, like Fujiko's hands. From somewhere deep inside him, tears rose uncontrollably to his throat.

Tabataba'i came every day during the following week, asked the same questions, received the same answers, and left again. Randall knew he would not kill him as he had threatened. He wanted information badly, and he was convinced that Randall knew enough to lead him to the people he sought. Once at the Comite, he could be broken effectively and the information extracted. The date for his transfer had been set as Sunday, 6 May. Randall knew that if he did not make his escape before reaching the prison he would never have another chance. Physically, he was stronger than he seemed, and during the past seven days, the threat of danger had made him mentally alert as well, but his position still seemed hopeless.

On the Saturday morning following Tabataba'i's last visit, Randall was examined as usual by Dr. Quchani. The doctor was a Sorbonne-educated psychiatrist in his mid-forties who had returned to Iran seven years before to look after ageing parents. His conversations with Randall had been restricted by the presence of the various nurses assigned to the room, all of whom were committed revolutionaries, but the American had grown to like Quchani. The day before, Randall had whispered his fears of secret execution to him, but the psychiatrist had only nodded and returned to his tests. Now, halfway through the examination, Quchani straightened up and said that he had forgotten to bring an important file. He turned to the nurse and asked her to fetch it from his office. She seemed reluctant to go, but the doctor snapped at her impatiently and told her to hurry; years of deeply ingrained hospital discipline overcame somewhat newer instincts of revolutionary suspicion, and she left the room. Once she was gone, Quchani spoke quickly to his patient, his voice low because of the guard at the door outside.

"Listen, I won't have time to repeat this, so you must listen carefully. At three o'clock this afternoon, you're to be taken to the treatment room on the ground floor for your final physiotherapy session. There'll be one doctor and one nurse only in attendance, and no guards at the door. Watch the nurse, she'll be armed. The doctor's not a revolutionary, he'll not try to stop you. Outside the treatment room, turn left along the corridor, then second right. That'll take you to an unguarded side entrance; it can be opened from the inside. If you make it, go to number 12 Halali Street, apartment 4. I'm sorry, but this is the best I can do for you."

The door opened and the nurse entered, carrying the missing file. Randall wondered if she would be on duty that afternoon.

She was not, but it made little difference. In tight head scarf and glasses, they all looked much the same to Randall—sexless vestiges of women. They said they wore the head scarf or the chador to prevent men being distracted by their beauty; Randall had seen very little beauty and certainly nothing to distract. He didn't think removing the head scarfs would make much difference.

At three o'clock, the doctor in charge of the session came into the room and, with the nurse's help, lifted Randall from the bed. Together, they supported him to the lift, then into the ground-floor corridor that led to the treatment room. Randall knew that he could walk without their assistance, but he had feigned a degree of weakness for just such an eventuality as this. In the treatment room, he was asked to strip and lie down on the low massage couch in the middle. As he did so, he tensed himself, knowing that he had to act quickly, before the treatment began to tire him. The nurse came toward him, then bent down to lift him to a sitting position. As she did so, he reached up and grabbed for her neck; her reflexes were fast, and she was able to fasten both hands around his wrists, but his training and experience proved more than a match for her superior physical strength. His fingers found her carotid arteries and jabbed expertly; she blacked out instantly, and he held the pressure for several moments more to ensure that she would remain unconscious for some time. The doctor had started toward him, but Randall hissed at him, "If you come any closer, I'll kill her! Now back away!"

His hands moved quickly across the woman's inert body, finding it hard and unfeminine, the breasts strapped down to avoid their unseemly emphasis. He found the gun, a small automatic, in a holster at her side, retrieved it, and leveled it at the doctor, letting the nurse's limp body slide to the floor with as little noise as possible.

He turned his attention to the doctor, the gun still pointed toward him.

"Quickly—take off your clothes."

Reluctantly, the man began to strip.

"That's enough," said Randall when he had reached his briefs. "Keep those on in case Bluestocking here wakes up and has a heart attack. Now, I'm sorry about this, but it's really for your own good."

Randall stepped toward the frightened man, raised the gun, and struck him on the left temple. He would wake up in about an hour with a nasty headache, but at least he was in the best place for it. And more to the point, he would not be suspected of collusion. As he dressed quickly in the doctor's clothes, putting on the white physician's jacket over the neat blue suit, Randall felt energy begin to surge through him. He had been inactive for so long, but now adrenaline charged his system again. He knew the euphoria would not last, that he had to find a place of safety quickly, before the inevitable lassitude set in. But for the moment, he felt alive again and ready to fend for himself in order to stay that way.

Cautiously, he eased open the door into the passage and looked to right and left. The corridor was empty, but sounds of activity came from both directions. Closing the door quietly, he hastened to the left. A walk was normally safer in such situations, but he reasoned that no one would find it unusual to see a doctor running in a hospital. Nevertheless, he wished he knew in which direction the casualty unit lay, whether he was rushing toward it or away. Taking the second turn to his right, he soon reached the side entrance described by Quchani. He grasped the handle and pulled it hard toward him. It would not move. He tried again, pushing and pulling, but it was evident that the door was locked. Behind him, he could hear the sound of footsteps and a trolley being pushed along the corridor. Panting, he removed the white coat, wrapped it several times around the automatic, and aimed the gun at the lock, between the door and the jamb. There was a thud, but the door jerked as the bullet sheared through the lock. Behind him, he heard the trolley drawing near the entrance to the side corridor in which he stood. Without pausing, he pulled the door toward him, praying there was no one outside. He slipped through, breathing heavily, and closed the door behind him.

The rays of the sun, already falling low toward the horizon, caught him full in the eyes, making him squint. He had come out on the western side of the hospital, facing the main street known at this section as Parkway. Quickly, he glanced around. There was no one nearby. He unwrapped the gun and rammed it into his inside pocket, dropping the medical jacket behind him as he did so. He smoothed the suit jacket and straightened his tie, heading for the side gate that led on to Parkway, hoping that the guards he expected to be on duty there would be more suspicious of those coming in than those going out.

Two floors above him, three men stood at the window of a small office. Molla Hasan Tabataba'i turned to the man on his left and smiled.

"Thank you, Dr. Quchani. It has all gone as arranged. I am sure your son will be released from custody within the next few days. I have already spoken with Mr. Lajevardi, the Revolutionary Prosecutor. Please tell your wife there is nothing more to fear."

The smile left his face and he turned to his right, where the third man, a corpulent cleric in heavy black robes, still stood gazing from the window.

"Don't worry, excellency," Tabataba'i said. "He can always be picked up again at any time we wish. He will be under constant surveillance. But for now, he is our bait. A little time and he will lead us directly to them."

"How can you be so sure, Molla Hasan?" the fat man asked, his lips scarcely moving behind the thick mat of his mustache. "How can you be certain that he will not go to his own people, try to flee the country? That is what I would do, were I in his position."

"He will not do that, sir; rest assured. He has scores to settle, revenge to seek. He is thirsty and he has to drink. I know he will look for them, and when he finds them, we shall be close behind. After that, he is yours, I promise."

The fat man still stared after the diminishing figure of Randall.

"If the Revolutionary Guards do not get him first."

"Yes," agreed Tabataba'i. "There are factors even we cannot control."

13

TEHRAN
5–6 May 1979

The sun sank rapidly, seeming to drag with it part of the thin fabric of the late spring sky. Darkness rushed to accomplish its nightly mission, settling over the city like a huge hand. And with the darkness, fear that daylight had in part dispelled returned with its former strength, for, by night, Tehran had become a city of fear. People stayed at home, dreading the footsteps of Khomeini's Revolutionary Guards, the knock at the door and the sudden arrests. After midnight, the Revolutionary Courts would sit, their deliberations swift, their verdicts immediate, and the executions that followed pitiless.

Peter Randall was exhausted, hungry, and frightened. For two hours, he had walked through central Tehran, resting frequently to conserve his strength, observing, thinking, trying to decide what to do. He had expected changes, but nothing had prepared him for what he now saw. Everywhere he went, he saw banks and cinemas burned out and boarded up, foreign shops and businesses gutted, photographs of Khomeini and slogans, women in head scarves, and on almost every street, men with guns, the Revolutionary Guards about whom Tabataba'i had once spoken. He felt conspicuous, his pale skin and blue eyes marking him out as a foreigner and therefore a possible spy. He had never felt so totally alone before, so completely exposed. The automatic weighed heavily in his pocket, and he knew that if he were searched he could be killed on the spot for possessing it. He had some money in the pockets of the suit he had taken, but none of the identification cards were of any use to him. The address given him by Quchani he would use only as a last resort: it was too close to his old apartment in Kakh and was probably too closely connected to the doctor to be entirely safe if he were suspected.

He had headed north after a little, away from the main streets, into the middle-class area of Yusefabad, taking a taxi as far as the east end of Aryamehr. Here he felt less exposed, among the suburbanites in their Western clothes, their eyes less suspicious of him in their midst. But even here safety could not be prolonged indefinitely. There were several CIA safe houses and dozens of emergency contacts, but Tabataba'i had implied that the security leaks through SAVAK had been heavy, and he had no way of knowing where and who was really safe any longer. His cover had been blown, and now he was on his own. The embassy would already have denied all knowledge of him and his activities, and although they might still be willing to help him find a way out, he could not be sure. Better to stay and finish what he had started several months ago. Then, if there was an escape route, he would find and use it. But first, he had to get off the streets, find a safe place for tonight, and for longer if possible.

Suddenly, there was a shout behind him: "Hey, you!" A man's voice, harsh and imperative. Randall froze, his hand moving toward his gun, turning slowly.

He saw them on the corner of the side street he had just passed, three Revolutionary Guards, two armed with pistols, one with an AK-47. About to break into a run, he realized that they had not shouted at him but at a girl on the opposite pavement. She was aged about twenty, attractive, and dressed in Western clothes, a gray suit of trousers and jacket. The man shouted again, angrily beckoning to the girl to cross to where he and his companions stood. Hesitantly, she obeyed.

"What's this?" the first man screamed at her as she came up. "Don't you understand anything? Are you stupid?"

"You know that women are expected to dress modestly in our society," shouted a second man, grabbing the girl as she came within range and beginning to shake her. Randall watched, horrified at what was happening. On the other side of the road, passersby hurried on, away from the street lights illuminating the scene.

"You are filth, cheap trash to dress like this, without shame," the first man snarled. Randall saw that he had ripped open the front of the girl's jacket and was pawing her breasts while the others looked on, fascinated. The third man held her from behind. She had begun to sob, though Randall could see that pride and anger fought with her fear for mastery over her.

Suddenly, the man brought his fist low and began to punch the girl in the groin, sharp, painful blows. "You want to display your legs, your private parts, so everyone can see?" He went on punching. Randall began to edge toward the group, fury rising in him like a tide. They did not notice him, so preoccupied were they with the girl.

"And why are you on the street alone after dark? I know why. You're a prostitute, a cheap whore. I've seen you before here, walking the streets, day and night. That's what you are, a harlot."

Fahisha! The word rang out, echoing across the brickwork around them, singing in Randall's ears. Before he even realized that he had acted, the automatic was in his hand, he was raising it. The man died on the first shot, a bullet in his brain. The girl screamed and Randall ran toward her. The other two guards moved away from her, turning toward Randall. The one with the AK-47 fired, wide of his target. Amateurs, their weapons looted from military barracks during the February takeover, they were no match for the American, tired as he was. Two further shots disabled them.

The girl stood frozen, rooted to the spot. Randall rushed up to her, ramming the gun into his pocket, and took her by the arm.

"Quickly," he said, "we must get away from here. Where can we go?"

Though still shocked, she was intelligent and able to assess the situation. She nodded and pointed up the side street.

"Here, this way first, then left."

They began to run, Randall slowly, his breathing difficult. His legs, already drained of strength, felt like lead and pounded with pain. The girl turned to him, puzzled.

"I'm sorry," he said, "I'm ill. I've been in the hospital. I can't go quickly."

"We must get away," she cried, taking his arm and supporting him. They reached the first turn. Here, in the smaller streets, lighting was poor and everywhere there were shadows in which to hide. The girl knew the way. Her house was close, a new house set behind a high stone wall. She rang the bell, jabbing it urgently. The speaker at the side crackled.

"Baleh! Ki-e?"

"Man-am. Zud bash, dar-ra baz kon."

A buzzer sounded and the girl pushed the gate open. They rushed inside and closed it behind them. At the top of the steps leading to the front door, the girl's mother stood, frightened by the tone of her daughter's voice. Seconds later, her father appeared. The girl ran

forward, sobbing, into her mother's arms. Randall came up the steps
more slowly and they entered the house together. Once inside, the
girl was taken away by her mother, while Randall was ushered into
the living room by the father, a man in his late forties with a receding
forehead and an intelligent face that at present betrayed considerable
concern and perplexity.

"Please, sit down," he said, motioning Randall toward a chair. The
room was well furnished, the result of taste rather than limitless
money. Exhausted, the American sank into the chair, feeling his legs
give way beneath him.

"I'm sorry," he said, "but I don't think I can talk much. I'm ill.
There was trouble. Revolutionary Guards."

The man frowned and took a deep breath.

"Are you hurt? Wounded?"

"No, but tired, very tired."

"I have a friend nearby who is a doctor. He can be trusted. Don't
worry, you're safe for the moment. We'll learn what happened later,
after you've rested. Vida will tell us when she has recovered."

The man turned and left the room. Randall caught sight of his stiff,
worried face in a mirror by the door. He felt overcome and sank back
into the chair, falling into darkness and silence and nightmare.

It was already nine o'clock when he woke the next morning. His body
ached and his head thudded with pain. With difficulty, he opened his
eyes. He was in a strange bed in a strange room. This was not the
hospital. Then the events of the previous day flooded back into his
mind. What had he done last night? In all his years in Tehran, he had
never killed in so thoughtless a manner. Since he had been in Iran, he
had only killed six times and always through sheer necessity, driven by
situations that had passed out of his control. But now that armed men
roamed the streets, a state of anarchy had been loosed in which violence would breed violence and death engender death. He sensed that
it was out of control and that it would take him deeper and deeper
into its dark heart.

But he should not have interfered last night. He had put his own
life and the life of the girl in jeopardy. They would link the shooting
of the Guards to him, an armed foreigner. The hunt would be intensified and the noose around him grow tighter hour by hour. Would it

not be better to start looking for that escape route now, before it was too late? If it was not too late already.

The door opened and the man he remembered from the night before entered the room. He smiled and came across to the bed, but beneath the smile Randall could detect anxiety.

"How have you slept?" he asked. "Are you feeling any better? My friend examined you last night; he says you have been very ill. Vida tells me that you mentioned you had been in the hospital. My friend says you have scars from gunshot wounds, a few months old. Who are you? Why did you become involved in what happened last night?"

Randall tried to sit up but found he could not. His mouth felt dry and it was painful to speak.

"I'm sorry," said the man. "You must eat and drink something before we talk. My wife will bring breakfast. Do you drink coffee? We have some freshly ground."

Randall nodded and tried to smile. The man rose and went out. His feet sounded loudly on a stone staircase outside, and Randall realized he had not even told him his name.

After a light breakfast, during which he learned that his host's name was Rustam Kayvanpur, a banker, Randall was able to sit up and talk.

"My name is Mason, Norman Mason. I'm an American, a representative for General Motors here in Tehran. I was injured during riots in December; I got mistaken for a demonstrator and shot. I was only released from hospital yesterday. I plan to go back to the States as soon as possible, but I have affairs to wind up here. I was on my way home last night when I saw your daughter being assaulted and something in me snapped. Anyway, she'll have told you what happened."

"A little, yes. Thank you, thank you for going to her aid. But I don't understand why you were carrying a gun."

"A friend brought it to me in the hospital before I left. He said I might need it, that Americans were unpopular and that I might be attacked."

"But Vida says you handled it like an expert, that you didn't miss."

"I was in the Army in Vietnam, and I was lucky last night; those guys were amateurs."

"Mr. Mason, if that's your real name, I don't think you're telling me the truth. Why were you alone in your condition? Walking. And why do you have papers belonging to a Dr. Khosravi in your pocket? Who are you? Where do you live?"

Randall breathed deeply, realizing that he could not hope to talk his way out of the situation. The papers had been his biggest mistake. He had been a fool not to get rid of them as soon as possible.

"All right," he said. "My name is Peter Randall and I work for the U.S. Government. I was being taken from the hospital to the Comite Prison, where I was to be executed. I escaped and came here yesterday evening while thinking about where to go. You know the rest. I don't know what your political views are, and I don't care, but I assure you that I am not an enemy of your country or your people. You must trust me. I need your help."

The Iranian remained silent, bent over in his chair, his head resting on his hands. After about a minute, he lifted his head and spoke in a quiet voice.

"Mr. Randall, I'm grateful for what you did last night. They are brutes, those guards. I have no strong political leanings, but I already hate this régime and what it is doing to this country, to innocent people like my daughter. But what you did was foolish. It has put us all in danger, serious danger. There were searches in this area last night; there will be more today and tonight until they find you and Vida. They can't have known her or we would have been arrested last night. I've sent Vida to the country, to her aunt in Ishtahard; she left early this morning with a friend. But you cannot stay here; if they find you, we shall all be taken and executed. You must leave today. Have you somewhere to go?"

Randall thought quickly. He could not risk telling this man anything of his plans nor put someone else in jeopardy by giving a false destination.

"Please, just take me into the city, near the American Embassy. I have no papers, but I'll find a way to get in. Will you do that?"

"Yes, that won't be difficult. I'll drive you there as soon as you're able to go."

Kayvanpur smiled and rose to go. As he did so, his wife came to retrieve the breakfast things. She was an attractive woman in her early forties, but she looked tense and upset. As before, she did not speak to Randall. They left together, shutting the door behind them. Randall lay back and shut his eyes, willing himself to recover, to regain what limited strength he had possessed yesterday. Half an hour passed in silence.

The click of the front door closing woke him, but it was the unmistakable sound of two rifle breeches being pushed back that alerted him to his danger. He had been a fool. The man had no reason to risk the lives of himself and his family for a stranger who might be a spy; far better to contact the authorities and hand him over in exchange for his daughter's safety.

He sprang from the bed, his stiff limbs protesting. Quickly, he jammed a chair against the door, then found his clothes, minus gun and papers, draped over the foot of the bed. He dressed rapidly, puzzled by the delay. Trousers, shoes were enough. Feet sounded on the landing, the men outside were cautious, afraid he might still somehow be armed. Moving as quietly as possible, Randall opened the small double window and swung himself out; it gave onto a small patio and lay about two feet under the flat roof. Thank God they had not had the intelligence to post anyone underneath.

With agony in every limb, Randall swung himself up and onto the roof, rapidly scanning his surroundings. The house was not close enough to its neighbors to allow him to cross to another roof. Thinking quickly, he lay down on the edge of the roof, near the window through which he had just escaped. There was a crashing sound from inside the room, then feet running. A moment passed, then a hand appeared on the roof, holding a submachine gun, followed by a second hand and a head. Simultaneously, Randall grabbed for the gun and began to leap to his feet. The guard's face gaped, his mouth wide open, then Randall's foot shot out, landing heavily on the man's chin. The guard gave a cry and fell backward, toppling outward from the window onto the concrete below. Without pausing, Randall lay down again, swung himself down and over the window, held the machine gun at the opening and fired rapidly, swinging the barrel in a wide arc. There were cries from inside.

Tensing himself against the protests of his muscles, Randall dragged himself back onto the roof, then ran hurriedly to each of the other sides and looked down. A single jeep was parked on the road outside, but there was no sign of any other guards. They must have sent three or four to arrest him; more would have been unnecessary. No neighbors had come onto the road to investigate the sound of gunfire; this time the terror instilled by the guards had worked to

Randall's advantage. He moved across to the back of the house again, looked over the roof, then swung himself down gingerly to the ledge of the window beside the one through which he had come. A heavy kick sent it flying open and he quickly maneuvered himself inside. Once there, he moved cautiously to the door and, sheltering by the wall, swung it open. There was no one on the landing. Flattening himself against the intervening section of wall, he moved to the door of the bedroom he had been in, the gun pointed ahead of him. Glancing inside, he saw two men on the floor, both badly wounded.

"How many were you?" he asked. "The truth, or I blow your head off."

One of the men stammered, "Three." Randall paused only to take their rifles, then slammed the door and made for the head of the stairs. There had been four, he was certain. The fourth man must have stayed downstairs to keep an eye on the occupants of the house. Where was he now? These guards were mostly amateurs, youths with guns they barely knew how to use. But sometimes amateurs could be more dangerous than professionals: they overreacted and made mistakes you didn't expect them to make.

The stairs led directly into the main room of the ground floor. Out there, Randall would be exposed, a simple target, easily picked off even by a child. He had to make the guard reveal himself first. He reached behind him for one of the rifles he had snatched from the bedroom, lifted it, and fired once into the ground, screaming as he did so, as if in pain. He then shouted loudly in Persian, "I got him," and began to run down the stairs. The door of the room facing the stairs across the living room opened and the fourth guard came out. When he saw Randall, it was already too late. The American fired from waist level, throwing the man back into the room, where he lay twitching for several seconds before giving a final jerk and lying still. Inside the next room, a woman screamed.

Randall checked that the guard was dead, then strode into the room. He thought his bones would break with the pain of moving and his head throbbed incessantly. Kayvanpur and his wife stood huddled together, fear creasing their faces. Randall was sorry for them. But he had no time to spare for pity.

"Where are your car keys?" he shouted. The banker, his eyes open in terror, jerked his head toward a low table beside the door. The keys lay jumbled with others on a ring.

"Which ones?" Randall asked, picking up the bunch.

"The largest two," Kayvanpur replied, his voice shaking. "Silver."

"Which way to the garage?"

Kayvanpur pointed. "Through the kitchen and down some steps. The door's unlocked."

Randall nodded, then went back to the living room. He saw the telephone on a shelf near the stairs, crossed to it, and ripped out the wire.

"Are there any more?" he asked brusquely. Kayvanpur and his wife both shook their heads fiercely.

"I hope not. Now, listen to me. You're going to give me at least ten minutes before going for help. Do you understand? If I have any reason to believe you haven't stuck to that, I'll come back." He knew they would obey his instructions; they were too numb with terror by now to do otherwise. He headed for the garage.

14

TEHRAN
6–16 May 1979

It was out of the question to drive anywhere near his real destination, so he left the car on Pahlavi, five minutes away, at the first public telephone kiosk. He had made up his mind to contact Sirus Rastgu, a lawyer who lived in Tajrish in the far north of the city. Rastgu was a deep-cover agent for MOSSAD, the Israeli intelligence service, who had been living in Tehran for fifteen years. His real name was Ilyahu Elghanian, and his family were Iranian Jews who had emigrated to Israel in 1949, when he was ten. Elghanian's cover was excellent, making use as it did of the extensive family connections of his pretty Muslim wife, whom he had married one year after his arrival in Tehran, and who had no idea of his undercover activities. He owed Randall several favors, some of them big ones, but he would still need persuading to take the risk of sheltering him.

Randall breathed a sigh of relief when Rastgu answered the phone in person. It was a Sunday, a full working day here, and he had expected the wife to answer and to give him her husband's office number. He spoke softly and rapidly.

"Is this line sterile?"

"Yes."

"When was it last checked?"

"Yesterday. Who is this?"

"Randall. Meet me on the corner of Takht-e Ta'us and Nader Shah. Hurry."

He hung up, leaving no time for questions or protests. Those could be dealt with later, in person. His first priority was to get off the streets. He began to walk slowly to his rendezvous, about ten minutes away. Elghanian would be there in a quarter of an hour, perhaps sooner.

He only had to wait three minutes before the Israeli's Jaguar pulled up at the curb. It was a conspicuous car here, but fast and consistent with the lifestyle of a jet-set lawyer. Rastgu scowled as he opened the door for Randall. As soon as the American was seated, he let in the clutch and roared out into the sea of traffic on Takht-e Ta'us, heading east.

"I'm taking you to a safe house in Majdiyye. We'll move you in a few days. Now talk. What the hell are you up to? You could blow my cover. When did you get out of the hospital?"

"Yesterday. It's a long story. Didn't you read about it in the papers, hear anything on the radio?"

Rastgu shook his head. "No, nothing. Should I?"

Randall was puzzled. "I would have thought they'd have had my description out by now. Sirus, I need a doctor, and I don't want Straker or anybody else to know my whereabouts. Not yet, anyway."

"Straker's gone. They've been pulling people out since February. The British as well. And ourselves. Everybody, for God's sake; this place has gone crazy. What's happened? Why aren't you on an escape line?"

"I've told you, it's a long story. There was a little fracas. Sorry, two: one yesterday, another less than half an hour ago. Both involving Revolutionary Guards."

"Shit. You want to stay clear of those bastards."

"That's precisely what I've been trying to do. Sirus, you owe me. I could cancel, but I need your help. And your people are partly responsible anyhow."

"But things have changed, Peter. There's never been anywhere like this before, it's completely insane. But what the hell! We're in the same filthy business, we're on the same side—some of the time—and we've been good friends. Yes, I'll help. You look as if you need it. But first, I'll take you to your new residence and a very discreet doctor."

It was not until the following evening that Rastgu came again, under the cover of darkness, to the safe house in Majdiyye. Randall was by then much recovered, though still a little groggy from the painkillers the doctor had administered. Rest and relief from tension had helped a lot. Randall explained as much as he could about what had happened to him, and Rastgu filled him in on events since January.

The Israeli did not attempt to question Randall about the motives for his evident determination to stay in Iran, nor did he try to dissuade him from his chosen course of action. Since last year, everyone had been behaving strangely and it was futile to try to resist the tide. He himself would hold out only as long as it seemed possible or advisable to do so, then break in the end, but whether to return with his wife and family to a new life in Tel Aviv or to die smuggling Jewish refugees out of the country, he did not know. For his part, Randall volunteered only what he knew, not what he felt. In all honesty, he did not know what his feelings were, but they had little to do with revenge, with the simplicity of retribution; he understood that now. The deaths of Iraj and Fujiko were unreal events, fragile as dreams; his own near-death had followed them so closely that he had not yet had time to formulate clear thoughts or clear emotions about them.

He would stay and he would track down the group responsible for their deaths, not because of those deaths but because of all the other brutal, senseless killings that were washing this country in blood. Or not, perhaps, even for that. It was his means of defending himself against the almost irresistible sense of failure that at times threatened to engulf him. For years, he and his colleagues had done all they could to protect Iran, to defend it against subversion from within and from outside aggression, to engender stability, a basis for democracy and freedom. He had committed abominations in the belief that they served a higher cause, had convinced himself that noble ends justified often terrible means. But what had it all led to?

Greater megalomania on the part of the Shah, greater repression, greater injustice, and, in the end, the inevitable revolution, which marked the defeat of all they had worked for. He could not resist or change that, not alone, not even with battalions of tanks and men. But he might be able to destroy something within it, something that instinct told him was more deadly than all the rest. He did not know its real identity or even possess an inkling of its true purposes, but it stood for all he most loathed and feared. Like a beast of prey or a giant spider, it was waiting in its lair, biding its time, preparing to strike. He would track it down to its source and destroy it there or die in the attempt. It really mattered very little whether he lived or died.

Then Rastgu's voice broke his reverie.

"First of all," said the Israeli, "we have to get you out of here. I'm working more or less alone since the closure of the Israeli Mission in Tehran, but I can't risk keeping you in this house. I'm moving you tomorrow to another house in Darband, in the foothills to the north of the city. You'll be safer there. But I can get you into the American Embassy just as easily; it's time you were out of Iran."

"No, thanks. There are some things I have to do here first. I want you to get me information, as much information as possible. I want to know about the brothel where the shooting took place—who owned it, everything about it. Then I'd like details about the house in Qolhak where the shootings took place in October 1977—the same thing: owner, previous owner, everything you can get. And I want files on all members of the department of Persian studies at Tehran University. And everything you can find on Masood Heshmat. That'll probably be enough to start with."

"It's plenty. I can't promise too much, Peter; you've no idea how difficult it is even to find the names of streets nowadays. Too many questions, too much curiosity, and you end up in Evin or the Comite, and before twenty-four hours are up you're staring down the barrel of a Mauser. People are betraying their friends, their relatives. I've heard of parents informing on their children, children on their parents. Nobody seems to be quite sane any longer. I'll do what I can, but no promises."

The following day Rastgu took Randall to Darband as he had promised. Up here, where the Elburz foothills began, the air was fresh and strong. It was a popular spot for picnickers, hikers, hill climbers, busiest in the evenings when people drove out from the heat of the city to enjoy a walk by the small river that flowed down through the center of the defile. The house in which Randall lived was hidden behind trees, quiet and invisible from the road. He spent his days exercising and reading, pushing body and mind in an effort to regain a peak of fitness. He was recovering rapidly now, but he never smiled and never referred to the past. Deep inside him, thoughts were buried that not even he knew were there. With Rastgu, who came regularly with supplies, he was outwardly present but inwardly withdrawn. Both men were worried by the fact that nothing had been written in the papers or said on the radio or television about Randall's escape from the hospital, although there had been lengthy reports about the shootings of the Revolutionary Guards in Yusefabad in which mention had been made of a foreigner.

It took Rastgu a week to track down his first item of information.

The brothel in Mortezavi Street had been owned by SAVAK. It was a popular haven for state officials and military men, as well as SAVAK agents, who had free access to the girls. There had been several important people there on the night of the massacre, one of the reasons for the complete clampdown there had been on references to it in the media. The girls were carefully picked and groomed and were paid well to remember interesting items of pillow-talk—it was cheaper and more efficient than bugging. Naked and relaxed after an exhausting session in bed with one or more of the house's skilled young ladies (or, on occasion, young men), all but the most tight-lipped of men could be cajoled into dangerous indiscretions. More than one customer over the years had paid for the thrills of a night with weeks in the torture chamber and a bullet at the end.

Two days later, Rastgu returned with more information. He had copies of all the files Randall had wanted from the University Secretariat, and had details about the house in Qolhak.

"The house, Peter, belongs to a certain 'Abbas Pakdini, who lives in a small village called Vakilabad, about one hundred miles southeast of Kerman. He's a rich farmer, with acres of pistachio trees. He has owned the house for nine years, during which time he has rented it out to large numbers of people, mostly Americans and Europeans, for unearthly rents. But for about a year leading up to the raid in '77, the house was rented by an Iranian called Farhad Rezapur. Does the name mean anything to you?"

"Yes, of course. He was General Naseri's chief assistant at SAVAK HQ."

"And he was also the man responsible for running the brothel in Mortezavi."

"Can he be contacted?"

"I'm afraid not. He was executed in early March, along with about a dozen other SAVAK officials. It's not much of a lead, I know, but it's the best I can do."

"That's OK. Just leave these files with me. I may find something, though I wish to God I knew what I was looking for."

When Rastgu had gone, Randall began the task of reading through the twenty thick files that the Israeli had left on his desk. Somewhere in here, he told himself, lay information that would link one of these names to the death of Iraj Ashrafi. He was certain of it.

Hour after hour, he read and reread the material in each folder, most of it trivial, some of it sordid, and none of it seemingly relevant to his purpose. Several lecturers had at different times shown political leanings of one kind or another, and more than one was deeply religious, but over the years anyone with serious oppositional tendencies had been arrested and incarcerated and his file removed to SAVAK headquarters. These files, like all files of their kind, were indiscriminate collections of the crucial and the meaningless, from a man's political opinions to his taste in underwear, and the garbage obscured anything of real value that might be lurking underneath.

And yet it was in the so-called garbage that Randall found what he was after, at about three o'clock the next morning. His mistake had been the assumption that he was looking for one man. In no one file was there anything of obvious significance, anything that would qualify as unduly suspicious. But in three files there was one small item, of no value in any one instance, but highly curious when linked to three separate individuals in one small establishment. The item in question occurred in the small personal details card pinned to the outside of every file and overlooked by Randall at least a dozen times. The three entries in question read as follows:

Name: Mo'ini, Jaafar (Professor)
Date of Birth: 16 Khordad 1297 (6 June 1918)
Place of Birth: Tehran
Name of Father: Mirza Ibrahim Khan Qazvini, Mo'in al-
Dawla
Name of Mother: Fatima, daughter of Mirza Muhammad
'Ali Nayyir Tehrani
Date of Appointment: Start of academic year, 10
Shahrivar 1349 (1 September 1970)
Last Place of Residence: Bam
Present Address: Apt. 3, 12 Vaziri Street, Pahlavi Avenue

Name: Rustamzadeh, Kayvan (Dr.)
Date of Birth: 9 Mehr 1326 (1 October 1947)
Place of Birth: Hamadan
Name of Father: Firuz Rustamzadeh
Name of Mother: Goli Rawhani
Date of Appointment: Start of academic year, 10
Shahrivar 1355 (1 September 1976)

Last Place of Residence: Bam
Present Address: Apt. 7, 49 Yaghma Street, Shah Avenue

Name: Amiri, Reza (Dr.)
Date of Birth: 3 Aban 1327 (25 October 1948)
Place of Birth: Shiraz
Name of Father: Asadollah Amiri
Name of Mother: Mehri Aqazadeh
Date of Appointment: Start of academic year, 10
     Shahrivar 1355 (1 September 1976)
Last Place of Residence: Bam
Present Address: Apt. 4, 17 Istakhr Street, Sepah Avenue

It was extraordinary, thought Randall, that three members of one small academic department should all share the same precious place of residence, when the town in question was scarcely more than a large village, a date-growing oasis on the edge of the desert in the Southeast of the country.

It was also curious, Randall reflected, that all three should have addresses in the center of Tehran, in what was a decent but far from popular neighborhood. Not only that, he realized with a shock as he pictured the area in his mind's eye, but within a few blocks of one another.

The system of academic appointments in Iran, where new universities were being established more quickly than capable native teachers could be found or trained to staff them, differed from that of most Western countries, where it is difficult for those outside the university system to compete for academic jobs. Nevertheless, it was still curious that all three of these men had experienced a hiatus in their academic careers before being appointed to posts at Tehran. There is no university or equivalent institution in Bam. Whatever they had been doing there, it had not been academic teaching. Further study of their files revealed that Mo'ini had taught for fifteen years at what had been Shiraz University before its transformation into Pahlavi University in 1962. In 1968 he had resigned his position there to take up residence in Bam, apparently to carry out research on local history. Both Rustamzadeh and Amiri had been educated at Pahlavi, where they had studied under Mo'ini. Following the completion of their doctorates in 1973 and 1974, both had gone to Bam to assist Mo'ini. The latter had been wealthy enough to finance two research assistants, and the whole thing seemed perfectly plausible. But Randall could find no record for any books, monographs, or papers published or presented by any of the three concerning the history or dialect of Bam.

There had been something else too in the back of Randall's mind, and now he remembered what it was. Vakilabad, the home of the man who owned the house in Qolhak, was only about ten miles from Bam.

15

TEHRAN
16 May 1979

A discreet check carried out by Rastgu later that same day confirmed that, although the university had been officially closed, the three academics were all still in Tehran and living at the same addresses. Randall chose Mo'ini. He was obviously the leader, would be better informed, and probably lived alone, as his wife had died three years earlier. Randall would need Rastgu's help to bring the professor to Darband, but from then on he would handle the interrogation alone.

At seven o'clock the same evening, Rastgu telephoned Mo'ini, explained that he was a lawyer who wished to discuss an urgent matter on behalf of a client, and asked if the professor would see him alone that evening. Mo'ini was suspicious at first, but Rastgu's explanation of the affair was so convincing that, in the end, Mo'ini agreed reluctantly to meet him, saying that he was already alone and expected no visitors. Five minutes later, Randall and his companion were on their way into Tehran. When they reached Vaziri Street, it was already quiet; Revolutionary Guards patrolled in squads of three or four, roaming the streets in search of antirégime terrorists. They had been stopped once on their way into the city, but Randall's new credentials, identifying him as John B. Royce, an American consultant working with Rastgu's law firm, proved acceptable.

Mo'ini had only a moment to betray his shock at seeing Randall when he opened the door. The American was ready with a chloroform pad, swinging in and behind the old man as he stood confused in the doorway. Together, he and Rastgu carried the inert body, propped between them, down to the car waiting below. It was all over in two minutes.

Back in the house in Darband, Mo'ini came to half an hour after their return. By then, he was firmly strapped in a chair; Rastgu had gone, leaving him alone with Randall. Wet towels and black coffee revived the professor sufficiently to begin the interrogation. Mo'ini looked older than his sixty years, white-haired and slightly frail. But Randall had met him often enough to know that he had a strength of personality, even of physical endurance, that belied the scholarly appearance. Mo'ini would not be an easy man to question.

"I want you to listen carefully, Professor Mo'ini," Randall began. "Your life may depend on how attentive and willing you are to answer my questions honestly. You know who I am and why I have brought you here. We once shared a friend who is now dead. You were responsible, whether directly or indirectly, for his death. I know that, and I am not interested in discussing the matter. Iraj was killed because he had information for me concerning a group of terrorists, seven of whose members died in the course of a SAVAK raid on a house in Qolhak over a year ago. I want you to tell me all you know about this group, what connections you have with it, its leadership—everything."

Mo'ini struggled vainly against the straps that held him to the chair. He was frightened and still befuddled by the effects of the chloroform. He shook his head as if to clear it.

"You are not Randall. You can't be. He's dead, killed four months ago. You are an impostor."

"You know me well enough, Professor. I haven't time for identity games. I've killed many times and I will have no hesitation in killing you if that proves necessary. Perhaps I shall do so anyway—you have a life to answer for. What do you know about this group?"

Mo'ini threw his head back, his face suffused with sweat.

"I know of no groups, no killings. You're insane, whoever you are. I'm a professor of literature. My job has nothing to do with killing."

"What do you do in your spare time, Professor?"

"I write poetry," the professor snapped.

"This is a country of poets, everybody writes poetry in his spare time. Bank clerks, teachers, policemen, generals—they all write poetry. What did you do in your spare time at Bam, Professor?"

Mo'ini was caught off guard. His eyes flashed, then grew dull again and veiled.

"I spent some years in Bam. I did some research there, on local history, on dialectic histories of the region written in the last century. It is an extremely interesting place. The ruins are fascinating. And the dialect is quite intriguing; several archaic agricultural terms have been preserved there." Mo'ini was relaxing, gaining confidence. He had to be shaken again, put off his guard.

"Did you learn those from 'Abbas Pakdini? Does his name have any special significance? What does it mean exactly? 'Of the Pure Faith', I think."

Mo'ini's eyes flashed again, betraying his uncertainty. His confidence had given way once more to his mounting fear. How much did the American know? Good God, what had he been told? What had Heshmat discovered, God curse him?

As if he read the old man's mind, Randall went on remorselessly.

"When did you last meet the German? What is he planning?"

The prisoner's control broke.

"How . . . how do you know? What do you know of him?"

"You're not here to ask me questions. What I know and what I do not know are not your concerns. What was your connection with Farhad Rezapur? What do you know about the house he rented in Qolhak? The brothel he ran in Mortezavi Street?"

Mo'ini almost panicked again, but this time he fought for and gained control of himself. As Randall had suspected, he was a man of unexpected resources and considerable resilience.

"I think, Mr. Randall, that you are bluffing, that you know very little. Otherwise, you would not have brought me here tonight, you would already be elsewhere. You are wasting your time, I will tell you nothing."

"You will tell me everything before you leave here. Or you will not leave here. You have not understood me properly. I am not only capable of killing, I am capable of hurting. I am trained in the art of making the dumb speak. I can make them speak in whatever dialect I please. When I finish what I intend to do with you, you will not stop talking, nothing will be able to make you stop."

Beads of sweat stood out on Mo'ini's forehead and upper lip. He was fully conscious now. It was not the content of what Randall said, but the tone of his voice that terrified and bewildered him. Randall's voice went on, soft, but cruel and insistent.

"Professor Ashrafi was not the only one to die that day, as I am sure you know. Perhaps you had nothing to do with the woman's death, perhaps you did. But she meant a great deal to me, and I assure you that there are no lengths to which I am not prepared to go to find her killers and revenge her death."

Mo'ini tried to twist himself away from the voice, the insistent, hurting voice, and struggled to press down the growing panic he felt. His voice came, deep in his throat at first, rising as he spoke.

"It is too late for revenge, nothing can defeat our purpose now. We have power and we are ready to strike. The Seven are ready, they only await their orders. The Lances are ready, they only await his hand. The Sword is ready, he will soon be unsheathed. Your day is finished. Our day is about to dawn."

Mo'ini's mouth set and his eyes became glazed. He seemed to clamp his jaws together, as if clenching his teeth in defiance of Randall. Suddenly, his body became rigid and his eyes widened in horror. Strapped as he was in the chair, he began to jerk spasmodically, his limbs straining against his bonds, the chair rocking, then tilting and falling to the floor. Randall watched aghast as the professor rolled in his bonds, his head thrown back wildly, his torso convulsing in spasm after spasm. Then, as suddenly as it had begun, the thrashing stopped. Randall stooped over and touched him. He was dead. The American placed his nose against the man's mouth, then pulled it away abruptly. Cyanide. He strained to lift the chair with the body in it, raised it on to two legs, then righted it. He undid the straps and carried the body to a couch on the other side of the room. He would have to ring Rastgu.

16

TEHRAN
17 May 1979

There was no point in trying to return to Mo'ini's apartment that
night. It was late, and they would be certain to be stopped by Revolutionary Guards and taken into custody. After phoning the Israeli,
Randall went to bed and tried to sleep, but he did so only fitfully. He
was on the threshold; he felt somehow that the secret group was
almost within his grasp, and yet something told him that there was
more, more than he could ever guess.

Rastgu came at first light, and together they concealed the body in
the cellar before setting off for the city. They drove past the house in
Vaziri Street three times before deciding that all seemed quiet enough
to risk an entry. While Rastgu kept watch downstairs, Randall went
up to the apartment and opened the door with a key he had taken
from the dead man's pocket. He entered cautiously, aware that someone might already have discovered that the professor was missing,
that his friends might be on the alert. But the apartment was empty
and profoundly silent. Randall made for the study and began his
search of Mo'ini's papers.

An hour later, he had found nothing but notes on Persian language
and literature. Whatever materials Mo'ini had possessed relating to
his group had not been kept in his apartment, or else were hidden
there in a secret safe or drawer. There was no time to commence the
kind of search needed to find something so well concealed, and Randall suspected that it would prove a waste of time anyway. Angrily, he
thumped his fist down on the desk. To be on the threshold and yet
thwarted again. Would the professor's colleagues prove any more cooperative? As he struck the desk, his eyes fell on a small black book
that he had not noticed before. He glanced inside and saw that it was
Mo'ini's diary. As he flicked through its pages, however, he noticed
nothing that seemed unusual. The entries were humdrum: times of

seminars, departmental meetings, deadlines for articles. Then, as he was about to close the book, he paused at the last entry. It was for that evening, 17 May. Written in Arabic, a language Randall knew a little but not well, it would not ordinarily have attracted his attention, but at his second glance, he felt his heart pound. One word leapt at him from the page, and he knew he was on the track again. The entry read in full: *"Yawm mawlid hadrat sayyidatina Fatima; yajtama'un al-sab'a fi dar al-shidda"*—"The day of the birth of our Lady Fatima; the Seven shall meet in the land of violence."

The Seven. Mo'ini had spoken of them last night. Who were they? Were they successors to the seven who committed suicide in Qolhak? He closed the diary and put it in his pocket, thinking hard. He had to discover when they were meeting and where the "land of violence" was. Could Mo'ini's associates tell him?

Locking the apartment door behind him, Randall descended the stairs and rejoined Rastgu. As they drove back to Darband, he described his discovery.

"Your Arabic's better than mine, Sirus. Is my translation accurate?"

"Yes, it seems to be. But I would have translated *'dar'* as 'house' rather than 'land' or 'region.' I don't know about *'shidda'*; it could be 'violence,' certainly, but maybe 'force' would be better, or 'strength.' It's impossible to tell without a proper context."

" 'House of force,' " muttered Randall. "A house would certainly be a more logical place for a meeting. Wait a minute, though. What about 'house of strength'? *'Dar al-shidda'* could be an Arabic translation for the Persian *'zurkhane,'* couldn't it?"

"I hadn't thought of it, but now you suggest it, yes, it could very well be that. A meeting in a *zurkhane* sounds very plausible."

Randall's mind raced with excitement. The chase was still on. The *zurkhane*, the "house of strength," is an ancient Persian institution little known in the West. It is a highly exclusive men's club, where athletes come to practice traditional feats of strength and skill, as well as to devote themselves to the virtues of patience, endurance, fortitude, and self-control. There were numerous *zurkhanes* throughout Tehran, including a well-known one belonging to the Bank-e Melli, and the meeting today could be in any one of them. He turned to Rastgu, who was concentrating on weaving his way through the teeming morning traffic.

"Which *zurkhane?*"

Rastgu changed up to fourth gear, the road ahead clearing for a stretch.

"I don't know. But we have some time. The meeting won't be until tonight."

"How do you know?"

"It's obvious. The anniversary of the birth of Fatima is the twentieth of Jumada II. Today's the nineteenth of that month—the twentieth begins this evening at sunset."

Randall had forgotten that the Muslim day began and ended, not at midnight, but at the setting of the sun. Since Mo'ini had entered the meeting for the seventeenth in his diary, it must be this evening. But where?

In the end, it proved easier to track down the *zurkhane* than Randall had at first thought. After some deliberation, he finally telephoned Farideh Ashrafi, Iraj's widow. He had not been able to speak to her since her husband's death, but he knew her well and could trust her. She answered the phone at the fourth ring.

"Hello," he said, "Mrs. Ashrafi, this is Peter Randall."

There was a long silence at the other end of the line. At last she spoke.

"Peter. Where are you? I tried to contact you after . . . You do know about Iraj?"

"Yes. I was there that day, at the university. I had arranged to see him."

"But I rang your apartment several times the next day; there was never a reply. I tried again on several occasions after that, and I wrote to you as well. Eventually, I heard you were missing. Because of the troubles, I assumed you'd left the country."

"I can't explain now, Farideh. Please trust me. Tell no one that you've spoken to me; no one. I'm in Tehran and I'm all right. I'll try to see you if I can, but there are things I have to do first. I need your help."

"Yes, Peter, of course. You know you can always come here for help. What do you want me to do?"

"Are you able to find out for me the address of the *zurkhane* that Professor Mo'ini goes to?"

There was another pause.

"Mo'ini is not an athlete. Even when he was younger, I'm sure he never attended the *zurkhane*."

"Not even to watch, to listen to the poetry?"

She hesitated.

"Yes. Yes, now you mention it, he sometimes does that. Iraj and he used to go together occasionally, sometimes just the two of them, sometimes with a group of friends. Maybe once or twice a year."

"Was it always the same *zurkhane?*"

"I think so. Yes, yes it was. It's on Hakimi Street, near the City Park. I don't know the exact address."

"That doesn't matter, I'll find it. Thank you."

He paused, uncertain how to continue.

"Farideh, I'm sorry about Iraj. And I'm sorry I haven't been able to visit you since his death."

"That's all right, Peter. I think I understand. Was there a connection? Was Iraj's death an accident?"

How could he answer her? There was silence.

"No," he said at last. "No, I don't think so. But I don't think it could have been prevented."

For a long time, she did not speak. Then her voice came again, as if from a long way away.

"Is what you are doing now connected with his death?"

"Yes, it's connected, closely connected. It may help to . . . avenge it."

"I don't want revenge, Peter. Iraj is dead, it's finished. No more deaths, please?"

"There have already been more deaths, more than you can imagine. But if I do not continue, there will be many more still."

"I don't understand, but I wish you good fortune. *Khoda hafez*, Peter."

She uttered the words of the everyday farewell, but with meaning and a special emphasis: "May God protect you." The phone went dead as she replaced the receiver.

Later that morning Rastgu found out that there would be a performance by the athletes at the *zurkhane* later that afternoon, after sunset. It was a small *zurkhane* that met weekly on Thursday nights, a fairly normal arrangement.

Randall and the Israeli spent the early afternoon disposing of

Mo'ini's body. During the quiet period after lunch, they loaded the corpse into the back of Rastgu's Land-Rover, the vehicle he used for out-of-town journeys, and drove into the mountains. There, they dumped the body by the roadside, then fired a bullet into the left temple. No one would ask many questions about such a corpse at the present time, and there would be no postmortem to determine the true cause of death.

There was time to rest before setting out for the *zurkhane*. Randall insisted on going there alone, with Rastgu to wait outside as backup in case anything went wrong.

"You're a fool, Peter," the Israeli told Randall. "One of them may recognize you—perhaps one of Mo'ini's colleagues. Let me go inside while you wait in the car."

"No, I want to see what happens in there for myself. I don't think the group will meet until after the performance; a *zurkhane* isn't something that can be kept secret or private. Farideh Ashrafi told me her husband and other friends used to go with Mo'ini. Iraj would have noticed anything out of place. But I want to go for the performance, to see the layout of the place."

He arrived at the *zurkhane* just before sunset and went inside. An old man sat by the door leading into the main room where the performance would take place. Randall explained that he was an American journalist who wanted to write a report on everyday life in Tehran after the revolution. The old man scowled and jerked his head up and back, angrily making a negative "tch" sound.

"You speak good Persian for a journalist."

"I've been in Tehran for several years."

"You can't come in, you aren't wanted here. This place is for Iranians only. No foreigners."

Randall produced a wad of one-hundred tuman notes, from which the portraits of the Shah had been carefully cut out.

"This is Iranian money, old man. I'll sit at the back, out of sight. They won't even notice me."

Dropping two notes into the doorkeeper's unresistant hand, Randall did not even pause for a reply, but went straight in. The room was dim, lit here and there by naked electric bulbs. It had a high, cedar-beamed ceiling and white walls, pierced here and there by niches. Photographs were hung at random: wrestlers, mustached athletes, soldiers; beside them were religious paintings: 'Ali with his twin-bladed sword, his sons Hasan and Husayn, Husayn alone on his horse at the plain of Karbala, and, above them all, a new painting of Ayatollah Khomeini. The floor of the room had been raised several feet and its center formed into an eight-sided pit, leaving a narrow area around the sides on which chairs had been placed for spectators. There were already several present, all men and boys, their clothing that of workers from the nearby bazaar. Randall found a spot away from the lights and sat down. His entrance had scarcely been noticed.

The *pir*, dressed in white, was already in the room. He was the master of the *zurkhane*, the center of all attention. He sat above the pit, a double drum, or *dombak*, on his lap, a small bell hanging on a stand beside him. At five o'clock, he began to beat the drum in a slow pulsating rhythm, then to chant verses from the epic poem of Iran, the *Shahnameh* of Ferdowsi. The strange, unearthly chanting, the heart of this remarkable ritual, and the steady thudding of the drum filled the domed chamber, lulling the watchers. A pause and the *pir* lifted a white swan's feather with which to strike the bell several times. He began his drumming and chanting again as a door opened below at the side of the arena. The athletes, preceded by a wiry white-haired man, came into the pit, half dancing, half leaping. They were naked to the waist, with broad belts and embroidered leather trousers that came to below the knee where they were fastened tightly around the leg. Most of them were extremely large and well-built, the normal physique of the strong man, the *pahlavan*, but a few of the younger men were thinner, their muscles developing only gradually to the desired strength and size. Yet there was nothing here of the grotesqueness of Western bodybuilding, or of a weight lifting competition. The *zurkhane*, its origins obscure, was a semireligious, mystical affair, and its emphasis was on the moral virtues that must be developed by the *pahlavan*.

The ritual began with floor movements, including "land swimming," the wielding of huge wooden shields, and a difficult exercise in which a number of the *pahlavans* spun themselves round and round, holding off the effects of dizziness by a sheer effort of the will; the old, white-haired man proved to be most adept at this, spinning for some two or three minutes without staggering or losing his balance. The next exercise involved the use of massive iron bows strung not with cord or wire but with a heavy chain. On these the *pahlavans* pulled as the drum beat its incessant rhythm and the words of the

Shahnameh rang out over their heads. When this was completed, they took down huge Indian clubs of varying sizes from racks around the sides of the shallow pit. The largest, wielded by the strongest man, was about four feet in length and correspondingly thick. Randall recalled picking up one of these clubs after a performance elsewhere; he had quickly realized that they are every bit as heavy as they look, the largest being almost impossible to lift. The *pir* rang the bell and started a rapid beat on the drums. A club in each hand, the men began to swing them slowly in circles, twisting their arms incredibly as the massive instruments turned round and round.

The last exercise involved the use of much smaller clubs, the type used by jugglers in the West. Three of the athletes were singled out by the older man to use these. In essence, the exercise was identical to a juggler's performance, except that here the clubs were thrown higher and higher up toward the lofty ceiling. It was superb, breath-taking, and Randall felt like applauding before he realized that such a response would be out of place. This was not a circus and these men were not performing for applause. They would come here, week after week, and go through their strange rituals even if there was not a single spectator to appreciate their strength and skill except God.

The performance lasted about an hour, at the end of which the spectators rose to go. Some of them would go home directly, others would remove themselves in small groups to a nearby teahouse to smoke the waterpipe, and a few would wait in the vestibule for friends among the athletes, to go with them to a mosque or the home of the *pir* to talk and drink tea or *sharbat*. Randall had noticed in the wall behind him a small opening like an unglazed window through to a room next door; now, as he rose, he glanced inside. The yellow light revealed what appeared to be a storeroom where the clubs and equipment were kept. He turned and joined the small group of men on their way out, attracting some curious and hostile glances. But no one challenged or even spoke to him, and he passed out of the main entrance into the street. Rastgu was still seated in his car, one hundred yards to the left on the other side of the street, well concealed in the shadows. Randall crossed the road and joined him.

They waited in the darkness, watching. In ones and twos, spectators, then athletes, left the *zurkhane* and moved off into the night. The lights were extinguished, the doors locked.

"Do you think we have come to the wrong place, Peter?" asked Rastgu.

"I don't know. But I plan to go back in and wait, all night if necessary. We've no other *zurkhane* to go to tonight, have we?"

Rastgu laughed softly. "No, Peter. I'm afraid we've made our choice. Be careful."

Randall had no difficulty in breaking in by a window at the back of the building. The bolt was a gesture rather than a barrier. There was nothing in a *zurkhane* worth stealing: not even the best-connected thief could hope to sell such specialized equipment. Once inside, Randall used a penlight to find his way to the small storeroom with the view into the main chamber. If there was to be a meeting, he was sure it would be there. To make his concealment more effective, he found a large piece of cloth and hung it over the small opening, fastening it with two lengths of string tied to hooks higher up the wall. He cut a long slit vertically along the fabric through which to see into the room beyond.

Time passed slowly in the dark. Half an hour seemed an age. The evenings were warm now, but here in this little-used building, squatting on the concrete floor, Randall became cold and numb. He moved quietly from time to time, to warm and loosen his limbs, but constantly listening for the sound of someone entering. Toward midnight, nearly four hours later, he had begun to despair. There could be no guarantee that the meeting would be held in the *zurkhane* favored by Mo'ini for his infrequent visits.

It was then that Randall heard a muffled murmuring from the direction of the main room. A door opened somewhere and he could hear feet moving across the floor in the room itself. A light went on, then another, and he moved rapidly to his makeshift curtain and peered through the slit. In the shadow-filled chamber in front of him, he could make out the shapes of men coming through the door and filing down the steps into the open pit.

There were seven, six of them dressed in white, as if in shrouds, the seventh a molla of about forty, dressed in black, his severe face framed by a closely trimmed jet-black beard. A ray of light caught his eyes as he descended the steps: they were cold, the deep black pupils like tiny chips of black ice in snow. Randall noticed that one arm ended in a stump. All seven entered the pit and squatted there in the traditional fashion, the six younger men facing the molla, who sat with his back to Randall. The American held his breath, conscious of the profound silence that filled the chamber into which he gazed, aware that he was an interloper whose presence would be paid for by his life were he discovered.

The molla chanted a prayer in Arabic, caressing the foreign words for their sacredness, molding them to his tongue, modulating and refining them as they rose into the vaulted shadows of the high beamed roof. He chanted for a long time, during which the others remained absolutely still. Their faces expressionless, their eyes fixed on him, they sat in a row, their stillness a disturbing counterpoint to the intensely controlled activity of the athletes who had exercised there not many hours before. The chanting ended at last on a wistful, trembling note that carried far into the darkness beyond the seated figures. In a low voice, the molla began to speak. Something in his tone made Randall shiver in the darkness where he sat.

"Tonight is a blessed night," the molla began. "Tonight is the celebration of the birth of her holiness Fatima, the daughter of the Best of Creation, the wife of the Prince of the Believers, and the mother of Hasan the Chosen and of Husayn the Lord of Martyrs. And tonight the Sword has been unsheathed and is preparing to strike."

On the faces of each of the young men seated before him, Randall could see the same look, a look of joy, triumph, and anticipation.

"Tonight," the molla continued, "the first of those who are to be sent has been chosen. Tonight the fates of men and jinn are being decided. Tonight the Imam is preparing his weapons and lifting his hand. Tonight the blessed are in Paradise and the damned are in Hell, and both are ready to receive more guests.

"I have brought you here tonight to explain this to you and to tell you that, when we leave here, we are invited to a house where we shall meet His Supreme Holiness in person. He is there already and awaits us. Even though I am not of your number, I have been asked to accompany you. But first, you must prepare yourselves with prayer and meditation."

He paused and then began to chant softly again. Randall recognized some of the words—it was a passage from the Qur'an. As he sat and listened to the voice reciting the sacred text, his mind raced with questions. He slipped his gun from his pocket, deciding that it would be safer to try taking one of them for questioning now, rather than to risk following them to their next destination, wherever it might be. He fingered the rubber pad he had brought with him to ram into his captive's mouth in order to avoid a repetition of last night's suicide. If he moved quickly enough, he could be out with his man and into Rastgu's car before the others could act. But he did not fool himself and realized that it was much more likely they would overpower him before he could make it to the door. Suddenly, he stiffened as he heard sounds from the vestibule. Was Rastgu making a move independently of him?

Without warning, the door of the main room was thrown open and armed men rushed inside, shouting at the seven men in the pit, ordering them to freeze. Ten men, all dressed in combat dress and carrying submachine guns, raced to surround the pit on all sides, their weapons leveled at those below them. Following them, unhurried and grimfaced, Molla Hasan Tabataba'i stalked into the room and stood by the door, eyes fixed on his prisoners. He spoke in a voice like a thin, well-honed knife.

"Please stand up slowly with your hands on your heads. I am arresting you in the name of the Islamic Republic of Iran. If you attempt to escape, you will be shot. Please stand and come to the door one at a time."

He paused, then lifted his voice, facing toward Randall.

"And you, Mr. Randall, will also please come out and give yourself up to me? You have been very useful, very useful indeed, but I have not yet finished with you. I have a friend who is particularly anxious to speak with you. Please leave your gun in the room where you are."

With a sense of panic, Randall realized that he had been set up, that he had been permitted to lead Tabataba'i and his men here tonight to make this arrest. He slipped his gun into his pocket and opened the door into the main room.

The seven prisoners were already standing, but instead of placing their hands on their heads as instructed, they moved together silently and calmly to form a rough circle, facing out toward the men surrounding them. Then, slowly and deliberately, they began to walk toward the guards, their faces set and grim, their eyes unflinching as they looked straight at the barrels of the guns that pointed at them.

Tabataba'i shouted again.

"Get back. Move back into the center and stay still. Place your hands on your heads."

But they kept coming, walking into the face of death, a look of unyielding determination in their eyes. Randall watched in horror, waiting for the guards to open fire, waiting for the carnage that he knew must come and that he was powerless to stop. But the guards held their fire, frozen, as if mesmerized by the men who moved toward them. Had their assailants been armed, they would have fired without hesitation, in simple self-defense. But to shoot down unarmed men, men dressed in white *kafans* like those they themselves had worn not many months before, and in which so many of their comrades had died, brought back sharp memories of the Shah's troops and the massacres of the revolution's early days. Their fingers froze on the triggers and they looked around in panic. The seven men facing them continued to advance menacingly.

"Shoot!" Tabataba'i screamed, his hand reaching inside his aba for his gun.

Randall could never remember clearly what happened in the next instant; the movements and the sounds all blurred together in his mind like a reel of film caught in a single frame. As if at a signal, the seven men leapt for the guards, their hands outstretched, clawing for the barrels of the guns. The guards panicked and opened fire at random, the roar of their submachine guns echoing like death itself in the high, domed chamber. Some of their attackers fell, their white robes exploding in stars of red. But one guard had hesitated a moment too long and fired too late. He was overwhelmed, his gun wrenched out of his hand and turned on him. Before the other guards realized what had happened, the survivor turned and opened fire in a steady scything motion. The bullets pumped into the circle of guards, mowing them down without discrimination and without pity.

Out of the corner of his eye, Randall caught sight of the black-robed molla rushing toward a curtain in the side of the chamber and passing through. Almost at the same instant, he saw Tabataba'i raise his pistol and fire at the man with the submachine gun. Without a cry, he fell, a bullet hole in the center of his forehead. The gun dropped from his lifeless fingers, clattered metallically on the floor of the pit, and was still. A single guard had survived. He opened fire into the pit, shooting again and again, sheer panic driving him, riddling the inert bodies on the ground below with a hail of bullets.

Randall looked up from the horror that lay beneath him. Tabataba'i having cheated death, stood facing him, his hand holding a Beretta leveled at his chest. To his right, the SAVAMA agent lifted his eyes and his gun and trained both on Randall.

"Please drop your gun, Mr. Randall. If you do not drop it, Ali will shoot you."

Then, from behind Tabataba'i, another voice interrupted him.

"I would prefer it if Ali did not try to do that. It would be best for us all if you dropped your own gun and told your friend to do likewise." Rastgu had chosen his moment well. He had not remained in the car, where he might be noticed by police or Revolutionary Guards, but had concealed himself in an alleyway facing the *zurkhane*, from which he had been able to observe the building. Unseen, he had watched the SAVAMA agents arrive. With extreme caution, he had followed them and observed the events of the past few minutes unroll like a film in the main chamber. Now it was his turn.

Tabataba'i and his man dropped their weapons as ordered; there was a cruel authority in the Israeli's voice which even the molla could not resist.

"Now, sir," Rastgu continued, "please be so good as to go down the steps into the pit. If you attempt to pick up a weapon or otherwise thwart me, the angels Nakir and Munkar will find you tomorrow in Behesht-e Zahra cemetery."

Tabataba'i did as instructed, his eyes filled with rage and frustration.

Rastgu spoke again. "Peter, come to the door. He has no one posted outside, but be careful anyway."

Randall made his way awkwardly past fallen chairs and bodies to where his friend stood in the shadows of the doorway. Rastgu stepped aside to let him pass, turning slightly as he did so. In the pit, Tabataba'i threw himself down, his fingers snatching for his fallen Beretta. Ali hurled himself down behind a chair, reaching for a machine gun. Tabataba'i lifted his arm, then jerked back and sideways as a bullet from Rastgu's magnum exploded through his skull. A second shot tore through the chair, taking part of Ali's head with it.

Rastgu shoved Randall and they ran outside. Three blocks away, a siren was wailing, maybe headed in their direction. They dashed across the road to the Jaguar and leapt inside. In seconds, the Israeli had started the engine and set the car hurling down the street, then up into a side street and eastward across the city, in the direction of the safe house in Majdiyye.

As their speed slackened now that they were away from the central area, Randall turned to the Israeli, shock still in his voice.

"They're dead, all dead. It was so quick, there was nothing . . . But, Sirus, it isn't over. Only six of the Seven were there tonight. The seventh man, the man dressed in black, survived, and he was older than the rest. He said he was not 'of their number.' And there's another still alive somewhere. He's the one they've chosen. I have to find him. I have to know what he's been chosen for."

"I'm sorry, Peter, but that's not possible."

Randall looked at his friend, puzzled.

"Not possible? Why not?"

"Because I'm taking you out. Tonight. I've already made the arrangements with your people. You're going home."

The American turned in anger, his eyes flashing.

"The hell I'm going home. I've got a . . ."

He never saw Rastgu's right hand as it jabbed toward his neck, striking him expertly on a nerve. He slumped forward on his seat and the Israeli straightened and put his foot down on the accelerator.

"Sorry," he said.

TEHRAN
17 May 1979

As Rastgu and Randall drove through the deserted streets of east
Tehran, two other men were sitting together in the old house in the
bazaar where the meeting for the death of Fatima had been held the
previous month. One was the old molla who had presided over that
meeting, dressed as before in a white aba and green turban. The other
was Husayn Nava'i, the chosen one, the man singled out to kill President Carter. He was twenty-eight years old, good-looking, with piercing eyes, a full black beard and sallow cheeks, and he was puzzled.
Originally summoned that night to the meeting in the old *zurkhane*,
he had at the last moment received a message asking him to go alone
to the house of the molla. Once there, he had been escorted by a
servant to the upper chamber, where he had found the old man
occupied in prayer. The holy man had neither paused nor acknowl-
edged his presence, but the servant had motioned him to be seated on
the carpet opposite. An oil lamp burned, its wick turned low, spreading a subdued yellow glow over the center of the room, bathing the
two men in its curious, ethereal light.

An hour had already passed, and still the old man sat, the chanted
words of prayer after prayer rising and falling like waves on an unchanging shore. As Husayn sat listening, the mood within the room
shifted and deepened, and he was drawn further into the circling
rhythms of the prayer. At last, the chanting stopped, and the silence
that followed was deeper than any the young man had ever experienced.

As if from a great distance, the voice of the molla called him back
to reality. Slowly, he became aware once more of the room, of the
flickering yellow lamp, the close-weaved carpet on which he sat, the
featureless white walls, and the old man seated facing him.

"You are welcome tonight," said the holy man, with much warmth and something more in his greeting.

"I am honored," the young man replied. It was not a pleasantry, but the truth.

"And puzzled," added the molla, a glint of amusement in his eyes.

"Yes . . . puzzled. I was expected . . . I have been summoned to the *zurkhane* to meet with Molla Ahmad. Why has there been a change? Why have I been called here? Have I committed some act that has displeased you?"

The old man shook his head and smiled.

"You have not sinned, my son. You have been chosen. You are to be the first to set out on his mission."

The molla reached inside the left sleeve of his voluminous aba, from which he drew out a folded sheet of blue paper. This he proceeded to unfold and flatten with his right hand while with his left he lifted a pair of thin gold-rimmed spectacles from the floor beside him. He looked up, cleared his throat, and addressed Nava'i.

"I have a letter written by His Supreme Holiness and addressed to you. He has asked me to read it in your presence."

Donning the spectacles, he began to read aloud in the incantatory manner favored by most Iranians when reading anything regarded as especially important or sacred. The letter was partly in Arabic, partly in Persian.

" 'In the Name of God. The blessings of God and His peace be upon Muhammad and the Family of Muhammad and upon the Imam of the Age, may God hasten his advent. O nameless and unnamed, know that your name is already inscribed in His Book and that His pen is ready to record your deeds alongside it. These are days of testing and trial, days of suffering and anguish. All that we have won we may yet lose again if the days of our final victory be not hastened. The forces of unbelief are neither defeated nor asleep and the armies of mischief are neither vanquished nor leaderless. If we do not act now in His name and for the sake of His cause, the moment of victory may pass, never to return. It is therefore time for you to make yourself ready for the service you have long been trained to render. I send you forth now in His name and with my blessing that you may be the agent of our greatest victory. Do not fear if you have to die, provided it be in His path. I assure you that such a death shall be accounted as martyrdom and you will die a martyr in the holy war, the *jihad* against the forces of darkness. May God send his angels with you. Praise be to God, the Lord of all worlds.' "

The voice of the white-bearded cleric halted, and he raised his eyes to meet those of the young man to whom the letter was addressed. The pale lamplight reflected devotion and awe in the eyes of the young man, compassion and understanding in those of his master. Commitment and fanaticism burned in the eyes of both men and behind the gaze, the old man was thinking, "My son, how little you know or understand of his real purposes, of the true meaning of the mission for which you have been chosen, for which you will die." And behind that thought, the old man felt a profound sorrow and a deeper exaltation. But now, a time of testing.

"You will leave here tomorrow," the cleric continued, "to travel by land and sea to Medina. You will spend the summer and autumn in the holy city, in a house of learning. There is one there who can teach you things I cannot, who will prepare you for the mission itself. You will stay there until the beginning of the month of pilgrimage. You will put on the white garments and go to Mecca to join in the rites of the pilgrimage, but you will not stay for the festival on the tenth day. By that date, you must be in New York, ready to go to Washington."

The old man hesitated, aware that there was yet more, that, as well as the joy of being summoned to his mission, the night held pain and suffering for the young man.

"Brother Husayn, before you set out on your mission, you will meet the Imam himself, here in this house tonight."

Nava'i's eyes lit with an indescribable radiance. To meet him was a privilege given to very few.

"But first, it is his command that your loyalty to him, your love for him, and your faith in him be put to the test. The last time you sat in this room, I explained that each of you had to pass through death in many forms that you might learn how to die. Your first death will be tonight. Please come with me."

The old man rose to his feet, a little unsteady after sitting so long, and reached for a simple wooden stick to assist his steps. Pale-faced, his heart pounding in his chest, Nava'i stood up also and followed him as he passed through the door and made his way slowly down the stairs.

It was now dark in the courtyard, but still hot. There was little light, for the moon, now in its last quarter, was almost fully waned, but a fabulous frosting of stars jeweled the sky. The molla, clearly visible, led Nava'i across the courtyard toward the illuminated square of an open door. Close behind him, the young man passed through the door into a dimly lit passage, whitewashed like the chamber from which they had just come. A low ceiling caused him to bend, even though it was in reality just high enough to permit him to stand erect. At the end of the passage was set a heavily built low wooden door with a massive lock. The molla made his way forward to the door, producing from a large pocket a ring carrying several heavy keys. With the largest of these, he struggled to unlock the door, which he then pushed open against the creaking resistance of unoiled hinges.

It was dark inside the room, the faint illumination of the oil lamp at the far end of the passage scarcely penetrating its shadows. The old man returned for the lamp and came back again to the door of the room, carrying it at shoulder height. The sickly yellow light now fell inside, casting crazy shadows over floor and walls. Against the far wall sat a man wearing a shirt and trousers. His hair was unkempt, his beard several days old, and his eyes strained and bloodshot; his wrists were bound on either side by tightly lashed ropes tied to iron rings set in the wall.

Nava'i entered the room and remained standing by the back wall, as if afraid to approach the bound man. In the narrow confines of the tiny room, even at this distance he could smell the sour foulness of the prisoner, a smell combining sweat, urine, vomit, and fear. As Nava'i walked into the room, the eyes of the prisoner—which until now had been averted slightly—fell on him sharply, opening a fraction as if in recognition. But again they resumed their glazed, almost vacant look; the man sagged on the ropes, seeming to ignore the pain as they cut into wrists already bloody and sore.

On Nava'i's face a look of dawning recognition appeared to echo the flash in the prisoner's eyes. Rapidly, it changed to horror and was then replaced by an emotionless mask as he sought to control whatever feelings seethed within him.

The bearded cleric stepped forward and walked across the small room to stand beside the prisoner. Clearing his throat, he addressed Nava'i, who was standing, his head bowed and his back pressed to the wall, as if trying to distance himself from the man opposite. "Brother Husayn, I told you that your loyalty would be tested tonight. The moment for that is come. Do you recognize the man beside me?"

Nava'i looked up and nodded.

"You are surprised to see him here? It is perhaps a year or more since you last met, but I know you and he were the closest of friends."

"He was . . . I thought he was in the United States. I have written several times in the last year, but have never received a reply. I could not understand it—Faridun was my closest friend. We have known each other since childhood; we were like brothers. And now I find him here like this. What is happening to him? Why is he tied up?"

"Your friend was indeed in America. I have no idea why he did not reply to your letters, but I think he had his reasons. He tried to betray our cause, to destroy the Imam himself. I can't tell you the details, but we discovered that while in the United States he made contact with the enemies of Islam with the aim of revealing information to them. We found out about this before he was able to tell them anything. Through his wife, whom he had left here in Tehran, we called him back to this country. He was arrested by us shortly after his arrival, taken before a court set up by the Imam and presided over by him in person. The Imam sentenced him to death three weeks ago, but then instructed us to delay the execution. We now know that his reason for this was to provide you with an opportunity to prove your loyalty to him and to demonstrate your faith in Islam. You are to be your friend's executioner."

Nava'i stood frozen, unable to move or speak. The old man held out his hand, beckoning him to the side of the condemned man. It was as if the figure in the robe and turban personified duty, faith, loyalty—all the virtues the years had striven to inculcate in Nava'i. He moved like a sleepwalker, stopping only inches in front of the prisoner's face. The emaciated man before him raised his head slowly, as if it caused him much pain to do so. His sunken eyes flashed for a moment with an old fire and his cracked lips moved soundlessly.

From a wide pocket in his aba, the old man brought forth a length of fine rope. He handed it to Nava'i, saying, "As you know, the condemned man is a sayyid, a descendant of the Prophet like myself, and it is forbidden by the law of Islam to shed the blood of such a man. The Imam has commanded that he be strangled. He is weak and will not take long to die."

Nava'i took the rope numbly, no longer able to think or understand. To avoid his friend's eyes, he tried to move behind him, but the ropes were in his way. Like a man in a dream, compelled by forces beyond his conscious control, he lifted the thin cord and turned it about the prisoner's neck, twisting the ends around his hands, then pulling with all his force. He could see the whipcord cut into the man's neck, the eyes bulge, the constricted veins rise; he could hear the rasping, tearing sound as his victim struggled hopelessly for breath. As if fascinated, Nava'i could not tear his eyes away even as his hands performed their deadly function. He could not feel the cord as it cut into his own flesh, bringing blood to the surface of his hands. The man's face turned blue, then purple, and the eyes seemed ready to leap from the sockets. It was all over in a matter of minutes, the pain and the struggle and the dying.

Nava'i released his grip, dropped the ends of the rope, and stepped away from the limp body of the dead man who had been like a brother to him. Taking him by his upper arm, the old man led him from the body toward the door. All was silent again after the roar of death that had seemed to fill his ears and echo wildly about the tiny room.

As they stood there, the sound of voices could be heard from the corridor outside. Footsteps sounded on the flagstones. Suddenly, both men in the room faced the door and bowed, hands on their breasts. In the doorway, a second old man had appeared, with a long gray beard and flashing eyes, and dressed like the first in turban and aba. He spoke the ancient greeting of Islam, *"Al-salam alaykum,"* and the others replied as one, *"Alaykum al-salam."* There was a reverential hush as he held out his hand for each in turn to kiss the ring on it in token of respect and humility. Their heads were bowed and they stood before him in silence, hands folded across their chests.

"Husayn," the new arrival said in a voice that carried like the wind, "you have done well. You have fulfilled your trust tonight. And now I wish to lay upon you an even greater trust and a much higher responsibility. The time has come for the waging of the last holy war. All mankind is ready for it, and I swear that it will come soon. The events of the past few months have prepared the way, but there remains much to do. Go tomorrow with my blessing and carry my greetings to the one you will meet in the sacred enclosure. Learn what he has to teach you and obey him as you obey me, in all things. And when you have performed the rites of pilgrimage, all save those of the festival, fly like the angel of death to the land of Satan and begin the task I have laid on you. You are to be the first blast of the trumpet mentioned in the Qur'an: 'The day will come when the first blast shall reverberate, then the second will follow close upon it.' May God and the Prophet and the blessed Imams go with you." The speaker lifted his hand in a gesture of benediction.

Nava'i fell on his knees before the Imam, taking the hem of his aba in his hand and kissing it. He understood nothing of what was happening—his mind was in chaos—but he knew more surely than he had ever known anything before that he would kill or die for the man at whose feet he knelt.

18

MEDINA
2 June 1979

The Prophet Muhammad lies buried in Medina with his two companions, 'Umar and Abu Bakr, in a grave beneath what was once the floor of the house of his favorite wife, A'isha. His resting place is marked by a small green dome over what is now the southern section of the Prophet's Mosque. The grave is surrounded by a massive enclosed railing of brass and iron adorned with the finest calligraphy, to which pilgrims cling as they make their way round the tomb, seeking blessings in this world and the next.

The dawn prayers had just ended, and crowds of worshipers filed into the cloisters leading to the tomb. All around them pillars of rose-colored stone cut from the hills of the Aqiq Valley rose in columns to soar into a tracery of softly pointed archways. Rich Persian and Turkish carpets lined the floors of the colonnades. Unnoticed among the press of silent pilgrims, two men walked slowly together. They did not touch, but an unseen bond joined them as they walked. Unconsciously, the other pilgrims kept their distance, opening a small space around them, allowing them to pass freely as they moved toward the mausoleum.

Husayn Nava'i had arrived in Medina from Jidda the previous day and had been ushered immediately into the presence of Muhammad ibn 'Abd Allah, who was living in a house near the mosque. They had spoken in private for over two hours. No one knew or dared ask what had passed between them in the course of their conversation, but that evening when they came together to dinner, Ibn 'Abd Allah's closest followers had been astonished to observe a deep intimacy between them, as if they had been brothers or lifelong friends.

The next morning, they had gone together to attend the dawn prayers at the mosque, and now the young Arab was leading Nava'i to pay homage at the tomb. They moved around the railing until they came to the southern side, in which a brass disk had been placed to indicate the level of the Prophet's head. As they passed, pilgrims reached out to caress the object, seeking contact with the unseen powers it contained. As he came abreast of the disk, Husayn Nava'i reached with his right hand to touch it, sobbing gently as he did so, his left hand outstretched to clasp the hand of Ibn 'Abd Allah. A steady stream of pilgrims passed as Nava'i turned and spoke in a low and solemn voice to his companion.

"I swear by God and His Prophet, upon whom be peace, to aid you in all things, whether in life or in death, in this world or the next. I give myself wholly into your hands, and I submit myself unreservedly to your decree. Whether I live or die, it is all one to me, so long as, in living or in dying, I may serve you."

For a moment, they looked into one another's eyes, then the press of anxious pilgrims began again and they resumed their circumambulation of the tomb. But that moment of silence by the side of the Prophet had been enough. Not even death could sever the bond they had forged in that moment of deep solemnity: neither their own nor the deaths of thousands.

PHASE FOUR

19

NEW YORK CITY
1 November 1979

Early in the morning of Thursday, 1 November 1979, a Boeing 747SP bearing blue and green Saudi markings landed at John F. Kennedy Airport. The passengers, many of whom had boarded the plane in London where it had stopped off for two hours, disembarked and proceeded to the terminal building. Unnoticed among them was Husayn Nava'i, thin and dressed in a heavy overcoat the color of burnt cinnamon. He carried one of the new Iranian passports issued by the revolutionary authorities, which held a three-month visa, stamped by the U.S. Consulate in Jidda on 24 October. In his possession was a cleverly forged document, produced by him four days previously, which purported to be from the assistant governor of the Saudi General Petroleum and Minerals Organization. It identified Nava'i as a Sunni Muslim from Abadan who had previously worked as a mineralogist for the NIOC, the National Iranian Oil Company, but had recently come to work in the Kingdom in order to escape from the Shi'i-inspired revolution in his own country. He had been sent to the United States for a period of six months' advanced study at the Massachusetts Institute of Technology; a forged letter from the head of the department of mineralogy there confirmed his acceptance for the course. He also carried numerous other papers setting out his qualifications and the details of his earlier employment. All in all, Nava'i seemed to possess impeccable credentials as a nonrevolutionary Iranian unlikely to cause distress to U.S. immigration officials.

In spite of all this, it took a long time for him to pass through customs and immigration control: since the transfer of the Shah to New York Hospital ten days earlier, U.S. port and airport control officials were more than usually attentive to Iranian nationals seeking entry to the country, especially through New York.

It was 8:45 A.M. when he entered the central concourse carrying a single leather suitcase and a black shoulder bag. He proceeded to a row of telephone booths on his left, found an empty one, and made a single call lasting exactly thirty seconds. Emerging from the booth, he exited through a pair of automatic doors, above which was a sign indicating a taxi rank, and took the first yellow cab available in the line. Nava'i spoke good English with an American accent. He had spent several years in the States as a student at the University of Colorado, where he had been known—under a different name—as a close friend of Faisal ibn Musa'id, the Saudi prince later responsible for the assassination, in 1975, of his uncle, King Faisal. Nava'i instructed the cab driver to take him to an address in downtown Manhattan, then sat back, exhausted after his long journey.

As they sped along, the vast city began to engulf him and, with its glass towers of silence rising brittle and bloodless all around him, made the sprawling roar of Tehran seem puny and insignificant. He himself was not a native Tehrani, but a farmer's son from Yazd, a dusty, ocher-colored city at the western edge of the great salt desert, the Dasht-e Lut. The desert was like the moon: pitted, dead, and bleached. Just outside Yazd, the main center for Iran's remaining Zoroastrians, stood two great *dakhmes*, the original "towers of silence," where the followers of Iran's ancient faith had until recently exposed the naked bodies of their dead, and where vultures circled endlessly over white bones. To the young man, set down so suddenly in the midst of New York, the great city seemed as dead as the desert, its twisting freeways as lifeless as the bones in the *dakhmes* which had terrified him as a child. Or was this sense of death merely a response to his knowledge that he, the killer, was already dead, that the angels Nakir and Munkar, who question the body in the grave, already hovered over him with the dark wings of vultures, ready to swoop when his task was done?

Thoughts of the desert, of towers of silence, and of black angels ceased abruptly as the cab drew up outside a tall building on West Twenty-third Street. He paid the fare, stepped out, and retrieved his luggage. Before him was a shop front, a wide window containing paintings, bowls, pen cases, small rugs, and articles of inlaid wood. Above the door was an ornate sign: Mohammad Ahmadi and Co., Persian Carpets and Antiques. Specialists in Miniatures and Illuminated Manuscripts. Nava'i stepped up to the glass door, set down his case, and pushed. It was locked. Inside, there were lights; he tried again. Still nothing. Then his eye caught the sign: Please Ring for Admission. Locating the bell push, he pressed once and waited. This was nothing strange to him: most houses in north Tehran have the same bell and speaker system at the door or gate, such was the fortress mentality of the nouveaux riches. A voice crackled through the speaker, "Yes, who is it?"

"*Aqa-ye Ahmadi? Man-am Husayn-e Nava'i. Az forudgah telefon kardam.*" It was suddenly easier to speak in Persian; the disembodied English of the speaker intimidated him.

"*Baleh, Aqa-ye Nava'i. Montazer-e shoma budim. Befarma'id.*" A buzzer sounded, the lock gave a faint click, and Nava'i pushed again. This time the door opened to his touch. With some awkwardness, he maneuvered his suitcase between door and jamb, pushed it ahead, then followed. The door closed behind him with a sharp locking sound.

A plump man of about forty advanced like a well-fed lapdog from the back of the elegant gallery. For a long moment, he stood facing Nava'i, appraising him as if he were a figure in a gold-bordered Safavid miniature he was admiring, a courtier from Tahmasp's luxurious *Shahnameh* come with a message from an eastern potentate. At last, he came close, embraced him, kissing him on both cheeks, and again. Stepping back, he held him by the upper arm with a firm grip.

"Welcome, welcome," he said effusively, "I am Ahmadi. I have been expecting you, you are most welcome. I am very happy to see you. I am very glad you have come." Ahmadi was punctilious in the profusion of *ta'arof*, the elaborate banter of Persian etiquette.

"Please, leave your case and come with me," continued Ahmadi. Taking the young man by the hand—thirteen years in the West had not taught him that this was a gesture which brought curious glances —he drew him to the small doorway leading into the back of the shop. At a desk inside sat a young woman of about twenty; she rose as they entered.

"My daughter, Fereshteh," Ahmadi explained. "Fereshteh-jan, this is Mr. Nava'i, the young man we have been expecting."

"I'm very happy. You are most welcome," she said to the stranger. She spoke with an American accent, but without awkwardness. Nava'i shook her hand, smiled, and became serious again. She sensed his strangeness, his unresponsiveness to her femininity: it was as if he were shaking hands with another man. Yet it was not the unresponsiveness of a homosexual, it was something quite different. And his eyes . . . For many months afterward, they would haunt her.

"Fereshteh," her father prompted, "would you be so good as to go to the front of the shop and bring Mr. Nava'i's case in here while he and I go to my office. Unless, of course . . ." He looked at his visitor, but Nava'i shook his head and said, "No, I don't need it. I have what I want in my shoulder bag."

"Ah yes, fine. Please come with me then." At the other end of the room was a second door, leading to a flight of steps that rose to a dark, brown-painted door marked Private in both English and Persian. The English was indifferently executed in straightforward store-bought lettering, slightly curling at the edges, but the Persian had been done very carefully by hand in a graceful *nasta'liq* style, blue letters on a cream background, each letter flowing into the next to form a single pattern.

Ahmadi took a key from his right inside pocket, inserted it into the lock and turned. *"Befarma'id,"* he said politely as he gestured his guest ahead of him into the office. Following, he locked the door behind them, then turned and, with more cries of *"befarma'id,"* motioned the young man toward a comfortable chair. The art dealer took a chair facing him, sat back, and smiled.

The square-shaped room in which they sat had been transformed from a dingy New York office into an evocation of the Persian spirit. Its dark walls were hung with bright, gilt-bordered miniatures taken from illustrated manuscripts of the works of Hafez and Nezami, replete with scenes of princes and princesses, warriors on horseback, dark-eyed youths, slender maidens, and pious Sufis. The floor was covered with layers of antique carpets and rugs from Kerman, Tabriz, and Mashhad, woven by hand in wool and silk, elaborate traditional patterns in colors mellowed by the years. It was a collector's paradise, worth a fortune if ever the contents were put up for sale. But it left Nava'i unmoved. The luxury in which this man walked ran counter to the principles of Islamic purity. The Prophet had slept on a reed mat and banned all images, all paintings of men or beasts, as blasphemous imitations of the handiwork of the only creator. Nava'i's eyes fell instead on a portrait of the Imam that hung in mute contradiction to the rest of the room on the wall behind the desk.

"You must be tired and perhaps hungry," said Ahmadi. "And a little disorientated—these long flights are always disturbing."

"Thank you. I slept on the plane. I am tired, but it will pass."

"I have not been in Tehran since the revolution. How is the city? How are the people? One hears so many rumors."

"We survive."

"Yes, of course, that is always true. Always survival. Yes. And now, perhaps, something more."

"Perhaps."

"The Imam. You met him in Tehran before your departure?"

"Yes. He spoke with me about my mission and gave me his blessing. He mentioned you—your work for the cause, your sacrifices."

The young man glanced with pointed irony around the room. His eyes met Ahmadi's and held him fixed in his uneasiness.

"Listen," said Ahmadi, a nervous tremor in his voice. "I know nothing of your mission, except what I have been told, that it is vital to the cause, to our people, to the true faith. My task is to help you here in New York as far as I can. I will sell the merchandise you have brought with you—it is safe, I trust?"

Nava'i nodded.

"Our organization here in the United States is small but extremely efficient, and our people are utterly dedicated. But once I have supplied you with money and given advice and information, there is little more I can do. If you fail, nothing, absolutely nothing must lead the American authorities from you to us. Do you understand?"

Nava'i did not move. "I shall not fail," he said.

"No, of course not, I am sure of that. You will not fail. I pray God that it will be so. They have told me that the fate of Islam may depend on your mission. That is a heavy responsibility—you are in my prayers. Now, do you have the merchandise with you?"

"It is here in my bag. The customs officials searched it, quite thoroughly, but they found nothing. Here, let me show you."

He unzipped the main compartment of the ample bag and drew out a large round tin marked boldly in Persian, "Pesteh-ye Arya," and in English, "Arya Pistachio Nuts." The lid showed scattered pistachios, buff shells with green and purple fruit protruding from their parted lips. The tape sealing the tin all around the side had been broken by customs and the lid removed. Inside, they had seen nothing but pistachios, as expected, and had replaced the lid. Most Iranians carry at least one box of pistachios or *gaz* (a pistachio-filled nougat) when they travel abroad, and neither Saudi nor U.S. customs had seen anything suspicious. Nava'i lifted the lid and showed the contents to Ahmadi.

"The Americans noticed nothing strange about these pistachios. What about you? You are Iranian. Can you see what they missed?"

Ahmadi looked closely. They seemed ordinary enough, but presumably they were not. What was wrong? Something nagged and tugged at the edges of his mind, but he could not place it. He gave up.

"You can't see?" Nava'i smiled, without warmth, sadly almost. Something akin to triumph shone in his eyes. He was like a child demonstrating his new conjuring trick to parents and friends. "Look more closely. How often do you see a tin of pistachios in which every nut is closed? These are like unripe, unroasted nuts. Let me explain. I bought a tin of normal pistachios, removed the kernels and kept each pair of half shells together. I then filled a bowl with the substance I had been asked to smuggle to you and filled each complete shell by pressing the two halves together in the powder. I applied quick-acting transparent glue to the join. When all the nuts had been filled, I rolled them in the wet salt used to coat pistachios after roasting."

The older man looked curiously at the tin of nuts, picked one up, and weighed it in his hand.

"The weight is about right."

"Of course: a pistachio kernel is lighter than most nuts."

Ahmadi licked the nut.

"And the salt tastes as it should."

"It is perfectly genuine."

Ahmadi reached for a bowl on the desk to his right and placed it on his lap. Taking the nut in his right hand, he placed it between his teeth, keeping the center ridge vertical, and bit down hard. The nut cracked, more easily than an unopened pistachio will normally crack, but not enough to spill the contents. Holding it in his hands over the bowl, he used his fingernails to pull the shell apart; a white powder cascaded, fine as dust, into the waiting bowl. Number-4 heroin, 99 percent pure for injecting, worth a fortune on the American market. The kilo Nava'i had brought would fetch one hundred thousand dollars on the streets.

Ahmadi stared, impressed in spite of himself. Over the years, he had handled many imports of heroin brought from Tehran to obtain dollars for the cause. But he had seldom seen such a large shipment so cleverly concealed. He smiled, took the box, and replaced the lid. Picking it up, he walked across the room and swung aside a miniature of Khosrow and Shirin to reveal a wall safe. Rapidly spinning the dial of the combination lock, he opened the safe and placed the box inside. Turning, he smiled again at Nava'i.

"Thank you. You can be assured that a sale will be made tonight. I have already made an appointment with my contacts. Some of the money will be given to you to finance your mission, the rest will be transferred to Geneva and from there to Tehran. Now, you must rest. You are more tired than you think. Let's leave the pistachios where they are and go to my house. I live with my wife and daughter in the Chelsea section, quite near here. You can have something to eat, then bed and sleep. A long sleep."

Nava'i nodded and rose.

"I shall be glad to rest. But, please, nothing to eat yet. I have made a vow that I shall eat nothing from dawn to sunset each day until I have completed my mission."

Together, they crossed to the door. Behind them in the room, a clock ticked remorselessly.

It was 3:00 A.M. and heavy frost lay like a caul of frozen breath on the streets of New York. In the brownstone apartment where she lived with her parents, Fereshteh Ahmadi woke with a start. Something had invaded her dreams and tugged her senses back into the cold and dark of the early morning. Lying still and tense in her bed, she strained eyes and ears to detect the source of the disturbance. Something told her it was not in the room with her, but outside, beyond her door. Almost imperceptible in the distance, she could hear a muted sound, rising and falling through the layers of silence that filled the sleeping house. Rising, she found her robe and hurriedly put it on. Going to the door, she opened it gently and stepped outside.

Across the passage and several doors down, a dim light shone from behind the partly opened door of the room in which their guest was staying. The faint noise, clearer now, like sobbing, came from there also. She tiptoed down the passage, listening intently as she approached the doorway and the steadily growing sound. Now she could identify it. In a subdued yet musical voice, Nava'i was chanting a prayer. In the dead silence of the night, the sound carried. It was plaintive and infinitely sad. Her trepidation mixed with curiosity, Fereshteh moved to the narrow opening, gently pushing the door open to see more clearly into the room.

Through the gap, she could see him kneeling upright on a prayer rug, facing her, a candle placed on the floor before him. He was dressed in white, a specter in the pale unearthly illumination. With a shock, she realized what he was wearing. It was a *kafan*, a shroud, such as is worn in Iran by old men within sight of the grave or, more recently, by young men with their hearts set on martyrdom in the blood-filled streets of Tehran. His face was firm, his cold black eyes fixed ahead not seeing the room or the open doorway or her frightened features but turned inwardly toward the shrouded black cube of the Ka'ba, the point of adoration thousands of miles away in Mecca. His soft voice rose and fell gently, imploringly, and tears, made bright and tremulous by the flickering light of the candle, coursed unceasingly down his cheeks. The heating had been switched off and the room was bitterly cold.

Shivering, her bare feet as cold as ice and her heart beating wildly, Fereshteh went back to bed. But sleep would not return, though she tried to summon it, and dawn was long in coming.

WASHINGTON
3–15 November 1979

On his second day in New York, Nava'i bought a wallet-sized photograph of President Carter in a store on Fifth Avenue. He wanted to study the face of the man he had come to kill. It was important to have a clear mental picture of his intended victim. He arrived in Washington by plane two days later, on the evening of 3 November.

On arriving at his hotel, he passed his bags to a porter, received his key, ordered a light meal to be sent to his room, and took the elevator to the third floor. On reaching the room, he placed his shoulder bag and suitcase on the bed, removed his overcoat and hung it on the door. Then he unzipped the back compartment of the shoulder bag and drew out a sizable manilla envelope. From this, he took a large leather-bound copy of the Qur'an, two photographs, a letter, and a calendar. The Qur'an he laid on the small walnut desk beside the window, open to the third chapter at the words, "And do not think that they who have been slain in God's path are dead. Indeed they are not: they live with their Lord and are well sustained." The photographs he set up on either side of the Qur'an; one was of the one-handed molla who had so shaped his destiny and who had trained him to be what he was; the other was of the Imam, a full-face portrait from which the intense gray eyes peered out into the world as if challenging it. The letter he carefully unfolded and placed on the desk below the Qur'an. From his pocket, he took a *tasbih*, a long amber rosary with ninety-nine beads on which he counted off the corresponding Most Beautiful Names of God in the course of the supererogatory prayer he always performed after the ritual *salat*. He carried the rosary with him at all times when he went out, silently fingering it in his pocket or on his lap as he walked or sat.

He lifted the calendar and folded back its sheets until he came to November. On the large page were three units of dates: in the center, the standard Common Era calendar for November 1979; to the left, the Iranian solar calendar giving the months of Aban and Adhar 1358 from 23 October to 21 December (the old Persian calendar runs like the signs of the Zodiac used by Western astrologers); and to the right, the Muslim calendar with the months of Dhu'l-Hijja 1399 and Muharram 1400.

Taking a thumbtack from a box in the shoulder bag, he hung the calendar on the wall over the desk. From his pocket, he took a red felt-tipped pen with which he drew a large circle around the first of Muharram 1400, the first day of the fifteenth Islamic century (not in strict fact—that would not be for another year—but in popular belief). He then drew a circle around the corresponding date on the Christian calendar: 21 November. Lifting the pen again, he drew a second circle around the tenth of Muharram—the anniversary of the martyrdom at Karbala in the year 680 of the Imam Husayn, grandson of the Prophet and prince of martyrs of the Shi'i world, after whom Nava'i was named. He marked again the corresponding date: 30 November. As he stepped back, pen in hand, there was a knock at the door; it was the late supper he had ordered.

He ate quickly and called room service again to take away the dishes. Having washed his hands and face thoroughly, he opened his suitcase and took out a long white garment and a small box. He undressed and put on the thin cotton robe, his *kafan*, which he had worn for prayer since being chosen for his mission. In the box were another rosary, made of clay beads from the soil around the grave of Husayn at Karbala, and a small clay tablet of the same soil on which he rested his forehead when prostrating himself during the rituals of prayer. He now lifted from the suitcase a small, fine prayer rug, a *janamaz* from Kerman, which his father had given him when he reached the age of maturity at fifteen. Laying it on the floor, facing the point of adoration, the Ka'ba, he began to pray.

After an hour spent in devotions, he rolled up his rug, replaced his tablet and beads, and removed the *kafan*. Yet somehow he wore it always in his heart. He was tired; he had rested in New York, but not enough, and at last the strain of facing his task entirely alone was beginning to tell. Now he went straight to bed and fell asleep within minutes. His dreams were silent and awful.

While he slept, a mob of about four hundred Iranian revolutionaries stormed and took possession of the U.S. Embassy in Tehran. Arriv-

ing in Taleghani Avenue—the old Takht-e Jamshid—before noon on
Sunday, 4 November, they told the Revolutionary Guards posted at
the embassy gate to stand aside. Everywhere, photographs of the
Imam Khomeini were brandished like weapons, talismans powerful
against the evil of the Great Satan, America. Even the girls wore
photographs pinned to the fabric of their black chadors. Once inside
the gates, the students broke into two main groups, one entering the
consulate section of the compound, the other attacking the two-story
chancellery building, known to the Americans as Fort Apache because
of its highly developed security reinforcements. Inside the building,
Marine guards put on flak jackets and gas masks and ordered the
diplomatic staff to the top floor. But all proved useless against the
determined onslaught of the mob, and by 4:00 P.M., the entire compound was in the hands of the students, whose numbers had now
risen to about six hundred. Not long after the final seizure of the
compound and the capture of the sixty-one embassy staff, including
the Marine guards, the students issued a communiqué under the
name of the Muslim Students of the Imam Khomeini Line. Before
the evening had passed, the Imam himself gave his blessing to the
seizure of the embassy. It was the first anniversary of a bloody massacre of students in Tehran by the Shah's troops and the sixteenth
anniversary of Khomeini's exile to Iraq. An auspicious day forever-
more in Iranian history. Within hours, as news reached Washington
and then other capitals, a new sort of tension began to build throughout the world.

Nava'i woke at 8:00 A.M. the next morning, unaware of what had
happened in Tehran. Fifteen minutes later, President Carter arrived
at the White House by helicopter from Camp David, where he had
gone to spend a quiet weekend—the last such weekend he would
enjoy for some time to come. Under the direction of Zbigniew
Brzezinski, the National Security Council went into one of its longest
and most critical sessions. Oblivious to all this, Nava'i performed his
morning devotions, turning his face to the southeast, past Capitol Hill
to Mecca. As he prayed, it was early evening in Tehran and the
students holding the embassy laid rugs on the ground throughout the
compound, turning to the southwest, also in the direction of the
forbidden city of Islam. Nava'i was hungry after his traveling and
sound sleep, but he did not head down to the breakfast room. Instead,

he dressed in a suit and overcoat he had bought on Fifth Avenue. He felt strange in the expensive clothes, purchased with money from the heroin sale, but knew that he had to avoid looking conspicuous.

Before coming to the States, Nava'i had devised several possible methods for carrying out the assassination. But all depended on unknown factors, so he now had to spend a week or two in Washington, observing, weighing possibilities, one after the other. He now set out for his first inspection of the capital. In the hotel lobby, he bought a copy of the Washington *Post* and a Rand McNally map of the city. Placing the map for the moment in his coat pocket, he glanced at the newspaper and stiffened as he read the headline on the special edition that had just started appearing in place of the normal morning edition. Very little was known as yet about the embassy takeover or the fate of its personnel, but Nava'i immediately realized the possible implications of what had occurred. Folding the newspaper, he slipped it under his arm, retrieved the map from his pocket, and stepped into the street.

Turning to the left, he headed down Connecticut Avenue. Beyond the stretch of statue-studded lawn at the bottom of the avenue, he could see part of the long north face of the White House. As it grew before him, a massive symbol of the unbelieving West, a sense of impending triumph began to surge, wave upon wave, within his heart. Unnoticed, Nava'i walked on, savoring the mood of the capital, observing its buildings and people with the piercing eyes and ascetic mind of a boy brought up in the desert. The air was cool and crisp; an east wind blew unhindered from Chesapeake Bay across to Washington. In the sharp morning sunshine, braced by the edge of fall turning to winter, Nava'i felt invigorated and confident.

During that first day he just walked, viewing the main sights of central Washington like any tourist. He bought a Pentax camera and several rolls of film in a shop on Virginia Avenue and began to take photographs everywhere he went. He walked several times around the White House, through the Ellipse, across Constitution Avenue to the Washington Monument, then down the Mall past the Smithsonian to the Capitol. Everywhere, his camera clicked, but most of the views he took were not those of an ordinary tourist. He took shots of windows, roofs, corners, street angles, shots designed to show height and distance, shots illustrating lighting effects and areas of shadow and darkness.

He spent the next week familiarizing himself with the layout of the capital. On three separate occasions, he visited the White House, mingling with tourists, carrying his camera. Each afternoon he took the exposed films he had taken that day to a drugstore on 14th Street near Franklin Square which provided a speedy developing service. When he called, he would pick up the batch from the previous day. After this, toward sunset, he would head for the mosque at the Islamic Center overlooking Rock Creek Park on Massachusetts Avenue; he would join in the evening prayers there, but afterward headed straight out and back into the street. He spoke to no one, not even the numbers of Iranian students he heard talking in small groups together. Following the prayers, he would return to the hotel and eat dinner, his first and only meal of the day, after which he went to his room to pray, meditate, and plan. He met no one, he received no mail or telephone calls, he avoided cinemas, theaters, and other places of entertainment, he never turned on the television set in his hotel room. He was a loner, a man pursued in his mind by the black wings of angels, dreaming dreams of an Islamic millennium, and set to shape the destiny of the world. He was not demented, or deranged, and that was precisely where the danger lay.

During his second week in the capital, Nava'i set off regularly every morning to the Library of Congress on Capitol Hill, where he had succeeded in obtaining a temporary reader's permit. He spent hours each day reading there, almost without a break, generally consulting reference works on the organization of the Washington administration, the presidential staff structure, the Secret Service, and the FBI, taking care never to ask for anything that might be classified and consequently arouse suspicion. When he asked for works on American-Iranian relations and current Iranian affairs in general, he encountered considerable difficulty. Just about everything available was being used by State Department staff, journalists, lecturers from Georgetown and other universities, and congressmen, who have priority on all materials in the library. The Persian language material was less in demand, so he concentrated on that. He did not know exactly what he was looking for, but he read and thought and read some more. Ideas came and went, plans floated in and out of his mind, always to be rejected as impractical. But he was slowly narrowing down the area of possible approaches. He was systematic and thorough, and no detail escaped sifting in the fine meshes of his brain.

It was an editorial in Thursday's Washington *Post* which finally suggested the answer. He had bought a copy as usual in the hotel and had read, as he did every day, the numerous articles dealing with Iran and the hostage crisis. The piece in question dealt with the difficulties faced by Carter and his staff in initiating negotiations in the absence of any clear authority in Iran. If only someone with influence in the right places would come forward, the article argued, Carter would certainly meet with him in the hope of at last bringing pressure to bear on the situation. Nava'i read the article twice, closed the paper, and left the library, his thoughts racing.

That night as he sat in his hotel room meditating, Nava'i pondered on the words of the article: "I have no doubt but that President Carter would meet and talk with such a person straightaway. As the days pass, the need for political initiative becomes increasingly pressing, and it can only be in the interests of influential factions in Iran to help close the gap of understanding between the U.S. Government and the students of Khomeini." He began to see a path toward his goal. He sat up until the early hours of the morning, thinking, planning, and making notes. Before going to bed, he wrote a letter to Ahmadi in New York, sealed and addressed it, and laid it on his desk.

Nava'i spent the morning shopping. Posing as an Arab businessman, he hired a car and made several trips to shops and warehouses throughout the city. He bought Arabic and Persian printing type and a small home press to use it on, an IBM golf-ball typewriter with reversible carriage and three different balls of Arabic letters, blocks and tools for cutting rubber and metal stamps, paper, ink, Arabic Letraset, calligraphic pens, and sundry other small items. His last purchase was a small item bought in a music store near the John F. Kennedy Center for the Performing Arts.

That afternoon, before prayers at the mosque, he had gone to the Library of Congress again. There, he ordered a copy of the collected poems, the *diwan*, of Hafez, the great fourteenth-century poet of Shiraz, the inspiration of Goethe's *West-östlicher Diwan*. Half an hour later, he collected the book, a heavy late-nineteenth-century lithograph edition, and took it to his desk in a remote corner of the main reading room. He sat in silence, his eyes closed. There were few readers about that afternoon, and no one passed by where he sat, breathing an inaudible prayer, an invocation before taking the *fal*, or an augury from the pages of the book—the Iranian version of consulting the *I Ching* for advice. He held the book with both hands and opened it at random. His eyes fell on a couplet on the left-hand page and he read it slowly. He paused, read it again, and closed the book. The words sang in his head, throbbing, throbbing.

> For Assaf's pomp, and the steeds of the wind,
> And the speech of birds, down the wind have fled,
> And he that was lord of them all is dead;
> Of his mastery nothing remains behind.
> Shoot not thy feathered arrow astray!
> A bowshot's length through the air it has sped,
> And then . . . dropped down in the dusty way.

The *fal* was ambiguous. It seemed to offer him victory and failure in a single prophecy.

He stood up and walked out into the cold air; his face was pale and he shivered at the touch of the north wind, but his mouth was set and his eyes blazed with a violent inner heat.

17 November 1979

On Saturday, Mohammad Ahmadi boarded a British Airways Concorde on the first leg of the long flight that would bring him, after a change in London to a 747, to Tehran by the following day. He carried with him two coded messages that Nava'i had written for his chiefs in Tehran and that could only be transmitted to them in this laborious but secure manner. The code was a simple one agreed on before Nava'i's departure and was unknown to Ahmadi, who was merely acting as a courier, whatever his position in the American side of the organization. Most letters in the Arabic/Persian alphabet incorporate dots, grouped singly, in pairs, or in a pyramid of three. The key to the code was carried in the first words of two lengthy but apparently innocent letters from Nava'i to his "Uncle Farhad" and "Cousin Behruz" in Tehran: the number of dots indicated the interval of words which carried the real message. "Uncle Farhad" worked in the central telegraph office located in the main post office building on Sepah Avenue. "Cousin Behruz" was someone in a much more exalted position.

WASHINGTON
17–18 November 1979

None of the people who sold equipment to Nava'i suspected for a moment that he was not an Arab. Few people can see the facial differences between the Semitic Arab and the Indo-European Persian, and the marked dissimilarity in accents is only obvious to someone familiar with at least one of them. To all intents and purposes, an Arab had bought Letraset, type, and a typewriter for the purpose of printing and typing in Arabic. There was no hint of a connection with

Iran, which, given the mood of the times, might have made someone suspicious.

Secure from interruption in his hotel room, the young Iranian worked throughout Saturday and most of Sunday at his task, pausing only briefly for prayer, an evening meal, and a little sleep. A large part of his training in Tehran had been in the forging of documents. Since it had been decided that it would be best to determine the final plan when actually in Washington, it would have been pointless even to attempt the preparation of documents in Medina; only now did he know what he needed.

He worked quietly and rapidly at his desk. By late Sunday afternoon, he had prepared a set of papers that would satisfy even fairly close examination. There were flaws here and there, but he was confident that no one could detect them without subjecting the documents to intensive analysis, which would take time. And time was precisely what the Americans did not have.

It was near sunset on Sunday when Nava'i left his hotel to attend evening prayers at the Islamic Center. He had not eaten since his evening meal twenty-four hours before, and when the prayers were finished, instead of taking a cab straight back to his hotel, he headed for a small Lebanese restaurant on Massachusetts Avenue, near the Center. The restaurant served halal meat—the Islamic equivalent of kosher—and was filled with Muslims from a variety of countries who had also been attending prayers at the mosque. Nava'i sat alone at a small table toward the back of the restaurant, ordered tersely in Arabic, and made it clear that he did not want company. Halfway through his meal, however, the manager asked if he would object to another customer sharing his table since the place was so full. Nava'i nodded abstractedly and continued eating.

He glanced up as the chair opposite was drawn back with a scraping noise. The new arrival was a woman, a small Indonesian in her early twenties who wore a full-length traditional dress and a long head scarf that framed her pretty oval face and fell below her shoulders. Shocked, he returned his gaze to his food. It was unseemly for a Muslim woman to come to a restaurant like this unaccompanied, without a husband or brother. He looked up again. She was still there, seated in the chair facing him, her lips forming a tentative smile.

"I'm sorry to disturb you," she said in English, "but there was no other table free. If you would prefer me to leave . . ." She shifted in her chair, ready to stand up. Helplessly, he gestured to her that she should remain, then returned his attention to the food. There was no point in drawing attention by making a scene. He would finish his meal and leave. But the woman made him uneasy. It was difficult not to raise his eyes to catch another glimpse of her face. She had the open, childlike look so characteristic of oriental women, but her eyes were feminine and amused, and he felt drawn to them against his will. He wanted to gulp down what was left of his meal and get up to go, but found himself instead toying with the food on his plate, eating it in small, tasteless morsels. The woman spoke again.

"Forgive me," she said, "I don't think I've seen you here before. Have you just come from the mosque? You were at the evening *salat?*"

He nodded.

"I was in the women's section," she went on. "I attend the prayers regularly and come here afterward sometimes. I like the mosque. It reminds me of home."

He looked up again.

"You go to the mosque alone? You have no father, no brothers, no husband to accompany you? A woman should not go alone to the house of God."

She looked down at the table, then said in a low voice, "My father and brothers are in Indonesia. I have no husband. I have no relations here in America." Silence fell again as she raised her dark eyes to him. At last he spoke again.

"Then you should go to the mosque with other women. It is not right for a woman to be alone outside her house."

She smiled and shook her head.

"Where I come from, the women often go in the streets unaccompanied. They even go to the mosque alone. We are good Muslims, but we have our own ways too, we observe our own customs."

Nava'i frowned. He should not be talking with this woman in such a manner. He ought to get up and leave, go before he brought shame upon himself. And yet he found himself speaking, drawn somehow to continue the conversation. His behavior was not normal and he knew it. The strain of the past weeks and the tension he now felt on the eve of his mission had finally worn him down.

"It is not Sunna," he said. "It is not the way of the Prophet. Have you no scholars where you come from to explain these things to you?"

She shrugged, her small shoulders rising and falling gracefully.

"Yes," she answered. "We have scholars. And holy men, dervishes who can perform miracles."

"Then why do they not do their duty? It is their duty to forbid wrong and enjoin right. God's law should be enforced." Even as he spoke, it seemed to him that his words came out stilted and forced.

She smiled, it seemed a little ironically.

"There are people like you where I come from. They tell us we are doing wrong when we do not follow the letter of the law, they say God will punish us. Do you think He will really punish me for going to the mosque alone?"

He did not answer her; what could he say, after all? But finally he spoke again.

"Where are you from? Is yours an Islamic country?"

"From Indonesia," she replied. "Yes, it is an Islamic country. Most of the people are Muslims. But we also have Hindus and people who believe in the old religion. My family have been Muslims for almost three hundred years, since the time when Arab traders first opened our country to the faith. We come from Modjokerto in Java. It's a small provincial center, but we have scholars and schools where Islam is taught. My father is a trader. He's wealthy but he tries to be a good Muslim, a *santri*. By that, we mean someone who doesn't mix his faith with the old religion. You would like him: he has been to Mecca for the hajj four times." She stopped abruptly, then changed the subject.

"Where do you come from?"

Nava'i wanted to resist. He knew that the talk had gone far enough. But her face drew his eyes and loosened his tongue. It was as if he really had no will power left, no strength with which to resist her. Her eyes were green and very beautiful. A lock of hair had edged its way outside her scarf and hung softly against her cheek. As if speaking from far away, he replied.

"I come from Iran, from a desert town called Yazd. It's a provincial center as well, but very isolated. My father was a farmer; he had a small holding in Maryamabad, just outside the town. We were very poor; most of our money went to the landlord. But we lived as good Muslims. They call Yazd 'the Abode of Piety.' It's true, the people *are* very pious. My father always longed to go to Mecca, to put his lips against the Black Stone and walk with the pilgrims to Arafat. But he died without even having been to holy Mashhad. He looked like an old man when he died, but he was only forty-seven years old. May God have mercy on him." His voice fell silent as he repeated the well-known Arabic phrase, and he looked away from her. He remembered the years he had spent after his father's death, saving every penny to have his bones taken overland to Karbala, to be buried near the shrine in order to ease his way to the next world. He felt so close to his father now.

She echoed the words he had spoken in Arabic, *"Rahimahu 'llah"*: "May God show him mercy." She wanted to weep, there was such sadness in his voice, sadness she somehow felt was less for his father than for himself.

"My name is Fatimeh," she said, "Fatimeh Natsir. What is your name?"

His food had grown cold. He laid down the knife and fork and sat back in his chair facing her. He felt pinned there, helpless.

"Husayn," he told her, almost in a whisper. "My name is Husayn Nava'i. Your father did well to call you Fatimeh. Are you Shi'is?"

She smiled and shook her head.

"She was the Prophet's daughter," she said. "Even Sunnis may use her name."

"But she was the wife of 'Ali," he added. "The mother of Hasan and Husayn. She has a special place in our hearts. We call her al-Zahra, 'the Beautiful.'"

Around them, the noises of the restaurant rose and fell: the clatter of utensils, the hum of voices, the bustle of waiters hurrying to and fro. But none came to their table. They sat as if in a circle of silence, her bright eyes holding him unmoving. His hands felt clammy and his heart was beating like a deep drum rolling in his breast. His thoughts were confused. He tried to pray, to ask God or the Prophet or one of the Imams to come to his aid, for he no longer wanted to leave the restaurant alone. But every time he beseeched them, his mind was filled with the image of her face and his nostrils with the fragrance of the perfume she wore. Again and again, there returned to him a saying of the Prophet that he had never understood before: "Three things have been dear to me: prayer, women, and perfume."

"Why do you close your eyes?" Her voice came to him as if from a great distance. He opened his eyes and she was looking at him, smiling wistfully.

"I was thinking," he said.

"Of what?" she queried.

"Why do you want to know?"

There was a pause. Still looking at him, she replied.

"You interest me. Interest and puzzle me. You are a strange man. I would like to know your thoughts, your secrets."

He said nothing. He felt as if she could see inside him, as if a glass window had been placed in his eyes through which she could see straight into his inmost thoughts. All the black memories welled up inside him, as if rising to overwhelm him: the hot sun parching their crops year after year; the grinding poverty of the farm and their landlord's fine house in town; his father old and tired and wasted, dying because he no longer had any will to live; his mother old and wasted at fifty; his three brothers and his sister all dead in infancy, their thin bodies returned to the dry dust of the desert; the vultures circling the empty towers of silence, day in, day out, searching for carrion; his meeting with Molla Ahmad; and the years of pain and sacrifice that had brought him here, within days of his death. What would he remember as he died? In all his life, he had never seen anything so beautiful as the woman sitting opposite him.

"You're far away again," she said. "I think we should go. We can't sit here. We can't talk properly. Will you walk me home? It's the custom here in America because the streets are so dangerous for women. It's dark now and I don't like to walk back alone. I don't live far away, just a short distance from the Islamic Center, on Wyoming Avenue."

Her eyes seemed to dance, beckoning him. He said nothing, but when he stood up, she rose also and he did not try to stop her. At the counter, he paid his bill and they went together into the freezing night air. Nava'i turned at the door and looked back into the restaurant. He had expected to see the eyes of all the customers turned in his direction, watching him leave with the woman. But no one was looking, no one cared how he came or went, or even who he was.

They walked slowly down to Belmont Road and followed it a short distance before turning east toward Wyoming Avenue. Their feet echoed in the darkness, her footsteps light and ringing on the frosted pavement. She was so small, he felt a giant beside her, awkward and uncouth. As they walked, he spoke about himself, about Yazd and his parents. But there was so much he could not tell her, so much of him that must remain forever secret. Above all, he could not reveal to her that she was walking with a man already dead.

When they reached her apartment, he lingered as she took the key from her bag and opened the door. He wanted nothing, he had no expectations. But he could not bear to leave her. If he left, he could not return. Tomorrow it would begin; by Wednesday, by the end of the month at the latest, he would be dead.

She turned to him, a little frightened by his spells of abstraction. "You're cold," she said. "Come inside with me, warm yourself before you leave."

Nothing seemed to matter to him now but to be with her. Even the hope of Paradise was trembling like a dying mirage. Since childhood he had been warned, as generations of his people had been warned, that men and women were as magnets and iron filings to one another. At last he understood. He could not resist. Magnetized, he flew to her. Irrevocably, he stepped across the threshold and he closed the door behind them.

Her apartment was on the second floor. It was warm and bright, its furnishings and colors imprinted by her personality. He stood clumsily in the middle of the living room, uncertain what to do or say. She laughed and asked for his coat. Numb, he shuffled it off and handed it to her. She told him to sit in a large red armchair by the window and, like an obedient child, he sat. His eyes followed her as she left the room to hang up their coats.

When she returned a few minutes later, she had removed her head scarf. Her long black hair fell across her shoulders like silk shot through with bands of light. He wanted to touch it, to bury his face in its perfumed darkness and escape the nightmares that surrounded him. Time passed and neither of them spoke. She sat silently, watching him, her eyes intent upon his face, following the shifting expressions that moved across it in constant succession. At last she broke the silence and they began to talk again.

She asked no questions, made no demands on his privacy. Instead, she told him about herself, about her childhood, about life on Java. He drank in her words as if thirsty for them and no others. Never before had he sat in a room and spoken with a woman like this. And at last he spoke, revealing to her facets of himself that had been buried deep inside him for years. There was much he could not tell her: his true identity, the nature of his mission, his imminent death.

But he spoke about everything else, as if longing to unburden himself of his memories before his life ended. She listened in total silence. Time passed unnoticed, hour after hour through the evening and into the night.

Several times he came close to telling her what it was that was driving him so inexorably to his coming encounter with death, but each time he pulled back, unable to betray himself to her. She sensed that there was more and that the things he had not revealed to her were more important than those he had. Finally, a deep and atmospheric silence fell, broken only by the sound of their breathing. Minutes passed, then she leaned forward and spoke, her words gentle, her voice full of concern.

"Husayn," she said, "why are you so sad? When I sat with you in the restaurant tonight, I saw terrible things in your eyes. Is it a memory? Or are you afraid of something? Please tell me, perhaps I can help."

He stared blindly, his eyes filled with impossible appeal. If only there was time.

"There is nothing you can do," he said, his words almost lost in the stillness.

"Perhaps I can comfort you."

He shook his head slowly from side to side.

"There is no comfort you can give me now. Perhaps . . ." His voice broke off and he looked away again.

"Perhaps . . . ?" She urged him to continue.

"If this had happened before, while there was still time . . ." He looked into her eyes, his gaze burning, penetrating her.

She stood up slowly, as if in a dream, and came toward him. Her skin was the color of amber and she smelt warm and fragrant. She was alive and fragile and he was afraid of his longings for her. She bent down softly over him, her hair falling across his face, and kissed him on the forehead, her lips moist and gentle, her breath warm and delicate. The kiss was like nothing he had ever felt on his skin before. The blood pounded in his veins and tears pressed hard against his eyes. He could not see her as she bent again to kiss his lips, softly, as a mother will do with her child. Her kiss was almost imperceptible at first, the faintest touch. And as he sat in mute astonishment, it grew from such a little thing to a living pressure that sent its ripples down to nerves throughout his body.

He did not know how she came onto his lap, her small, almost weightless limbs insinuating themselves until she was curled there, her arms encircling him, her lips on his, her tiny tongue trembling moistly on the edges of his open mouth, her breath entering him. She felt so light, so vulnerable, a flower he could crush in his clumsy strength. He hardly understood how his arms moved as if of their own accord to hold her there, to press her against him. Blinded with tears, his heart leaping, he slid his lips across her parted mouth to kiss her cheeks, her nose, her eyes, his kisses falling again and again upon her upturned face.

Like snow melting, she slid from his lap and stood, her arms extended to take his hands and raise him to his feet. Unprotesting, he bent to her will and stood, his legs trembling like the limbs of a fawn. He was hers, and she could lead him to Hell and its nineteen gates if she pleased. Without a word, she took him by the hand and led him step-by-step in silence across the floor to the door of her bedroom. The door opened to her touch and she brought him inside, closing it behind them. She reached out her hand and a soft light fell on them from the lamp beside the bed, casting shadows over her face. He sat down on the edge of the bed, his eyes fixed on her, all thoughts of sin and impurity gone. All he felt was the blood pounding in his temples. Her scent was stronger in this room, overwhelming him, filling him with her.

The movement was so simple: her hand seemed barely to touch her dress and it fell away from her shoulders, dropping all at once in a crumpled heap to the floor. She wore a simple white cotton bra and small white pants. No lace, no silk, no elaboration. Without either coyness or embarrassment, she reached behind her back and unfastened the bra, removing it in a single, uncomplicated motion. She wanted to show herself to him, to offer her body to him simply and artlessly. He watched in growing wonder as she slipped out of her pants and stood naked, her body shining quietly in the gentle light. She stood before him, her arms by her side, unclothed, defenseless, presenting herself innocently to his troubled gaze. He could not take his eyes off her; he feared to close them lest she be gone when he opened them again. Her loveliness held him fascinated. He had never seen a woman's body before, but now that she stood undressed before him, her nakedness awakened in him feelings that had waited for this moment. He had so few things of beauty in his memory with which to compare her.

At last she came to the bed and sat beside him, the fragrance of her body lifting to his nostrils. She looked into his eyes, and saw them filled with a pain she could not understand, then bent once more to kiss him, taking his hand and placing it on a small shadowed breast. He felt her nipple harden beneath his fingers as he held her, marveling at the firm softness of her skin, the warmth radiating from beneath its surface. With her help he undressed, awkward, shy, his hands shaking, his fingers clumsy on the buttons. When he was naked, she lay back on the bed, pulling him gently down to lie beside her.

"Touch me," she whispered, her breath brushing against his ear. The soft light dappled her limbs, transforming her for him into a flowing pattern of light and darkness. As if independent of him, his hands reached out in search of her, caressing her without the awkwardness of thought or learned, tired responses. She became tense, then relaxed as he stroked her gently, his every movement expressive of the wonder and joy he felt. His hesitant gentleness rendered his touches more erotic for her than those of the most skilled lover. Her eyes upon his, she turned and stretched out her hand to him, her fingers encircling his penis before running beneath with small, lingering strokes. He cried out with the unaccustomed pleasure of her touch and rolled toward her, his body all instinct now, his whole being centered in the one desire to clutch her to him and be one with her.

Her fingers guiding him, he began to enter her. But his heightened tension pushed him instantly over the brink into a quick, wracking orgasm. Exhausted, overwrought, and cheated of a total entry into her, he rolled back onto the bed and wept. Wave after wave, tears of bewilderment and dismay washed through him. Fatimeh lay beside him gently stroking his back, whispering his name, easing him back to her.

At last he sat up, his tears spent, his mind becoming clear once more.

"Don't worry," she said, her voice soft and encouraging. "We'll try again, tonight or tomorrow, it doesn't matter. It'll work next time, you'll see." She paused, her eyes seeking his, holding his hand in hers.

"This was your first time, wasn't it?" she asked, wondering within herself how a man of his age could have remained so wholly without experience.

After what seemed an age, he nodded his head. "Yes," he replied. Just "yes" and nothing more: no comment, no explanation. A silence fell and long minutes passed while he looked intently at her face. At last he spoke again.

"I'm not the first man you've been with, am I?" he asked. But he did not need to ask; he already knew the answer.

She returned his gaze, then shook her head wearily.

"Have there been many others before me?" he continued. "Have you slept with many men?"

Turning her eyes aside, she nodded and her voice came in a barely audible whisper.

"Yes."

It was as if, with that single whispered word, she had slapped him full in the face. He could not bear to look at her. When her words came at last, flat and devoid of the vibrancy her voice had held before, he wanted to press his hands over his ears in order to blot them out. But his hands were lifeless and numb and he could not lift them.

"I came here three years ago," she said, "with my husband. He was much older than I, a man of more than fifty. My father had known him since he was a boy and there had always existed an agreement that I should become his wife. We were married when I was fifteen. I knew nothing then of men and I was not prepared for what would happen. He was like a beast, he cared only to satisfy himself. But by the time we arrived here, he had almost lost interest in me. He took no other wives, but he was rich and could afford other women. It was no secret, he never tried to hide them from me."

She paused, her eyes filled with an inner pain that her words had brought to the surface again. His gaze averted, he failed to notice. She went on.

"He spent his time at his office, dealing with the business he had come to this country to establish. I was left at home most days. He didn't like me to go out, he was extremely old-fashioned in such matters. But there were some other Indonesian women living near us in Georgetown, and I began to spend time with them. They were my age or a little older. Mostly, they came to my house at first, but after a while I found it was possible to go out with them, shopping, visiting restaurants, even seeing the sights like tourists. I was free. Can you understand what that meant? You're a man, you've never known anything but freedom. How could you understand what it's like to be without it?"

He made no response but went on staring in front of him like a man lost in a dream. She did not even know if he could hear her, but she continued.

"I wanted to go places by myself, to be fully independent, but my English was too poor. I had never been given proper lessons. So one of my friends arranged for her teacher to visit me. He was a young man, a graduate student at the university, and he came to my house when my husband was out. I paid him with the money I was given to spend on clothes.

"At first we were very formal, but when my English improved, we came to enjoy one another's company more and more. He was funny, he made me laugh constantly. I looked forward so much to the days when he would come; sometimes I lay awake in bed at night when I knew he was due the next day, thinking over the things I was going to say to him. He wasn't very good-looking or witty or sophisticated, but he was kind and good-natured, and I started to love him. One day—it was two years ago, in winter—he came back for his gloves, he had left them behind. He found me crying, weeping because he had gone. I said nothing, I needed to tell him nothing; he understood.

"He came often after that, sometimes to make love to me, sometimes just to sit and talk with me. But we were careless. I became pregnant and my husband discovered what had happened. He had not slept with me for months, there was no mistake. I think the thing that made him angriest was the fact that he had been unable to give me a child but another man had done so. He wanted to have me killed, but friends interfered and he was persuaded to abandon me instead. He pronounced the words of divorce three times in front of witnesses, and I was no longer his wife or he my husband. It was that simple. He left that night on a flight to Jakarta. The next week I learned that my father had disowned me. I could never return home. The house was sold and I was forced to move in with Paul, my lover."

She stopped speaking as her eyes clouded with tears. She was talking for her own sake now, not for his, explaining for the hundredth time what had happened and why, reliving the misery of her past.

"One month later, Paul was stopped on the edge of Georgetown by muggers. He put up a fight and one of them stabbed him. He died that same night in the hospital. Four days later, I lost the baby.

"When I recovered, I had nothing, no one. My old friends had deserted me, even the most emancipated ones. They called me a fallen woman and said their husbands would not let them even talk to me. Before that, they used to boast about how they had their husbands under their thumbs, how they could do as they liked. When I got out of the hospital, Paul's apartment had been rented to someone else. In the end, I went to the Islamic Center and asked for help. They told me they could do nothing for me, but I could see straightaway that it was not lack of means but of will. Then, as I was leaving, one of the men I had spoken to, an Arab from Kuwait, came after me and said he could arrange accommodation and a little money. I thought he was kind, that he had taken pity on me. But he soon made his conditions clear. I had no choice. Where else could I go? I slept with him.

"When he finally grew tired of me, I realized that I could at least choose the men I gave myself to. I never asked for money in return. Once I did that, I knew I would have to make myself available to any man who could pay. Instead, I let the men I met decide what they wanted to do. I lived with some of them for a while. One bought me this apartment—he said I could keep it when he returned to Bahrain. Others bought me clothes or put small sums in my bank account. How else could I have stopped myself from starving? I had no choice. A woman has no choice. I was an outcast and I found people who would take me in, each for a little while. I loved each of them a little and I let them love me in return. Was that wrong? Is it wrong? When I met you tonight, I wanted you. I wanted to sleep with you and be with you. You seemed so sad, sad and distant, and I wanted to help you if I could. I still want to. I don't want money from you; I'm not a prostitute. Stay with me tonight. Let us be friends if nothing else."

She looked directly at him, trying to penetrate the shell that seemed to have grown up around him. She thought he had not heard her, but every word she had spoken had entered his thoughts and lodged there, growing like seeds in the darkness of his mind. He lifted his eyes, helpless in the grip of the black feelings that surged inside him. How could someone so lovely, someone so seemingly pure, be so foul? She had caused him to sin, to jeopardize his soul and his mission. She had awakened feelings in him that he had succeeded in suppressing for so many years and with so much unhappiness. His heart lurched as he thought about what had just happened. She had forced him to reveal his weakness and had humiliated him. The blood rushed to his cheeks as he remembered the shame: at the very moment when his manhood had been about to take possession of her, he had failed. In seconds, his strength and virility had been changed to powerlessness and impotence, and he knew that inwardly she was mocking him, comparing him to the numerous other men who had made love to her—and satisfied her. Suddenly, Nava'i felt terrified as he confronted his own despair. He could no longer control the turmoil of his thoughts and knew only that she would lead him on to further, darker sins. He realized also that he had told her too much, that she knew enough to be dangerous. Should anything go wrong with his mission, she might realize what had happened and tell what she knew to the American authorities. They would make the connections she was unequipped to make. The mission was once more at the center of everything for him. It must not be endangered. He would have to undo the evil he had done if there was to be any hope of success.

Her right hand had grasped his and held it now, the warmth of physical contact bringing him back to her again. She felt desire for him, the slow, trickling onset of arousal creeping once more across her breasts and through her loins. With a gentle motion, she raised her left hand and brought it to his cheek as she bent to kiss him on the mouth. Uninstructed, his hands moved as she wanted them to move, to her slender waist, then up over her breasts and neck to her face. Slowly, tenderly, he caressed her cheeks and stroked her hair, his fingers soft and warm upon her skin. She drew away slightly to look into his eyes, seeing there an expression of deep longing mingled with the pain of an infinite loss. But even as she looked, his eyes changed and an icy chill shivered through her spine. His eyes were cold and implacable, and she knew in the very instant she gazed into their depths that she was going to die. Fear rose inside her, desperately urging her body to rise and run, but she lay, unable to move, as his hands rose slowly to her throat and meshed about it.

As his fingers pressed into the soft skin of her neck, Nava'i's eyes continued to gaze into hers, oblivious of their look of desperate entreaty. His hands were like steel around her windpipe. She could not cry out or plead. Her legs jerked uselessly and her hands pulled hopelessly on his wrists trying to break his iron grip, but he continued to squeeze, the pressure unyielding and merciless. As her body grew limp, he fell forward on top of her, pressing her down onto the bed in a grotesque parody of an embrace. Her eyes opened wider and wider, pleading hopelessly with him as silent screams reverberated deep inside her skull. The thrashing of her limbs grew weaker every second, and in a matter of moments, all movements ceased and her body lay limp and lifeless beneath him.

He lay for a long time on top of her, like a lover whose passion is spent but who cannot bear to break the contact of skin with skin. When at last he raised himself, he could not tear his eyes away from her face: her features had relaxed again in death, her dreadful stillness lending her a last beauty that had been unattainable in life.

He found his clothes and dressed. As he was about to leave, his eye caught sight of her dressing table in a corner of the room. Crossing to it, he picked up a small lipstick. On the wall above the bed, in large letters, he wrote a single Arabic word before tossing the stick aside. At the door, he turned and looked back once more. The tangled sheets, the small body lying wretched in death, the red letters above her on the wall, all combined to bring back to him the memory of another room, another woman he had killed. The thought of Tehran made it easier to leave. The fog had cleared from his mind and he was himself again. It was already the first day of the mission.

22

WASHINGTON
19 November 1979

Early on Monday morning, a telegram arrived in Washington. It had been dispatched from Tehran with priority rating a few minutes before and was addressed to the State Department. Minutes later, a motorcycle messenger turned out of the main postal services building onto Constitution Avenue, turned west, then north again along the overpass that leads onto the Theodore Roosevelt Bridge. A few seconds later, he was running up the steps of the State Department. It was all extremely unorthodox, and it was another fifteen minutes before the telegram lay at last on the desk of the Secretary of State. He read it twice, lifted one of the three internal phones in front of him, and asked to speak to Arthur Pike, director of the Office of Iranian Affairs. Pike was already at work in the Iran Crisis room set up two weeks before in the department for round-the-clock monitoring of the hostage situation. Leaving his deputy in charge, he hurried to Cyrus Vance's office, where the Secretary was waiting for him, the telegram held in his extended hand.

"Arthur, we've just received this telegram from Tehran. It is in English, but I want your opinion. Is it some kind of hoax or what?"

Pike read the telegram carefully.

PREPARED TO NEGOTIATE INDEPENDENTLY OF REVOLUTIONARY COUNCIL FOR RELEASE OF HOSTAGES THROUGH MUJAHIDIN LEADERSHIP STOP HAVE REQUESTED MUJAHIDIN REPRESENTATIVE IN WASHINGTON HUSAYN NAVA'I TO MEET PRESIDENT CARTER TO DISCUSS TERMS STOP NAVA'I INSTRUCTED TO NEGOTIATE ONLY WITH PRESIDENT STOP AUTHORIZED TO SIGN AGREEMENT ON MY BEHALF STOP NAVA'I WILL ARRIVE STATE DEPARTMENT MONDAY MORNING STOP CONFIRMATION OF HIS STATUS WILL BE PROVIDED BY AYATOLLAH SAYYID ALI MARVDASHTI STOP SIGNED MUHAMMAD 'ALI MEHDAVI KHANI.

Vance turned to Pike, querying, "Who is this Khani? Have you heard of him?"

Pike nodded. "I'd heard the name before, but I just learned this Saturday who he actually is. On Saturday, the Iranians made public the names of the fourteen members of the Revolutionary Council who took over the running of the country on 8 November, after Bazargan and his cabinet resigned. Among them was Ayatollah Mehdavi Khani, the member with responsibility for the Khomeini Committees."

"And Marvdashti?"

"I don't know much about him. No one does. He seems to have lived in Najaf in Iraq for a long time, where he was an aide to Ayatollah al-Qasim al-Musawi al-Khu'i, the supreme leader of the Shi'i world. He also had close contact while in Iraq with Khomeini and was sent by him to Iran in 1977 to help orchestrate the growing movement against the Shah. He isn't a member of the Revolutionary Council, but I have heard rumors that he is more influential than many who are."

"OK. What about Nava'i? It says here he's the Washington representative of the Mujahidin. Have you ever met him?"

"No, sir, I haven't. In fact, I've never heard of him before, or of there even being a Mujahidin representative in this city."

"Could he be attached to the Iranian Embassy?"

"I doubt it, sir. We know fairly well who they have and that certainly doesn't include Mujahidin officials. And from the wording of the telegram, I assume this whole thing is being worked outside the official channels."

"Then how was this telegram transmitted?"

"That's just the point, sir. If this had official approval, it would have gone through the embassy as usual. Why a telegram? I imagine they have one of their own men at the telegraph office and that no record of this communication exists in Tehran."

"Right, it's unofficial. Now, what do you know about Khani's links with the Mujahidin?"

"Nothing. I'll have to check up as far as I can. If I don't have anything on file, perhaps the CIA at Langley will have data stored. I expect we'll have something, but you realize that there's just no way we can get hold of up-to-the-minute information from Iran. If we're in luck, the British may hold a file, but it's not likely to have much more than our own and they aren't in a much better position than we are for obtaining intelligence there at present."

"OK. Do what you can. Now, it says that Nava'i is coming here this morning. I take it no one has been in touch with your department to arrange an interview or anything?"

"No, sir, no one. It all seems pretty unorthodox, but I figure he'll just turn up at the front door and ask to see someone, probably you, sir."

"Well, if he isn't going through diplomatic channels, there's not a lot more he can do. In any case, at the moment this whole thing seems a bit vague, and obviously I can't see him until we've decided on a negotiation at that level—and that's if Nava'i has credentials we can accept. So I'd like you to see this man when he calls, check his credentials, put a team together to start investigating him—and his chiefs—and report back to me this afternoon. I don't expect you'll have any final answers, but I would like an interim report. And, of course, if you turn up anything definite, if you find out he's an impostor or anything like that, then contact me immediately. In the meantime, I'll speak with the President and fix up a provisional meeting of some kind for Wednesday. He's at Camp David at the moment for Thanksgiving week, but if there does seem to be a chance of opening negotiations, I've no doubt he'll want to see Nava'i as soon as he's been cleared. OK, Arthur, good luck."

At 10:30 A.M., Nava'i walked up the steps to the main entrance of the State Department. He had been up early that morning in order to drive out south of the city along the Potomac. He had headed into Maryland on the southbound Indian Head Highway as far as Fort Washington Forest, where he had turned off the main road and down toward Piscataway Creek. Here he had dumped into the river all the equipment he had bought on the previous Friday. He felt elated; everything had turned out perfectly: the seals he had cut, the letterheads he had set up, the letters he had typed, the stamps he had made to overprint photographs and signatures, the identity cards he had produced from card and ink and plastic film. Returning to the city, he had taken the precaution of going to a number of shops that provided a Xerox service, photocopying the various documents he had prepared over the weekend. He did not need the copies, which he later shredded and threw away. What he had wanted and what he had obtained was a variety of fingerprints on the papers. If only his own prints were found on them in the event of a check, they would immediately be identified as forgeries. He had then spent half an hour before going to the State Department sitting in his car outside the White House, gazing toward the windows of the Oval Office. Carter was not there, but Nava'i did not know that and it did not matter: he was not gloating over his anticipated victim; he was praying, rosary in hand, for divine help in his task.

A Marine guard had been posted at the entrance to the State Department with instructions to escort Nava'i on his arrival to Arthur Pike's office on the third floor. Having, after polite apologies for doing so, frisked the Iranian thoroughly and checked his black leather briefcase, the guard led him into the elevator, up to the third floor, and along a blue-walled corridor that traversed the long southern flank of the building. Through windows on his right, Nava'i could see the Lincoln Memorial, with its statue of the bearded champion of human liberty, and, beyond it, the Potomac shining in the sharp November light.

Arthur Pike was waiting for him in office 320, the center of what had become, for the present, the most vital section of the State Department. In the Iran Crisis room on the same floor, a team of experts struggled to extract from unusually limited sources information on developments at the midpoint of what had become known as the Arc of Crisis, stretching below the vast, sweeping belly of Russia from Turkey to Afghanistan. But it was here in the office of the head of the Iranian desk that the most crucial discussions were held on what information had priority for the Secretary of State or the President himself.

A thin, wasted man of forty-three, Pike was showing the effects of almost uninterrupted tension. The past two weeks since the start of the embassy takeover had been a constant nightmare, and still there seemed to be no end in sight. A Princeton man, he had degrees in politics and Persian; his doctorate, completed in 1962, had researched "The Distribution of Power within the Iranian Political System," but like most other commentators, he had failed to observe the true significance of the growing religious opposition to the Shah. For some months now, he had begun to regret bitterly his ever having become involved with Iran at all.

After the formal introductions were over, Pike invited Nava'i to explain the purpose of his mission. The young Iranian spoke in English, carefully weighing his words. It was, above all, vital to persuade this man of the authenticity of his credentials, to make him believe he really was a negotiator sent by the Islamic Mujahidin to discuss terms with President Carter. Otherwise, he would have no chance at all of meeting the President face-to-face. As Nava'i spoke, Pike listened with a mounting interest.

"I believe you have received this morning a telegram from Ayatollah Mehdavi Khani stating that I have been appointed by him to act as a negotiator on behalf of the Mujahidin guerrillas in Tehran on the issue of the American hostages held there by student revolutionaries of the Khomeini line. I have brought with me various papers to serve as credentials, which you will doubtless want to study later. Obviously, there is a serious problem here. I have not been sent through the normal diplomatic channels, nor am I acting on behalf of the Revolutionary Council at present controlling Iran. With the breakdown of satisfactory communications with my country, you will find it difficult to establish what I think you call my 'bona fides.' So it remains for me to tell you something about myself to help you decide.

"For several years I have belonged to a group of Mujahidin with its headquarters in south Tehran. When the original Mujahidin-e Khalq split in 1975 and the main branch claimed to have abandoned Islam for Marxist ideas, our group was one of those that remained faithful to the early principles and continued to struggle as Islamic guerrillas; for us, the fight against the Shah's régime remained a holy war, a *jihad*, and we were *mujahidin*, fighters in the holy war. The two words come from the same Arabic root—I am sure you know that already. The name of our group is Goruh-e Badr; Badr is the name of a battle fought by the Prophet, the first battle of Islam. Our leader is Molla Mohammad 'Ali Nayrizi, a very respected clergyman, a great scholar; he preaches in the mosque of Shah Abdol-'Azim in the south of Tehran and holds classes in Islamic law at a theological school there. He is very well known and was a student of Ayatollah Khomeini before the Imam was exiled to Iraq. Our group was very active in the revolution; several of us were killed, but we remained intact and took control of a high school to the north of the American Embassy, the Dabirestan-e Bahar-e Naw, off Karim Khan-e Zand Avenue. That is our headquarters now. When the ayatollah returned to Iran, he gave us some important tasks to perform, and a few of our number were chosen for his bodyguard.

"Although a great many members of the clergy are suspicious of the Mujahidin and Feda'iyan, Mehdavi Khani and several others are secretly sympathetic to our group because of our strict Islamic line. Many of the students now holding the embassy belong or have belonged to the group and probably the majority are sympathetic toward us. The proximity of our headquarters to the embassy has resulted in a great deal of contact between us and the students—we have even given them assistance in guarding the compound from time to time. We have enough influence to persuade the Revolutionary Council and the students to give up the hostages provided certain conditions are met by the U.S.A."

Pike interrupted. "What would those conditions be, Mr. Nava'i?"

"I'm sorry, I'm only permitted to discuss them with your President."

"I cannot guarantee that the President will speak with you. That will be his decision."

"He will speak with me."

"What makes you so certain?"

"He wishes to negotiate. He cannot find anyone with whom to do so. The Bazargan cabinet has resigned, leaving only the Revolutionary Council, and they will not negotiate."

"The PLO have offered to act as intermediaries."

"You know as well as I do that that will not work. It is politically too dangerous, too controversial. And the PLO have no real political influence in Iran."

"How much influence does your group really have, Mr. Nava'i?"

"Enough to sway the issue. We have influence with the students and, in this matter, it is they who really count, more than the Revolutionary Council. President Carter will talk to me because there is no one else in Iran willing to talk to him."

Pike caught Nava'i's gaze and held it, as if seeking to probe behind those eyes that stared but gave nothing away. Seconds passed in silence, then the American spoke.

"Mr. Nava'i, what are your reasons for coming here? Why does your group want to negotiate with us? Surely you will only destroy any influence you may have when it becomes known you have made approaches to my government. What do you hope to gain from all this?"

Nava'i returned the gaze, unperturbed.

"Leverage," he answered, "power perhaps. I use concepts you can understand, words that may make sense within the context of your culture. But they are distortions. We seek . . ."

He paused, as if collecting his thoughts and rephrasing them. "Let us say, we wish to make the truth manifest. The phrase we use is a little different: 'to complete the proof,' to make perfect the evidences of Islam for our people. We can only do that if we have a vantage point from which we can influence minds and hearts. The revolution is more in danger with every day that passes. The different factions are beginning to tear at one another's throats, the jackals have already started to appear on the streets, hungry for what they can scavenge from the coming holocaust. We have to stop the decay before it goes too far. The leaders of our group are of the opinion that the business of the hostages will eventually backfire on the revolution. Our motives are not humanitarian. Such motives mean nothing to us. We would kill the hostages tomorrow if it seemed useful to the cause of truth. Human rights are your weakness: your obsession with them will destroy you in the end. We are concerned only with the rights of God. That is our strength.

"We will arrange to free your hostages in return for certain economic, political, and military benefits. For once, we are in a position of strength, and we will dictate the terms. As I have already told you, I can only discuss those terms with your President."

"Very well, let us assume that the President will be willing to talk. I shall have to assure him first that you are in reality an authorized negotiator on behalf of the Mujahidin. You will have to convince me of that yourself. You understand that I have no means of confirming your status through Tehran. What documents have you brought with you?"

From a briefcase by his side, Nava'i produced several papers. They included a letter from Ayatollah Mehdavi Khani, authorizing Nava'i to negotiate on his behalf; his Mujahidin and Goruh-e Badr identity cards; a statement signed by four members of the student executive at the U.S. Embassy in Tehran, expressing support for the Goruh-e Badr and agreeing to their acting as mediators between the students and the U.S. government; and a copy of a letter written by Khani, signed

by Beheshti, Khalkhali, and Hashemi Rafsanjani, and addressed to
Mohammad 'Ali Nayrizi, in which the signatories stated their
preparedness to cooperate with the Goruh-e Badr if they could send
someone privately to Washington to negotiate with the President.
Nava'i explained the nature of each document as he passed it to Pike
while the latter made notes for the benefit of his team of experts who
would be examining the papers later that morning. He was still asking
questions when the door opened and a secretary entered with a sealed
message.

"Excuse me, sir," she said, "this has just been sent urgently from
the British Embassy. Mr. Vance took delivery of it but he thinks you
should see it right away."

Pike opened the envelope and drew out a message marked "Urgent" and "Top Secret." It had been transmitted in code from the
British Embassy in Tehran to the Foreign Office in London and from
there to their Washington embassy, who had passed it on to the State
Department. Despite the circuitous routing, there had been the minimum of delay in the transmission of the message, and its importance
was immediately apparent to Pike. The report stated that the British
in Tehran had been approached that morning (it was now early evening there) by a young Iranian ostensibly applying for a visa. He had
brought a message asking for a British official to come in secret to the
home of Ayatollah Sayyid 'Ali Marvdashti in the southern sector of
the city. A Persian-speaking first secretary had volunteered to go and
had been taken by a carefully prepared route to the house. There he
met Marvdashti (whose face was familiar to him from television ap-
pearances) and spoke with him. The ayatollah asked him to pass on to
Washington confirmation of the status of Husayn Nava'i as a negotiator on behalf of the Goruh-e Badr and certain senior clergy. The
private and secret nature of the information had been impressed on
the diplomat who had returned without delay to his embassy.

Pike looked up at Nava'i.

"It seems that your position has been confirmed by Ayatollah
Marvdashti. But we shall still require some time to consult on your
offer and, of course, to put the matter to the President. It may well be
several days before we can arrange an interview, if at all."

"I understand you cannot do things like this immediately. But I do
urge you to act as fast as you can. It is urgent that I see the President
as soon as possible and place my proposals before him. There is dan-

ger to the hostages. Already there is talk in some quarters of trying them as spies. But there is also another danger which I have not mentioned. I have heard that a group of Marxist Feda'iyan are planning to storm the embassy and kill those held there. There may not be time to waste with diplomatic niceties here. The President must see me as soon as possible. I suggest you ask him for an appointment on Wednesday."

Nava'i picked up his briefcase, stood, and turned to go. The first step had gone well. Marvdashti had timed his part perfectly. Now, he was sure, the rest would be simple. Carter would be dead by Wednesday, the first day of the new century. And nothing could prevent it.

23

MECCA
Monday, 19 November 1979

As Nava'i sat in Pike's office at the State Department, dusk was falling over the domes and minarets of Mecca. The voice of the muezzin rang out clearly from a spot high up on the Masjid al-Haram, the Great Mosque. Behind the precipices of the Jabal Hind the sun slowly sank, and three miles to the north, the western flank of Mount Hira, the scene of the Prophet's vision of the angel Gabriel, was flooded with light. The pilgrimage season had just ended, the Ka'ba was decked in its new black and gold covering, and life was beginning to return to normal for the people of the city. But the day after tomorrow would be the first day of a new century; here, at the heart of Islam, there would be celebrations. Tonight many of those who entered the Great Mosque to pray hoped that this new century would see the resurgence of Islam, the end of centuries of weakness and indolence, perhaps even the final triumph of the faith.

In a small house in the Jiyad quarter, not far from the Bab Jiyad itself, a group of eight men sat on couches around a low copper table of North African manufacture. They spoke in Saudi Arabic, but one of them had a noticeable Persian accent. A man of about forty, he had been sent from Iran to direct operations here in Mecca. His Arabic was correct, if somewhat classical and bookish, but his vowels were open and liquid, and he experienced difficulty with the harsher consonants and the guttural sounds. In spite of this, his words had a strong impact on those around him; whenever he spoke, the rest fell silent.

Beside him sat Muhammad ibn 'Abd Allah al-Qahtani and his brother-in-law, Juhaiman ibn Saif al-Otaybi. The Iranian had first met the former two years earlier when he had come with several companions to perform the pilgrimage. They had encountered him at Muzdalifa on their way back from Arafat at the end of the hajj rites.

He had attracted their attention by his solitary manner among the
masses crowded there and they had entered into conversation with
him. All spoke Arabic, having studied it for many years at theological
school. At first, he had resisted their offer of friendship. They were
Shi'is, and he was a pious Sunni, and he was not eager to be so close
to heretics. But in the end, he had felt himself drawn somehow to the
oldest of them, a white-bearded man whom the others treated with
unusual deference. The Iranians had spent more than a month with
him. When they left, they were convinced that he was the long-
awaited Mahdi whom they had sought in vain elsewhere. And he, for
his part, believed that they, though heretics, belonged to a people
more ready to believe in him than the great mass of Sunnis in his
native land.

The Iranian, who had been sent several months before from Tehran to coordinate the efforts of al-Qahtani and his followers with
those of the Tehran leadership, was giving the group leaders their
final instructions. When he finished speaking, Muhammad ibn 'Abd
Allah addressed them briefly.

"Above all else," he said, "we must respect the sacred enclosure.
We must act with speed, using surprise to avoid unnecessary violence.
It must all be accomplished in the shortest possible time. Once we
have taken the mosque and hold hostages, we will be safe from immediate assault. The government will have to consider how to overcome
us without damaging the sacred precincts or harming the hostages.
We will be armed—the consignment of submachine guns from Tehran will give us a considerable advantage in the course of a siege. We
only have to hold fast until the tenth of Muharram; by that time
other events will have occurred elsewhere which will ensure our final
victory. Before long, the world shall hear of our seizure of the mosque
and its true significance. Soon, a holy war will begin between Iran and
America, and in a short time, the Islamic world will enter the conflict.
The unbelievers will be defeated, in spite of their weapons and their
material wealth, and we shall leave Mecca as conquerors and rulers of
the world. I promise each of you the governorship of a seventh part of
the earth. May God be with you tomorrow."

Outside, the call to prayer died away. Lights flickered on in the
Grand Mosque. Under the cover of darkness, small groups of men
made their way to different houses scattered through the city. With
tens of thousands of others, they had entered Mecca two weeks be-

fore as pilgrims. A large number were Otaybis; others had come from
Iran with a large contingent of Shi'i pilgrims, some from Bahrain,
Kuwait, Yemen, Egypt, Morocco, and Saudi Arabia itself—from Riyadh, Jidda, Medina, and even Mecca. As the teeming thousands of
pilgrims left for Medina, having completed the rites of circumambulation, running, and stoning in Mecca and its vicinity, no one had
noticed those who stayed behind. Tonight their excitement was infec-
tious. Weapons had arrived as promised from Tehran, and the Mahdi
would be visiting each cell in the course of the evening. As the last
group passed by the Bab al-Safa, they could hear the sound of the
evening prayer intoned by those inside the Great Mosque. The Islamic day begins at sunset. This was the last evening prayer of the
fourteenth century.

WASHINGTON
19 November 1979

Nava'i left the State Department and returned to his hotel. He was
aware of the FBI tail that followed him all the way, but it was of no
concern to him at this stage in his plan. Back in the State Department, his departure sparked off a flurry of activity. Through lunch
and all of that afternoon, telephones rang, telexes clattered, and couri-
ers sped back and forth with packages between the department, CIA
headquarters at Langley, FBI headquarters on Pennsylvania Avenue,
and, on one occasion, the Iranian Embassy on Massachusetts Avenue.
In a dozen offices, computers searched memory banks, microfilm cameras clicked, filing cabinets opened and shut, photocopiers flashed and
ran off sheets of paper, and Telecopiers whirred. The Iran Crisis room
began to resemble even more than ever a wartime operations center.
On the wall, seven clocks with white faces and black hands and figures inexorably moved toward a new Islamic century.

After a general consultation, the Nava'i documents had been divided among six "Iran hands" whom Pike had assembled for the job
of verifying them. Each of them had set about checking and cross-
checking names, signatures, dates, and facts. Helpers were conjured
up from obscure corners, but access to the Nava'i papers themselves
was rigorously restricted to Pike and his team of experts. Gradually, a
picture began to emerge, and by nine o'clock that evening, it was

agreed that enough basic information had been obtained to make an initial judgment. Cyrus Vance was contacted and agreed to come directly to the department.

When he arrived, he went straight to Pike's office, where the section chief and his team were waiting for him. Pike gestured him into a comfortable chair and asked for coffee to be brought.

"Well, sir," Pike began, "we've done the best we can for the moment, but we're seriously handicapped for an investigation like this. With the Tehran embassy out of action, all our agents in Iran out of the country or lying low, and the British having to be extremely cautious there, we're strictly limited in what we can dig up. We did put what was made to seem a routine request to the Iranian Embassy here for biographical information on the members of the Revolutionary Council, but Ali Agha, their chargé d'affaires, turned it down. A hell of a lot just can't be corroborated or disproved, but we've had positive results on everything that can. If he is an impostor, he's done his homework. There is a Goruh-e Badr with which Molla Mohammad 'Ali Nayrizi has connections, but we aren't able to confirm his leadership. We are also unable to confirm the occupation of the Bahar-e Naw school, although there is a school of that name in that location. The names of two of the student leaders check out according to one of our sources, but we have nothing on their signatures. The CIA has supplied us with a copy of a Mujahidin identity card, and Nava'i's is almost identical; the differences could be explained by a different date of manufacture and issue. We have quite a bit on Mehdavi Khani, and it seems he does have connections with Nayrizi and with various Mujahidin groups. Marvdashti is quite well known, and several reports indicate that he has had high-level involvement with more than one Mujahidin group—particularly in the years before the Mujahidin-e Khalq went Marxist. There is nothing in U.S. files on Nava'i himself, but that means nothing either way. He speaks excellent English with an American accent, so he must have been here before; FBI and Immigration have no record of a previous stay, but he may well have returned to the States under a false name or may have been here the first time using an alias. Considering his guerrilla affiliations, that isn't surprising.

"Our general conclusion is that you should take him seriously for the moment and contact the President to arrange an early meeting. If he is genuine, then something positive may come of it; if not, we won't have lost anything except time. Meanwhile, we'll continue our investigation as far as we can. The cousins in London may come up with something—they're proving unusually cooperative on this. Scared shitless it might happen to them, I suppose. If necessary—but only if absolutely necessary—the CIA has agreed to activate one of their agents in Iran. But they'll want very high authorization for that, probably the President himself, if not God Almighty. Here's our interim report, which could be shown to the President. It includes our recommendations for a meeting."

Vance picked up the report and rose to leave. Then, turning to Pike again, he asked, "And if he is an impostor, what do you think his motive could be?" Pike pondered for a moment. "Whoever he is, whatever he wants, I think we should take the risk. It's our only chance."

TEHRAN
Tuesday, 20 November 1979

As Pike was speaking, a cold, gray dawn was creeping over the roofs of Tehran. The hands of the muezzin were blue with cold as he gripped the balcony of the minaret, his face raised upward in readiness to begin the call to the dawn prayer, the call that contains the words *"al-salat khayr min al-nawm"*—"prayer is better than sleep." Below him, · a small group of men walked out of a door into a gray, cement-walled courtyard. Three of them carried submachine guns, one wore the gray aba and black turban of a molla, another was dressed in paramilitary uniform; in front of this last man was a sixth man, naked but for a pair of briefs, his hands tied behind his back. The military-looking man escorted his prisoner to the far wall of the courtyard, instructed him to stand with his back against it, and walked back to the wall facing it where the three gunmen were already lined up. Sharp in the winter air, the voice of the muezzin suddenly burst into life above them. The molla paused, as if caught unawares. He whispered briefly to the Revolutionary Guard commander by his side and then waited for the chanting to end. At the far wall, the prisoner shivered uncontrollably in the bitter cold. Minutes passed; the light grew, but it brought no heat. At last, the muezzin came to the end of his call. A profound silence filled the courtyard as pale shadows began to stir around it. The gray-draped priest approached the scantily clad man who stood trembling against the wall.

"By decree of the local Revolutionary Court of the Yusefabad District, under the presidency of Ayatollah Sayyid 'Ali Marvdashti Mojtahed, you have been found guilty of the crimes of waging war against God, of heresy, and of theft from the revolutionary forces. In accordance with the law of the Qur'an and the ordinances of the sacred code of the Ja'fari school, you have been sentenced to death, the sentence to be carried out at once under the direction of myself, Molla Mohammad Shahidi, and the Mujahidin commander attached to this court, Sadeq Namazi. Before you die, it is my personal wish to urge you to repent of your heresy and with your last breath to return to the faith of Islam. Today the angels Munkar and Nakir will question you in the grave: if you cannot satisfy them of your true belief in God, the Prophet, and the holy Imams, your punishment will be the fires of hell for all eternity. Surely you will not persist in apostasy at this last hour."

The condemned man strove to control his shaking and struggled to steady his harsh, asthmatic breathing. When he spoke, his voice was thin and reedy but it gained strength rapidly as if drawing from some last reserve of energy that a man about to die could afford to squander.

"Listen . . . Listen to me before you kill me. You . . . you most of all, Molla. You have understood nothing . . . nothing. He is coming now, the Imam, the promised one, the one you have been expecting. It may be today . . . it may be tomorrow . . . but his coming is near. I have helped prepare for his coming . . . I will be raised up again to be one of his soldiers in the last battle. You martyr me and you condemn yourselves. Listen . . . he is ready . . . he is coming . . . it is time . . ."

He broke off, wracked with coughing, scarcely able to stand. The molla glanced at the commander, nodded. The order was given. Three submachine guns stuttered, fell silent. The prisoner fell, writhed in blood, jerked, and lay still. A flock of startled pigeons, wings flapping, cooing frenetically, lurched into the sky from their roost beneath the roof of the mosque. They circled, and below, the courtyard emptied as the last two members of the firing squad exited, carrying between them the already freezing body of their victim, leaving behind on the cement a pool of blood that was rapidly turning to ice.

MECCA
Tuesday, 20 November 1979

The earth rolled, bringing light from the east. Dawn moved across the waters of the Persian Gulf and thence over the desert heart of the Arabian Peninsula until it began to rise over the eastern hills of Mecca. This was the last circuit of the sun in the fourteenth Islamic century, but the cycle of worship continued as before. As the first faint traces of dawn appeared against the horizon, the call to morning prayer was first raised from a minaret in the eastern wall of the Great Mosque. It was about 4:00 A.M. As the light grew, it revealed the dark, muffled figures of men and women making their way to the various entrances of the mosque in time for the first communal prayer of the day. Thousands flocked to be present on such an auspicious occasion. Among them were over two hundred young men, dressed in black robes and wearing the red and white checked headdresses of the National Guard irregulars, Prince 'Abd Allah's "white army" of Bedouins, the feared rival of the regular Army. Between them, they carried fourteen cloth-draped coffins into the precincts of the mosque. This attracted little attention, for it is customary to bring coffins into mosques and, in Iran and North Africa to the shrines of saints, in order to attract blessings—*baraka*—for the dead. But these coffins were not receptacles for corpses on the first stage of their journey to the grave. They contained pistols, rifles, submachine guns, grenades, and even daggers, enough to arm the men who brought them in. Having set down their coffins, which they knew would remain undisturbed, the men in black robes joined the other worshipers at the various fountains scattered around the mosque enclosure to perform the necessary ablutions prior to the prayer. But as the crowd thickened and people began to form rows facing the Ka'ba at the center of the vast arena, small groups of the rebel force stationed themselves at the gates of the mosque and behind the lines of the faithful, at whose head stood Shaykh Subayyal, the Imam or prayer leader of the Haram, the sacred enclosure.

The fading of the last notes of the call to prayer was the agreed

signal for action. In a coordinated movement, men rushed to close
and bar the huge gates that led into the Haram on all sides. Others
flung the heavy brocade covers from the coffins and began passing out
the weapons and ammunition to their fellow conspirators. The group
leaders made their way forward through the serried ranks of worshipers to stand, backs to the black-draped cube of the Ka'ba, awaiting the
appearance of Muhammad ibn 'Abd Allah. A shocked murmur began
to move through the crowd as people at the front and back could see
what was happening. In the women's section, screams were heard as
eyes fell on the stony-faced men in black with machine guns held at
waist level, pointed at the crowd. At the rear, a few people began to
run for the gates, but were turned back by barked commands and
leveled guns. One man was shot in the head trying to push his way
past—the first casualty. Another group of rebels, carrying high-pow-
ered rifles with telescopic sights, broke up and headed singly for the
entrances to the stairs leading up to the main minarets at the corners
of the enclosure.

A closely knit body of a dozen rebels made its way to the center of
the compound, coming to a halt by the small door of the Ka'ba.
Muhammad ibn 'Abd Allah and his Iranian deputy detached themselves from their bodyguard. Without preamble, the deputy began to
address the crowd. He called on the Imam of the Haram publicly to
recognize Muhammad ibn 'Abd Allah as the Mahdi, sent by God to
end injustice and bring at last the final triumph of the true faith. The
new century would soon be with them. Here, in Mecca, the birthplace of Islam, a new age was about to dawn. The promised Mahdi,
the guide to all truth, was here with them in the person of Muhammad ibn 'Abd Allah and would lead them this morning in the ritual
prayer, as prophesied centuries before.

Atop the minaret at the northwest corner, a black-robed sniper
could see soldiers moving from the army barracks in the north of the
city down toward the mosque. He made ready to fire on them when
they came within range. Another siege had begun.

Below, the bewildered multitude began to pray, many nervous and
out of line. At the end of the prayer, the self-proclaimed Mahdi stood
by the Black Stone set in silver mounting in the corner of the Ka'ba
and called on those present to recognize his authority. After he had
spoken for twenty minutes about his claims and the new age he had
come to usher in, he paused dramatically and placed his hand on the

hajar, the Black Stone, a meteorite that had crashed to earth nearby untold ages ago.

In a loud voice, he shouted: "As a sign and a token of my power and the truth of my claims, tomorrow, on the first day of this new century, the king and ruler of the Christian unbelievers, the President of the United States, shall be struck down in his palace by the hands of an angel sent by me to slay him. When you hear that he is dead, then you will know that my word is the truth and my cause the cause of God."

He stepped down and the crowd stood silent, uncertain what to do. From the northwest minaret, a rifle shot rang out over the valley, raising echoes from the hills.

24

Wednesday, 21 November 1979

In Qum, Imam Khomeini, the supreme religious and legal authority of the Shi'i community of Iran, sat in the small reception room of the house where he lived. A microphone stood before him, with a tangle of wires running outside to a mobile van belonging to the National Iranian Radio and Television Service. His speech was being relayed to the main transmitter of Radio Iran at Vanak in the north of Tehran, on the grounds of the former Shahanshahi Park. He had responded quickly to the news of the seizure of the Great Mosque and was now telling the world that the act was an American-Zionist plot. As transcripts of his broadcast were translated and disseminated, thousands throughout the Islamic world—and not only Shi'is—believed him. The dawn of the new century was marked throughout Pakistan by attacks on U.S. buildings and personnel. In Islamabad, the U.S. Embassy was burned to the ground and a Marine Guard shot as an angry mob surged about it. In Lahore and Rawalpindi, the U.S. information centers were set ablaze, and in Lahore the mob also turned its attention to the consulate general and put it to the torch. In Karachi there was widespread rioting, and a fanatical crowd was kept back with difficulty from the U.S. Consulate. The following day in Qum, Khomeini would declare that there was now a de facto "war between Islam and the unbelievers."

Early on Wednesday morning, news of the Pakistan incidents began to flow into Washington, and within minutes, the President had been notified at his retreat at Camp David. Cutting short his Thanksgiving holiday, he boarded a helicopter for the short journey back to the capital and was soon in the Oval Office conferring with Brzezinski and the members of the National Security Council. The situation was critical. Fears of further seizures of hostages haunted them all. The conference broke up after two hours with no picture emerging of what steps to take to prevent further outbreaks of trouble. As he was preparing to leave the Presidential Office, the Secretary of State turned and reminded Carter of the appointment which had been made for that afternoon with Nava'i, to discuss possible terms for the release of the hostages.

"Sir, in view of these developments, do you want to go ahead with the meeting with the Mujahidin representative this afternoon?"

"I don't see why not. If we do have further trouble and maybe even more hostages to deal with, the sooner we can get some initiative underway in Iran the better. Whatever the Iranian students do will be followed elsewhere, so their release ought to be our first priority even if there are other outbreaks. Sure, I'll see Nava'i as planned."

Nava'i had spent the whole of Tuesday in prayer and meditation in his hotel or at the Islamic Center mosque, where he had been tailed by FBI agents. During his absence at the mosque, his hotel room had been carefully searched, as he had expected it would be, but nothing of interest had been found. He had woken before dawn on Wednesday and had joined large numbers of his fellow Muslims at the mosque for dawn prayers. News of the capture of the Great Mosque had reached the world the day before, and after the prayers, all conversation was directed to that one topic. But Nava'i chose not to discuss it and left for his hotel, where he spent the rest of the morning reading the Qur'an. He had telephoned Pike at the State Department on Tuesday afternoon and had been told that a meeting with the President had been arranged at Camp David for Wednesday afternoon at 3:00 P.M. He was to go to the State Department at 1:00 P.M. and from there transport would be arranged to Maryland.

When he arrived at one, however, he was notified that the President had returned to Washington and that the interview would now take place in the White House at the time already arranged. Unperturbed, Nava'i was shown to a sitting room on the first floor to wait until it was time to leave. At two-thirty, he was brought by Pike to the Secretary of State's office and introduced to Mr. Vance. After a brief discussion, the three men, escorted by a member of the Secret Service, headed down the front steps of the building and into a waiting Cadillac limousine. It was two-forty.

At two forty-five, the car drew up alongside the west wing of the White House and parked discreetly away from the sight of tourists and journalists. Nava'i and his three companions wasted no time in entering the building by a side door, from whence they were escorted by a waiting aide along passages and through doors until they reached the corridor leading to the President's office. Before proceeding further, it was necessary to pass through a security check. This was not normal procedure with diplomats and others of similar rank visiting the President, but the irregular nature of Nava'i's credentials and the fact that he had been—indeed still was—a member of a terrorist organization had given several individuals in the higher echelons of the Secret Service the jitters, and they had insisted on a thorough check before the Iranian envoy could be admitted to see the President. In order to avoid embarrassment, however, it was explained to Nava'i that the check was standard procedure; Vance and Pike also submitted to a search to further mitigate any offense that might be caused. But Nava'i was completely clean: he carried nothing but a small amount of money, a wallet, a pocket prayer book, and his customary rosary. Without further ado, he was admitted with Vance and Pike to the Oval Office while their Secret Service escort remained outside.

They were met by a smiling President showing few outward signs of the strain he had been under for the past three weeks. The famous smile and southern drawl acted as always to put others at their ease as Carter introduced Nava'i to Mr. Brzezinski and to Howard Straker, described as a special presidential adviser on Foreign Affairs. Straker was in fact there to evaluate Nava'i's proposals in the light of his knowledge of the intelligence situation in Iran, as CIA opinion would have to be consulted before any action could be taken.

The meeting was to be conducted in comfortable chairs grouped about the large fireplace at the far end of the room. The principal participants took their places, Nava'i to the left of the President, Vance on his right. A male stenographer was seated discreetly at a table nearby. As soon as everyone had settled, Nava'i took a paper from his inside pocket on which the proposals he was to present on behalf of Ayatollah Mehdavi Khani were written down. These he read in full to the President before returning to the first for discussion. In the grate the firelight flickered, reflecting in small red points off the clicking beads that circled endlessly through Nava'i's restless fingers.

Even as he talked, Nava'i's mind was elsewhere. His thoughts turned toward death, and the many forms it could take. In his dreams he had seen the angel of death many times, his black wings unmoving, his face draped by a long crimson veil, an apparition of silent, brooding menace. During the last few nights, the angel had come to him time and again as he slept, but with his heavy wings now moving slowly up and down, beating the air with a low hissing sound, the bloody veil slipping inch by inch down his face, revealing the terrible eyes, and almost uncovering the mouth beneath. The Iranian shuddered involuntarily as the grim image rose again before his mind's eye. The President, noticing his apparent distress, leaned toward him solicitously.

"Is something wrong, Mr. Nava'i?"

Nava'i shook his head.

"No, I'm perfectly all right, thank you. Just a slight chill."

He continued talking, controlling himself once more. There was nothing to fear. The angel was waiting for the man in the chair opposite him. Not even a President could find safety once the moment of his death was upon him. No one could resist the onrush of the angel as he took the veil from his lips and swooped at last.

Peter Randall put down his coffee cup, pushed back his chair, and left the table. He had taken a late lunch and felt disinclined to return to work at Langley that afternoon. A telephone call would take care of the problem, and he could spend the rest of the day with his feet up. Since his convalescence during the summer, he had been working as an analyst on Middle East intelligence reports at CIA headquarters in Langley, but his heart was not in the job and he knew his resignation was only a few months away, perhaps even weeks. He still kept himself informed about events in Iran, but it all seemed like a dream world to him now, far away and blurred by more than just distance. He had invested so much of himself—hopes, fears, and memories—in the country and the people, but it seemed to him that he had lost all that again when he had left. It was like Vietnam all over again: nightmares in place of dreams, bitterness instead of the inner satisfaction he had once looked for. He felt as if he had been cleaned out and casually discarded.

The grim purpose that had been set ablaze in him in the hospital in Tehran had been horribly intensified as he had sat behind the curtains in the half-deserted *zurkhane*, watching the black-robed molla with his acolytes. For he had known then that he was looking at last upon the faces of the men he sought, that the source and meaning of

Fujiko's death lay in that domed and partly lit room. Randall knew that if Tabataba'i and his men had not come and brought the carnage that had followed, he himself might, in the end, have wrought the same terrible revenge. And none, least of all the one-handed man, would have escaped.

But his return to Washington after those events had been too soon, there had been no time for him to come to terms with what had taken place, to confront and master the violence—both what he had witnessed and what he had sensed within himself. Within a week of his return, a reaction had set in. He had become lethargic, passive, lacking in will or purpose and had allowed events and systems to shape and order his life. It was as if he was sinking ever deeper into a quicksand from which there could be no release. He had not lost his purpose wholly; it lay there unchanged within him still, but it was shrouded and weak and growing dim, and he did not know how it might be uncovered and set alight again.

He wandered over to his armchair, chased his cat from her favorite seat, and settled himself. He would make the phone call in a few minutes. Listlessly, he felt beside his chair for that morning's Washington *Post*. The headlines reminded him so much of work and of Iran that he scarcely read the main news anymore. He turned with little interest to the local pages, scanning them for something undemanding. On page 4, he came across an article about a murder in Washington. It read:

WOMAN FOUND MURDERED IN APARTMENT

The body of Fatimeh Natsir, an Indonesian resident in Washington, was found last night at her address on Wyoming Avenue. Mrs. Natsir, aged twenty-three, had been strangled by an assailant as yet unknown. Her naked body was found by a visitor who held a key to the apartment. A police report issued this morning stated that Mrs. Natsir, who was divorced and lived alone, had been sexually assaulted before being choked to death. Her body seemed to have been in the apartment for at least two days before its discovery. A full autopsy report is expected tomorrow. There were no obvious signs of a struggle in the bedroom, where the body was located, which suggests that the victim knew her killer and invited him into the apartment. The police report mentioned, however, that curious scribbles had been found on the wall above the bed, written in lipstick and resembling examples of Arabic graffiti found on buildings in the city.

Randall's heart stopped, then started again. Blood rushed to his head, and his hand began shaking. There were two photographs. The first showed the victim as she had been in life, smiling, at ease, beautiful, out of reach of the death that had overtaken her on Sunday night. The second showed the bed and the scribbling on the wall. It was blurred, but he did not need a magnifying glass to enable him to read the word written there. It was indelibly inscribed in his own mind: *fahisha*. The fear and the blood had followed him, even here. Panic gripped him for a moment, a dizzying sensation of utter vulnerability, to be replaced almost at once by something else, something he could scarcely put a name to. It was a feeling of exultation mixed with dread, the feeling the hunter experiences when he comes at last upon his prey. He had felt it only once before, as he had sat in the darkness of the *zurkhane* watching the white-clad men in the room beyond, waiting for the moment when he would open the door and walk out to meet them.

He got up and went to the telephone. Within seconds, he was through to Howard Straker's office at CIA, Langley.

"This is Randall. I want to speak to Howard, please."

"I'm sorry," the voice of Straker's secretary came back to him, "but Mr. Straker left over an hour ago for the White House. He had a meeting with the President at three o'clock. Can I take a message for you?"

"Can't you contact him at the White House?"

"I'm sorry, Mr. Randall, but he left strict instructions that he wasn't to be disturbed. If you'd like to leave a message."

"It's too important for a message, for Christ's sake. What's his meeting about? How long will it go on?"

"I'm afraid I'm unable to tell you, sir."

"Dammit, I rate a high enough security clearance!"

"You haven't been cleared for this, sir. I don't know anything about it myself. It's been listed on a 'need to know' basis. You'll have to speak with Mr. Straker himself. I can't help you."

Randall slammed the phone down in fury. He paused, then picked up the receiver and dialed again. This time he was put through to Brandon Stewart.

"Stewart speaking."

"Hello, Stewart, this is Peter Randall."

"What can I do for you, Peter?"

"I want to know what's going on this afternoon. Howard Straker's gone for a meeting at the White House. I need to contact him, but his smart-ass secretary tells me I have to leave a message."

"Hey, calm down, Randall. Is it anything I can help with?"

"Do you know anything about this meeting with the President?"

"Yes, but I'm not at liberty . . ."

"Look, I don't want to know what's being discussed, but can you at least tell me if it involves Iran?"

Stewart hesitated, then replied.

"Yes, I suppose I can say that much. Yes, it does."

"Stewart, are there any Iranians at that meeting?"

"I'm sorry, Peter, I can't . . ."

"Dammit, Stewart, this is important. Are there any goddamn Iranians at the White House?"

"Maybe if you'd explain to me why you want to know. You'll have to tell me what . . ."

"Listen, they're here in Washington."

"Who are in Washington? Who are you talking about?"

"The Qolhak Group. I don't know how many, I don't know why. All I know is they're here."

There was silence at the other end. When Stewart spoke at last, his voice had changed perceptibly: Randall could detect the fear. So there was an Iranian at the meeting.

"I'll do what I can to get in touch with the President. I hope to God you're wrong, Peter. I hope to God you're wrong." The line went dead. Randall replaced the receiver, grabbed his coat, and headed for the door. It was three forty-five. Five minutes would take him to the White House if he stepped on the gas.

At four o'clock it was agreed to adjourn the Nava'i meeting until the President and the Security Council could meet to discuss the proposals at length. The Iranian terms were the most reasonable so far put forward and included a readiness to admit the illegality of the seizure of the hostages. Carter was optimistic and relieved that a possible solution to the stalemate had offered itself.

An internal telephone rang and was answered by the stenographer, who listened intently but said nothing. As he put down the receiver, the President rose to his feet and, as the young Iranian followed suit, smiled and reached out his hand. In responding, Nava'i fumbled with the string of prayer beads he had been holding in his right hand and, in doing so, broke the cord at the end where the rosary came together in a long "handle" or toggle, into which a fine silk tassle had been inserted. The beads sprang free and tumbled, all ninety-nine of them, onto the carpet at the feet of Nava'i and the President, dancing and rolling in all directions across the room. Instinctively, all those present bent quickly to the floor, hurrying to capture the rolling beads before they were lost under chairs and tables. The President too stooped to pick up a handful of beads. As he did so, no one noticed the imperceptible movement made by Nava'i as he disengaged the upper half of the handle of the *tasbih* and pushed it along what was now revealed to be a two-foot length of piano wire until it caught on a tiny metal knob firmly soldered onto the other end. The beads, with holes of greater diameter, had passed easily over the end of the wire when Nava'i had released it, but the top part of the handle, bored to fit the wire snugly, caught tightly on the small knob. As the President straightened, his hand outstretched toward Nava'i, the assassin whipped the now lethal length of wire, held by the small handles at either end, over Carter's neck, sidestepped so he stood behind his victim, and pulled the wire tight, fast enough to slice through the President's neck in a single motion.

Everything happened at double speed. Nava'i had been trained to kill and was an expert in the use of the wire loop. He had killed several times with it before, silently and instantly. By all the odds, Carter should have been a dead man, his neck severed through windpipe and jugular vein. But even as he pulled on the wire, Nava'i was hit full in the upper arm, then in the side by two rapidly fired bullets coming from his right. Caught at close range, he was thrown sideways onto the floor, and in seconds Straker and Pike were standing over him, the former having retrieved the wire loop while the others hurried to assist the President. Within seconds, aides rushed through the door, followed by guards carrying magnums. Nava'i lay bleeding on the floor while, two yards to his right, the stenographer stood covering him with a .38 pistol. He was, in fact, a Secret Service agent placed in his position about one year previously without the President's knowledge as insurance against just such an eventuality as this.

Outside, it was dusk, and in Washington the first day of the fifteenth Islamic century was ending. A single star appeared faintly in the sky over the Capitol. Over Mecca, the sky was long awash with stars.

25

WASHINGTON
Wednesday, 21–Sunday, 25 November 1979

That evening in Washington, a subdued but not visibly shaken President Carter made his first public reference to the possibility of the use of force by the United States in the hostage situation. Unless the hostages were released unconditionally, he said, he might order military action against Iran.

Within an hour of the announcement of this warning, the Pentagon stated that a naval task force was now on its way from the Philippines to rendezvous with other U.S. warships patrolling in the Indian Ocean. In March, a task force had already left the Philippines for the area, following an outbreak of fighting between North and South Yemen and, in mid-October, a naval battle group led by the 51,000-ton USS *Midway* had entered the region. Three B-52 sea surveillance and three airborne warning and control (AWACS) missions had already been flown. The 60,000-ton aircraft carrier *Kitty Hawk*, accompanied by an escort of destroyers, left Subic Bay that night, heading west. In Norfolk, Virginia, the nuclear-powered carrier *Nimitz* weighed anchor for the Gulf of Oman; with over 90,000 tons displacement at full load and a length of 1,092 feet, it was the largest warship in the world. It carried eight squadrons of attack, fighter, and antisubmarine aircraft, together with a number of E-2C early warning planes—over ninety planes in all. Like the *Kitty Hawk*, it operated three Sea Sparrow Basic Point Defense Missile systems. On board was a sea crew of 3,300 and an air group of 3,000 men. Khomeini's "de facto war" looked like becoming more than a war of words.

Nava'i, unconscious and still bleeding profusely, was rushed to the D.C. General Hospital beside the north-bank sector of Anacostia Park, where he underwent immediate surgery. The first bullet had torn through his upper arm from a forward angle, glancing off the

lower humerus bone and through the brachial artery, first passing into
the chest from the side above the eighth rib, then behind the right
kidney, and exiting through the lower back. The second bullet had
taken him lower down, in the waist, striking the second of the floating
ribs and being deflected through the back, again without passing
through a vital organ. His situation was serious but not critical, and
after the operation, he was moved to a room on the third floor. News
of the assassination attempt was kept from the media, and Nava'i's
wounds were explained in the hospital as having been sustained at
National Airport while trying to escape after attempting to carry a
gun on board a plane to Los Angeles. Hospital staff were asked to
cooperate in keeping quiet a story which, if it leaked out, might cause
violence toward perfectly innocent Iranians throughout the United
States. A round-the-clock guard was posted on Nava'i's door, and at
FBI headquarters and the State Department, preparations were made
to interrogate the prisoner once he recovered consciousness. Agents
were sent to his hotel room, where they found none of the equipment
he had used in preparing his documents but discovered a number of
papers, overlooked as unimportant in the earlier search, all of them in
Persian. These were brought to the Iranian Office at the State Department for Pike and his team to examine.

The would-be assassin was not long in recovering consciousness,
but the doctors would not allow him to be interviewed until late on
Thursday. When it began at last, the interrogation was carried out by
Straker, with the assistance of Peter Randall, in the presence of representatives of the FBI, the Special Service, and the State Department.
Straker had been shaken more than anyone, not only by the events in
the Oval Office, but by Randall's information that Nava'i must be a
member of the very group they had been chasing in Tehran. The
Iranian's fingerprints had been checked positively with some found on
items in Fatimeh Natsir's apartment, including the lipstick used to
write on the wall over her bed. Neither Straker nor Randall could
begin to guess the exact motives behind the assassination attempt,
but they and others in Washington were in no doubt that had Nava'i
succeeded, an announcement would have gone out from a group
somewhere in Tehran, claiming responsibility. Whether that group
was made up of guerrillas or members of the provisional government,
the result would have been the same: war between the two countries.
Nothing could have prevented it.

Straker spoke for a while with Nava'i, expecting resistance from the Iranian, but there was none. He wished to speak, to make things clear. Straker switched on a tape recorder and held the microphone close to the man's mouth.

Nava'i talked freely, although he was still in pain.

"You know now that much of what I told you was false. Several of the documents I gave you were forged. But a great deal was just as I explained it. I do belong to the Goruh-e Badr and I have been a member of the Mujahidin for many years. The connection between Ayatollah Mehdavi Khani and the Mujahidin is much as I stated, and he was responsible for the telegram which alerted you to my mission. It is also true that Ayatollah Marvdashti is connected with our group. But I originally came here as part of a special Mujahidin task force on an entirely different mission. You know that, on 13 May this year, Ayatollah Khalkhali issued a *fatva*, a pronouncement of the death sentence on the Shah and members of his family. About a month later, he offered a reward of $140 million to whoever carried out this sentence and stressed that anyone who died while trying to carry it out would be regarded as a martyr to the cause of Islam. Then, on the first of August, he formed what he called his Red Army, the Jashn-e Sorkh, and gave its members responsibility for carrying out the execution of the Shah and other enemies of the revolution. I was one of the first recruits to the Red Army.

"Several members of the Goruh-e Badr joined Khalkhali's army together and we originally planned to travel as a group to Mexico, where the Shah and his family were staying. But a month ago we heard that he had been transferred to New York Hospital–Cornell Medical Center and was being guarded there on the seventeenth floor. Our first reaction was to continue with our original plan of going to Mexico where we could execute the Shah's wife and the so-called Crown Prince Reza, but then we thought that if we could kill the Shah himself in the heart of New York it would be a very great triumph for our cause. So we traveled separately to New York at the beginning of this month, met together, and began to make plans. We obtained guns and explosives through contacts in New York, and every day some of us would join the Iranian students protesting outside the hospital. In that way, we gained a general picture of the layout of the building and realized that our attack would have to be by night. We had only been in New York a few days when the American hostages were taken in Tehran, and we immediately realized that the incident would cause a dramatic change in relations between our countries. We discussed how we could show our solidarity with the students, and it was suggested that if we could execute both the Shah and the President of the United States, it would be a symbolic act of unusual significance.

"Half of our group elected to stay in New York while the rest of us came here to Washington to devise a plan. We had agreed on the first of Muharram, the beginning of the new century, as the most appropriate day for the executions, and made our plans accordingly. In the end, we agreed on a scheme that involved only myself. If it went wrong—as it has done—then I alone would be killed or arrested, while the others could return to New York, regroup, and continue the struggle. You know the rest."

To Randall, Nava'i's story sounded plausible, but it left obscure many points relating to the objectives and activities of the group. When the Iranian had finished talking, he was allowed to question him.

"Nava'i," he began, "I don't know whether any of what you've been telling us is true, but it certainly isn't the whole story. You're going to tell me what I want to know, even if I have to beat it out of you slowly. I don't think any of these gentlemen here will stop me. First, I want to know who the Seven were and what their purpose was."

Nava'i looked in surprise at the American, then smiled. "They were chosen to carry out missions similar to mine."

"Were you one of them? Were you the seventh?"

The Iranian nodded.

"Were you the first to be sent?"

He nodded again.

"Who were the others supposed to kill?"

Nava'i remained silent, staring at his questioner.

"Was one of them Sadat?" Randall pursued.

The Iranian shook his head. "I don't know."

"Have they been replaced, the way the original Seven from Qolhak were replaced? Or are you the last?"

"There have been many Sevens. There is never a last."

"You're lying, goddam you."

Howard Straker moved forward, catching Randall's arm, steadying him.

"Peter, don't let him rile you. Keep it cool."

"It's OK." Randall suppressed his anger, returning to the questioning. He thought back to his interrogation of Mo'ini. "What is the Sword?"

"Al-Sayf."

"I don't want an Arabic translation, I want to know what it is."

The Iranian smiled at him, a knowing smile. "Not what. Who."

"Who, then?"

"He has been unsheathed."

"Where?"

"In the Sanctuary."

Randall frowned, then his eyes hardened as he realized what Nava'i meant.

"In Mecca? The Mahdi? He belongs to your group?"

The Iranian said nothing, merely smiled.

"What are the Lances? Or who are they?"

The silent figure on the bed continued to smile. Randall went on, "Are they his soldiers, the ones who took over the mosque?"

Nava'i's eyes were unmoving, his lips firm.

Straker returned to Randall's side and whispered to him, "Let's leave it at that for today, Peter. He's withdrawing, mentally and physically. You won't get much more out of him. Let's go over what we've got."

Three days later, Straker called a briefing with Randall, Arthur Pike, and representatives of the FBI and the National Security Agency. Overall authority for the investigation rested with Pike and the Iranian desk, but Straker had been delegated to deal with its day-to-day running. Drawing on the information extracted from Nava'i during interrogation, Straker had tried, so far without success, to build a profile of the group to which he belonged. Details had been passed to intelligence services throughout the world, but the overriding need to keep many aspects of the affair under wraps had resulted in minimal feedback. More significant results were obtained from investigations centered on a single item found by FBI agents in Nava'i's hotel room.

This was a photograph of a young man wearing American academic robes and inscribed, "For my dear friend Husayn, from Faridun, on the occasion of my graduation, July 1975." On the back, in a different hand, was a verse from the fourth chapter of the Qur'an: "God does not love anyone who is a traitor, a sinner," followed by the words "Nothing must be forgotten." Copies of the photograph were made and distributed widely, and it was not long before the subject was identified. Someone recognized the graduation robes as the doctoral gown for the Massachusetts Institute of Technology. The Cambridge-based institute was able to identify the man in the photograph as Faridun Amirzadeh, an Iranian born in Tehran in 1948 who had studied at Pahlavi University in Shiraz before going to MIT to do graduate research in nuclear physics. He had returned to Iran with a Ph.D. in 1975, but early in 1977, he was in Cambridge again, asking a number of his old professors about how to report an important matter of international concern to the U.S. Government. Before his queries could be followed up, however, he was called back to Iran—it was believed his wife had contacted him to say that their daughter was seriously ill—and had not been heard of since.

Two days after the arrival of this information from MIT, a report was received from the West German Office for the Protection of the Constitution, the Bundesamt für Verfassungsschutz (BfV)—in effect, the internal security police. Their report had been sent in response to what was seen as a routine request for information sent out to all major Western intelligence and security agencies. West Germany, with its high proportion of Iranians and the threat posed by Iranian Marxists living in East Germany, kept a close watch on people of that nationality living or traveling within its frontiers. The Confederation of Iranian Students in West Germany had been one of the most militant anti-Shah groups in Europe before the revolution. Conversely, action taken by the West German police (acting under orders from the pro-Shah government in Bonn) against Iranian protestors had been noted for its particular brutality.

The BfV computer in Cologne had been fed information from the INPOL computer of the Federal Criminal Investigation Office in Wiesbaden, identifying Faridun Amirzadeh as a terrorist suspect. The first link in a long chain had been made.

Howard Straker surveyed the faces of the men in front of him. Each man here was worried, each had superiors waiting impatiently for hard information, for results that would allow them to rationalize what had happened and to apportion blame—preferably outside their own departments. Straker himself was under precisely the same pressures, but he at least had previous experience in Iran and had learned at first hand just how elusive Nava'i's group could be. He dared not hope for fast results—uncertain anyway that they would be useful ones—but at least he had something of value to report at last. He opened the slim file containing what little material he had been able to assemble so far. He cleared his throat and an expectant silence filled the room.

"Gentlemen," he began, "you've all seen copies of the photograph found in Nava'i's room, and you've heard the earlier MIT report. What we've just heard from the Germans is much more interesting, but also a little disturbing. Amirzadeh, the man in the photograph, was registered by their Criminal Investigation Office under their Befa-K terrorist category following a visit he made in 1977 to Hamburg where he had a meeting with Professor Ernst Kleiber, head of a private West German rocket company called DRASAG. The initials stand for Deutsche Rakete und Satellit Gesellschaft—German Rocket and Satellite Company. DRASAG was founded in West Germany in the late sixties by Kleiber and a number of other scientists to manufacture and market a modified version of the V-2 rocket that von Braun developed at Peenemünde during the war. DRASAG's rocket is cheaper. It's made from mass-produced components and is built around two tanks with small twin-engined modules which can be clustered in stages. DRASAG scientists overcame a basic cost factor in ordinary rockets by replacing the use of solid fuel combined with liquid hydrogen and oxygen with a new technology based on the use of nitric acid and paraffin.

"A couple of years before Amirzadeh made contact with Kleiber—it may not have been his first contact, of course—the company had reached an agreement with President Amin of Uganda which gave them absolute authority over a tract of land about thirty thousand square miles in size on the central plateau around Lake Kyoga. The region was supposed to be a testing ground for DRASAG's rockets, but the company managed to obtain some pretty staggering rights. They could construct airfields, erect launching ramps and power stations, put up observation posts, telecommunications and radar installations, build roads, railways, hospitals—in other words, just about run the damn place. In return for all of which, of course, our friend Amin was to be given the first rockets to be made operational.

"The company claimed its rockets were being developed for eventual sale to Third World countries which wanted to place communications and surveillance satellites in orbit, and maybe they were. But the fact is that these rockets can be adapted to launch missiles. The largest vehicle planned by them was to have a cluster of six hundred engines, which could take a ten-ton payload into orbit. As far as we know, some of their rockets have an effective range of around two hundred miles. And none of you needs to be told that anything capable of launching a satellite can be fitted with a warhead without any sweat. And anything that can be fitted with a warhead can be fitted with a nuclear warhead. Recent reports suggest that, even before Big Daddy's overthrow, the company was negotiating a move up north to Libya, where Qaddafi plans to give them a home.

"For obvious reasons, the West Germans have been keeping an eye on DRASAG's activities. The BfV had been carefully watching the movements of company officials and their contacts inside Federal frontiers, so Amirzadeh's visit to Kleiber in '77 was recorded as a matter of routine. It seems that, after he left Hamburg, Amirzadeh was observed by the Federal Border Control Force at Frankfurt Airport, boarding a Lufthansa Airbus en route to Entebbe. The FBCF makes copies of suspect passport photographs, and they sent a shot of Amirzadeh for storage by the BfV. The BfV says it checks with the shot we sent them: it's the same man. The Germans have been very helpful. They've sent us a copy of their file on Amirzadeh, and I've made extra copies for each of you.

"I've also got copies of four very brief files kept by the Germans on four other Iranians connected with DRASAG. These don't tell us much, and they don't give any clues as to whether there are links between these four and Amirzadeh or Nava'i. And, incidentally, the Germans don't think they've got anything on Nava'i himself—at least, not under that name. It's my recommendation we ask the Intelligence Board to request further help from the Federal Intelligence Service, the Bundesnachrichtendienst, asking them to cooperate on this with us and the BfV. Do I have your approval?"

Hands were raised by all present and Straker recorded his recommendation. He nodded and sat down. At the back of the room, Peter Randall raised his hand again.

"Yes, Peter?" Straker prompted.

"Howard, these missiles. It sounds like a wild idea, but do you

think that's what could be meant by 'the Lances'? Mo'ini said, 'The
Lances are ready.' "

Straker half rose from his chair, his hands on its arms, his eyes fixed
on Randall. If Peter was correct, the terror was only about to start.

26

Straker, Randall, and their colleagues interrogated Nava'i several times but, although he spoke freely and openly about many things, he would give no further details on the membership and plans of the group which he claimed was in the United States. Apparent confirmation of his story came with news that the state police in Minnesota had arrested four Iranians on a charge of plotting to kidnap the governor. Three days later, eight young Iranians were arrested by the FBI as they were about to board a flight to New York at Baltimore/Washington International Airport. They were carrying rifles, telescopic sights, and ammunition. But confidence began to falter again when the stories of the twelve new terrorists were found to differ widely from that of Nava'i. A team was still going through his original documents, as well as the few papers found in his apartment, but little progress had been made.

Every evening, Randall would return home from his office or from the hospital more worried than he had been before. Something was nagging him that he could not name or isolate. Recent events in Iran had frightened him, even though he understood more than most people the causes and significance of those events. The trouble was not only from Iran, but wider, spreading through the entire Islamic world. Something ugly and unprecedented was threatening civilization, democracy, and the whole liberal tradition of the West. The growing fury and arrogance of militant Islam caused him to lose sleep at nights, much as the rising terror of Nazism had troubled his father's dreams in the mid-thirties.

Straker and the others directing the interrogations wanted to administer truth drugs or use a lie detector on Nava'i, but the physician in charge would not permit their use while he remained a patient in the hospital. After a provisional release date of 3 December had been fixed, arrangements were made to transfer Nava'i to a top-security unit at the Marine Corps headquarters in Arlington, where more persuasive techniques could be used. Straker made it clear to the Iranian that they would resort to harsher measures if he continued to evade their questioning. Nava'i simply smiled at him and said nothing.

HAMBURG
Monday, 26 November 1979

Kurt Müller, director of the Hamburg division of the Bundesamt für Verfassungsschutz, opened the 132nd file of the day. Since Washington had put through their request for assistance on the Amirzadeh/ DRASAG case, he had put in hours of extra time to follow up every available lead. For the present, he concentrated all his energy on the new case. Strictly speaking, the matter was nothing to do with the West Germans. Amirzadeh and his friends had committed no known crimes in the Federal Republic, and DRASAG was a legitimate—if suspect—company. But you do not have to commit or even plan a crime to find your name and details in the Weisbaden computer, or to become the object of intense interest on the part of the BfV. For all that they had tried to play things down, it was obvious that the Americans were on edge about something, something big. And Müller had been deeply interested in DRASAG and its activities for several years.

He had known that one or two of the scientists involved with the development of the DRASAG rockets were former Nazis, as were several of the company's financial backers: nothing illegal, and certainly not unusual in West Germany, but not, at the same time, reassuring. Over the years, individuals of several nationalities had visited the company's offices. They generally came from developing countries with a large military budget—Libya, Pakistan, Uganda, Kenya, Brazil, and Indonesia. In all but a few cases, they had come as official representatives, eager to discuss the potential of the rockets for what were euphemistically called "satellite surveillance programs" being set up by their home governments. But the five Iranians who had visited DRASAG between 1976 and 1979 had puzzled the security police by their apparent lack of any connection with the Shah's régime. The usually cooperative Iranian Embassy in Bonn had claimed to have no knowledge of their presence in the country and to know nothing of them or their activities.

Since starting work on the files, Müller had discovered very little. Two of the Iranians had visited DRASAG in May 1976 and July 1977 respectively. Following their visits, they had been watched by the BfV and observed making contact with leading members of the Deutsche Aktiongruppe, the largest of the twenty-three or so West German neo-Nazi organizations. Following the meetings with the fascist group, each had gone on to Switzerland, where he had stayed two nights in Zurich before flying back to Tehran via Frankfurt. Amirzadeh—who had visited Hamburg in August 1977—and another of the five had both followed their visits to DRASAG with trips to Uganda, presumably to inspect the company's site there. The fifth man had gone on to New York, thereby providing the first direct link with the United States.

What had been the business of the two Iranians who had gone to Zurich? Alerted by Bonn of the Swiss connection, Washington had asked the proper authorities in Bern to carry out urgent investigations in the hope of bringing something to light. Under Swiss law, such investigations would be far from easy, but the Swiss Government had already shown its concern for the American position with regard to Iran by allowing its embassy in Tehran to represent the U.S., and the present case appeared sufficiently related to warrant some small degree of connivance with the work of the American intelligence bureau.

In all likelihood, the Swiss would never have found any traces of them. But the moment Müller opened his file, he knew he had the lead they were waiting for. It was a personal file on Hellmut Schleicher, treasurer of the Deutsche Aktiongruppe. Müller's hands shook with excitement as he sifted through the contents of the file. Even a week ago, none of it would have attracted special attention; now it made sense, urgent sense.

In early June 1976 and August 1977, Schleicher had received checks on behalf of a Zurich-based charity known as the Organisation Charitable de l'Aide Musulmane (OCAM), with offices registered on the fashionable Bahnhofstrasse. For some reason, the two payments—50,000 and 60,000 Swiss francs respectively—had attracted no attention. Müller cross-checked quickly and discovered that precisely these amounts had been paid a few days later in each case into the Aktion-gruppe's own account, registered as private contributions from Schleicher. Müller picked up his telephone and dialed a friend at the Federal Taxation Bureau.

As a result of a long conversation, he learned within hours that between 1975 and 1979 at least twelve payments, totaling 500,000 Swiss francs, had been made into DRASAG's Hamburg account by OCAM. In accompanying tax statements, these payments were justified as contributions to relief work being carried out by DRASAG in Uganda, while OCAM was described as a charitable organization established in 1970 by several Iranian businessmen with the object of providing aid to poor Muslims in developing countries in Africa and elsewhere.

27

MECCA
Monday, 26 November 1979

For days now, a bloody battle had raged between Saudi government forces and the band of rebels led by Muhammad ibn 'Abd Allah and his brother-in-law Juhaiman. Action against the insurgents had been swift but uncertain and ineffective. Under the direction of Prince Sultan ibn 'Abd al-Aziz, C-130 Hercules transports had been sent to Tabuk and Khamis Mushayt to ferry in troops, and by midafternoon all six hundred men of the Special Security Forces were in Mecca. Reinforcements of police and National Guard were sent in from Riyadh. As evening fell, orders were given to cut off communications with the mosque and to sever all power and electricity. In the gathering darkness, soldiers had ringed the sacred building, only to be picked off by sharp-eyed snipers perched in the minarets.

The following day, a disastrous helicopter assault had been launched in the hope of penetrating the mosque itself. As the Sultan's troops swung defenseless over the open courtyard, the Mahdi's snipers had opened fire with devastating accuracy. Time and again, the helicopters had swung in, desperately trying to drop men into the courtyard, but every time the Saudis had been repulsed with many casualties.

By Friday, the government forces, supported by a declaration from the Saudi clergy conceding that military action inside the mosque precincts was now permissible, invaded the building in force. Canisters of gas supplied by the U.S. Embassy were used against the rebels, who were forced down from the minarets and the upper stories of the building and thrust back to the entrance to the cellars that lay deep beneath the courtyard. Throughout Saturday and Sunday, rifle and submachine-gun fire cracked and rattled through the hollow spaces of the great shrine. Behind makeshift barricades, the Mahdi and his followers held back the forces of their enemy, taking a terrible toll for every man they lost.

The rebels knew nothing about what was happening outside, but the Mahdi spoke to them when there were lulls in the fighting, encouraging them to struggle to the end. He claimed that the Saudi authorities were concealing the fact that the President of the United States had been assassinated and that a war between America and the Islamic world was already beginning. If they could only hold out for a few more days, until the tenth of Muharram or a little longer, the great jihad would be underway and they would be called forth from the Great Mosque to lead the armies of Islam against the forces of the Infidel.

Now, on Monday, the remnants of the Mahdi's group, still almost two hundred in number including women and children, were huddled deep inside the maze of subterranean tunnels and cellars that weaved and crisscrossed the regions below the mosque like giant warrens. These underground chambers, known as *khalawi* or retreats, numbered as many as three hundred. They had been hewn out of the grey lava on which Mecca was built centuries before, insalubrious holes designed for the austere meditations of puritan devotees.

Whenever there was a lull in the shooting, the silence seemed almost unbearable. It was not one silence, but many silences, each with a texture of its own. There was neither day nor night, only brief snatches of sleep and the pangs of hunger, increasing as the stores of rice and dates gradually petered out. The stench was terrible, the musty smell of the tunnels mingling with the reek of makeshift latrines and the all-pervasive odor of fear. From time to time, wisps of tear gas would drift through the tunnels and force the rebels to clutch rags to their mouths and noses in order to breathe. The darkness clung all around them, broken only by flashes of fire in the moments of battle.

The Mahdi was everywhere. He never seemed to sleep or to lose hope. Time and again, men on the edge of despair were lifted back by a few words whispered by him or by the touch of his hand. He played his part in the constant fighting, running down galleries unseen to snipe at the misty shapes of government soldiers, calling on them to lay down their arms and fight with him on the side of truth. Sometimes they could hear his voice ringing out through the echoing tunnels, its tone of confident authority intimidating the enemy and boosting the confidence of his own followers.

Late that night, he was sitting near their forward position with Juhaiman ibn Saif and his Iranian adviser. Each attack forced him and his men deeper into the tunnels, blocking off all hope of escape, killing one man here, wounding another there, wearing them down. Yet there was no choice but to go on fighting to the last reserves of their ammunition and their strength. They had no illusions about the fate that would await them once captured.

Muhammad ibn 'Abd Allah was tired. Things had not gone according to plan, and his mind was filled with fears and doubts that he dared not voice to those around him. He could not guess what had happened. Had God abandoned him in spite of everything? That was the one thought he could not bear to entertain. Or had Husayn Nava'i failed in his mission? Was Carter still alive, war still undeclared? He had played his part, rising up in the Sanctuary at the appointed time; but now he waited in vain for word of uprisings elsewhere, for news that the hour had truly come and the final battle commenced. His greatest fear was to be taken alive, to be mocked and reviled and beheaded while crowds stood by jeering.

So far, the government troops had been held back from making an all-out assault, uncertain of the numbers in the tunnels, under orders perhaps to bring the rebels to the surface alive, so that they could be tried and sentenced publicly under Islamic law. But Muhammad ibn 'Abd Allah knew that the moment would come when the patience of their commanders would run out and the final struggle for the control of the mosque would begin. They would use gas, small hand grenades, possibly even flamethrowers. And no one would escape.

Suddenly, a cry went up to the left, followed by the sound of gunfire. There was a heavy rumbling sound, a hollow booming that echoed dully through the cavernous underground chambers. Exhausted though he was, the Mahdi leapt to his feet, followed moments later by his two companions. They picked up their guns and ran in the direction of the noise. The troops were bringing in heavy equipment of some kind. A fresh assault was about to begin, and even as he ran through the tunnels, Muhammad ibn 'Abd Allah offered up a silent prayer.

"Oh God," he pleaded, "come to our assistance. Do not let me die down here in the dark. You brought me out of the desert and carried

me here to your House. Now, with victory at hand, do not abandon
me."

There was a great, blinding flash as a battery of arc lights was
switched on, bathing the tunnels in a white radiance brighter than
the midday glare of the sun.

28

WASHINGTON
Tuesday, 27–Wednesday, 28 November 1979

Information on OCAM and its dealings was sent from Bern to Bonn and from there to Washington on Sunday, 25 November. At FBI headquarters, an emergency meeting was called to evaluate the new data. So far, only one rather intangible link had been found between the DRASAG/Deutsche Aktiongruppe pattern and the United States: the visit to New York in 1975 of one of the five Iranians. But it was clearly worth following up. Several suggestions were made as to the nature of the business involved, but all were agreed that OCAM was little more than a slush fund set up to distribute money to individuals and groups requiring payment. The question at the front of everyone's mind was—who had set up OCAM? Swiss law prohibited disclosure of such details and, however cooperative Bern might prove to be, there were too many legally enforceable restrictions to allow them to obtain such information quickly, if at all.

There seemed to be a strong possibility, in view of the Iranian links, that the slush fund might be connected with a drug ring, and the FBI was asked to furnish data on all Iranians in New York convicted or suspected of links with drug smuggling, peddling, or pushing. By Sunday afternoon, a long list was run off. Leaving aside all small-time operators, pre-1975 convictions, and deportees, there were still seventeen names on the list. Ten of these represented recent convictions, the other seven suspects.

Among the seven suspects was Mohammad Ahmadi. He had been of interest to the FBI for some two years now, and they had more than enough evidence to haul him in. They had held off, however, for two reasons. One was that, from time to time, he would unwittingly lead them to one of his contacts in the New York drug market. The other was that his lifestyle, bank balance, and business interests simply did not reflect the large sums of money which the FBI was certain passed through his hands; they preferred to wait for a lead on the destination of the money before pouncing.

Now, it seemed, they had their lead. Ahmadi's home and office were raided simultaneously on Tuesday evening. Ahmadi, who had returned to New York from Tehran two days before, was arrested on charges that had been reserved over the past two years, and masses of documents were taken. Acting on instructions from Washington, the New York FBI section forwarded all the papers found at Ahmadi's house and office to headquarters.

One packet of documents was given immediate scrutiny. This was a bulky file found in the wall safe in the office. It was labeled in Persian and English "Muslim Aid Organization" and contained a detailed breakdown of monies paid into and out of the charity's account in Zurich. Several other files also found in the safe provided additional information on DRASAG and related matters.

It took a day to construct a provisional assessment of the contents of the file and other papers. The completed report was shown immediately by the agent in charge of the investigation, Frank Brightman, to the director of FBI internal operations, Marvin Taylor. Taylor, an unimaginative man who had worked his way up in the Bureau by advocating policies of caution, ever in line with the views of his superiors, felt an acute sense of dread growing within him as he read the brief summary.

"Is this for real?" he asked, hoping to God it was not.

"I wouldn't show it to you if I had any doubts," replied Brightman. "It's not complete. We still have a lot of work to do on these papers, and even then there'll be plenty more research on the European end. Ahmadi won't talk. His wife and daughter aren't very cooperative, but they say they don't know anything and we think they're telling the truth. Even so, what we have gives a fairly clear picture."

"One hell of a frightening picture. But, OK, I'll arrange a meeting of intelligence chiefs to hear the report and let them make the decision. Have enough copies made and be sure they're classified. I don't want word of this getting to the wrong people."

On Wednesday evening, Carl H. Manning, the director of the FBI, asked for an emergency meeting of the principal members of the U.S. Intelligence Board. This institution has been described as the "Supreme Court" of the U.S. intelligence community. It meets weekly and is chaired by the director of the CIA, who also acts as the President's intelligence adviser. At the meeting held later that evening were the head of Central Intelligence, the directors of the FBI, the National Security Agency (NSA), the Atomic Energy Commission's intelligence unit, and the Bureau of Intelligence and Research at the State Department (INR), together with representatives of the Defence Intelligence Agency and the various advisory councils of the CIA. The meeting was addressed by Manning, who had been fully briefed on the affair.

"Gentlemen," he began, "as you all know, an attempt was made six days ago on the President's life. The would-be assassin was an Iranian, and in view of our relations with his country and the problems facing us internally given the large numbers of his fellow countrymen throughout the States, it became top priority to discover just who had sent him and to try to assess further security risks from the same quarter. Our first lead was this photograph."

He held up the graduation photograph of Amirzadeh and proceeded to give a rundown of the information which had come to light through Bonn and to describe the events that had led to the arrest of Ahmadi and the seizure of his papers.

"We've just heard this morning that Ahmadi has committed suicide while in custody. Apparently, he used a cigarette to set fire to his mattress and inhaled the fumes. So all we have to go on are the papers found in his safe. But I think they will be sufficient to give us all the new leads we require.

"First of all, we now know that Ahmadi was a key figure in an extended heroin-smuggling chain running from Tehran via London and other European cities to New York. For a period of at least ten years, Ahmadi appears to have guaranteed regular sales of top-grade heroin to five or six important narcotics dealers in New York, although there is no evidence to suggest that he was more directly involved in the market there. Figures paid for all shipments to him are recorded in full; a small portion of the money from each sale would be placed in his own bank account or in other locations such as safe-deposit boxes or with investment brokers. The rest—and it adds up to quite a bit over the years—was sent in various ways to the Zurich account of the Organisation Charitable de l'Aide Musulmane, a charitable organization which he established in 1970 together with three other individuals, all Iranians with addresses in Tehran.

"We estimate that, over the years, something like two or three million dollars earned from heroin shipments must have been paid into this account. During the same period of about nine years, Ahmadi also made deposits to DRASAG totaling a further two and a half million dollars, but it is still unclear where this money came from —certainly not from his own antique business. A separate batch of papers indicate even more deposits to the DRASAG account. These were not made by Ahmadi himself, although he kept a full record of them, but so far we haven't been able to establish just who was responsible. But we do know the places they were made from, and that is one of the most worrying aspects of the whole thing. Ahmadi has records of payments—some in thousands of dollars, some in hundreds of thousands—from Amsterdam, Istanbul, Buenos Aires, London, Rome, Munich, Hong Kong, and, in particular, Tehran.

"The indications are that OCAM is at the center of an international drug ring. But that may only be the tip of an iceberg. Quite obviously, the man who tried to kill the President wasn't acting on behalf of a gang of heroin smugglers, however international. The drugs are obviously only a means—probably one among many—of securing funds for a political organization with much wider aims. The most powerful evidence for this view is to be found in a second file containing records of OCAM transactions. These are the payments out: several of them are extremely interesting.

"We already know that large sums were paid out to DRASAG and to the Deutsche Aktiongruppe, both in West Germany. But there are also records of other payments, several of them to private arms dealers in Paris, Lyons, and London. In 1976 several large sums were paid directly to George Atiyah, one of the leading arms purchasers for the Christians in the Lebanese civil war. These payments were made directly to his own bank account in Zurich.

"Finally, there are references in yet another file to contacts with a number of European fascist movements in France, Italy, Spain, Belgium, and Great Britain. We're particularly worried about the British connection, because the Secret Intelligence Service in London tells us they have evidence that their groups have been undergoing paramilitary training and weapons-testing exercises. Closer to home, Ahmadi had in his files the name and address of Hal Brewster, leader of the White Supremacy Party based in Macon, Georgia. So it looks as if we have an international neofascist network centered, like the drug ring, on OCAM.

"Just how all these loose ends tie together, we can't say. Obviously, OCAM has been operated as a slush fund into which money from drugs and other sources has been paid over several years. Money has then gone out again, mostly to finance arms purchases but also, it seems, to assist various neo-Nazi groups and possibly the Christian militia in Beirut. Where the connections lie, God knows. Perhaps we'll learn something more once we can really get down to interrogating this man Nava'i. It's my opinion that his story so far is another fabrication. So I want your permission to take him out of the hospital and get to work under more suitable conditions. I also want to recommend that further investigations at the international level be authorized and carried out as soon as possible."

29

WASHINGTON
Thursday, 29 November 1979

On the twenty-eighth, Nava'i, now recovering and soon to be moved from the hospital for interrogation, asked Straker if he would bring him the copy of the Qur'an he had left in his apartment. Straker saw no reason to refuse the request; the book in question had been checked by him personally and had proved to be exactly what it appeared—a large, well-printed edition in a heavy leather binding with the usual Shi'i appendices at the end, probably a family heirloom from the late nineteenth century. When he came to visit Nava'i on the twenty-ninth, Straker brought the book with him.

As it drew toward midnight in Washington, it was already early morning in Tehran. Since shortly after sunrise, large crowds had begun to gather in the streets, forming processions that slowly wound their way across the city. At sundown the evening before, hundreds of thousands had marched in a cold drizzle, beating themselves as they walked to the stroke of muffled drums. Morning brought them onto the streets again. Red-eyed and filled with religious fervor, they marched through the streets in memory of the death of Husayn thirteen hundred years ago. They carried chains with which they whipped themselves, first across the left shoulder, then the right. The more fanatical had placed razor blades within the links. Others beat themselves repeatedly on the bare chest or forehead until they drew blood. All their sins, all their sorrows would be expunged today, and they would be purified for the holy war against Satan America. The procession wound on, snakelike, toward the west of the city. Outside the American Embassy, a crowd of several hundred thousand stood and chanted, an unchained monster with a multitude of mouths. In the south of the city, smaller processions moved through the narrow streets. And in a house near the Shah Mosque, eight men sat listening to the cries outside.

The night nurse had made her rounds at 10:00 P.M. Outside Nava'i's room, a new guard came on duty; he would be there until his relief showed up at eight the next morning. The wards of the third floor were quiet, the corridors empty of staff, the patients asleep. Inside his room, Nava'i got out of bed, went into the small adjoining bathroom, and performed the ablutions necessary for the ritual prayer. Although the doctors had expressly forbidden him to do so, he had risen at midnight for the past three nights to perform the *salat.* The guard had come in the first two nights and found him prostrating himself on the floor; knowing nothing of the medical prohibition, he had said nothing, and by the third night, he had lost all interest in the proceedings. Once again, he could hear Nava'i's voice inside the room muttering the refrains of the prayer. Half an hour later, all was silent again.

But inside, Nava'i sat upright and unmoving on the floor. He began to breathe in and out slowly and deeply. In his mind he was once again in the shadow-filled valley deep in mountainous Kurdistan where he had lived for a year with dervishes of the Ahl-e Haqq sect together with his teacher, Molla Ahmad, who had trained for many years with them in his own youth. It was as if he could see the black-robed molla sitting before him now, his handless arm lying unmoving in his lap, his eyes closed in deep meditation. For twelve months, they had sat together while Husayn learned the higher dervish techniques of self-hypnosis, of breath control, and of total inner concentration. Night after night, he and Molla Ahmad had gone to the main lodge of the order to watch men enter trances in which they ate ground glass or razor blades, pierced their cheeks with knives or skewers, or exposed themselves to the bites of poisonous snakes or heavy charges of direct electrical current, enough to kill an ordinary man. And in the daytime, Husayn had slowly acquired the power to perform these acts himself. His teacher had pushed him to the limits of his endurance and then beyond, guiding him with an instinct born of a lifetime's devotion and training. And he had learned quickly and thoroughly, though it had cost him much to do so. He was still imperfect, but with a determined effort of his will, he could achieve considerable control over the pain centers of his body and even prevent wounds from bleeding. Now, at last, his powers were to be put to the supreme test.

Hour after hour, he sat motionless and silent. About an hour before dawn, he began to chant in a low voice a *dhikr* ritual, repeating over and over again the words *"Ya 'Ali, Ya 'Ali."* After half an hour, he changed the words to *"Ya Husayn, Ya Husayn."* Each phrase was punctuated by sharp, deep breaths, rhythmical and disciplined. At dawn he was already entering the first stages of a semitrance state. Now the chant changed again, this time to *"La ilaha illa 'llah."* Then to *"Huwallah."* No one interrupted, and the guard, tired after his night's vigil, assumed that Nava'i had begun the dawn prayer. Quiet fell again. Inside the room, Nava'i was silent and still. He sat unmoving, his eyes shut, his muscles locked yet relaxed, his heartbeat controlled, slower and ever slower. As the faint light of dawn began to touch the sky, he opened his eyes, stood up and walked to the table beside his bed. Picking up the Qur'an he unrolled from it the silk cloth in which it had been wrapped several times, as is customary still in many families. Holding the book open near the middle, he bent it back until a gap appeared between the spine and the back of the pages. Slipping his fingers down into the gap, he pulled the *shirazeband*, the headband or strip of cloth at the top of the back binding, and tore it away from the book. Behind it was revealed a flat strip of metal. Carefully inserting his nail behind the metal, he pulled it back. It tore the paper of the binding, enabling him to hold it more firmly between finger and thumb. He now drew it out, a thin blade of the finest tempered steel, nine inches in length. Carefully replacing the headband, which grew sticky when wet, he closed the Qur'an and replaced it in its silk wrapping cloth. On the table were several rolls of unopened bandage. Tearing open one package, he cut himself a suitable length of cloth and wrapped it tightly around the top section of the blade, where it had been blunted.

Raising the point of the knife to his right cheek, he began to press it hard against his flesh. It penetrated the cheek, and he pushed it through until it touched the inside of the cheek opposite; he continued to press until it pierced the left cheek and emerged on the other side. Not a sound escaped his lips as he pressed the knife through; not a drop of blood appeared on either cheek. He then slowly withdrew the knife back through the left, then the right cheek. There were small puncture marks where the blade had passed through, but no blood.

Stepping to the door, knife behind his back, he opened it and called to the guard. Unsuspecting, the man walked forward to the door against which Nava'i was leaning, apparently ill. As the guard moved toward him, the Iranian moved like lightning, slicing the front of the man's unprotected throat and pulling him forward into the room in a single action. Spurting gouts of blood, the guard fell to the floor as Nava'i closed the door. Leaving the body where it lay, he crossed again to the middle of the room and knelt on the rug he had moved there. Again he began to chant the word *"Huwallah,"* stopping after only five minutes. Prepared, he applied the point of the blade to his stomach and pressed hard. Sharp as a razor, it slid in almost without a sound; he removed it quickly, leaving a neat cut in the cloth of his night-robe. Again he applied the point, pressed, and pulled the blade out. No blood issued from the deep wounds. Again he pressed and again. Seven times in all, each time easily, without a sound escaping him, without a drop of blood. But his forehead and body were perspiring freely. He got up, tottered, regained his balance, and walked to the side of the bed. There, he picked up the rest of the length of bandage he had unwrapped together with the wrapping paper and, clutching them, made his slow way into the bathroom. He flushed the two strips of bandage and the crumpled paper down the toilet, then lifted the lid of the cistern, dropped the blade inside, and replaced the lid. Turning back into the bedroom, he knelt again on the rug. The sun's first pale rays were falling through the window. Nava'i heaved a great sigh, shouted *"Allahu akbar,"* and with an immense effort, released every block, every hold over his body, his veins and arteries. Blood came welling out from seven wounds simultaneously, his white gown was drenched in crimson, and streams of the hot red liquid poured out upon the floor. The sun had not yet fully risen.

TWO

QIYAMA

PHASE FIVE

30

TEHRAN
Thursday, 6 December 1979

In a room in the house where Nava'i had been told of his mission, eight men sat in silence. Six were dressed in traditional Islamic fashion, some in black, some in white, with neatly trimmed beards. Their ages ranged from about thirty to perhaps sixty or seventy. Beside them sat a seventh man older than the rest of the group. White-haired and blue-eyed, he was clearly not an Iranian; his features seemed more Nordic, although his skin was deeply tanned from many years in a hot climate. He wore Western clothes, a neat white cotton suit and shoes of soft black leather. Two thin scars lined his right cheek. These seven men sat in a row toward the back of the room; on cushions facing them sat the Imam himself, gray-bearded and bright-eyed, wearing a dark green aba and a green turban that signified that he was a descendant of the Prophet. Each member of the group bore on his face signs of the tension and pain of the past fifteen days. On several occasions during the last fortnight, they had had cause to weep. But their tears had not been for Husayn and his martyred family; they had wept for the participants in the tragedy that had taken place in the Great Mosque of Mecca.

Word had just reached Tehran that early on the morning of the day before, the last of the rebels hiding in the cellars beneath the Great Mosque had surrendered. Altogether 60 had been killed and a further 170 captured alive. According to the Saudi authorities, among the dead was Muhammad ibn 'Abd Allah, the self-proclaimed Mahdi. Whether or not that was true, the capture of the mosque and the ensuing seige had already had wide repercussions throughout the Islamic world.

The failure of the Saudi Government to release clear information only fed the flames of speculation elsewhere. The Mahdi's prophecy of holy war seemed about to be fulfilled. On 23 November, there had been anti-American rioting in Turkey, where students tried to storm the residence of the U.S. consul-general in Izmir, and in Bangladesh, where three hundred students demonstrated in front of the U.S. Embassy in Dacca, accusing the CIA, that demon-of-all-plots, of complicity in the mosque attack.

On the twenty-fifth, Rear-Admiral Ahmad Madani and Admiral Mahmud Alavi, the joint Iranian naval chiefs, had placed the Iranian Islamic Navy on battle alert as news came that the aircraft carrier *Kitty Hawk* and its escort were expected the following evening in the approaches to the Gulf. On the twenty-seventh, the U.S. State Department had warned American citizens against visiting several Islamic countries and had begun to withdraw dependants and nonessential personnel from the United Arab Emirates, Iraq, Lebanon, Syria, Qatar, Kuwait, Oman, Libya, Bahrain, South Yemen, and Bangladesh. By the twenty-eighth, an American fleet was being assembled in the Arabian Sea, off Oman. That same evening, word came that the Shi'i villages of al-Hasa were in flames following rioting during the Muharram processions. Juhaiman and his three companions had done their work well that summer. On the twenty-ninth, fifty-four members of the U.S. House of Representatives had demanded that the President issue an ultimatum for the release of the hostages in Iran. If they were not released, he was urged to "initiate specified military operations against Iran."

Each of these incidents had given renewed hope to the men now sitting in that upstairs room in south Tehran. The possibility that jihad might still be declared and that Muhammad ibn 'Abd Allah would soon be recognized by the Muslim world as the divinely appointed Mahdi sent to lead the war had every day been a living reality in their minds and hearts. They knew that Carter had not been assassinated, although they did not know just how Nava'i had failed; it was even possible, some of them thought, that he was still alive and preparing to make a later attempt.

But the news that Muhammad ibn 'Abd Allah had been killed and his followers put to death or taken prisoner dashed whatever hopes they had held. It was in a mood of deep despair that they met toward sunset on 6 December. Yet, as they looked at the Imam, they realized that he did not seem to share their mood; a gentle smile at times played over his face, and he sat calmly and at ease, watching them. At last he spoke.

"I understand the sadness on your faces, and I feel the pain that you feel. Many have died and many of those who have been arrested will die. But surely we are not grieving for them: those that die in the path of God are martyrs. No, I think we are grieved because our hopes have been dashed. We thought that by now, Muhammad ibn 'Abd Allah would have been proclaimed Mahdi and leader of the forces of the Islamic world in a last jihad against unbelief and tyranny. Instead, he and his followers have been hunted down in cellars and tunnels and have been killed or taken prisoner by Muslim soldiers. But it would be wrong to believe that all is, therefore, lost, that our hopes have been crushed forever. I remain hopeful and I believe that much is yet to happen. What has taken place is surely *bada'*, the changing of the Divine Will for purposes not revealed to men. There are reasons why I say this.

"Let me begin by telling you a story—a story I have never mentioned to anyone before. During the past few days, I have often thought of it as a symbol of hope for our cause. Its meaning for us is profound. I want you all to return to your homes tonight and to meditate on what I have to tell you. Tomorrow I want you to communicate my words to those you consider ready to hear them.

"Listen carefully. In the summer of 1977, the Mahdi was traveling in the eastern part of Saudi Arabia with one of our people from Makran. They were preaching to the Bedouin of the region, encouraging them with words and money to join them when the time came. Eventually, they were arrested and Mahmud Shaybani, the Iranian, was executed at a place called Abu Faris. Muhammad ibn 'Abd Allah was tied to a camel and sent out into the Rub' al-Khali. He wandered for days without food or water and on the fifth day was on the point of death. As he lay dying in a wadi, he was found by riders from a tribe encamped nearby and brought back to their tents. After his recovery, he converted many of them to his cause and, with their help, was able to return to Mecca in time for the pilgrimage, when he met and preached to Muslims from many countries. The hand of God snatched him from the jaws of death. All this he has told me with his own lips.

"Do you not see what has happened? When Muhammad ibn 'Abd Allah realized that President Carter had not been killed and that the Will of God concerning his prophecy had been changed, he and his closest followers went underground, into the tunnels beneath the mosque. Can you not see the reason for this? Do you not recall that there are prophecies in all the books of Shi'i tradition that the Hidden Imam will come again from the underground cellar into which he first vanished when he went into occultation? Has it not always been assumed that those prophecies refer to the twelfth Imam of the Twelve Shi'is, the child Muhammad ibn Hasan who disappeared in the year 260 of our calendar? But you know and I know that such assumptions are false. To whom, then, do the prophecies refer? Is it not clear that Muhammad ibn 'Abd Allah, the true Mahdi of the last days, went into hiding, into spiritual concealment from the physical eyes of men in the cellars beneath the Great Mosque? That he is the Muhammad al-Mahdi whose return from the cellar is prophesied? We have not seen his body. The photograph they have printed is not of him. The description they have given is not his. They think he is dead. But we know that he is still alive, hidden from our eyes, waiting to return to us once more from the depths of the earth."

The Imam stopped speaking. He could see that they were still uncertain but that the seeds of hope had again been planted in their minds. These men were eager to believe that the Mahdi had only vanished again briefly, ready to appear once more as soon as the signal was given. One of them, the old man who had brought Husayn Nava'i to the execution of his friend, looked at the Imam.

"I beg pardon, holiness, but can you say when he will come? Shall I yet live to see his day?"

The Imam looked benignly at his old disciple, smiling.

"Sayyid 'Ali, my old friend, you have waited very long and very patiently. You have not seen him as some of us have, and you have not witnessed the day of his triumph as you had hoped. But I assure you" —here his voice grew loud and ringing and his eyes flashed as he looked about the room—"that you shall not die nor even lie upon your deathbed before you have seen him rise up for the last time. The times are propitious and he is waiting for us to act. There is fear in the world; we must work on it. There is growing tension; we must increase it. There is suspicion; we must feed it. There is mounting anger; we must fuel it. There must be a war, first a war between the great powers to weaken them, then a jihad between the united nation of Islam and the rest of the world. Already the tension is high. I can feel it. And it is growing."

The atmosphere in the small room grew more and more charged as the Imam continued to speak, his flashing eyes and small fluttering hands holding the attention of all who listened. At last, he fell silent and rose to his feet. The rest of the group stood as well, then waited for him to lead the way outside. But instead, he turned to one of them, a thin man dressed in black who stood somewhat apart from the others, his lined face and handless arm reminders that he was not like them.

"Molla Ahmad," said the Imam in a low voice, "please stay with me. There is a matter I wish to speak with you about."

One by one, the other men filed out of the room, backs first, their faces turned at all times to the Imam. When at last they had gone, the old man sat once more on the floor and gestured to Molla Ahmad to be seated beside him. Without preamble, he began to speak.

"Ahmad," he said, "I have bad news, news that concerns you deeply. One of our people in Washington has passed a message to me that Husayn Nava'i is dead. He took his own life several days ago in a hospital where he was taken after his attempt on Carter's life. They shot him before he could fulfill his mission. He did not disappoint you, Ahmad. He was the best of your pupils. There will not be another like him. I know he was precious to you, as you are precious to me. But you will find comfort in the manner of his death."

Molla Ahmad's face showed no trace of emotion, but in his eyes, the Imam could see the grief he felt, and he knew it was as if he had lost a child.

"Now that he is dead," the Imam continued, "I need you to carry out a mission on my behalf, a mission that will take you to America in his footsteps. Are you willing to go there for me?"

The molla bent his gaze to the floor. "You know I would never refuse you, lord, not to the ends of the earth."

"Very good. Now listen carefully. All is not right in America. Husayn is dead. Mohammad Ahmadi has been arrested, his papers have been seized, and he too has committed suicide. Peter Randall, the American agent responsible for so much damage to our cause, is still alive in Washington and is again involved in this matter. Someone must go to New York to contact our group there, to find out what is happening, and, if possible, to prevent further information falling into the hands of the Americans. I want you to leave as soon as possible, tomorrow if you can. There is no time to lose. They must be stopped. Do anything you can, take any measures, however terrible, to ensure that nothing jeopardizes the great work. I have always depended on you, Ahmad, and you have never failed me. Do not fail me now."

The molla raised his eyes and gazed steadily into those of the Imam. "I shall not fail you, lord," he said.

31

WASHINGTON
Tuesday, 18 December 1979

As the Imam had predicted in Tehran, tension was indeed growing. The American hostages stayed under guard in the embassy compound in Tehran; photographs of them, blindfolded and humiliated, appeared in the world press and sparked off anger and indignation throughout the West. In the United States, there was talk of an Entebbe-style raid on the Iranian capital, of a knockout attack on the oilfields of Khuzistan. On 29 November, the students holding the hostages had stated that if the Shah were to leave the United States for any destination other than Iran, they would put forward the date of the threatened spy trial. Three days later, the Shah left the Cornell Medical Center in New York for La Guardia Airport, where he boarded a plane that took him to Lackland Air Force Base near San Antonio, Texas; there he was admitted to Wilford Hall Hospital on the base. His eventual destination was still undecided. On 4 December Sadeq Qotbzadeh, the acting Iranian Minister for Foreign Affairs, announced that the hostages would definitely go on trial on espionage charges. On the same day, President Carter announced to an increasingly impatient public that he intended to stand for reelection.

In the Indian Ocean, U.S. warships patrolled uneasy waters. To the north, on the borders of Afghanistan, Russian troops began their buildup in preparation for the invasion that was still three weeks in the future. The first significant increase in Soviet troop activity occurred on 8 and 9 December, when a special brigade of Russian airborne soldiers arrived at Bagram Air Base.

In Europe, NATO defense and foreign ministers prepared for a major conference in Brussels, at which they were to discuss the American proposal to base 464 Tomahawk Cruise missiles and 108 Pershing II ballistic missiles in Britain, West Germany, Holland, Belgium, and Italy. From Russia, Gromyko warned the Europeans of the dangers of a renewed arms race. From Lakenheath and Upper Heyford airfields in England, F-111s, armed with nuclear warheads, roared into the sky on their daily missions.

Intelligence services in ten countries checked and cross-checked their files. Names, places, and dates were exchanged time and again in a crisscross of information, and a pattern began to emerge. But only in Washington did anyone know the full extent of the danger. It was here that all the strands were pulled together, and it was only here that the details of the attempted assassination of the President were known.

In a small room at CIA headquarters, three men sat hunched over a table littered with papers, files, and tagged documents. Howard Straker and Peter Randall both recalled a similar meeting almost two years earlier, only this time Brandon Stewart was absent. Arthur Pike had not been part of that fraternity, but he had watched their doings from afar, had received their reports, agonized over them, acted on them, advised on the strength of them. Until recently, the three men had never met together, but they were meeting today to try to put together more pieces of the enormous jigsaw of information that seemed to be growing more formless and surreal with every addition their hands brought to it. Straker shuffled a pile of papers and began the conference.

"From what intelligence we've been able to gather, it looks as if our charity organization OCAM is at the center of one hell of a conspiracy, and we can't even begin to guess just how wide. Drug trafficking seems to be just part of its activities, and as far as we can see, that side of their business exists purely for the purpose of securing money, which in turn is being used for others aims—aims which have very little to do with charity. The UN narcotics bureau has been very helpful, and yesterday they were able to give us an important link in the chain.

"You already know we found records of large payments into OCAM's account from companies based in Hong Kong. It seems that all of these belong to one or other of just five families, and the families all happen to be of Iranian origin. They're all well-established Hong Kong residents, very big in business over there. The chief family members all own expensive, heavily guarded homes up on Victoria Peak and have plush offices on Pedder Street. They have weekend houses at Mui Wo on Lantau Island and factories on Kowloon, and they're familiar faces down at the Hong Kong Club and Happy Valley Racecourse. In other words, they're respectable. And they're crooks.

"It seems that members of the five families, who all happen to belong to the Ismaili sect, arrived together in Hong Kong during the last century. Nothing unusual in that—a lot of Iranian merchants set up trading emporia there around the same time. There was quite a lively trade between Hong Kong and the port of Bushehr in southern Iran, on the Gulf. Persian carpets, cloth, turquoise, and so on went out to China, and they sent back Chinese ceramics, silks, and tea. But one of the biggest exports from Iran was opium. The trade was perfectly legal then, of course—back in Iran they called the drug *taryaq*, 'the remedy,' because of its use as a medicine.

"In this century, most of the old Iranian families cleared out of Hong Kong. Business was no longer so good, especially since the trade in opium had been made illegal, so they wanted to make killings elsewhere. But our five families stayed put, apparently trading in silk, jade, and ivory. In fact, they really continued the opium trade, but in reverse. Our report suggests they've been diversifying into manufacturing and distributing heroin since the sixties. They used to have close links with a large British company, Banner Wilson, but for some time now they've formed a kind of syndicate, small but effective, and independent of the triads or anybody else. If they're helping finance OCAM, this is getting to be one hell of a network.

"The original opium supplies get to the syndicate from the Golden Triangle, from Laos, Thailand, or Burma. They smuggle it over the Thai border in little images of the Buddha, as customs officials are forbidden by law to inspect religious artifacts. Most of it's shipped from Bangkok straight to Hong Kong, where it's split up among the various drug clans. Our five families run a joint manufactory in Kowloon, making heroin from the raw opium. You can guess how they manage to keep the police from making raids—or at least from making them at inconvenient times. Anyway, they ship both opium and heroin on ships sailing for the Gulf. At the Strait of Hormuz, small dhows make contact, take the drugs aboard in tiny packets, and take them across to small anchorages on the Iranian coast. Sometimes, a few small fry get arrested, maybe executed, but nobody ever gets to the big dealers in Tehran or the shippers in Hong Kong. Incidentally, Peter, your old friend Hajj Reza Turk was one of the main importers dealing with Hong Kong shipments.

"Some of the drugs are sold in Iran, as you know, but the rest is smuggled out again overland, usually on the Tehran–Istanbul train. It goes into Turkey, where a fascist group called the Gray Wolves buy it up to ship out to Holland. And now it looks as if some of it's been going straight from Tehran through London to Mohammad Ahmadi in New York."

Straker paused, his fingers drumming on the table. He took a deep breath before continuing.

"There's more," he said. "We've been able to get help from the British. They looked up some papers in the British Library, old files belonging to the Banner Wilson group which are normally kept under lock and key. There were a couple of dossiers on our five families right up to the last war. The really interesting one dated from the thirties. It seems that in 1932 the Nazi Auslandsorganisation started building up a complex of party branches in the Far East. There'd been German communities in China from the late nineteenth century, mostly in Tsientsiu, Tsingtao, Hong Kong, Hankow, and Shanghai, where they usually worked for the German-Asiatic Bank, I. G. Farben, or Krupp—the latter companies both developed major interests there. The first Nazi Party organization in the region was set up in Hankow, but it moved a few months later to Shanghai, where a man called Franz Hasenöhrl was in charge. Hasenöhrl managed to get branches going in several other places, including Hong Kong. And it's here we come back to our five families.

"They already had trade links with German companies, but now they got involved with Hasenöhrl's little Nazi group. It was said that a large amount of the Nazi Party funding in Hong Kong and Shanghai came from the families, in return for some pretty exceptional trading concessions with I. G. Farben. We don't know what happened to these links after the war, but the British authorities in Hong Kong don't seem to have taken any action on the issue. Added to what we know about the neofascist groups already involved in this business, I'd say we've got something. And I don't much like what we've got."

As Straker finished speaking, there was a knock on the door and one of his assistants came into the room.

"I'm sorry to disturb you, sir," he said, "but we've just received that report you wanted from Lebanon."

Straker nodded and motioned the man to a chair. "Is there anything in it, Harper?" he asked. "I'll read it later, but now just give me a rundown of anything worth mentioning."

Intelligence services in several countries had been asking questions of arms dealers, so far without result. The answers were always much the same. No sales had ever been made knowingly to representatives of fascist groups, German or otherwise. Even arms dealers have their code of ethics. Yes, there had been inquiries at different times from Iranians, some on behalf of the Shah's government, others for private organizations. And yes, payments for some shipments had been made through the Organisation Charitable de l'Aide Musulmane—it had been explained that this was a European front set up by the Pahlavi Foundation on the Shah's instructions. The arms sold in this way had not been shipped directly to Iran but to government officials in Afghanistan, who, it was believed, had arranged for their clandestine transfer across the border. Why the secrecy? Ah! That was something one never asked in this business.

Then someone had remembered Mikhail Antonius, a former associate of George Atiyah, the Lebanese Christian arms purchaser. They had been involved together in the purchase of arms for the Christian side of the early days of the Lebanese civil war. From late 1975, Beirut had become the center of a vast and complex arms trade that circled the globe. Whereas the Palestinians had relatively easy access to weapons supplied to them directly by Syria, Iraq, and Libya, Christians had been forced to fend for themselves, bringing arms from abroad by sea. A lot of money had passed from hand to hand—estimates varied from $200 million to $600 million—in return for vast quantities of arms and ammunition. No one knew where most of this money came from, but among the speculated sources were the CIA, Israel, banks located in Beirut itself, West German financiers, the Vatican . . . and Iran.

Antonius, it was said, knew more about the international arms trade than any living man and in the past had always proved cooperative with the CIA—though some people suspected he was just as cooperative with the KGB. Instructions had been given to the CIA station in Beirut to arrange a meeting with Antonius and find out what he knew. From Harper's version of the report, it seemed that, as always, he knew a great deal.

"Sir, according to Antonius, OCAM in Zurich gave quite large contributions to the Lebanese Christians, specifically for arms purchases."

"To the Christians? Are you sure?" It sounded back to front.

"Ah yes, sir. It's quite clear, sir. There's a note explaining that OCAM told Antonius they were Shi'is and preferred to help the Christians rather than the Sunni Muslims. But in any case, they don't seem to have been doing it out of disinterested motives. In return for making contributions, they wanted Antonius to buy arms over and above his own needs. He says these were to be shipped to Iran."

Straker whistled and leaned back in his chair.

"It's perfect. What a front! Everybody knew the Christians were in the market for arms here and in Europe. They were fighting a war, so nobody thought of surpluses going somewhere else. Any details about how they organized it?"

"Yes, sir. They used to get weapons routed out of Marseilles, Spain, Italy, and Greece. Lebanese ex-pats in West Africa also handled a lot of the trade, sending stuff through Casablanca and into the Med. Apparently, a lot of these shipments were sidetracked out of the Med over to Turkey, where they were moved overland through Anatolia and into Iran. What happened after that Antonius doesn't know."

"And none of these shipments was ever stopped?"

"Not as far as Antonius knows, sir."

"Any idea what sort of stuff went through?"

"Yes, sir, it's quite a list. A lot of submachine guns—French MAT-49s, German Heckler and Koch MP5-A3s, with some of the new short version of their MP5K, and large numbers of our own Cam-Stat X-9111s. Antonius says there were several large shipments of 9 mm Parabellum cartridges—all the guns I mentioned take them. There were also batches of the Soviet 7.62 mm AK-47, our Armalite AR-18, and some Belgian Browning pistols. And there's one other thing, sir."

"Yes?"

"Antonius says that in '78 two shipments were sent from Sierra Leone across Africa, over the Red Sea to Saudi Arabia. He says they included grenades and submachine guns."

Straker whistled again, but his mouth was dry and the sound was broken.

"Any particular type?" he asked.

"Yes, sir, the same type used in the mosque siege this year."

When Harper left with instructions to type up the report in full, Straker turned to the others.

"Where do we go from here?" he asked.

Pike shook his head. He was already far out of his depth, and he knew it. The emphasis had shifted away from Iran to Germany, Hong Kong, Turkey, Beirut—God knew where.

"Beats me," said Randall. But he knew that the answer was in Iran, where it had been all along. He wanted to go back there, to go right to the heart of this unending web, though he realized that without the right information to return would be not only dangerous but also futile. He leaned back in his chair and cursed loudly.

32

WASHINGTON
Tuesday, 18 December 1979

When Pike had left, Randall returned with Straker to his office. A long, low-ceilinged, white-painted room, it was comfortable in the impersonal manner of a hotel suite or an airport VIP lounge. Straker worked there, all but lived there at times, but he had brought nothing of himself to the room. The furniture, the desk equipment, even the plants by the window were all bought and placed there by the Agency. Straker had added nothing. There were no paintings on the walls, no photographs on the desk, not even a trophy or a good-luck piece or a favorite pen on the desk. There was nothing with which Straker tried to impress something of himself upon the room's neutral space, and had he died or gone abroad tomorrow, the room would have been available for its next incumbent almost immediately.

As he sat down in one of the room's three armchairs, Randall thought it made sense that it should be so. He had known Straker for several years, first in Iran and now here since his return, but in all that time he had never been able to come close to him, to know the man behind the official. Straker was forty-five, unmarried, friendless, and taciturn. He neither visited nor was visited. He never talked about himself, seemed not even to have a personal life. There were no rumors about Straker in the department, no gossip, no history, either true or false. Randall knew he was good at his job, careful, accurate, the master of his feelings, a control on whom an agent could depend. If he harbored passions, they were deeply buried, out of sight, decorous.

But now, thought Randall, something was disturbing him, setting him on edge. Straker was worried, preoccupied. And it had to do with the present case, Randall was sure of that. Did Straker know something, suspect something that he would not tell his colleagues? That he could not tell them?

Straker sat down facing Randall and closed his eyes momentarily. Yes, it was time, they had to act now or not at all. It would have to begin that night; there was no time to lose. There was so much Randall did not know, did not suspect; so much he must never know, never suspect. But he was their key and they had to use him. Randall's problem was that he had become involved. Almost from the beginning, he had allowed personal feelings to cloud his judgment, blur his vision, and deflect him from his course. It had almost cost him his life. Such involvement always carried that penalty. An agent must never feel, must never care, must never become personally involved. That was Straker's creed, it had been his creed for twenty-five years, and it had never been found wanting. Randall was a problem, but he must be used at least once more. As soon as he had established the link, they could bring him in again, tell him he was still unwell, that he had never recovered from the physical and mental scars of Iran, retire him from the Agency. It would be discreet, of course. It was always discreet.

"Peter," he said, uncertain how to begin. A pause. Randall waited, not knowing what purposes Straker could have in mind. He could not read his face; he had never been able to do so. It was featureless and closed, like the room. Straker continued, his voice controlled and flat.

"We have a problem, Peter. It's a minor problem, but one with which you may be able to help." He paused again. He had used the word "problem" twice: once would have been enough. He must not overemphasize the difficulty. Rising, he went to his desk and opened a drawer. From it, he drew out a dull red folder.

"I received this a few hours ago," he said, sitting behind the desk, thus distancing himself from Randall. "It's a report from the FBI in New York. They're being cooperative in this matter. I thought it"— he hesitated, then resumed—"preferable not to mention it during our meeting with Mr. Pike. He does not need to know everything.

"The report concerns the Ahmadi family in New York, the wife and daughter. It seems that Miss Ahmadi has been missing since late yesterday afternoon."

Randall's eyes opened a fraction wider. Otherwise, his face showed no reaction.

"Her name's Fereshteh," Straker continued. "According to this report, she's been looking after her mother ever since the father's arrest. The past few weeks have been difficult for the family. Ahmadi died in custody, so there had to be a postmortem. But the FBI had his papers, and the family lawyer made a fuss, dragged things out, caused an irksome delay. It took until a few days ago to sort everything out, so the funeral was only held yesterday morning. Afterward, Fereshteh Ahmadi went back to the family house with her mother and some relatives. Some time in the afternoon, she went out to pick up some tranquilizers for her mother from a drugstore. She hasn't been seen since. No one's seen her and no one's heard from her."

Straker fell silent. Yes, it must be tonight, tomorrow at the latest.

"Yes?" Randall's query was neutral, undemanding. He wanted to know.

Straker looked up, puzzled.

"What can I do?" asked Randall. "You said I could help. What do you want me to do?"

"Go to New York. Find her. Find the girl." Straker had not intended his phrases to issue as imperatives. Mentally, he had prefaced each one with "I want you to . . ." But that wasn't right. It was not he, Straker, who wanted Randall to go to New York. Straker was indifferent. He just passed on the wish, transformed it into an imperative. Wishes, orders, where was the difference in the end? He had learned not to distinguish them, had learned simply to obey. Randall had not learned. Randall would be difficult.

"I want you to try, Peter, try to find her." Straker said it, but he wanted nothing. Or obedience, perhaps.

It made no sense to Randall. There were men in New York to do that—the police, the FBI, even private agencies. What could he do? Where would he go? He said so.

Straker nodded.

"I know, Peter. The police are already looking for her. And the FBI. But you can speak to her mother in Persian, make her confide in you, tell you what she knows. She can lead you to the girl."

"How do you know?"

"I'm sure of it. The mother knows where the girl is. Speak to her."

"And if I find the girl? If she's still alive?"

"She left for a reason, Peter. Discover her reason and you may discover what lies behind all this, who lies behind it. She knows who they are, she must know. She left because she knew. Go to New York this evening, Peter. Take as much money as you think you'll need.

Keep in touch with me direct. I'll be here. Ring me when you know something, keep me informed."

Randall could think of nothing more to say. He stood, his eyes on Straker. What was Straker thinking? Why did he want him in New York?

"Can I have this?" he asked, pointing to the folder on the desk.

Straker opened the drawer, drew out a second file, passed it to Randall.

"This is a copy, you can have it."

So Straker had known he would say yes. What else did he know? Randall picked up the report and left, closing the door quietly behind him. As he did so, the other man lifted one of the two phones on his desk and dialed a short internal number. There was someone waiting at the other end.

"He's on his way," he said, then replaced the receiver. A moment later, the other receiver was also dropped back into its cradle. He knew Randall might be on his way to his death, but what could he do? A decision had been made, and he had to abide by it. Randall would be bait, he would draw them, he would make the link. Far greater issues were at stake than the life of a single agent.

NEW YORK CITY
Tuesday, 18 December 1979

It was late when Randall reached New York, but he headed straight for the Ahmadi house in Chelsea. At the airport, he had hired a car, paying for one week's rental in advance. He hoped he would not be in New York that long, but he was equally aware that this could be a tedious operation, inconclusive and time-wasting. He wondered why Straker had bothered to send him at all.

Heavy snow had fallen earlier that day, and progress through the streets was difficult. Twice he was sure he was being followed, but each time when he looked back, he saw different cars. He had been out of practice far too long, he thought. His nerves needed to settle down.

The house was dark when he arrived, and at first, he thought of returning in daylight. But it was only ten o'clock and he wanted to start his search for the girl as soon as possible. He was sure she had

disappeared of her own accord, maybe because she felt bad about her
father's death and wanted to be by herself, or perhaps because she
thought somebody was out to kill her. If someone had been going to
snatch her, they would almost certainly have done so earlier, after her
father's arrest. But if she even thought they were trying to murder
her, she must know enough to make it necessary. Straker was probably
right—find her and he might find the group, if she would talk.

He rang the bell and waited. There was no answer. Perhaps Mrs.
Ahmadi had moved in with a relative. He rang again. This time the
communicator crackled and an angry voice blared out.

"Yes! Who is it? What do you want?" It was a woman's voice, the
accent Iranian.

"Are you Mrs. Ahmadi?" he asked.

"Who wants to know?"

"My name is Peter Randall. I have to talk with you."

"Mrs. Ahmadi, she is ill. Her husband they buried yesterday, she is
upset, needs rest. No visitors."

There was a click and the apparatus went dead. He hesitated, then
rang again. Another click and the voice came again, angrier this time.

"Listen, go please. She is sleeping, you wake her. Go please."

He spoke rapidly in Persian.

"I have to talk with her, about her daughter, about Fereshteh."

There was a long silence, but the woman at the other end did not
switch off the communicator. At last, she answered, also in Persian.

"Is it bad news? Is she dead?"

"It's not news. I don't know where Fereshteh is or how she is. But I
want to help find her. Please, I need to talk with Mrs. Ahmadi."

"I am her niece, you can talk with me."

A loud click and a buzz announced that the door had been unlocked. Randall pushed it open and stepped into a wide, expensively
decorated hallway. It was as if he had crossed thousands of miles in a
single step, walking into the house of a wealthy family in Tehran.
Rich Persian carpets covered the floor, framed miniatures hung on
the walls, three enameled lanterns hung from the ceiling. At the head
of the stairs stood a tall Iranian woman of about thirty, dressed in a
black mourning dress with a black chiffon scarf tied on her head.
Randall closed the door and moved in her direction. She said nothing,
merely stood watching as he climbed the stairs toward her, her face
expressionless, her eyes cold and set. She was thin, with well-shaped

features and black penetrating eyes. Randall thought she would be attractive if it were not for the hard line of her mouth and the uncompromising firmness of her expression.

"Thank you for agreeing to see me," he said, his voice politely deferent. She nodded silently and led him to a small sitting room off the second-floor landing. Closing the door gently, she motioned him to a chair. All around him was the atmosphere of Iran. It made him uneasy.

Seating herself opposite him, the woman spoke at last.

"Who are you, Mr. Randall? Why do you come here? Who sent you?"

"I'm from . . . the government. I've come to make inquiries about Fereshteh, to find out what I can, anything to help me find her."

"You speak good Persian. You've lived in Iran. What government department do you work for, Mr. Randall?" Her face was set, giving away nothing.

"I was with the embassy in Tehran for several years, Mrs. . . . . ?"

"Navabpur. Nushin Navabpur. What interest does the State Department have in my cousin's disappearance."

"She may have become involved with an extremist group working in this country. We're concerned for her safety."

"You don't have to lie to me, Mr. Randall. You're not from the State Department, and your interest in Fereshteh has nothing to do with her safety. You think she belongs to a terrorist organization and you want to find them through her."

Randall knew he would gain nothing from evasion. Iranians are too much masters of that art to be easily taken in by others.

"That's one motive, yes. But she herself may be innocent; she may know things connected with other people. As a result, she may be in great danger. If you know where she is, please help her by telling me."

"I don't know where she is, but even if I did, I'm not sure I'd tell you. The police are already looking for her. Why don't you ask them?"

"We're already cooperating with them. But it's possible that Fereshteh may not want to get involved with the police, that she's trying to avoid them."

"What makes you think she isn't running from you?"

"I don't think she knows we're involved." Something about the

woman worried Randall, nagged at the back of his mind, just as a
small cut will snag on everything it touches and draw attention to
itself. But he could not identify it. She picked up a pack of cigarettes
from a low table beside her, shook one out and lit it, inhaling deeply.
She did not offer one to Randall.

"Mr. Randall, we do not need your help. If Fereshteh is . . . if
she is still alive, the police will find her. Her mother and I pray she is
found before she comes to any harm."

Suddenly, it came to him: her eyes. In spite of the black clothes,
the funeral the day before, and the mourning ceremonies afterward,
this woman had not been grieving. There was no sign in her eyes of
tears recently shed, of concern, of anxiety for her cousin. Perhaps she
had felt little for her uncle and cousin, even hated them, but Iranian
traditions of mourning would demand that she make a show of grief,
even if she did not feel it. Randall thought quickly. There was something more, something she had said that was wrong, that had alerted
him but refused to come to the front of his mind. As he thought, he
continued speaking.

"I have been authorized to look for your cousin. My orders are to
find her and help her, but first I need your assistance."

Even as he spoke, he realized what it was. Persian words like
"niece" and "cousin" are much more precise than their English
equivalents. At the door, just before she let him in, when she had
called herself Mrs. Ahmadi's "niece," the words she had used were
"sister's daughter"; but later, in the room, she had referred to her
"cousin" as "the daughter of my father's brother." Fereshteh could
be either her cousin on her mother's or her father's side, but not both
simultaneously.

"Who are you?" he asked. "You can tell me the truth or wait till I
have you checked you out. But first I want to speak with Mrs.
Ahmadi. Now."

As he spoke, her face told him that he was right, but her eyes
continued to bore into him, holding him.

"I'm afraid that's impossible, Mr. Randall. I cannot permit it. You
will have to leave, otherwise I shall be forced to call the police."

What was she hiding? Why was she trying to stop him from seeing
Ahmadi's widow?

"I wouldn't do that, Mrs. Navabpur. Nor would I advise you to try
to stop me from speaking to Mrs. Ahmadi. Where is she?"

He had not noticed her hand move slowly to the pocket of her dress. The past year had taken its toll of him. With an even movement, she brought her hand out again, her fingers clasped around a small but lethal automatic pistol.

"I think, Mr. Randall, we have talked enough. This isn't the first time you've tried to interfere with us. The last time cost valuable lives, lives whose importance you could never hope to appreciate. Mrs. Ahmadi is in her room; she had an unfortunate accident. I think it will be necessary for you to have one as well. Please put your hands on your head, then stand up very slowly. This is a small gun, but I'm sure you know exactly what sort of injuries it can inflict at this range."

He knew. Slowly, keeping his eyes on the gun and the hand that held it, he raised his hands and placed them on his head as instructed, then began to lift himself out of the chair. She held the gun steady; there was no risk of her firing accidentally or prematurely. He would have time to think.

"Now, Mr. Randall," she continued, "using your left hand, please take your gun out of its shoulder holster and drop it gently onto the floor. If you move too quickly or too suddenly, I will shoot you."

He edged the gun out of its holster, gripping it backward, his movements slow and reassuring. The weapon fell with a soft thud onto the thick pile of closely woven carpet at his feet.

"Now put your hand on your head again, then walk to the door. But don't try to open it."

He obeyed, remembering the instructions he had been given years before at training school on how to deal with a situation like this: "Do what they tell you, do it slowly, don't do anything to panic the person holding the gun, give yourself time to think, and don't act until you're absolutely ready."

"Now," she went on, "stand by the door and open it slowly with your left hand. Don't move into the opening until I tell you." Her hand never wavered and the gun stayed pointed directly at his head. He had to get her closer.

"Who are your people?" he asked. "I have a right to know, don't I? We've been fighting each other for two years, and I still don't know who you are."

"Keep quiet!" she snapped. It was the first sign of nervousness she had betrayed. "Open the door toward you slowly."

He reached the doorknob and turned it, then swung the door open.

"I don't care to be quiet," he said in a soft voice. "If you're going to kill me, it'll do no harm to tell . . ."

"I said be quiet and I meant it. The Secret is never to be revealed to outsiders, never." She spoke with passion and intensity, her voice ringing out in the silence of the empty house.

Randall glanced down at the carpet near the door. It was just as he had thought it might be. It is not uncommon for wealthy Iranians to invest their money in good carpets as a hedge against inflation: they are awkward to steal, easy to store, and always increase in value as they get older. A good carpet should be walked on—it improves the nap, gives it a patina, and mellows the colors. The best method of storage is to pile carpets three, four, or even half a dozen thick. Here there must be about three—the door had been cut by about half an inch to allow it to ride over them. Randall opened the door fully and stood waiting for the woman's next instructions.

"Now, stand in the doorway, but don't move. Keep your hands on your head."

This was the most difficult moment for her, and the most dangerous for Randall. He could make a dash for it, to right or left, possibly find shelter in a room before she could get to the door and shoot. Possibly, but not certainly—and if he guessed wrongly, he would not live to regret his mistake. He moved his foot slightly, pushing his heel against the top carpet, slipping it back gently.

"Kneel," she said, "then move your knees toward the banisters."

He bent his knees slowly, pushing the carpet up into two low ridges. Her eyes were focused on his head and hands, the gun dropping to stay aimed at her preferred target, the nape of his neck. He moved awkwardly across the landing on his knees, the polished wooden floor painful underneath. When he reached the banister, the woman started forward toward the door. He tensed, not knowing where she would tread.

The gun fired abruptly as she tripped over one of the ridges in the carpet and pitched forward onto her face, her left arm thrown out awkwardly to break her fall. The bullet went wide, ripping into the wood of the banister three feet away from Randall. In seconds, he was on his feet, kicking the gun from her hand and reaching down to immobilize her with a sharp blow to the side of her neck. He bent down and rolled her onto her back before lifting her to a sitting position, then hauling her to her feet. She was light, but her height made her awkward to move.

Once he had her seated in a high-backed chair inside the room, Randall bent her head forward and probed inside her mouth with his fingers. He found the capsule behind the last lower tooth on the right. Reaching into his pocket, he took out the small Swiss army knife he always carried, pulled out a small file, and carefully began the business of removing the capsule—a task made more difficult by the necessity of keeping her head well forward in case he should accidentally break what he was anxiously trying to keep intact.

Five minutes later, the capsule lay safely in his hand, a small gray cylinder of frangible metal holding enough cyanide to kill in seconds. He placed it in his pocket and sat opposite the woman, waiting for her to recover consciousness. After another ten minutes, her eyes flickered, then opened. She gazed at him, the hatred in her eyes bringing vitality to them more quickly than the mere recovery of awareness. He saw the hatred replaced by something else, something he had seen once before in Professor Mo'ini's eyes before he had died at Darband. Her eyes closed, and she flexed her jaw, once, then again.

"You're wasting your time," he said. "I have it here. I took it out while you were unconscious."

The eyes opened, the hatred now clouded by despair.

"I asked you to tell me about your group," he continued. "Now I'm ordering you. If you know who I am, you will also know that I don't give two fucks what happens to you so long as I get what I want."

She stared at him, her eyes fixed at a spot above his head.

"It may take all night or longer, but I'm going to make you talk. First, I want to know where Fereshteh Ahmadi is."

She continued to stare, her eyes unblinking, her breathing shallow.

"Do you know where she is?" he pressed. "Did you kill her when you killed her mother?"

She said nothing in reply, staring ahead, her eyes vacant, her face drained of all expression. How long can she keep this up? he asked himself.

"When did you come here? Yesterday? Last night? Today? This evening? When was Mrs. Ahmadi killed? How many others are there in New York? Is Fereshteh Ahmadi a member of your group?"

He flung the questions at her, knowing that this barrage could go on all night and all day. Very soon, he would have to hand her over to someone else, but now she was his to interrogate. He leaned forward and slapped her face hard. Her head jerked sideways, and remained there. No movement of her features showed she had even felt the blow. Her eyes continued to stare ahead without expression. He frowned and slapped her again, and again she did not register the blow, although her head was snapped forward once more, still staring in front with unseeing eyes. He began to shake her. Randall got no response and heard only the sound of her shallow breathing and the unrelenting gaze. Her skin was growing paler and cold to the touch. He lifted her right arm, then released it. It remained where he had left it, suspended in the air. He repeated the process with her left arm, then pushed both arms back to their original positions by her side. She had entered a deep state of cataleptic trance and was rapidly going deeper into it. Defeated and frustrated, he sank back into his chair. To have come close so many times and to have been cheated so often! How many places they found to hide from him: in ciphers, in silence, in death, and now in a mockery of death. Dammit! He would get her to talk. He reached for the telephone.

33

NEW YORK CITY
Tuesday, 18–Wednesday, 19 December 1979

"There's nothing I can do, Mr. Randall," the doctor said, leaning back and pursing his lips. He had been sent directly from the New York office of CIA, who paid him as much for his discretion as for his medical services. He replaced his equipment in his small gray bag and snapped it shut. There was a sense of finality in the motion.

"She's cataleptic all right," he went on. "Very deeply. I've never seen anyone quite like this. And I've never heard of anyone putting themselves into a trance as easily as that. I would have said it was impossible. It's as if she'd been programmed and only had to press a sort of internal switch for it to take effect almost at once. We'll have to take her back to headquarters and see what we can do with drugs. But it may take time, and there's a possibility that the treatment will kill her. Or she may be brain-damaged if and when we bring her around. You're going to have to wait some time to interrogate, and even then she may just go back into trance again, unless we can find some way of inducing an internal block. I'd say you've lost this one."

"Dammit!" Randall exploded, throwing himself out of his chair. There was a knock at the door and one of the two CIA officers who had come with the doctor entered the room.

"We're ready to move the body from the bedroom, sir," he said to Randall. They had found Mrs. Ahmadi on her bed, strangled with a stocking. The doctor estimated that she had been dead about five hours.

"OK," Randall said, and turning to the doctor: "You'd better arrange to have this one removed as well. I'll arrange for her to be kept under lock and key, but I want you to do all you can to keep her alive. She has information I mean to get. Please contact me as soon as you think she can be questioned."

He left the doctor in the room and went upstairs. Fereshteh

Ahmadi's bedroom had already been ransacked by the woman downstairs or by her friends. Its contents were strewn wildly across the floor
—bedclothes, clothing, makeup, books, papers, photographs. He began to pick his way through the mess. Had Nushin Navabpur been
looking for something in particular, or just searching haphazardly?
Perhaps she had found what she was seeking before he arrived and
had already sent companions after the girl. Or perhaps he had interrupted her in her search. He picked up papers, mostly letters and
what seemed to be old college notes, and began to skim through
them.

According to the file he had consulted before leaving Washington,
Fereshteh Ahmadi was twenty-three, unmarried, and worked as a cat-
aloguer in the Museum of Modern Art, just off Fifth Avenue. She had
originally studied at the National Academy of Design, where she was
still registered as a part-time student in graphics. Some of her time
she spent helping in the family antique gallery. An American citizen,
she had lived in Iran until the age of ten before accompanying her
parents to New York in 1966. Her photograph showed an intelligent,
unusually attractive woman, whose eyes and mouth suggested an independent spirit, tinged perhaps with frustration. He had seen the same
look before on the faces of Iranian women whose brains and looks
were passports to all kinds of success, but whose families held them
tied to the demands of tradition and a bleak conformity. Sometimes
they became political activists.

Now, as he read through letters and memoranda in a room cluttered with what he guessed were the mere externals of a more complex life, Randall felt a sense of desolation overcome him. Why had
he not resigned when he came back from Iran? It was just like returning from Vietnam—that had been the moment to get out. But
he had stayed on, toying with resignation, knowing it was there to
turn to if he needed it, leaning on it as a possibility, until now he had
been sucked back once more into this greedy vortex of intrigue, sor-
didness, and violence. The phantom he had been chasing since last
year still eluded him, slipping like smoke from his grasping fingers
each time he came face to face with it.

At the bottom of a pile of letters, he came upon one, folded carefully and replaced on its envelope, that suggested a line of search. It
consisted of only a few lines: "My darling, I am sorry everything had
to end like this, so completely and so suddenly. Perhaps all will be for

the best. You know I could never hurt you. You will know where to find me if you ever look for me again. Russ." The note was brief and it had no address and no surname, but it was a beginning. Randall located an address book, thick, filled with names, some entered alphabetically, others seemingly at random. There was no one under "Russ." He started at "A" and began to work through, reading each entry. After a few minutes, he had found him, or so he hoped: "Russell Fernwell, 49 Grove Court, Greenwich Village." To be certain, he checked on through to the end, but there were no more Russells. He closed the book and tossed it onto the small desk by the window. As he did so, his eye was caught by a piece of paper that rose slightly in the current of air created by his action. He crossed to the desk and picked it up, his hand trembling slightly as he touched it.

He had seen one like it before: a pale blue sheet covered in mysterious symbols and a swathe of almost indecipherable characters along the bottom. He could not be sure that the letters were all the same, but it was in all other respects identical to the sheet that had been found in Masood Heshmat's file, which Heshmat had picked up from the floor of the house in Qolhak and which had already led to so many deaths. Silently, he folded it and placed it in his pocket.

From the house in Chelsea to Greenwich Village was a drive of only a few minutes. Grove Court was a group of small brick houses off Grove Street, all looking onto a central garden. From having been New York's bohemian quarter up through the sixties, the Village had become a hideout for the wealthy and successful with artistic pretensions. It was still lively, but a sedate air had fallen on the area, muting the strident rebelliousness of its earlier decades. Grove Court was secluded, silent, and on its guard against intruders. It was after midnight when Randall swung open the heavy gate that protected the little sanctuary from the uncertainties of the street outside. It clanked behind him, leaving the traces of its closing in the air around him.

Russell Fernwell had been awake, but he was clearly not happy to have been disturbed at a late hour. Fortyish, graying, with a receding forehead and long hair, he dressed as an artist. But Randall's sharp eyes detected in his casually expensive clothes the signs of a man who had made it in life and wanted to let others know, yet did not wish entirely to sever token links with a past when he had struggled. Noticing Fernwell's patrician features and confident gaze, Randall did not

think he had had to struggle very hard. Showing his identification, he asked if he could come in.

"You may," Fernwell replied, his voice affectedly languid, "but I want you to know that there is a lady in my living room, and that she will not leave to suit you. If that is understood, by all means come in." He gestured flamboyantly, almost as if he expected his words to throw his caller off balance. Obviously, Fernwell was a man who sought after effect. Randall stepped inside. Fernwell closed the door, locked and bolted it, then led the way into a spacious, sparsely furnished room on their right.

The "lady" was a girl of about eighteen, dark-haired, pale-skinned, and almost pretty. She lay on a long leather couch, watching the two men enter, her eagerness to seem unconcerned apparent in the unfocused shifting of her eyes. Randall ignored her, his eyes traveling instead to the walls of the room, hung with paintings and photographs. He recognized the styles of several well-known contemporary painters—Rivers, Rosenquist, Lindner. The two Warhols and the Hockney were rather more obvious and their position on the wall opposite chosen accordingly. The photographs were mostly nudes, for the most part of women, and all apparently by the same photographer.

"A drink?" queried Fernwell, nodding toward a table in the corner covered with colored bottles and glasses. "Or perhaps something else?" His eyebrows lifted. Randall shook his head and sat down on the nearest chair. "Please, make yourself at home," said Fernwell, the words coming just too late to be effective. He crossed to the table, poured himself a whiskey, and returned to sit facing his guest. The girl followed him all the time with her eyes.

"So, what can I do for you?" Fernwell asked, his nervousness betrayed only by a constant flicking of the fingers of his left hand. "It can't be dope, it can't be porn—the Feds look after all that for our great nation. It must be an international art-smuggling racket. Or fakes."

Randall was tired, and Fernwell irritated him.

"I'm here to ask about Fereshteh Ahmadi."

Fernwell froze momentarily. His fingers stopped their ceaseless flicking and his eyes became sharp and focused.

"Jesus," he said, "the father hasn't been making some crazy complaints, has he?"

"Complaints?" echoed Randall. "What would he have to complain about?"

"Shit, I don't know. Anything. What should I know?"

"You tell me. I want to find out where she is and if you've seen her since yesterday."

"Seen her?" Fernwell almost laughed. "How should I see her? I'm the last person she wants to see, or so she told me. I haven't seen her since August. The fifteenth of August to be precise. But what do you guys want to find her for anyway? She's lily-white, I assure you."

"She disappeared yesterday." Randall explained about Fereshteh's father's arrest and death, but he kept to himself the possible connection with a terrorist group. If Fernwell knew anything, he didn't want to put him on his guard. When he had finished, the artist whistled softly, then shrugged.

"Hell, if she's running from something or just gone off for a spot of deep thinking, this is one place she won't be coming to."

"Why not, Mr. Fernwell?"

"Why not? Because the last time she and I met, she said she never wanted to see me again. At my age, I know when a woman means it, and she meant it."

"How long had you been together?"

"On and off, about three years. I met her at a gallery downtown. They had an exhibition of Tobeys, just after he died in '76—mostly white writing. I wanted to buy some. Anyway, Tobey'd been mixed up with Baha'ism, some sort of Persian cult, and a lot of people at this show were Iranians. Fereshteh was there, though she and her people are regular Muslims, and we got to know each other. She was at the National Academy at the time and knew my work, liked it even. I'm a photographer—this is some of my stuff on the walls. I used to paint, but I went over to photography about ten years ago. We met a few times after that, and I made love to her one evening after dinner here. I wanted her to move in, but she was still into this heavy Iranian thing about the family, so we just kept things quiet and spent time together when we could. Anyway, after about a year, she started modeling for me—some of those on the wall are photographs of her. She was one of the best models I ever had. But she wouldn't let me exhibit any of the work I did with her—said her parents would kill her or something. I thought it was stupid, but the kid was frightened, so I did like she said. Pity, though—some of my best work was done in those sessions. She was an inspiration. I mean it."

Fernwell paused, glancing at the wall. Randall followed his gaze. From where he sat, he could not see clearly, but the photographs did seem good. He suspected that Fernwell was actually brilliant at what he did and that there had been a time, perhaps not long ago, when people had bought copies of his prints because they were exciting, and not because they were Fernwells.

It had not taken Randall long to guess that what he had seen of Fernwell so far was mostly an act, and an unconvincing one at that. The brash exterior covered something else, and Randall guessed that Fereshteh Ahmadi knew what that something else was. He had formed a mental image of her while going through the things in her room, and that image did not include an affair with a middle-aged sophisticate. Fernwell was hiding himself. His hands betrayed him most of all, moving nervously to his mouth, not quite under control. The man was vulnerable, and he compensated for his insecurity by telling strangers he had a right to be where he was. There must be a lot of strangers in his life.

"What happened in August?" Randall asked, digging for more information. Somewhere there were answers that would lead him to Fereshteh. He had only to find the right questions.

"August?" Fernwell shrugged, as if to dismiss the matter lightly, but the gesture went awry. Whatever had happened, it had been important to him. "There wasn't any one thing," he said, "no specific incident. Things just came to a head, that's all. Our relationship had been going downhill for the past six months or so. I'd been changing. My work was getting tired, repetitive; I was selling to a ready market. I still did good work with Fereshteh, but the rest was trite. She said my photographs were becoming banal and that I was getting banal as well. 'Banal'—that's the word she used. It hurt at first when she said that; I was angry. But she was right.

"We started arguing. She didn't like my friends or my clients. She had friends of her own—younger, more idealistic. She started cutting dates, and then one day in August she showed up here. She was tense, angry; she said it was no use, it was finished. I never saw her after that. That's the truth."

Randall nodded. He wondered how much Fernwell had deteriorated since then.

"Aside from art, what else was she involved in?" Randall asked. "Politics, religion, anything like that?"

"Hell, no!" Fernwell's rejoinder was emphatic and spontaneous. "She hated politics. Her parents were religious, but she had no time for it. No, she loved art, the theater, and modern dance. She also liked Japanese food, Vonnegut, and discos," he said flippantly, and then changing his tone: "Listen, you told me her father was arrested on a drug charge. Now you're asking about politics. What is this? Is she in some kind of danger?"

"She may well be, so if you've any idea where she might be, you'd be doing her a favor by telling me. She was close to you: if she's in trouble, perhaps she'll come to you for help."

"I doubt it. But I'll let you know if she does."

"Where would she go? Does she have friends, people she'd feel safe with?"

"Nobody I can think of. She had friends from the academy, and there were students from Columbia she spent a lot of time with. But I was never much part of that side of her life. What we had was separate, cut off from everything else."

Randall nodded. There was nothing more he would learn from Fernwell, and he got up. The girl on the couch followed him with her eyes, uninterested. Randall turned to leave.

At the door, Fernwell drew back the bolts that gave him security from the desperate world outside and Randall stepped into the frostbitten night. The door began to close, then opened again. Fernwell called to him.

"I've just thought of something. I have a loft over in Soho, on Wooster Street. I bought it as a studio during the late sixties, when people started moving into Soho because of the cheap rents, and I still use it when I need a large space. Fereshteh went there a lot—I gave her a key, and she still has it. It's just a chance, but she might be there. Hang on, I'll get you another key." Fernwell slipped back inside, leaving Randall alone on the step. He returned quickly, two keys in his hand.

"It's 15C Wooster Street; this key lets you in downstairs, this one opens the door to the loft. Let me have them back some time. And listen—if you find her, no rough stuff. If she needs anything—money, legal help—I'll fix it for her."

Randall nodded. He knew the word "fix" hadn't been used by chance.

34

NEW YORK CITY
Tuesday, 18–Wednesday, 19 December 1979

In spite of the cold, Randall decided to walk. He wanted to clear his head, shake it free of the fumes that seemed to snake through it and fog his thoughts. Around him he could feel the city, wrapped in snow and darkness, but not asleep. From a deep, dark heart somewhere, hidden to him, it seemed to throb with quiet, unceasing life. Cars and people passed him, the doors of bars and nightclubs reassured him of humanity within, the sounds of music and laughter broke out and faded again as he passed. They came down to him in streams—streams of music, streams of voices, streams of colored and pale lights, washing him as he walked in his own silence. In a rock club, someone was singing a Patti Smith number, maybe in the same spot she had first sung it herself. The words came to him on the night air, sharp and distinct, the music raw and violent. He walked on and the music rose to its crescendo behind him, growing dim at last as he moved away. More than once, he had the sensation that he was being watched; once he heard feet behind him, but when he turned around he saw no one and the echoes were gone.

Wooster Street seemed deserted, even stragglers from nearby Broadway gone for the night. Randall felt hemmed in by the low, confining walls, the heavy cast-iron façades of old commercial buildings transformed by time and money into artists' studios and rehearsal rooms for New Wave bands. Fifteen C was narrow, a single unit slotted between two wider frontages. The window above was dark: no one was there. He turned the key in the lock; it moved easily between his fingers and he pushed against the door. His hand reached out into the dark and fumbled against the wall, finding a switch and pressing it down. Light flared in the hallway. A flight of steep metal stairs led abruptly upward to the doorway of the loft. He climbed, fearful of the dark metal beneath his feet lest the sound of his footsteps announce his arrival to anyone who might be upstairs.

He unlocked the loft door, which swung back slowly. A shaft of pale, nacreous light fell across the wide wooden floor of the vast, cold room. He could sense its stretching emptiness as it remained huddled in darkness. His hand reached for the light switch. As it did so, a woman's voice rang out from the shadows far to his left. The words were Persian, the tone sharp and edged with fear, but dangerously controlled.

"Stop where you are and raise your hands. Slowly. Clasp them together upside down and hold them there over your head. I'm pointing a gun at you and you're framed perfectly in the light behind you, so don't even think of moving. Come inside very slowly and stand in the middle of the room."

He did as she said, feeling a fool to have been caught like this for the second time in the same night.

"Just stop there!" the voice ordered. "Take your gun out with your left hand and throw it on the floor. Don't be misled by my voice—the echoes in here make sounds change direction. You wouldn't hit me." He did as she said, dropping the gun as gently as possible to the floor.

"Now," she continued, "who are you? How'd you get in here?"

He decided to shift to English. "My name's Peter Randall and I've come here to find you, to help you if you need help. And I think you do."

She switched to English as well, speaking it much more fluently than she spoke Persian. "You aren't a cop—they don't speak Persian. But don't bother to tell me, I can guess who you're with. Why don't you leave me alone? What does the CIA want with me? I told you I know nothing."

"I think you're mistaken, Miss Ahmadi. We've never spoken to you. We left all the questions to the police and the FBI. I'm here now because something else has happened, something that's sent you running. I want to help."

"Don't lie to me. The CIA have been right on top of me ever since this whole thing started. Once the cops and FBI had finished, your people moved in."

Randall was perturbed. Not even the CIA had been notified about this case.

"Who did you speak to?" he asked. "What were their names?"

"They called themselves Agent Gorman and Agent . . . I forget. They carried CIA IDs, said they'd come up from Washington. What am I telling you this for anyway? You know it already."

An icy cold stabbed through Randall. There was a Gorman at the CIA; he'd met him once or twice during his training. What was going on? Why hadn't Straker told him they'd already been in on the questioning?

"Listen," he pleaded, knowing he had to convince her. "I didn't know anyone else had been sent; I just came to New York to find you. You have to believe me. You need my help, but I need yours too—I have to know what they asked you about, what they wanted to know."

"Look," she said, "do you really think I'd swallow that?" But he sensed the hesitation in her voice. "Even if I believe you, that you know nothing, what does that change? One of your departments doesn't tell another what it's doing. So, what's new? It's all part of the same little game."

"No, tell me what they wanted—it's important."

"Look, this conversation isn't going anywhere. If you want to know, they were asking about a terrorist group. Listen, I didn't even know my father was involved in drug peddling till he was arrested. And now people come around saying he maybe had links with some nut cases back in Iran and am I a member of this group as well? What am I to believe? Something's going on here I just don't want to be part of."

"What else did they ask you about?" insisted Randall.

"They said that if I had any contacts with this group I should tell them the Agency was ready to make a deal. They were willing to cooperate with them in order to help them get into power. Gorman told me to say that this country needed influence in Iran and this group needed resources to take control there. They could be of use to one another. In return for certain privileges, the CIA would supply them with anything within reason—money, arms, people. You'd think your people had burned their fingers so badly over there they wouldn't want to dip into all that again. Don't you ever learn?"

Randall could feel his heart thumping in his chest. His mind was reeling at what she was telling him. The bastards wanted a deal! They'd sell out to anyone, anywhere, for the sake of another day's influence. She was right: they never learned.

"Fereshteh, listen to me and listen carefully. I believe you when you say you know nothing of the group your father belonged to. You have to believe me when I tell you I knew just as little about this crazy plan to arrange some kind of deal with them. We have to talk, we have to help each other find out what's going on."

"How do I know I can trust you?"

"You don't. But you've got no choice. You aren't going to kill me, and you can't stay here pointing that gun at me forever. Turn on the light, get some chairs, and if you've got any heat in here, for God's sake put it on."

There was a long pause, then movement, and a light went on at the far end of the loft. Randall blinked his eyes, then looked toward the light. She stood facing him, the gun raised in her hands, her eyes alert, watching, waiting. She was dressed in jeans and a heavy sweater. Now that he saw her, he knew that the photographs had told him very little indeed. The Patti Smith song came back to him, and he saw in Fereshteh that same lean, tormented look, feminine beauty and male strength in the same face.

They sat down on chairs underneath a huge canvas that dominated the studio, white background covered with black strokes, the same shape repeated, merging and merging again with images of itself, now light, now heavy. With a start, he realized that the repeating shape was the Arabic and Persian letter *ayn*, a short half circle with a deep hooked tail. He looked at it, then at her.

"Yours?" he asked.

She nodded.

"It's good."

She shrugged.

"Listen," he began again, "I have to know all that's been going on here. First of all, why did you try to disappear yesterday?"

"It was a choice between that and what I believe your people would call 'elimination with extreme prejudice.' "

He smiled and shook his head. "They only talk like that in films. Who wanted to 'eliminate' you?" He hoped to God it hadn't been Gorman.

"Friends of my father," she said in a quiet voice that was still filled with disbelief. "It was after the funeral, not even two days ago. We went back to the house—mostly relatives, some business associates, but mainly Iranians. My parents never really got to know Americans, they stuck to the Iranian community here. Anyway, I slipped out of the living room after about fifteen minutes; I wanted to get away, be on my own for a bit. The whole thing had been too much; I still can't take it all in. And I was worried about my mother, how she was taking it."

She paused. "Have you seen my mother? Is she all right? I wanted to get a message to her, to tell her I'm safe." Then she caught sight of his eyes. He had tried to lie with them, but was no longer capable of it. She stopped, already pushed near her limits, unable to accept much more. When she went on, her voice changed but steady, his admiration for her grew. She knew when it was better not to ask.

"I went to the library. We call it a library—it's a small room downstairs, next door to my father's study; the two rooms have separate entrances but they connect. I went in quietly, not wanting to let anyone know I was gone, and sat down. I suppose I just wanted to cry or something, but I couldn't, not then. So I sat there a while, just thinking. Then I heard the study door open, and I realized that the door between the two rooms hadn't been closed properly. I couldn't see clearly, but when they spoke, I recognized one of their voices. It belonged to a man called Hushang Khodadust, an old friend of my father who visited him at his shop from time to time. Always at the shop, never at home. I'd never heard the other man's voice before, but there was something about it that made me shiver. It was cold, icy . . . emotionless. Then he passed by the door again and I caught a glimpse of him. He was dressed in the clothes of a molla, all in black, with a black turban, small, tightly wound. I only saw him for an instant, but I'd know him if I ever saw him again."

Something indefinite clutched at Randall's heart.

"What was he like?" he asked. "Was there anything distinctive about him?"

"Oh yes," Fereshteh replied. "It was his face that drew my attention, but there's an easier way to recognize him. His right hand was missing."

Randall drew in his breath sharply. He was here, here in New York, the man he had seen in the *zurkhane.*

"Is there something wrong?" Fereshteh asked.

"No, it's all right. I'll be all right. Go on."

"I got up to leave, but they'd started talking about my father, and something made me listen. After about a minute, I didn't move or try to leave because I knew they hadn't wanted to be overheard. They began by talking about my father, about whether he might have told the police anything. They seemed uneasy. One of them mentioned the CIA and said they'd interfered already in Iran. I realized they must be talking about the group Gorman had referred to. Then they started talking about my mother and me, about what we knew and whether we could be trusted. I think it was Khodadust who said my mother was safe, she knew nothing at all, that my father had never told her anything, but that I might be a risk to them. He said that my father had mentioned to him that he planned to get me involved by telling me about the group. He didn't know whether I'd been told anything yet or not, but it was too great a risk and it would be better to get rid of me. The phrase he used in Persian was 'Mahvash konim,' 'let's wipe her out.' The other man agreed and said he'd arrange it. After that, they left. I stayed in the library for a while, then I left, got my coat, and came here."

She saw him glance at her clothes, obviously not funeral wear.

"I keep some clothes and things here for when I come down to work. That reminds me, how did you find this place?"

"Your friend Russell thought you might be here. He lent me his key and told me to let you know that if you need any help, money or anything, you can go to him."

Her face changed and her eyes seemed to cloud over.

"I wouldn't go to that bastard if I was drowning and he sold life belts," she said, the bitterness in her voice raw and undisguised.

As she spoke, he raised his hand, his body tensing, his senses alert. He whispered quietly.

"Is there another way in here?"

Instinctively, she too lowered her voice.

"Sure, there's a fire escape; it leads down to the back of this block. Why?"

"I heard a noise from back there. Get up slowly and head for the light switch. When I say 'Go,' put the lights out."

She stood up, the fear on her face visible. He moved for his gun, still lying where he had thrown it on the floor. Too late. The door at the back of the room crashed open and a man stood framed in the doorway, an M-16 machine gun held at waist height in two hands.

"Go!" Randall screamed at the girl. She threw herself at the switch, and the studio was instantly plunged into near darkness as the gunman opened fire, bullets ripping like a flock of angry hornets into the wall. Firing on full automatic, the clip was emptied in a second. Randall heard the man disengage the first clip and throw it to the ground. He had about three seconds. Skidding across the floor, he grabbed his gun, swung around, and aimed at the light on the landing outside. The bulb shattered at the second shot and total darkness enshrouded them. The gunman paused, listening. Randall cupped his hands and shouted, "Here, you bastard!" The echoes rang from the wall and the machine gun blazed again, its muzzle illuminated across the room. Randall knelt and aimed just above the spot where its light had been. He fired: a single shot, sharp and clear in the darkness. There was a cry and the sound of metal crashing to the ground, followed by the thud of a body. Randall shouted to the girl.

"Are you all right?"

Her voice came, shaking but direct, out of the darkness to his left.

"Yes. Did you get him?"

"I got him but he may be alive. Can you find the light switch?"

"I think so." There was a sound of her hand slapping the wall, then the light flashed on again. Against the far wall, a man lay crumpled, his machine gun out of reach. Randall crossed to him and pushed him over with his foot. A glance told him that the man was about thirty, probably Iranian, and dead. The magnum had torn a hole the size of a baseball through his upper chest. Randall turned to check that the girl was all right.

She was still standing by the light switch, her face frozen with terror. A row of bullet holes ran in an undulating swathe all along the wall against which she stood. Randall put his magnum in its holster and walked over to her, standing between her and the man on the floor behind him. "It's all right," he said, knowing it wasn't. She turned her eyes on him and looked angry, sad, and frightened, all in quick succession. With a small cry, she threw herself toward him, clung to him, not because he had saved her but because there was no one else and there had to be someone. He cradled her in arms grown weary with emptiness.

"We have to get out of here," he said quickly.

35

NEW YORK CITY
Tuesday, 18–Wednesday, 19 December 1979

Randall was sure now that he had been followed to Wooster Street. What he was not sure of was the identity of whoever had followed him. It might have been the Iranian gunman, but he could not be certain that the Iranian had been the only one looking for him. Knowing what he now knew, he realized that he had been set up, and that Straker might have sent a man to tag him until he found the girl. He might have been followed all the way from the airport after all— maybe even from Washington. He could afford to take no chances. From now on, he was on his own.

He and Fereshteh left by the front entrance, taking precautions in case the gunman had been covered by a friend outside. The street was empty, but Randall knew that a police car might appear any moment if someone had heard the shooting and taken the trouble to telephone. Randall had no definite plan other than to get away from the neighborhood as quickly as possible. For all he knew, he was still being followed by Gorman or one of his pals. But that was a problem that would have to wait its turn.

They got to Broadway. Walking fast, their footsteps raised echoes. A light snow had begun to fall, the white flakes silent, caught in the last moments of their long descent by streetlights and the headlamps of cars racing by. Randall stopped and turned to Fereshteh.

"I want you to think quickly. We have to find somewhere to disappear, a crowded, noisy place—a bar, club, somewhere we can get lost easily."

She didn't even have to think; the answer came in a flash.

"CBGB's, over on Bowery, near Third. Let's go."

He nodded and took her arm, letting her take charge, knowing it was the best way to help her recover control and master the rage of emotions inside her. Emotions were luxuries for later, if indeed there would be a "later." Now she had to kill her feelings in order to stay alive. They found a cab on Broadway and drove east. Randall kept watch behind as they moved quickly through the dark streets. He could not throw off the sensation of being followed. Somewhere behind them, eyes were watching, a car was keeping pace with theirs, carefully staying out of sight. Once ready, they would move in, whoever they were.

CBGB's was New York's most famous New Wave rock club of the moment, a narrow, renovated hellhole filled with smoke and noise and a freaky clientele, some of whom could be dangerous and most of whom wanted to look it. The men at the door looked oddly at Randall, prepared to turn him away; out-of-town thrill seekers or executives on the prowl for cute young hookers were not welcomed. It was Fereshteh who got them in. There was no mistaking her for anything but a hard-bitten New Yorker. Randall watched her precede him into the depths of the club and wondered if this was the same woman who had needed his comforting half an hour before.

Inside, the noise was deafening, the crowd seemingly impenetrable and the air unbreathable. On the stage far down the hall, a British punk band was halfway through its set, the voice of the singer strident and insistent, the music menacing. The audience was standing, many of them dancing where they stood, most of them high and oblivious of all but the music and the pulsing lights. Randall and Fereshteh pushed into the crowd, feeling it close behind them as they threaded their way through the jerking bodies. They reached the stage, where the crowd was packed densely up against the high platform, the music pouring down on them from above. Randall glanced backward. In the distance, toward the door, he could make out the signs of a commotion. They were moving in.

A line of heavyset men was ranged along the stage, keeping fans from trying to climb up. Randall forced his way through to the front row, to the side of the stage, Fereshteh close behind. Right in front of him was the last bouncer in the line, a tall, beefy man, sweat pouring from his face. Randall turned to Fereshteh and shouted, "We're going up, get ready!" He turned to the man, kneed him heavily in the groin, and cracked his hand sharply into the side of his neck as he jerked forward, collapsing with a grunt and sliding into the crowd.

Randall leapt for the stage, pulling himself up in two coordinated movements, then turned. The next bouncer made a grab for his legs.

Randall's right foot struck out fast and heavy, taking the man clean in the throat, sending him crashing back down into the first row of fans. There was a shout and a sudden surge toward the stage, throwing Fereshteh forward and pinning her against the side of the platform. He reached down and found her hand, then held her wrist and pulled her up. Behind him, a stagehand ran forward and grabbed him, trying to drag him back. Fereshteh pulled free of the crowd and clambered up, pitching forward onto the platform. Randall released her, reached behind for the clinging stagehand and broke his grip without difficulty. With a second movement, he threw the man backward into another man just behind him. Fereshteh was on her feet.

"Quickly," Randall shouted, heading offstage, aware that they could now be seen clearly from the back of the hall. Someone else rushed toward him.

"Where the fuck do you think you're going?" the man screamed. Randall crashed into him, sending him reeling into a block of colored lights. There were sparks and a shattering of glass; several of the lights went dead. Grabbing Fereshteh's hand, Randall ran for the stage door at the back. It opened at his first push, letting in a blast of icy air. They dashed out, slamming the door behind them. They were in a long alley, deserted except for garbage cans and cats. Even the bums were indoors tonight.

"Let's go," shouted Randall. "We've got to get off the streets. They'll have someone around here in minutes." They came out of the alley onto Third Street, checking behind that all was clear. On the other side of the street a line of parked cars stood patiently in a blanket of snow. Some looked expensive. Many of the punks in ripped clothes inside CBGB's obviously had fat bank accounts at Chase Manhattan and some of them would be careless. Randall crossed over and moved quickly along the row, trying doors. The door of the fifth car he came to, a white Morgan convertible, opened easily. Less than a minute later, the engine fired into life and they moved out into the street.

Randall headed north toward Lexington Avenue, a street with numerous hotels. At East Forty-second Street he turned left toward Grand Central Station. The car would attract little attention parked in that area and, even when found, would create considerable doubt as to their present whereabouts. Out of Grand Central they could travel on any number of suburban or long-distance trains, or take the subway system.

On foot again, they walked back to a hotel on Lexington where they would be safe for one night. Tomorrow they would have to move elsewhere, but there would be time enough to think about that when they had both slept.

At the desk Randall asked for two singles, adjoining. The desk clerk raised one eyebrow slightly, but said nothing. It was obviously beyond his comprehension why anyone in New York in 1979 should waste good money on a rather pointless gesture of propriety. He handed over two keys to 534 and 535, wished them goodnight, and returned to his novel, thinking what he would do if he had a girl like that in his room.

They took the elevator to the fifth floor without saying a word. In the corridor, as they were about to go into their rooms, Randall turned to Fereshteh.

"Listen, I'm going to open the connecting door. Keep it unlocked. If anything happens, if you hear anything, come in straight away."

She nodded, an ironic smile on her face.

"They could come in and kill me, I wouldn't move. I didn't get much sleep last night. Now I feel like something the morgue would turn away."

He laughed and opened his door. Five minutes later he was in bed, falling quickly into a heavy sleep, the darkness consuming him without the intrusion of dreams or even their shadows.

Perhaps it was a sound that woke him, perhaps an instinct. Before his eyes had opened, his hand found and clasped the gun beneath his pillow. He sat up, blinking the shadows away, his mind still somewhere in sleep. She was standing in the doorway, her slender body lit from behind by the bedside light in her own room.

"How long have you been there?" he asked, finding speech and slipping the gun back under his pillow.

"About five minutes," she replied. "I was afraid to wake you, you seemed so completely asleep."

"What's wrong?" he asked.

"I can't sleep. I'm worn out, but I can't sleep. The whole thing's just . . ." She stopped and the tears came, not violently as before, but gently. She made no effort to wipe them from her face. "Can I come in beside you?" she asked, her voice that of a little girl by her parents' bed. "It's not . . . I just can't sleep in there on my own."

He pulled back the covers and she crept in beside him. He wanted to hold her, to comfort her, but he was afraid. Instead, he smiled and stroked her hair and rolled over, saying "Goodnight." Sleep took him again, quickly, pulling him down in a rough embrace. And soon it came for her too.

When he awoke, it was already late, and she was gone. He panicked until he heard her in the bathroom. He called and she answered. She had been up for half an hour. The bathroom door opened and she came out. She had dressed, washed her hair, and put on some makeup she carried in the bag she had brought from the loft. She smiled at him, a trace of embarrassment visible at the corners of her eyes.

"It's all yours, I've finished," she said. "I'll be in my own room. I've asked them to send up breakfast in five minutes."

He looked at his watch. It was already past eleven.

"Why don't we just wait and have lunch?" he asked.

"No way. I'm starving. I hardly ate yesterday."

After breakfast they walked. Fereshteh seemed more relaxed now, less suspicious of him. She talked about herself, her family, her friends. However Ahmadi had worked it, his family had known nothing of his drug connections or his links with the Iranian group behind Nava'i.

"Didn't your father ever give any hints that he had political or religious leanings?" Randall asked at last.

She shook her head. "We never talked about politics at home, at least not in any serious way. My father always said he had no time for politicians, and since I wasn't really into that sort of thing myself, we never even had arguments. Back in Iran, he'd been a businessman, keeping his nose clean, saying the right things to the right people. And we were never a religious family. Technically, we're Ismailis, so we never got mixed up in the wilder stuff in Iran, and here we only went to small gatherings for the main festivals, like going to church for Christmas. My father had contacts with Ismaili businessmen in Bombay and East Africa, but he was never really involved in it. Except . . ."

She paused, a frown creasing her forehead, trying to remember. "About ten years ago, when I was thirteen or fourteen, I remember he seemed to change. For a time, he was very moody, very quiet, not himself at all. And then he started talking about God a lot more than usual, said things like 'We're all in God's hands,' corny stuff mostly. And then, after a month or two, he seemed to go back to normal. That was the nearest he ever came to being religious, as far as I know. Maybe something happened back then, maybe somebody died. He never talked to me about it, and I never asked him. But . . . there were some times, especially during the last year, when I got a feeling he wanted to talk to me about something. A few times he would start a conversation, then he'd stop and get up and leave the room."

She stopped speaking, her eyes thoughtful, memories of her father passing like phantoms through her brain.

"And then . . . A couple of months ago we had a guest, a young man from Tehran—I can't remember his name. He gave me the creeps, very intense, preoccupied. I heard him the first night he stayed with us praying in his room and crying. A real fanatic, I thought. But there'd been the revolution and everything, and somehow I never connected him . . . There was something else though. When I was going through some of my father's papers a few days ago, I came across something unusual. It was at the back of his diary, a sheet of blue paper folded over and tucked in. It had Persian writing, but nothing I could understand, and the names of Muhammad and some of the Imams at the top. It looked like a talisman or a mandala. I'd forgotten about it until now—I left it on my desk to look at some time."

Randall reached inside his jacket pocket and drew out a folded sheet of paper.

"Is this it?" he asked, unfolding it, knowing it was. She looked at him, the outrage of her privacy clear on her face.

"I'm sorry," he said, "I had to look. It's how I found you. I took this because . . . because I once saw it or something like it in Tehran. Some people I knew there died because of it."

Perplexity and something like concern replaced the anger in her eyes. He smiled and put the paper away.

"I'll tell you all about it another time," he said. "But we've got to get moving soon. I've decided where we'll go today. This little piece of paper's reminded me of someone."

36

THOUSAND ISLANDS
19–20 December 1979

At the northeast tip of Lake Ontario, where its waters start to flow into the St. Lawrence River, the Canadian-U.S. border is broken and confused by the inland archipelago of the Thousand Islands. Traveling on Interstate 81 through Syracuse, Randall and Fereshteh reached Cape Vincent at the head of the St. Lawrence by late afternoon. They had lingered in New York only long enough to take five thousand dollars from a safe-deposit box, buy some warm clothes for her, and hire a car using a false ID carried by Randall.

They stopped at a diner in Cape Vincent, and while Fereshteh ate, Randall made a telephone call. Five minutes later, he came back to the table, smiled, and sat down.

"It's on," he said. "He's there and he says he'll pick us up in his jeep in half an hour."

"Did you tell him what's been happening?" she asked, still chewing a piece of steak.

"No. He thinks I'm up here for a break. He'd heard about my accident and knew I'd been recuperating. But I can trust him. I'll tell him when we get there."

"He" was Juliusz Rostoworoski, one of Randall's former teachers in his training days back in Washington. Rostoworoski was retired now, but in his day, he had been the best of his kind. A Polish refugee, he had originally been recruited as a young man to work for the OSS in Poland toward the end of World War II. Already something of an expert on Oriental languages, he had been sent to Iran in 1946 and had become one of the most valuable American agents in the country. In the end, he was forced to leave Tehran after the fall of Mossadeq in 1953, an event he himself had been closely involved in organizing. Back in the States, he had retrained as a cryptologist specializing in Arabic and Persian codes before being appointed to the National

Security Agency next door to Fort George Meade, just outside Washington. At the NSA, he had quickly acquired a reputation for brilliance both in deciphering and encoding messages in either Persian or Arabic and, until his retirement in 1974, he had presided over his esoteric realm like a king. Randall knew that materials were still sent to him, but he often wondered whether the breakdown in the quality of U.S. intelligence in Iran during the late seventies did not have something to do with his departure from full-time work. Since his retirement, he had come to live on one of the Thousand Islands, a small islet originally bought by him as a holiday home, with a single house that had been let out to tourists when he was not there. His wife had died years before and he lived alone, something of a recluse. Randall had visited him on his island once or twice during vacations and had grown to like the old man. He still held him and his brilliance in great awe.

They finished their meal and went outside. Rostoworoski's jeep was already there, the old man behind the wheel waiting patiently. As they came up, he rolled down the window.

"It's good to see you, Peter. And you, Miss . . . ?"

"Ahmadi, Fereshteh."

"I'll call you Fereshteh, if I may. I've always liked the name. Peter, I suggest you leave your car in Dan Willis' garage just down the road and come back in my jeep. We've some rough ice to cross over to the island."

It took Randall fifteen minutes to garage the car and return. By that time, Fereshteh and the old man already seemed the best of friends. They smiled as Peter climbed into the jeep.

"Peter," said Fereshteh, "Juliusz has just been telling me that he knew some of my relatives in Tehran back in the fifties."

Randall smiled and slid into the seat beside her. Old Juliusz had charm, and he hadn't lost his old trick of seeming to know something about everybody and everything. Peter sometimes wondered if he made half of it up.

The journey to Rostoworoski's was straightforward, except for the last stretch, which involved driving out onto the frozen waters of the St. Lawrence. In spite of the Pole's assurances, Randall felt uneasy as the jeep skidded its way across the packed crust, its headlights stabbing a way ahead, the ice sparkling and shimmering in the white, bobbing beam. Randall could never work out just how the old man knew his way across the unmarked vastness of frozen water.

They sat for hours that night, warm and comfortable beside a large open fire of logs, while Peter recited the story that had brought them there. Somehow it was more difficult in the warm security of Rostoworoski's home to talk of the dreadful days and nights in Tehran, of the deaths and tortures that he had thought he had left behind him forever. He spoke of Fujiko and Iraj Ashrafi, of the attempt that had been made to kill him, of his escape and his encounter with Mo'ini, of his discovery of the seven men in the *zurkhane*, and of what had happened there. He then went on to explain what he could about Nava'i and his attempt on the President's life, and to describe as clearly as possible the web of complexities that had been partially unraveled since then. He could see that Fereshteh was bewildered and frightened by his story, but Rostoworoski sat without moving, years of experience helping him fill in details, confirm the accuracy of what Randall was saying. He told the old man everything, including his information that the CIA was trying to make a deal with the Iranian group.

When he came to explain how he had found Fereshteh, however, he hesitated for the first time. She saw his hesitation and asked the question she had so far refrained from putting to him.

"Peter, how did my mother die?"

He answered her as simply as he could, knowing it would be more cruel to keep her in ignorance. She fell silent and remained pensive for the rest of the night, but she did not ask to be excused, and time and again as Peter glanced at her, he felt he could see a new strength building up in her, a capacity for cold anger he had never guessed she might possess.

When he had at last come to the end of his long narrative, Peter took the blue paper from his pocket, unfolded it, and passed it to Rostoworoski.

"Juliusz," he said, "if anyone can read this, you can. It may be important, it may be nothing. But it's the only link we've got between the group here in the U.S. and the people I was after in Tehran."

Rostoworoski nodded. "I can't promise much, Peter. I've got no real computer here, just a small Apple that I use to play about with; it won't handle complex cryptological programs. But I'll give it a go. It may not even be in code, of course. A lot of Islamic talismans use letters in groups that mean nothing at all, just look or sound impressive. This could be something like that."

"No," said Randall, "it means something, Juliusz. Iraj Ashrafi died because he was able to crack it, because it meant something to him. And if he could do it, I'm sure you can."

"All right, I'll try. But now it's time for bed. You two must be very tired and we've been talking for hours."

Neither Peter nor Fereshteh needed further prompting. They rose and followed Rostoworoski to their adjoining rooms on the next floor. They said good night and watched him go down the stairs again. When he was gone, Fereshteh turned to Randall and said, "I like your friend, Peter. I trust him."

"Do you trust me?" he asked.

She smiled. "No," she said, and closed the door of her room.

Randall woke at eight the next morning. Downstairs, he could hear the sound of typing and then, listening more carefully, the noises of someone cooking. He rose, washed and dressed, and went down. In the main room, Juliusz was sitting at a desk, his fingers striking the keyboard of an old Olympia portable. Randall had the feeling that Juliusz had been there all night. The old man looked up as Randall entered.

"Good morning, Peter," he said, "Fereshteh's fixing us all some breakfast. We'll eat, then I have something to show you."

Even as he spoke, Fereshteh called from the kitchen. "Peter, Juliusz. Breakfast's ready." He followed Juliusz and felt soothed and buoyed up by the smells of hot coffee, fresh waffles, and syrup which filled the room. They all sat down at the wooden table and began to eat. Throughout the meal, Peter kept eyeing his old friend, wondering what it was he had to show them, detecting in his eyes more than a hint that something was disturbing him.

At nine o'clock, they retired into the living room. Juliusz stoked the fire, piling fresh logs on top, the flames leaping for them, hungry and impatient. The old man went across to his desk, picked up some papers, and returned to the fireside, where he sat as before in his deep leather armchair. He held out the blue paper Randall had handed him the night before.

"While you kids were asleep last night," he began, "I made a start on this. I hadn't intended to do more than glance through it, get a feel of it, but once I started on it I couldn't leave it alone. It bugged me. It was obviously in code, but nothing resembling any code I'd ever seen before. And yet something about it seemed familiar, as if I should have recognized it.

"Frankly, it seemed a mess. The top's just rather pretty calligraphic arrangements of the names of the Prophet Muhammad, his daughter Fatima, his cousin and her husband 'Ali, and their two sons, Hasan and Husayn. There's nothing odd about that. But the lines at the bottom made no sense at all. You've both seen them: just strings of letters joined together, no beginning or end forms except for the lines or letters that can't do without them, and no obvious way to split the text into words. I wasn't even sure if I was dealing with a piece of Arabic, Persian, or maybe even Urdu or Ottoman Turkish, or a European language transcribed in Arabic characters. It could have been anything, and nothing I tried made sense.

"Then it occurred to me I'd read about something like this before. It took me a while to track down my reference, but I got it in the end. It's an old code, dating back to the eleventh century. Actually, it's very simple. Whenever one of the letters from the five holy names occurs, the next letter but one is part of the message, then it repeats in reverse. Everything else is garbage, like the tinfoil that bombers chuck out to trick radar. It took me a while to transcribe it, but here it is, along with a translation."

He passed two sheets of paper to Randall. The younger man glanced at the transcription, then read Rostoworoski's translation:

> My brother Muhammad. The bearer of this message is the young man for whom you and your companions have waited. He brings tidings of the Holy One in Mecca. Ensure that all is made easy for him and give him whatever assistance he may require in his mission. These are days that will not be seen again. The final victory is near, so let not your hand nor your heart nor your will falter in this mighty task. He is the last of the Seven, whose mission is to make ready the way for the unsheathing of the Sword. And the Sword is the first of the swords to be drawn from their scabbards. In the days of Alamut, my namesake, Lord Hasan, sent out his *feda'is*, the elite of the *hashshashin*, to destroy kings and princes and to bring fear to the hearts of

governors. Those days are come again. I that bear his name have taken up his task once more and shall bring it to its completion. It is the time of the final holy war, the last crusade against the forces of darkness and unbelief. Have complete faith, for the resurrection is near and the day of our everlasting kingdom is upon us. You have done well in all the years before this. Do well again and claim your reward when you come into my presence. Praise be to God. Hasan.

Randall frowned and passed the sheets to Fereshteh.

"I don't understand this, Juliusz. It doesn't make sense to me."

The old man raised his eyebrows. "It'll mean something to Miss Ahmadi, I think." He watched her as she read, her brow furrowed, a look of comprehension coupled with puzzlement in her eyes. When she had finished, she passed the pages back to the Pole without saying a word. The old man held her gaze as he took the papers, then turned to Randall.

"What do you know about Ismailis, Peter?"

Randall shrugged. "Not a lot. They used to be an important sect back in—what? The eleventh, twelfth century? Nowadays they've got a few communities here and there, but I've never heard much about them. Fereshteh here can tell you more, I'm sure. Literature's more my field than history or religion."

The old man nodded and returned his gaze to Fereshteh.

"The letter means something to you, my dear?"

She nodded. "Some of it, yes. But it doesn't make any sense; it reads like some kind of sick joke, like something out of the past. Ismailis don't go around killing people like that, they don't wage holy wars. It's crazy. How could my father have been mixed up in something like this?"

Rostoworoski smiled, seeking to reassure her. "I agree, it is crazy. When I was in Iran, I knew some Ismailis in Tehran—your relatives were among them. They were gentle, kind people, not the sort of people to get involved in affairs of this kind. But I'm afraid there is a certain sense to all of this. Your father was an Ismaili, the five families in Hong Kong that Peter mentioned last night belong to the sect, and this letter certainly came from someone who looks back on the days of Alamut with pride." He stopped and shifted his position. Randall

could tell that, in spite of his efforts to cover it up, the old man was
tired after the intellectual struggle of the night. Randall watched him
raise himself to his feet with an effort, walk over to the bookcase to
the left of the fireplace, and, after a few seconds' hesitation, take
down an old leather-bound volume. He passed it to Peter, his hand
shaking slightly as he did so.

"I want you to read this, Peter. You can finish it this afternoon, it
isn't very long. It's a bit out of date now, but most of it's still accurate. It's a history of the Ismailis of the early Middle Ages, but you'll
notice that the author doesn't refer to them very often by that name.
He usually calls them by their more popular title: the Assassins or, if
you prefer the Arabic, the *hashshashin*.

"The Assassins were one of the earliest secret societies in the world,
with an astonishing organization that covered most of the Middle
East and even parts of Europe. They were founded late in the eleventh century by Hasan al-Sabbah, an Ismaili missionary to Iran, who
started preaching new doctrines and winning converts. His sect
spread pretty quickly by all accounts and, before long, the authorities
made the usual attempts to stamp it out. In order to protect themselves, Hasan and his Assassins took over a number of strongholds in
different parts of Iran—the best known is Alamut, the 'Eagle's Nest,'
which was perched on a high rock in the mountains near Qazvin. It
was virtually impregnable, a natural fortress manned by religious
fanatics trained as soldiers."

Randall reached across for the transcript of the letter. "So that's
what you think this is a reference to, this sentence about 'Alamut' and
'Lord Hasan'?"

The old man nodded. "I don't think, Peter; I know. The code the
letter was written in originally came from Alamut. That's how I remembered it: I'd read about it in this book. Hasan used to send his
missionaries out from Alamut to spread the word; but he also sent out
killers, men called *feda'iyan*, 'the ones who sacrifice themselves,'
young fanatics, prepared to obey him to death and beyond, if necessary. It was the *feda'iyan* who gave the sect the name *hashshashin*—it
means 'eaters of hashish'—but it quickly came to mean what it means
in almost every language today, 'assassins.' "

Fereshteh shook her head, puzzled. "I don't understand. What had
hashish to do with the sect? I've never known Ismailis who smoked
grass."

The Pole nodded again. "You're quite right, they don't nowadays—and maybe they never did. The hashish may just be part of the legend."

"The legend?"

"Oh yes. A great many legends grew up about Hasan and his Assassins. Here, let me read you an example." Rostoworoski rose and went to the bookcase again, taking down another volume, a larger one this time. Standing by the fire, he opened the book and flicked through its pages until he found the passage he was looking for.

"This," he said, "is a copy of *The Travels of Marco Polo*. He visited Iran in the late thirteenth century, not long after Alamut had been destroyed by the Mongols. He left the following account of what he'd heard there about the activities of the Lord of Alamut:

" 'The Sheikh was called in their language Alaodin. He had made in a valley between two mountains the biggest and most beautiful garden that was ever seen, planted with all the finest fruits in the world and containing the most splendid mansions and palaces that were ever seen, ornamented with gold and with likenesses of all that is beautiful on earth, and also four conduits, one flowing with wine, one with milk, one with honey, and one with water. There were fair ladies there and damsels, the loveliest in the world, unrivalled at playing every sort of instrument and at singing and dancing. And he gave his men to understand that this garden was Paradise . . . The Sheikh kept with him at his court all the youths of the country from twelve years old to twenty, all, that is, who shaped well as men at arms. These youths knew well by hearsay that Mahomet their prophet had declared Paradise to be made in such a fashion as I have described, and so they accepted it as truth. Now mark what follows. He used to put some of these youths in this Paradise, four at a time, or ten, or twenty, according as he wished. And this is how he did it. He would give them draughts that sent them to sleep on the spot. Then he had them taken and put in the garden, where they were wakened. When they awoke and found themselves in there and saw all the things I have told you of, they believed they were really in Paradise . . .

" 'Now the Sheikh held his court with great splendour and magnificence and bore himself most nobly and convinced the simple mountain folk round about that he was a prophet. And when he wanted emissaries to send on some mission of murder, he would administer the drug to as many as he pleased; and while they slept he had them carried into his palace. When these youths awoke and found themselves in the castle within the palace, they were amazed and by no means glad, for the Paradise from which they had come was not a place that they would ever willingly have left. They went forthwith to the Sheikh and humbled themselves before him, as men who believed that he was a great prophet. When he asked them whence they came, they would answer that they came from Paradise, and that this was in truth the Paradise of which Mahomet had told their ancestors; and they would tell their listeners all that they had found there. And the others who heard this and had not been there were filled with a great longing to go to this Paradise; they longed for death so that they might go there, and looked forward eagerly to the day of their going.

" 'When the Sheikh desired the death of some great lord . . . he would take some of these Assassins of his and send them wherever he might wish, telling them that he was minded to despatch them to Paradise: they were to go accordingly and kill such and such a man; if they died on their mission, they would go there all the sooner. Those who received such a command obeyed it with a right good will, more readily than anything else they might have been called on to do. Away they went and did all that they were commanded. Thus it happened that no one ever escaped when the Sheikh of the Mountain desired his death.' "

Rostoworoski grinned and closed the book.

37

THOUSAND ISLANDS
20–21 December 1979

When he had replaced the book, Rostoworoski returned to his armchair. He sat for a moment, as if in thought, then spoke.

"That, of course, is mostly legend," he said, "but it was based on some hard fact. Hasan's *feda'is* were very well trained for the tasks they had to perform. They were taught foreign languages, the ceremonies of other religions, the etiquette used at different courts, how to use disguises. As Marco Polo says, their chief would send them to the palace of an enemy of the faith; the chosen assassin would play a part there as a servant or a musician or whatever, win people's confidence over a period of months or, in some cases, even years, until the command came to strike down the victim.

"If you think back to our friend Polo's account, you'll see that his version of things is just an exaggerated reflection of the truth, blown up out of proportion by the real terror the Assassins inspired everywhere they went. It wasn't long before any suspicious death was laid at their door. Nobody felt safe, nobody was safe. Maybe they got high on hashish, maybe not. But it wasn't a drug that made the *feda'is* such deadly killers, it was their sheer fanaticism, their ruthless dedication to a cause, and the totally systematic way they went about the job of murder. There'd been assassins all through history, but it was the Ismaili *feda'is* who gave us the name.

"But," said the old man, changing his tone abruptly, "if no one objects, I'd like another cup of coffee. And perhaps just a drop or two of whiskey in it."

Randall and Fereshteh smiled and stood up. Rostoworoski led them into the kitchen where they brewed coffee. Rostoworoski poured three cups and added more than a couple of drops of whiskey to each. They knew it was not intended just to keep out the cold. After about a minute, Randall broke the silence.

"Juliusz, what you've been telling us sounds almost unbelievable. But surely there aren't any Assassins, Ismaili Assassins, still around today."

Rostoworoski sipped his coffee thoughtfully before speaking. "I don't know, Peter, I just don't know. From what you've been telling me and from the content of the letter I decoded, it wouldn't seem very farfetched to say that there are. But who they are, where they've come from—that's another question, and one I can't answer.

"Of course, the original Assassins died out, more or less. By the thirteenth century, the groups in Iran had lost much of their strength; then, in 1256, the Mongols invaded Iran and destroyed all the Ismaili fortresses in the process, Alamut included. Those Ismailis who survived went underground or fled to India, where they made converts and became known as Khojas, a peaceful community who preferred to forget the ways of their ancestors. A few stayed in Iran, as I said, but they kept themselves pretty much to themselves. Then, in the 1830s, the leader of the Iranian Ismailis, a man called Aga Khan Mahallati, became governor of Kerman. In 1843 he rebelled against the central government, but he was defeated and fled to Bombay. The present Aga Khan is a direct descendant, and he's recognized as Imam of the Ismailis throughout the world.

"Nowadays you can find Ismailis in India, East Africa, Syria, Afghanistan, and in quite a few other places. As Fereshteh knows, they're completely quietist. They don't mix in politics, they keep a low profile, and avoid religious extremism like the plague—the diametrical opposite of Hasan al-Sabbah's Assassins.

"But since last night, I've been asking myself one question: what if a group still existed, faithful to Hasan's policies and methods? Or what if someone had decided to revive them? If that's what's happened, this could very well blow up into something very serious."

The old man stopped talking and stared into space ahead of him, his mind held by thoughts he could not bring himself to vocalize. Moments passed during which no one spoke, the eyes of the younger man and the girl focused on Rostoworoski's face. When he spoke again at last, there was a tightness in his voice, a deep seriousness in his tone which caused goose pimples to rise on the backs of Randall's hands.

"Peter, you told me last night that when you were interrogating this man Nava'i, the one who tried to kill the President, he admitted the Mahdi and his followers in Mecca were members of his group. What else did he tell you about that?"

Randall shook his head. "Nothing. Even that was mostly our interpretation of what he said, his talk about the Sword being unsheathed in the Sanctuary, about it being a person. But he told us nothing else about it, and Saudi intelligence isn't very cooperative over the issue. There was a big shake-up in their General Intelligence Directorate two years ago, and we still haven't been able to reestablish good contacts at all the necessary levels."

The old man tapped his fingers slowly on the table. "If the two events were coordinated, it implies a mastermind planning things on a massive scale, much wider than we think. What you've told me about drugs and arms deals suggests something like that. Look what happened after they took the mosque in Mecca—it damned near sparked off a holy war against this country. I dread to think what might have happened if Nava'i had succeeded.

"Just look at what's been going on and see if it doesn't make some kind of sense to you. For years these people have been buying enough arms to equip a small army, and you tell me they may even have some rockets from this West German outfit. I don't know what they plan to do with them, but it isn't going to help the situation down in the Gulf. The Saudis have been building up their arms as fast as possible; the Kuwaitis, the United Arab Emirates, they've all been rushing to arm themselves to the teeth—Skyhawks, Mirages, conventional missiles of just about every type, Chieftain tanks; you name it, they've got it. The Russians have been piling stuff into Iraq for years till they've nowhere left to put it. Turkey's unstable, Pakistan's in an unholy mess, Afghanistan's been taken over by Marxists, the Communists in Ethiopia seem ready to take over Somalia. The whole stinking region's one big powderkeg and it's ready to blow up in all our faces.

"And right in the middle of all this we've got a highly organized group of religious lunatics who look as if they want to spark off some kind of final holy war. They may be crazy, but they may actually succeed in doing just that. It may not be the holy war they envisage, but it could be the one war that really will end all wars."

That afternoon, Randall read the book he had been given on the Assassins while Fereshteh and the old man laughed and chatted in the kitchen. Their gloom of the morning had worn off, but Peter's deepened as he read. At times, it was hard to believe that he was reading sober history, not legend, and by the time he had finished, he understood why the Pole had been so worried. If someone had brought back the methods and the fanaticism of Hasan al-Sabbah and his bands of devotees, then the danger for the world was immense. Randall remembered the faces of the seven men in a blood-soaked room in Qolhak, the cold desperation of the seven captured in the *zurkhane*, the look of calm detachment in Nava'i's eyes as he lay in his hospital bed, and he knew that no force on earth could stop such a group should it achieve a major breakthrough. They were not finished; of that he was certain. The scale and range of their arms deals alone told him that they were far from small in numbers, that for every one killed, dozens, perhaps hundreds lay waiting for their turn.

It was in those moments that Randall's sense of purpose was renewed, his determination resurrected. The desire for revenge, the need to restore a balance that had been a memory for a while became a necessity once more; but it was not mere revenge that drove him now. He now knew a different fear from the kind he had experienced in Vietnam. That had been raw, metallic, centered in the longing to come out alive. This was smooth and almost delicate, insidious as poison, and all-pervading. It threatened more than his personal survival. Now, as he sat in Rostoworoski's cabin, he realized that he could only master his fear by bringing that vision out of the shadows in which it lurked and confronting it in the full light of day.

When Rostoworoski and Fereshteh came back into the living room, they found Randall gazing into the fire, his thoughts far away.

"Are you all right, Peter?" the girl asked, concern in her voice. Her talk with the old man had straightened out several things for her. She now understood much that had previously puzzled and confused her. Rostoworoski had told her what he knew about Peter's last months in Iran, about Fujiko, about his long conversation with Death. He did not know all the details, and there was much he had left unsaid, but what he had said had brought her a certain peace. The night when she had gone to Randall's bed, she had clung to him, not caring who he was or where he would go when the morning came. Her hands had fallen away and she had slept, and in the morning, she had risen and dressed, embarrassed somehow by the sharing of his bed, even though they had shared nothing more. But now she began to see him more clearly, as a man, not a CIA agent.

Randall started, then sat up and smiled. "I was miles away," he said. "I'm sorry. Is it late? I should have come for you, told you I'd finished."

"And what do you think, Peter?" Rostoworoski asked, his voice even, the question pitched neutrally, as if by an academic tutor with no personal interest in the matter one way or another.

"I agree with you. They could be very dangerous. We have to stop them."

"How do you propose to do that?"

"Go back to Iran, pick up the trail there, finish what I began a year ago."

Rostoworoski said nothing. There was nothing he could say to dissuade Randall from what seemed a futile and dangerous gesture. The younger man knew already all that he could say, knew the risks, knew how little or how much chance there was of success. The Pole knew better than to try talking him out of it. In his years with the OSS and CIA, he had seen many men with the same look on their faces, and he knew that for such men there could be no turning back. It was something he had learned to live with, watching in silence as someone went out to meet an almost certain death. Few of them had ever come back, and those that had had been changed. It was another sort of death, gentler perhaps, but more cruel.

Fereshteh sat beside Peter, conscious that here was a territory into which she could not venture. She was not excluded because she was a woman—that was something she knew and recognized immediately, something her upbringing in an Iranian family had taught her to understand and at least tolerate, though never quite forgive. But this was something different, something she had seen only once before, in the eyes of a boy she had known when she was sixteen, when he had come back from Vietnam. She knew that now, as then, she could not intrude, but she could try to help.

"Peter," she said, "I don't know what sort of plans you have, what you intend to do once you get to Iran. But I think you need more information. You need to be able to find them—not just a handful in a room somewhere, half a dozen at a time, but the heart, the center. I've been thinking about how you could get that information, and I think I know the answer.

"In New York there's an institute that carries out research into Ismailism. It's called the Ismaili Research Foundation, and it's attached to Columbia University. They have offices on Riverside Drive. Some of the academic staff are American, and I'm sure they'll cooperate. If anyone knows about the people we're looking for, they will."

Randall grew thoughtful. He knew Fereshteh was right, that they needed information above all, and that without it there was no hope of success. But now that he had decided to go back, he wanted to leave for Tehran immediately, without any detours. It was left to Rostoworoski to make up his mind for him.

"She's right," said the old man, "without more information, you're as good as dead. They've been ahead of you all along, protected by your ignorance. Now it's your turn. Learn everything you can, find out where they are, who's behind them, what their strengths are, their weaknesses. Go back to New York, Peter. Begin the hunt there."

Rostoworoski was right. Randall lifted his head and nodded. He was an intelligence agent, not a hit man. He was trained to outthink his adversary, not outbludgeon him.

"Juliusz," he said, "I'll need your help. I must have a new passport, one that will get me into Iran without trouble. And I'll need backup documents to go with it. Money I can fix in New York. I have safe-deposit boxes there that I can draw on. Nobody else knows they exist. But I need a contact for the papers—can you do that for me?"

Rostoworoski nodded. "That's easy; I can arrange it this evening. I know someone in New York who can do that sort of work. His prices are high, very high. But he's good, the best. No one has ever been arrested for carrying documents he's made. He'll start work tonight, finish the job tomorrow, except for your photograph. You can take that when you go to see him."

"There's just one thing," Fereshteh broke in.

The Pole raised his eyebrows. He knew what it was.

"He'll need two passports," she said. "I'm going too."

The knocking came at two that morning. Randall woke at once, alerted by the vibrations dying away through the empty house. It came again, sharp and insistent. Someone was hammering at the door. He heard the door of Rostoworoski's room open and the sound of slippered feet on the wooden floor outside. He climbed out of bed, shivering in the unaccustomed cold, and put on his coat, slipping his gun into the pocket. When he opened the bedroom door, the old man had already gone down the stairs and was walking through the living room. The knocking went on: whoever it was didn't intend to go away. Randall started slightly as the door of Fereshteh's room opened and she too came out onto the landing.

There was the sound of voices, soft at first, then rising. With a shock, Randall recognized the voice of the caller. It was Howard Straker, insisting that he be allowed in, that he knew Randall and the girl were with the Pole. Rostoworoski indignantly denied that he had seen Randall or that he was staying with him, but Straker was determined to come in and search the house for himself, and in spite of the old man's protests, he pushed his way into the house. Randall turned to Fereshteh and told her to pack two bags quickly, then headed for the stairs and went down.

"Hello, Howard," he said, "it took you a while. I thought your boys were better than that. Now that you've found me, you can leave again, because I'm not coming back to Washington with you."

Straker took a step toward Randall, then paused, uncertain of the other's mood.

"Peter," he began, "I don't understand. Why did you run? What made you try that stupid getaway after Wooster Street? Why didn't you just bring the girl back to Langley like we asked? We only wanted to help her, talk to her."

"Like hell you did," said Randall. "She told me all about Gorman's stinking offer, about your plan to make some kind of deal with those scum back in Tehran. How long have you been playing your little games, Howard? When did it all start? After Nava'i got to talking? Or before that, at the start of the hostage crisis maybe? Or even earlier, back in Iran, while I was still in the hospital? Or were you and Stewart planning it all from the very beginning and just forgot to tell me— was that it? You can tell me now, Howard, and then you can get out."

Straker grew pale. He had not expected this barrage from Randall.

"It wasn't like that, Peter," he protested. "You don't understand. This is something recent. It wasn't my idea. I hate the whole thing, but I'm . . ."

"Just acting under orders, Howard? Seems like I've heard that somewhere before."

"It's true, Peter, I swear it. This goes high up, at policy level. We want to get the hostages out, and then we have to get a foothold in the country again. The stakes are very high, you've no idea . . ."

"So you thought you'd make a deal with people who just tried to kill the President! You guys amaze me, you really do. But you can count me out. I've more important things to do. I've got scores to settle."

Straker's face altered, grew hard. He shook his head gently from side to side. "That's all in the past, Peter. We're in the present now, and you're coming back to Langley with me: you and the girl. I've got two men and a jeep outside. Don't make things difficult for me, Peter. I'm not in charge of this operation, I have no authority. They sent me because I know you, because I asked them to. The men in charge don't give a damn about you, Peter. They'll kill you if you threaten to make a break, tell anyone what you've heard about the operation. If word gets out that we've been planning this, all hell could break loose —not just in Iran, but throughout the Middle East. Not to mention the liberals here as well. So please, Peter, just cooperate with me, come back to Langley and bring the girl, and everything will be OK. We'll forget this, put it down as a temporary lapse, the effect of the shooting last year. Go upstairs, get dressed, then tell the girl she's coming along too. And I'm afraid you'll have to come with us as well, Juliusz," he continued, turning to Rostoworoski.

He stopped dead, frozen in his tracks. The old man was standing face-to-face with him, a gun in his hand pointed directly at Straker. Randall noticed that his hands were no longer shaking.

"Peter," said the Pole, "go upstairs for Fereshteh. I'll keep Straker occupied until you're well away. You'll have to deal with his friends on your own."

As he spoke, Fereshteh appeared at the head of the stairs, dressed in outdoor gear and carrying two bags. Draped over one bag were Randall's clothes. She came down quickly, her eyes on the strange group by the door. Randall turned to meet her, grabbed his clothing, and dressed rapidly. When he was ready, he took one of the bags.

"The jeep's out at the back, Peter," said Rostoworoski, his eyes still fixed on Straker. "The key's in the ignition and there's plenty of gas in the tank. Keep the front of the house to your back and drive straight ahead for half a mile, then go right at forty-five degrees. After another quarter mile, you'll make out the land in the distance. There's a moon tonight so you should be able to see well. Look out for a single tree, much higher than the rest, right on the bank. Keep straight for it. Whatever you do, don't get far off that line; the ice is weak in parts and you'll go straight through. Goodbye, Peter, Fereshteh. And good luck."

They headed for the kitchen. At the door, they turned together.

"Thank you, Juliusz," Randall said. "Thank you for everything. If I make it, I'll try to let you know. If I don't . . ."

Straker's voice broke in suddenly.

"Miss Ahmadi," he began, "I trust you know what you're doing. Or have these gentlemen here explained exactly what they're getting you into? If you come back to Washington with me, I can guarantee immunity for you and complete safety. You can have protection from whoever you're running from. But once you go out of that door, I can't guarantee anything. Do you understand what I'm saying?"

"I understand perfectly." The hardness in her voice surprised even Randall. "Why don't you save yourself a lot of trouble and go find some sucker who doesn't understand?"

Outside, the cold was fierce and the moon shed a brilliant, uncanny light over everything. They found the jeep and climbed in, throwing their bags into the back. Randall turned the ignition key and prayed silently that the engine would start first time; it did. The wheels spun on the frozen ground as he pushed down on the pedal, heading past the house and down toward the river. He caught a glimpse of Straker's jeep as they rushed past, then they were at the river and running out onto the ice. Beneath them, the wheels began to drum on the close-packed surface, raising soft echoes from the water that flowed by underneath. Just how far underneath Randall did not like to think.

Lights flashed on and the engine of the other jeep roared into life. Seconds later, the beam of its headlamps flashed in Randall's driving mirror as they spun around in pursuit. Grimly, Randall clutched the wheel and pressed harder on the pedal. In spite of the chains around his tires, he had to fight to keep the wheels under control. The steering wheel bucked and tried to wrench itself away from him as the jeep fought against the line of travel, trying to tear itself off into a deadly spin across the ice. They were going much too fast for safety. He glanced at the milometer: the half-mile point was coming up rapidly.

Ten seconds later, Randall turned the wheel, heading the jeep right at forty-five degrees. Suddenly, the wheels locked and the vehicle, still doing over sixty, was thrown into a vicious spin. Desperately, Randall fought to steer into the spin, the wheel wracking in his hands like a wild animal, the jeep careering madly across the ice, at every moment threatening to tilt and topple over. It seemed endless, but it was only a matter of half a minute before the spinning and the lurching ended and they came to a halt.

"Are you all right?" Randall breathed, unable to see clearly in the dark.

"Yes, I'm fine," replied Fereshteh. "But don't do that again, please. I gave up roller coasters when I was fourteen."

The engine had died, so he reached for the ignition. As he did so, he caught sight of headlights to the left, coming straight for them. There was an explosion and a side window of their jeep shattered. They were shooting! Straker had been telling the truth. They would kill him rather than let him escape with his information.

Randall switched off his lights, opened the door, and leapt out onto the ice, feeling it crunch and crack beneath his feet. How far had they come from the safe areas? He ran around the jeep, his eyes on the lights rushing toward them. He could not judge how far away they were, but they were closing quickly. Without pausing, he took his magnum from his pocket, aimed low in the direction of the oncoming jeep, and fired rapidly, emptying the chamber, bullet after bullet in quick succession. He could not see what effect, if any, his shots had had. Quickly, he reached for fresh cartridges and began reloading, his eyes fixed all the time on the lights ahead, which were eating up the gap between them with immense speed.

It happened too quickly for the men in the other jeep to take evasive action. Randall's bullets had smashed the ice directly in the path of the oncoming vehicle, weakening and splintering it. As the jeep reached the point at which he had fired, its front left wheel slammed into the broken ice, shattering it further with the impact of its tire chains, throwing the fast-moving vehicle heavily over. It hit the ice with great force, setting up fast-widening cracks that joined with those already made by Randall's bullets. The thick ice buckled and cracked, then gave at the center with a loud breaking noise, and the jeep disappeared into the deadly, freezing waters below. Within seconds, the lights had vanished, submerged in the darkness of the river beneath, and Randall could see nothing of them. It was as if they had never been. He wondered if Gorman had been a passenger. He hated Straker and Straker's superiors back in Washington for what they had just made him do. He had had no wish to kill Americans.

But there had been no choice. Slowly, he returned to the jeep and climbed in. Fereshteh sat immobilized, her face frozen in shock. There was nothing he could say to ease the horror she felt. He switched on the lights, turned the ignition key, and let in the clutch. "Which way?" he asked.

She turned and looked at him, her eyes seeking reassurance that he could not give. He let out the clutch and drove off to the right, hoping it would bring them to land.

38

Friday, 21 December 1979

Peter and Fereshteh had abandoned the jeep as soon as they arrived in Cape Vincent and had retrieved their hired car from Dan Willis' garage. Willis had been none too pleased to be woken at such an hour, but a sizable tip soon made him feel a lot better about it. As they were about to leave, Randall took him quietly aside.

"Listen," he said, "I'd as soon you didn't say anything about us being here. If her husband gets to know about it, there'll be big trouble; I'm sure you understand. So if anybody comes snooping around, you haven't seen us."

Willis nodded, his hand still clutching the bundle of notes Randall had passed to him. He wasn't sure he much approved of what this man and woman were up to. But he didn't like snoopers either, and he didn't like trouble. Why should he say anything to anybody?

Driving cautiously, they arrived in New York after 10:00 P.M. and abandoned the car on the Upper East Side before taking the subway and then walking to West Twenty-third Street in Chelsea, where they checked into the Chelsea Hotel. Randall chose the Chelsea for its special brand of anonymity, an anonymity guaranteed by the hotel's strange and varied clientele. Mark Twain had stayed there, as had Dylan Thomas and Arthur Miller. More recently Bob Dylan and Leonard Cohen had put up at the hotel and written songs about it. It was cheap and rambling, and no one cared much who anyone else was or, more importantly, what they did. No one raised their eyebrows at the Chelsea, and that was just what Randall wanted.

He booked two adjoining rooms without a connection. He could tell that Fereshteh needed to be alone, wanted privacy more than the sense of security a connecting room could offer. Last night she had seen him kill two men, albeit in self-defense. The fragile bond of trust that had grown between them at Rostoworoski's had almost been broken. She had learned that he was not working for Straker, but there were still barriers of uncertainty between them, and she needed time to think.

They spent the early afternoon resting, and after a very late lunch, they talked things over. Fereshteh still wanted to accompany Peter to Tehran; he was determined that she should stay in New York.

"I want to come with you," she said. "I can't do anything here on my own."

"No, Fereshteh, it's much too dangerous. What I have to do there will involve risks, serious risks. This business doesn't involve you as it involves me. And I need you in New York—there are things here that have to be done."

"Such as?"

"Such as getting a report about all this to the right people should the need arise. If anything happens to me in Iran, you and Juliusz will be the only people to know what's been going on. And Straker will make damn sure Juliusz doesn't speak to anybody. I'm going to write the report tonight. If we learn anything at your institute tomorrow, I'll add that to it. Then it'll be in your hands either until I return or until you know something has gone wrong—that I won't be returning."

Suddenly, she stretched her hand across the table and held his tightly.

"I don't like being left behind," she said, "like the helpless female in a B-movie. I can be useful in Tehran. Nobody knows me there; I can go places it might be dangerous for you to visit."

He took her hand and gripped it.

"I wish that were true. But it isn't. A woman on her own can't do anything in Tehran now, even wrapped in a chador. You haven't been there for years, you've no idea how to behave. You'd make mistakes. Fatal mistakes."

She took her hand away, resigned, unable to argue against what he said, what she knew was true.

"And if New York gets dangerous?" she asked, her voice almost inaudible to him across the table.

He frowned, then shook his head.

"Why should it?" he said. "No one knows you're here, no one has any reason to look for you."

"It was dangerous before," she said, her voice rising slightly. "It

could get that way again. There might be some people who don't
know I ever left."

"Maybe it would be better then if you left the city, went to Europe
perhaps." Why was he sending her away, distancing her, when he
wanted her to stay?

She flared up suddenly, the strength of anger and frustration in her
voice taking him by surprise.

"And just when the hell do you expect me to get back to some sort
of normal life? Jesus, I've been chased by gunmen, my mother's been
killed in our own house, I've got the CIA breathing down my neck,
and you tell me just to go away and forget about it! New York's my
home! I have a house here and a boss who hasn't heard from me in
days. I attend classes in the evenings, I have friends I spend time
with. You're a professional, they pay you to do this kind of thing.
You're probably good at it. I kind of think you are. You can go on
running for the rest of your life and it's still all part of the job.

"But I am scared—scared and angry and alone. This business does
involve me, it involves me more than it does you, because until it's
finished I can't even walk down the street I've lived on since I was a
kid, without looking over my shoulder and jumping every time a car
slows down behind me. I can't go to my friends, because there's no
way they can understand and because I have no right to risk their lives
by getting them involved. My parents are dead. And any one of my
relatives could belong to this sect. So now, Mr. Intelligence Agent,
just what do you suggest I do?"

She was shaking and her eyes were filled with tears. He looked at
her, knowing there was no answer, that words of comfort would be
ironic and out of place. He had been so concerned with larger issues,
with the lives of presidents and the weaving of international plots,
that he had lost sight of her in the midst of them. As he looked at
Fereshteh, groping for a way to break the silence that had grown up
around them, he realized that, for him, her life had become more
important, more immediate than any of those other issues. She had
become a focus for his concern, just as all that had mattered in the
beginning had been Fujiko and her death, that small death that everyone but Randall had forgotten.

"Listen," he said at last, "stay in New York, here in the hotel, for a
few days, a week perhaps. Once I know how things are in Tehran, I'll
contact you, and if it seems safe, you can fly out. If anything happens

here, I'll give you a number through which you can reach me. That's the best I can suggest. Will it be enough?"

She nodded, the sudden anger subsiding as it had flared up. She did not smile, but reached out her hand once more, and this time he held it without speaking.

Randall left Fereshteh in the hotel that evening in order to call on Rostoworoski's friend. A visit to a safe-deposit box he kept in a twenty-four-hour facility gave him enough money to make a down payment for the documents he would need. The man lived in the Williamsburg section of Brooklyn, the old Jewish quarter, and was identified only by the name Yaakov. Randall felt oddly conspicuous in this part of New York, with its tightly packed streets punctuated by signs in Hebrew and Yiddish. Most of the shops were closed for the Sabbath, which had begun at sunset, and the streets were almost empty.

Randall found the address without difficulty. It was a small Hebrew and Yiddish printing shop on Lee Avenue, the sign indecipherable to Randall and the window grimy with years of dust, the mezuzah on the doorpost rusted in place. He knocked and waited. Yaakov was a long time in coming, but at last a shape appeared behind the net curtain that covered the door. The lock turned and the door swung open slowly. Yaakov was, as Randall had suspected, a Polish Jew who had worked with Rostoworoski during the war. Bent now and white-haired, he appeared frail and unwell, but the eyes that looked Peter up and down were sharp and the hands that he held to his chest did not shake.

"Yes," he said, "what is it? Don't you know *Shabbes* began this evening? Come back tomorrow night or Sunday morning. Come tomorrow after *Habdala*, I can see you then."

The old Jew made to close the door, but Randall placed his hand on it, a look of urgency on his face.

"Please," he said, "I must see you. I've come from Juliusz Rostoworoski; he sent me to you. I need your help, and it must be tonight."

The man's eyebrows lifted as he looked more closely at Randall.

"You've come from Juliusz?" he said. "Why did you not say so? If he thinks it is important, it must be so. Is a life in danger?"

"Yes. Many lives."

"In that case, come in. For many lives, for even one life, the *Shabbes* may be broken."

Randall stepped into the shop. Yaakov ushered him through a small door at the back, into a storeroom, and then through a second door into the room that served as his kitchen, dining room, living room, and study. On the bare wooden table stood candles, the remains of two challah loaves, and a small, unpretentious *Kiddush* goblet. The old man's wife had died three years before, but he continued to observe the Sabbath meal here in her memory, as if she were still with him. He motioned Randall toward a chair and sat opposite him.

"You need papers, yes?"

Randall nodded.

"Many?"

"Not so many. One passport, two, possibly three others."

"For when?"

"Tomorrow, Sunday at the latest. Can you do it?"

"It depends how difficult they are, how good they have to be. Will lives depend on their being good?"

Randall nodded. "Yes. My life."

"And on your life?"

"Other lives, perhaps a great many others. I dare not think how many. There have already been deaths. Too many deaths."

Yaakov frowned and shook his head sorrowfully.

"It still continues. The killing and the waste. It is endless, it is the one thing that never dies. You know Juliusz?"

"Yes, I know him. He is a close friend."

"Is he well?"

"Yes," Randall lied.

"I am glad. I care for him deeply, like a brother." The old man paused, memories in his eyes. There was a silence, then Yaakov spoke.

"It is late. Let us begin."

As Randall spoke with the old man in New York, a top-level meeting was being held at CIA headquarters at Langley. Those present were the Agency's six top policy men. It was they who had decided several days earlier to go ahead with the plan of making direct contact with the group behind Nava'i, and it was to them that Howard Straker had been made directly responsible for the running of the operation. Now he was attempting to explain what had gone wrong. He spoke in a low but firm voice.

"We were lucky to find Randall. The local police still send routine reports on anyone who visits Rostoworoski, and we file them for future reference. I ran a check on anyone Randall might contact and came across a note saying the Pole had had visitors the day before, a man and a woman. We found both Randall and the girl there, and I think I could have persuaded them to come back but Rostoworoski interfered."

"Do you have any idea why he should have done that, Mr. Straker?" asked one of the six men, a gray-haired Negro with a serious, lined face familiar to generations of international politics students at Harvard.

Straker shook his head. "I can understand his interfering maybe, but not the way he did it. He would have shot me, I know that."

"You think he was outraged by our proposal to collaborate with this underground organization, that he disapproved?" This time Straker's questioner was a younger man, a lawyer who had chosen some three years earlier the anonymity of behind-the-scenes decision making in preference to the seat in the Supreme Court that he had always known would be his one day. Moral issues were still his principal preoccupation.

Straker shook his head once more. "No, sir. Rostoworoski has been involved with worse than this. He played a major part in the coup that overthrew Mossadeq and put the Shah back in power, and during the years he worked here, he handled much more sensitive material. He was a pragmatist, a man who took the widest possible view."

"Then it was something else, something he knew perhaps."

"I think so, sir. He's being questioned downstairs now. I don't think he'll hold out on us for very long."

A third man leaned forward, his eyes fixed on Straker, as if seeking to hold the agent immobile in his chair. General Burton was the military representative on the panel, and his priorities did not include moral niceties.

"I understand, Mr. Straker, that Rostoworoski has already told you quite a lot. I have a report here which gives a verbatim transcript of his first interview; it makes interesting reading. Do you believe any of it?"

"Sir?"

"Do you believe any of this stuff about Assassins and an Eagle's Nest and the Lord of Alamut? Does it make any sense to you?"

Straker returned Burton's gaze without flinching. He knew what to say.

"No, sir. No, it doesn't make any sense to me. It's like something out of the Arabian Nights, pure fantasy. Maybe the historical portion is true, but it's crazy to imagine anything like that now. I think Rostoworoski's covering something. Or else he's cracked."

"What could he be covering? What would he have to gain?"

"Time, sir. Time for Randall and the girl to make their getaway."

"And if they get away, what happens then?" The black academic spoke again, his face creased more deeply than ever. He had a good idea what might happen then.

Straker paused before replying. They all knew the answer already, but it had to be spoken all the same.

"I'm not sure, sir. They may just be escaping, thinking of nothing else. Or they may plan to go public, to reveal what we planned to do."

"Would anyone believe them?" asked the lawyer.

"Some people, yes. Enough. But what happens here doesn't matter. It's in Iran that it really matters. Khomeini will believe them, Khomeini and anyone who follows him. It could sound the death knell for the hostages. It could even lead to war."

There was a silence in the room. Then a fourth voice rang out, the voice of the Policy Committee's leading strategist, John B. Fitzpatrick.

"So Randall is dangerous. He will have to be found and stopped."

"And if he can't be stopped, sir?" Straker asked.

"Then he must be eliminated."

39

NEW YORK CITY
Saturday, 22 December 1979

Fereshteh spent Saturday morning at the Iranian Consulate making arrangements for obtaining a passport to replace the one she had "lost"; a lot of money passed hands before the surly clerk there would agree to her legitimate request. Should it at any point prove necessary for her to leave the country, she could do so without dangerous delay once the passport was ready. The clerk told her to call back on Monday. After a quick lunch near the consulate, she went shopping in midtown Manhattan, buying clothes, luggage, and the numerous other things they both needed.

At ten o'clock on Saturday, while Fereshteh visited the consulate, Randall arrived at the Ismaili Research Foundation on Riverside Drive, behind Barnard College. He was tired. The past few days had taken their toll, but he knew that much worse lay ahead of him, that there would be little or no time for rest until he had found and acted against the people whom he sought. It was like climbing a mountain in a fog, with no way back and the summit hidden and out of reach. There were so few footholds, so many places where he might slip and fall, and at times he wanted that. He wanted to relax, let go his hold, and fall effortlessly into the abyss.

Randall had telephoned on Friday afternoon to make an appointment with the director of the foundation. He had said as little as possible on the phone, telling the director's secretary only that he had an urgent matter to discuss and that he required advice on an aspect of Ismailism. She had asked his name and institution, and he had told her he was Dr. James Saunders, formerly with the University of Tehran. He did not think they would be able to check that.

He was met by the director in person, a tall, graying man who looked like a successful diplomat or a lawyer. Randall saw immediately that he was less an academic than an administrator. He appeared to

be an Arab, possibly an Egyptian or a Syrian. His jet-black hair was
winged with gray streaks that had been brushed back carefully as if to
render their possessor more distinguished. Randall guessed he was
about forty-five and that his manners would be impeccable.

"Dr. Saunders?" he asked, one hand extended in greeting. His
gestures were polished and mannered, the rituals of a confident and
accomplished man. But Randall began to distrust him almost from
the start. "Please," he continued, "do sit down. I'll have some coffee
brought in. Make yourself comfortable."

At once, Randall recognized the Oxford intonation, the breeding
that the rich of other countries could still buy in England. How hard,
he wondered, had this man worked to become an English gentleman?
He would not be easy to judge, not in the short time Randall had
available. There were layers to him, and Randall would have to move
carefully, revealing as little as possible, probing the man without
knowing whether he could trust him in the end.

Randall had taken a tremendous risk by coming here. If Rostoworoski was right, any member of the Ismaili sect could conceivably
belong to the subgroup whose existence he had postulated. There
would be no way of knowing in advance who or where they were.
Randall already knew they had eyes and ears everywhere. He could be
walking into a trap, one that he might not even hear as it closed
behind him. But there was no option and no time now for more
roundabout enquiries.

The director returned in moments, his practiced smile ready for
Randall.

"I'm terribly sorry," he said, "I forgot to introduce myself. My
name is 'Abd al-Latif al-Shidyaq, the director of the foundation. You
must forgive me, but I doubt very much if I will be of much help to
you. That is, if your problem relates to Iranian Ismailism. You will, of
course, have realized that I am an Arab. I come from Salamiyya, to
the east of Hama in Syria. Most Syrian Ismailis come from around
there; it's been our main center since the middle of the last century.
But you will know that already, of course."

Randall could not be sure whether al-Shidyaq was merely being
polite or whether he was testing him. He shook his head.

"I'm afraid not. My knowledge of the Arab world is very limited. I
lived in Iran for a long time, but I've only made brief visits to some of
the countries on the Gulf."

"A la tatakallumu 'l-'Arabiyya?"

"No, I'm afraid not. I can read some Arabic, of course, but not speak it." Why had he sprung that on him? Was it another test? Or was Randall becoming paranoid, seeing traps where there were none?

There was a knock at the door, then al-Shidyaq's secretary entered carrying a tray of coffee and sweetmeats. The girl walked self-consciously across the room and set the tray down on a low table in front of the director's desk, between the chairs on which the two men sat. Randall noticed that she seemed ill at ease—whether on his account or the director's, he could not tell. She straightened, smiled nervously at Randall, and left the room.

Al-Shidyaq poured the coffee from a tall silver pot with an elegant, elongated spout. "I hope you like coffee in the authentic Arab fashion, Dr. Saunders," the director said. His hands moved efficiently, economically, manipulating the small handleless cups. The smile never left his face. Nor did it warm it. "Milk and sugar ruin good coffee; I like to drink mine as the Bedouin drink it, unsweetened. If it is too strong for you, I can ask Fatima to bring some milk."

Randall shook his head and smiled though he hated unsweetened Arab coffee. He found it strong and bitter and almost undrinkable. He lifted the cup and sipped. It tasted like medicine. He smiled again and reached for a piece of *halwa* from the plate in the center of the tray.

"How can I help you, Dr. Saunders?" It was the question for which Randall had been waiting, and it had come a little sooner than he had expected. Much would depend on how he answered it, on the care with which he broached the subject. Where to begin? How to begin? Move inch by inch, reveal a little at a time, probe gently until he found an opening. That had been his first thought. But then? Should he press harder into that opening or draw back if he found resistance? If he sensed danger, would there still be time or opportunity to withdraw?

"Initially, Dr. al-Shidyaq, I would like to know something of the Ismaili community here in New York. What percentage, for example, are Iranians or have contact with Iran."

"There are very few, Dr. Saunders, very few. A dozen, two dozen perhaps, who are known to us, that is. There may be more, those who are not active in the faith, and . . . others." Al-Shidyaq smiled and raised his cup to his lips.

"'Others?'" Randall responded, the question terse, probing. The *halwa* crumbled between his fingers onto the plate. Al-Shidyaq moved his head to the side, put down his cup, and refilled it.

"Yes, others," he said. "When I speak of ourselves, I mean Nizaris, of course. Khojas. But there are other Ismaili groups apart from ours. There are Musta'lis—they call them Bohoras in India. We have little contact with them."

"How many of them are Iranians, do you know?" Randall already sensed the distance in his host, a mounting reserve. Had he already touched a nerve?

"I am afraid I have little knowledge of these people, Dr. Saunders. But I think there are few Iranians among them. The Musta'lis live mostly in India. There are also some in East Africa and many in the Yemens." Al-Shidyaq felt a tiny stab of fear. Why had this man come? Where were his questions leading? "Perhaps if you explained the purpose of your questions, Dr. Saunders, I could be of more assistance. Is your interest centered mainly on the Ismaili community in New York?"

Randall put down his cup. He reached for a file he had brought with him. There could be no way around it. He had to show the papers. They were the way in. Saying nothing, he reached inside the file and took them out: the blue sheet with the cryptic letter, the full Persian transcription, and Rostoworoski's English translation.

"Perhaps these will simplify matters," he said, passing the sheets to al-Shidyaq. "Have you ever seen anything like this blue paper before? Does it mean anything to you, anything at all?"

The director's reactions were unmistakable: the sharp intake of breath, the look of recognition in the man's eyes. Recognition and fear. From the eyes, it flickered instantaneously across al-Shidyaq's face before being replaced as quickly by a look of impassivity, a vacancy of expression that tried to conceal some deep, hidden agitation. The Arab was frightened. What had frightened him?

Al-Shidyaq examined the papers as if scrutinizing them carefully, but Randall knew his mind was elsewhere, that his thoughts were whirling in an effort to find explanations and blocks for whatever questions were to follow. Half a minute passed slowly in tense silence, then al-Shidyaq shook his head with mannered deliberateness and passed the papers back to the American. His voice as he spoke was little changed, but Randall could detect a note of fear in it.

"I'm sorry, Dr. Saunders, but they mean nothing to me. I could not read the Persian, of course, but the English translation seemed quite clear. I have never read anything quite like it before. And I have never seen anything resembling the blue paper. It is certainly not an Ismaili document. May I ask where you found it or who gave it to you?" The stab of fear had grown to a scarcely controllable feeling of panic. He had difficulty maintaining his voice in the proper register. How had the American obtained such a document? What could his presence here mean?

Randall looked straight at al-Shidyaq, who was no longer smiling. The confident man of the world had been replaced by someone who was lonely and frightened. He knew something. And he was afraid.

"I'm sorry," Randall said. "I can't reveal that. But it was found in this country. In this city."

"Who are you, Dr. Saunders?" Al-Shidyaq's voice had grown cold. The urbane politeness had vanished, and had been replaced by a brusqueness edged with what was very nearly terror. "Where have you come from? Why have you come here?"

"I told you," Randall replied. "I came for information."

"I have no information for you. No information that can be of any help to you."

"I think you have," Randall retorted, his voice gentle but insistent. They were fencing now with sabers, not foils. "I think you have the information I need."

"You are mistaken, Dr. Saunders. Mistaken and rude. You have been misinformed. I have no information of the kind you seek. You will have to go elsewhere. There is no information here." Al-Shidyaq brought his hands together, held them tightly. A final gesture, precise and assured. He stood.

Randall nodded.

"I understand," he said. "I am sorry to have troubled you, Dr. al-Shidyaq. I shall not bother you again." It was a lie. He had to trouble him again. Al-Shidyaq was the key now; he must be persuaded to surrender whatever it was he knew. But not here. Not now.

Nothing more was said. Both men knew that the fear generated between them had become a bond to hold them together. Randall would try to draw the bond tighter, to use it as a weapon, a constricting, pressing force that would intensify al-Shidyaq's fear and uncertainty. The other would attempt to extricate himself from it, to escape Randall and thereby calm his own fears. But in so doing he would make mistakes, and when he did, Randall would be there, ready to profit by them. Except for one thing. There was no time, no time at all for such tactics.

Randall rose, shook hands with al-Shidyaq, and went to the door. He turned as he went out. The director stood, his eyes fixed on the American, watching him go. Randall noticed that one hand played nervously with the lapel of his immaculate jacket, rubbing a small spot where he had spilled a few drops of coffee. The coffee had been hot and bitter, and Randall could still taste it in his mouth where it had passed thinly over his tongue.

40

Randall waited behind the trees bordering Riverside Park on the other side of the Drive from the building housing the foundation. The icy cold clung to him like a blanket, chilling him, forcing him to move from time to time in order to keep warm. It was a long wait. Al-Shidyaq finally emerged just after one and headed east toward Broadway. Randall guessed he was going to take the subway home. He waited half a minute, then followed him.

The doctor walked nervously, glancing around from time to time as if afraid of being followed. Randall kept well behind but never let the man out of his sight. At Broadway, al-Shidyaq turned and headed directly for the nearest subway station. There was a short wait. A train arrived and he got on; he was going to downtown Manhattan. Randall jumped into the next coach and took a window seat, from which he could keep an eye on the door ahead.

At Columbus Circle, al-Shidyaq left the train. Randall waited a few moments, then followed, anxious not to lose him among the busy Saturday crowds. He changed lines, taking a northbound train up Central Park West and got out at the next station. Randall was still behind him. From time to time, the Arab glanced over his shoulder, but he was obviously inexperienced and knew none of the tricks that can force a tail to reveal himself. Randall shadowed him, still unseen.

When al-Shidyaq reached the corner of Seventy-second Street, he headed straight for the Dakota, a massive apartment building designed to look like a French château. Overlooking the park, it had been the first block of luxury apartments built in New York. Now, almost one hundred years later, it was still exclusive and expensive. Randall sighed. It would be almost impossible to get into the building unseen. Was this the man's home, he wondered, or had he come to visit someone? From the way the security guard in the lobby greeted him, Randall guessed the former.

He let a few minutes pass. Al-Shidyaq needed a little time to settle, to feel secure. Randall wondered again if he had a wife. A wife could be a complication. Or, just possibly, an asset. He waited. Finally, it was time. He took his official identification card from his pocket. There was a risk in showing it if the guard insisted on cross-checking, but it could save a lot of valuable time. He entered the lobby.

"Can I help you, sir?" The guard was polite but alert. Randall showed his card, a finger carefully obscuring his name. It was an official card; that was what mattered.

Before the guard could ask to examine the card more closely, Randall had replaced it in his pocket and started to talk.

"I'd like to have a word with one of your tenants, a Dr. al-Shidyaq. He isn't in any trouble but he may have information that could be useful to us."

"Yes, sir. Just one moment, I'll call him. What name shall I give?"

"It was on my card. Grant. Agent Grant." If asked, the man would say he had seen the name on Randall's card.

The guard went to his telephone on the lobby desk and dialed a number. There was a brief exchange, then he turned to Randall.

"Dr. al-Shidyaq would like you to explain the nature of your business, sir."

"I'm afraid I can't reveal that to a third party. I have to explain it to him in person."

A pause, another exchange. The guard turned.

"Very well, sir, he says he'll see you. Fifth floor, sir, apartment 511. The elevator's on your left, sir."

Al-Shidyaq was waiting outside the door of his apartment. When he saw Randall, he froze, but he did not go back inside.

"So," he said as Randall approached. "This is your true identity, Dr. Saunders. I take it your real name is Grant?"

"Grant will do," said Randall. "Let's go inside, Dr. al-Shidyaq. We have things to talk about."

"How did you find this place? Do you have authorization to enter my apartment? I'd like to see it first, please. Otherwise, I'll have to ask the guard to escort you out again." Al-Shidyaq was bluffing very well. But he was frightened.

Randall said nothing. He came up to the Arab, seized his arm, thrust him through the open door, and closed it.

"Sit down," Randall snapped. He had only one way of quickly overcoming the other man's fear, the fear that was holding him back from telling Randall what he knew. He had to frighten him more, make his own threat seem more real, more immediate, even if, as Randall knew, it was not.

"You can't . . ."

"Yes I can. Sit down." At all costs, Randall wanted to avoid force. He wanted cooperation, and he knew he would get it best if he first frightened then reassured his informant. He had to undermine his confidence to the point where he would need Randall to cling to. Only if nothing else worked would he consider violence. But now everything would depend on his voice and his eyes. Al-Shidyaq had to believe in him, had to be certain that Randall would do all he said he would if he did not tell him what he wanted to know.

Anger and fear battling in his eyes, al-Shidyaq sat down. Increase the anger, Randall thought; it will serve to sharpen the fear.

"You can't do this, Mr. Grant."

"I'm doing it. Or hadn't you noticed?" Randall's tone was insulting.

"You have no authority. I have rights."

"Not anymore, you don't. I just suspended them." Randall remained standing. The interrogator must always be higher than his subject. It was basic technique.

"I'm a foreign resident. I have a right to contact my consulate."

"Go right ahead. Just as long as you're sure you have good contacts back in Damascus, contacts in very high places."

"What do you mean, 'contacts'?" Panic was welling up inside al-Shidyaq. He felt paralyzed and disoriented. This could not be happening right here in his own apartment. What did the American mean? What did he want?

"I mean people who can explain to Syrian intelligence the nature of your links with the CIA, who can account for the extensive file we have on you, the work you've done for us back home."

"You're mistaken. There is no such file. I've never had contacts with the CIA. You have the wrong person." This was impossible; there were limits to what they could do. This was not Ba'athist Syria: this was America.

"What makes you so sure, Dr. al-Shidyaq? What do you know? What do you know of what we can and cannot do? You know nothing. Your file is being prepared at this very moment."

"You can't frighten me. I don't have to say anything. Your own law guarantees me certain rights. You are accountable, you are not above the law. No one is above the law." The American was bluffing, trying to scare him into talking. And if he talked, if he told him what he knew, it would be worse, far worse.

"You would be surprised at what we can do in the interests of national security. You are a threat to that security. The law guarantees you nothing." Randall paused, then recommenced.

"In just under one minute, Dr. al-Shidyaq, you are going to start talking. You are going to provide me with information, the information I asked you for this morning. Believe me, you will."

"I'm not afraid of you, Mr. Grant. You are overreaching your authority. I have nothing to tell you." Al-Shidyaq was growing confident. It was bluff, pure bluff. If the American had been about to do anything, he would have done it by now; he would not have wasted time making threats. He had not even raised a hand to hit him, had not even suggested violence. There were controls. This was America. He would be safe.

"In that case, Dr. al-Shidyaq, let me tell you what is going to happen to you. Please listen carefully, I shall not repeat myself. I will now pick up your telephone and dial a certain number. The phone will ring three times, then I will hang up. Five minutes later, a car will arrive outside this building. It will have tinted windows and untraceable number plates. Officially, it does not exist. Four men will come up to this apartment. The guard will not stop them; he will have received a phone call in the meantime. He will not even see them. The four men will escort you to their car and no one will stop them. If you try to signal to the guard, you will be amazed to find that he has become blind. If you try to call out, you will discover that he has gone deaf. You will be driven to a building somewhere outside New York and taken inside. It is a tall building, gray, windowless, with extremely thick walls. Like the car, it does not officially exist. Nothing can be heard through those walls, especially the screams of men in pain. They will put you in a small room, a very small room, without windows or lights. There is nothing in there, nothing. No one will come. No one will bring you food and water. No one will speak to you. They will leave you there for a day or three days or a week, perhaps longer. It will seem much, much longer to you. When they finally come for you—and they will come for you, they will not have forgotten about you—you will have lost track of time, you will be confused, you will be desperate to talk. They will talk with you for a little while. They will give you some food and water. And then they will return you to the little dark room. This process will continue until you tell them everything or you are dead. It really doesn't matter once you have gone there. You will not come out again in any case.

"In the meantime, other men will have taken your passport to a different building, this time in New York City. Tomorrow, your passport will have an exit stamp through John F. Kennedy Airport and an entry stamp through Cairo. There will be records of your having booked a direct flight there. There will be records of your departure and your arrival. Three days from now, your passport will be found in a deserted alleyway near the Hilton Hotel. There will be a record of your having stayed at the hotel. The Cairo police will make a search, but they will not find your body. That is not unusual. When your friends eventually make inquiries after you, they will be told what has happened. After a little while, they will pay for small advertisements in the papers. Do you understand me now, Dr. al-Shidyaq? Do you understand what we can and what we cannot do?"

Al-Shidyaq had become pale, like a man who has seen his own death in a dream. He wanted to be sick, but there was only the bitter taste of fear in his mouth. He sat absolutely still. His hands had stopped moving and his eyes did not blink. In his mind, he could see a car pass in Damascus, three men seated in the back, one of them wearing a white hood, like a flour sack. It was a memory that had long haunted him. When he spoke, it was almost in a whisper.

"You cannot do this. It is inhuman. You cannot do it." But he no longer believed himself.

Randall said nothing. He had taken away al-Shidyaq's last anchors, and the Arab turned at last, as Randall had known he would, to his tormentor for help. There was no other recourse. Where else could he go?

"Very well," he said, his voice dull and flat. "I will tell you all I know. It is not much, but you must be content with it. Please come with me. I have papers in my study that will help explain this matter to you."

Al-Shidyaq rose and Randall followed him to a small room lined with files. He switched on the light, took a key from his pocket, and opened a filing cabinet near the desk. From it he took several files and handed them to Randall.

"In these you will find a number of documents, several of them more or less identical to the talisman you showed me this morning. Most of these papers are letters from a man who calls himself the Imam Hasan al-Qa'im bi-amr Allah. He is the Hasan whose signature appears at the bottom of the letter you brought with you.

"Copies of similar letters have been sent to Ismailis in India, East Africa, and elsewhere—but to no effect. I have even heard that he has sent letters to the Musta'lis in India and the Yemens, but I have not seen them. Most of them are written in Arabic, but this man Hasan is an Iranian as, it appears, are most of his followers. That much you seem to have guessed.

"In these letters, he summons the Ismaili world to recognize him as the true Imam, their divinely appointed and inspired leader. As yet, however, he is only the head of a sect, a sect of which few of us had ever heard until quite recently. The first letters began to arrive in 1975. Last year he sent out a lengthy epistle in which he gives an account of his sect and its beliefs. You'll find a copy in that second file.

"They call themselves Irshadis. It seems they became a separate group in the middle of the last century. I will have to bore you with a little history, but I promise to be brief. In 1817, the head of the Ismailis in Iran was a man called Khalil Allah. He was killed in that year in a brawl in the city of Yazd. His successor was known as Aqa Khan Mahallati, who became governor of the province of Kerman for a time. He was dismissed on the death of the Shah who had appointed him, rebelled twice in an attempt to recover the governorship, and was finally defeated in 1842. He fled to India with most of his followers, offered his services to the British, and soon established himself as head of the Ismailis there. He was the first Aga Khan.

"It now seems that something curious happened among the few Ismailis who stayed on in Kerman. One of them said that the Aga Khan had forfeited his right to the position of Imam by abandoning Iran, which had always been the true home of the sect. This man was called 'Abd al-Husayn Khan Kermani, and he claimed that he was the true Imam. He was a young man, extremely intelligent, handsome, and very rich. He used his money and his powers of persuasion to spread the influence of the sect as widely as possible, mostly by infiltrating other groups. By the time he died near the end of the century, the Irshadis had become quite powerful, although their existence was known to very few people."

Now that he had begun to talk, al-Shidyaq was finding it easier than he had thought. There was no need for him to hold back anything now. He went on.

"Things seem to have gone on much like this until some time before the Second World War. 'Abd al-Husayn Khan's successor died in 1933, and he was followed as Imam by his son, Hasan, who took the title of al-Qa'im bi-amr Allah. Hasan was a new man, devoted to tradition like his father and grandfather but also fascinated by aspects of the twentieth century, especially by modern science. His letters reveal this time and again. Some of them reveal great sympathy with the European fascist movements of the 1930s—he seems to have admired their methods of organization and their messianic dreams.

"After the war, some Irshadi families invested heavily in the small industrial sector that was being developed in Iran and became unbelievably wealthy. Like a lot of other big families during the period, they pooled their resources and sold extensive landholdings outside the city. They invested in just about everything. After the Shah's so-called land reform, they cashed in on the real estate boom in north Tehran, and by the mid-seventies their combined wealth was estimated in billions of dollars, much of it in Swiss bank accounts and a great deal of it made over to Hasan to spend as he pleased.

"Whether or not as a result of this, in 1975 Hasan decided to come into the open and make himself known to Ismailis everywhere. Then, in 1977, he went even further. He claimed that the hidden Imam, the promised Mahdi whose coming has been awaited by Ismailis for centuries, was due to appear on earth. He wasn't referring to himself. He was speaking about someone called Muhammad ibn 'Abd Allah, who would be the true Mahdi for the entire world of Islam. When he appeared, Hasan would return the earthly leadership of the faith to him so that he could rule over the nations as was prophesied. He was to make himself known at the Ka'ba in Mecca and call for the launching of a holy war against the non-Muslim world. At that moment, Hasan said, the nations of Islam would rise up as a single nation and conquer the earth. He claimed to know this because he had in his possession a book of prophecies known as the *Kitab al-Irshad*, the Book of Guidance. That's where they get the name Irshadis, from the title of the book.

"But Hasan was not prepared to leave things entirely to God. Late in 1977, he said that some years earlier he had instructed members of his own sect to give a percentage of their income to a program which aimed to produce some sort of secret weapon with which the Mahdi would conquer the world. He never revealed the nature of this weapon or where it is supposed to be kept, and I'm not sure that it really exists. I think he spoke of it in order to encourage others to join him.

"When the false Mahdi appeared in Mecca last month, we were very nervous that it had something to do with this man Hasan and his group. If he was somehow involved and if word got out that there were Ismailis in the affair, it could be disastrous for all of us. People are not discriminating: they do not make distinctions between one group and another. To them, all Ismailis are the same. They would accuse us of engineering the rebellion in Mecca. They would hunt us down in packs and kill us. Our men, our women, and our children."

Randall listened with fascination. He was aware that, for the first time, he was hearing the truth about the group he had been chasing for so long. He was finished with speculation, done with conjecture: he knew now their name, their history, their aims, and the identity of their leader. He was no longer chasing a phantom but something tangible he could pursue to its lair and, if he was able, destroy.

"That is all I know, Mr. Grant," al-Shidyaq concluded. "There are more details, of course. You will find them in these papers. But the basic facts are those that I have just given you. Nothing is known of their location, except that their headquarters are still in Iran, nor can I tell you anything of their organization, their leaders, or their current activities. I have told you everything I know. You must believe me."

"I believe you," said Randall. "But I do not understand why you were afraid to tell me this."

Al-Shidyaq seemed to grow pale again. He looked away from Randall and said nothing. The American looked at him. He was untroubled by the man's fear. But he had to know the reason for it.

"You have met them," Randall said at last. It was a statement, not a question. "Here in New York. Recently."

Al-Shidyaq said nothing, but Randall sensed that he was right.

"Why did they come to you?" asked Randall. "What did they want? Why did they reveal themselves to you so openly?"

Al-Shidyaq trembled, then he spoke, his voice dull and weary.

"It was one man. He came to the foundation earlier this month and asked to see me. He said he had come from Iran on behalf of the Imam Hasan, that he had been sent to look after the interests of the Irshadis in this country. He said that the American Government had become interested in the affairs of their sect and that they did not wish any information to be passed to them. He thought someone might come to the foundation asking questions. If they did, I was to tell them nothing, to deny all knowledge of such a group. Otherwise . . ."

He fell silent.

" 'Otherwise'?" prompted Randall, even though he could guess the answer.

"Otherwise they would kill me. And my family in Syria. They know who I am, where to find me. They have people everywhere. There is no escape."

"Was he Iranian, this man who came to you?"

Al-Shidyaq nodded.

"Yes. He was a man of about forty, perhaps older. A molla. He wore black, and where his right hand should have been, there was a stump. It has been almost a month, but I can still see his face if I close my eyes. I will never forget that face."

"I know," said Randall, his voice almost inaudible. "I have seen him too."

A silence fell, broken only by the gentle ticking of a clock on al-Shidyaq's desk. It was time to leave. Randall rose. He picked up the files and reached out his hand to al-Shidyaq. The hostility that fear had provoked between them was gone, replaced once more by a cold formality. They shook hands briefly and Randall left. The door of the apartment was closed firmly behind him and he heard the sound of a lock being turned.

Randall went downstairs to the lobby, where the same security guard was on duty. He looked at his watch and saw that it was almost three o'clock. He had several things to do that evening. He asked the guard to ring for a taxi to pick him up at once. An ABC radio cab arrived outside the building minutes later.

As Randall drove away, the telephone on the desk rang. The guard picked up the receiver.

"Johnson," said a voice at the other end, "this is Dr. al-Shidyaq. I just noticed a cab pulling away from the curb. Was my visitor in it?"

"Yes, sir. I called it for him a couple of minutes ago."

"Thank you, Johnson. Can you tell me what company it was?"

"It was ABC, sir. Is anything wrong?"

"No, everything's fine. Do you happen to have ABC's number there?"

"Yes, sir. It's 492–4444."

"Thank you, Johnson. That's all I wanted to know."

Upstairs, al-Shidyaq put down the receiver. He hesitated for only a moment, then picked it up again. He dialed and a voice answered almost at once.

"ABC cabs. Can I help you?"

"Hello. My name is al-Shidyaq, a resident in the Dakota on West Seventy-second Street. A friend of mine left here a couple of minutes ago in one of your cabs, and I've just realized that I didn't check where he was going. I have to follow him there in a few minutes. Could you please tell me where he was headed? Has your driver radioed his destination in yet?"

"Well, sir, strictly speaking we're not supposed to do that."

"I understand perfectly. You're quite correct. But this is terribly important. We have a very important meeting. A lot of money is involved, and I daren't be late. Can't you just bend the rules slightly? You have my name and address. You can check with the security guard downstairs if you like."

"No need for that, sir. I've got a note of your name here. Your friend asked to be taken to the Chelsea Hotel on West Twenty-third Street."

"Of course, I remember now. He mentioned it. The Chelsea Hotel."

That evening, Randall picked up his papers from Yaakov. They seemed perfect to him, but the real test would come when he arrived in Tehran. He had already booked a seat on the ten o'clock flight to London that night and planned to leave England for Iran the following afternoon.

When he returned to the hotel, Fereshteh was waiting to say goodbye. She was pale and withdrawn and said very little. He told her about al-Shidyaq, about what he had told him of the Imam Hasan and his group. She listened, but what he said meant little to her. She could not hate an abstraction, and that was what they still were to her. She had seen them and fled from them, but she still could not believe in them, not even when Randall gave them a name and a history. She had spoken with Gorman and Straker, and she had seen Peter Randall kill, once in the loft on Wooster Street, once on the ice near Rostoworoski's place. She could believe in those things, in Straker and Randall, and Gorman dying in the ice. But these others were shadows that she had glimpsed out of the corner of an eye. She feared them and she longed to be done with them, but they were not quite real to her. She feared Randall too, not out of a sense of danger to herself, but because he was driven so, compelled to things she could not properly understand. For him, her shadows were real, and she feared that, through him, they would somehow become real for her too. She feared his hatred and his single-mindedness, for she had become part of it and could not break free. When he left, she sat for a long time in her room, afraid for him and afraid for herself. She did not sleep that night.

PHASE SIX

41

TEHRAN
23 December 1979

It was dark and bitterly cold when Randall arrived in Tehran. Snow lay thickly on the ground and the air was now clear and frosty. At Mehrabad Airport, an electricity failure had cut off all heating, but an emergency generator kept runway and other essential lights and communications equipment in operation, and the passport and customs control area was dimly lit by kerosene lamps. Despite this, the vigilance of the Revolutionary Guards in charge of security was, if anything, greater than usual. Many Iranians were returning from Europe for the Christmas vacation, though here in Tehran there was not now and never would be a Christmas.

Randall was traveling on an Irish passport under the name Sean Byrne, a freelance photographer based in Dublin. It had been stolen a week earlier in New York. Fereshteh had bought him a range of impressive secondhand photographic equipment at Willoughby's on West Thirty-second Street—enough to convince the casual eye. The choice of an Irish passport had been deliberate: Randall knew it would pay off once he reached Iran, and he had paid Yaakov to produce several other documents he might be able to use there. The passport itself had been provided with an absolutely authentic visa stamp from the Iranian Consulate in New York; Randall had no idea how the man had obtained it, but knew that it had added a great deal to the overall price.

Randall's Irish passport caused a little confusion at first. None of the guards on duty had ever seen one before, and none of them seemed even to know where Ireland was. Randall was constrained to use only English in speaking with them—any indication that he knew Persian would cause immediate suspicion. He knew from his stint at Langley that the CIA was thought to be moving agents into Tehran disguised as European businessmen, and Randall had to convince the aggressively suspicious guards that his credentials were bona fide. To his relief the visa passed scrutiny—an important first hurdle that would make the rest that much easier. He next presented a letter that he himself had helped forge, signed by Mehdi Rahmatollah, the Iranian consul in New York, confident that they would not bother to check its authenticity. It asked Iranian officials to cooperate with Mr. Byrne, as he was in Iran on important business.

Randall now produced what he knew would be the most crucial documents and passed them to the guard whose English seemed best, a man of about twenty-five who had evidently been educated abroad, probably in England. The first was a letter from Provisional Sinn Fein headquarters, identifying Sean Byrne as a political representative of the Irish Republican Army authorized to enter into negotiations with other anti-imperialist organizations for their mutual benefit. The second was a detailed receipt from NORAID, the North American organization that provided material assistance to the armed struggle in Northern Ireland, acknowledging that Sean Byrne had received and arranged for the transfer to Ireland of large sums of money collected among the Irish community in New York, together with two shipments of arms destined for Donegal.

When the Iranian had finished scrutinizing these papers, Randall tried to explain that he had been authorized by his superiors to come to Iran in order to meet with leaders of the revolution and to cement relations so that the two sides could give one another mutual assistance in the struggle against British imperialism. He was playing a long shot and he knew it. Ireland was virtually unknown to most Iranians. Many had only a vague idea of where England, France, or Germany were situated, but during the marches leading up to the revolution there had on more than one occasion been cries of *"Zendebad Irland,"* "Long live Ireland!" Word had got through that the Irish were somehow involved in a struggle for independence from the British; so long as they were fellow fighters in the battle against world imperialism, the Irish, whoever they were, must be friends. Randall now played on these sentiments, talking to the guard about the Easter Rising in 1916, the Civil War, the partition of Ireland by the British into north and south, the civil rights marches of the sixties which had ended in bloodshed, the entry of British troops, and the long war of attrition that had followed. These men, he knew from long experience, thought in black and white, and he, therefore, drew a picture that was stark, dramatic, and calculated to win their sympathy.

The guard to whom he addressed his words had, it turned out, been in England, as Randall had suspected from his accent, at university near Brighton, and he knew a little about the Irish problem. As he started to explain the matter to his friends, however, enlightenment began to dawn in the eyes of one of them. Randall, pretending to understand nothing, listened intently as they talked together in Persian. A few years ago, it seemed, Liam de Paor's study of the Northern Ireland troubles had been translated into Persian, and this man had read it. Randall himself now remembered having seen it on sale in Tehran in 1977, and he now offered up a silent prayer of thanks to the book's translator.

In the chaotic conditions still prevailing in the aftermath of the revolution, the Guards had retained a remarkable degree of autonomy. As an organization, they often acted independently of the government, even in opposition to official policy, and no one dared criticize them. The guard in charge of the interview walked over to a telephone and dialed a city number. Randall's heart was racing now. He realized that even though he had the guard's sympathy, the Iranian could not take sole responsibility for letting him into the country. He knew how these people worked, and in all cases of doubt, it was safer to obtain authorization for one's actions from above, rather than to risk taking action that might as easily lead to a firing squad as to a commendation. And if things went well, a favorably disposed superior might let some of the credit rub off; if not, a word in the right ear might put a man in his former commander's post.

Randall need not have worried. After a five-minute conversation with his superior, the guard replaced the receiver and smiled. Very courteously, he began to explain the arrangements for "Byrne's" stay in Tehran. As a representative of a friendly revolutionary group actively engaged in a struggle with one of the major Western powers, "Byrne" should not be kept waiting too long at the airport. Certainly not overnight. If necessary, one of the guards could accompany him to a hotel in the capacity of "official escort." That would be nothing more than a polite formality if the man were genuine, but if he should turn out to be an impostor it would ensure that he was kept under surveillance. Other guards could be sent from headquarters to help keep a watch outside the hotel. The commander agreed to this arrangement. Better to work out the details in the morning in person than give offense to an ally already tired by a long flight.

It was settled that the English-speaking guard should accompany Randall to the Gilan Hotel on Ferdowsi Avenue. They left the airport together, the guard helping to carry the heavy photographic equipment. It was an ideal way to enter the country, under official protection, but Randall would have to get rid of the man at the earliest opportunity.

They took a military jeep that stood parked just outside the main entrance to the small airport, one of a large number "liberated" from army barracks throughout the country in the last days of the great upheaval. The guard drove, his foot heavy on the accelerator, relishing the open road of early morning and the authority the jeep conferred on him. No one stopped them as they headed toward the center of the city. The streets they rushed through were dark and bleak, and Randall shivered from more than the cold.

The guard, whose name was Sohrab Qasemlu, talked freely with Randall, eager to know more about the Irish struggle against the English. The American had watched newsreels and read newspaper accounts of the troubles in Ireland and was able to bluff convincingly. He found Qasemlu likable and intelligent, in contrast to the thugs he had shot in Yusefabad so many months ago. When at last he spoke of the revolution and the part he had played in it, Randall felt almost ashamed of the deceptions he was practicing. Qasemlu was neither an opportunist nor a fanatic, but a young intellectual who had been appalled by the injustices of the Shah's brutal régime and who now hoped only to help build a just society in its place. Randall felt jealous of his optimism and his confidence. In his place, he would have believed and done the same things. But he felt sorry for Qasemlu as well, for he knew how little chance there really was of securing justice in the new world of the ayatollahs.

When they reached the hotel, it was dark and seemed deserted, but Qasemlu knocked loudly on the main door until a sleepy-looking porter appeared. Within minutes, the manager arrived, apologetic and deferential. He explained that as it was winter and there were no tourists, only a few businessmen, the hotel was virtually closed. A room could, of course, be made available right away, if the gentleman was willing to put up with a little discomfort until the morning.

Randall was allocated a room on the fourth floor, overlooking the main street. The elevator was out of order so the manager led them with repeated and profuse apologies up the stairs. A small, rotund man, he chattered incessantly and fluttered his soft white hands as they went up, trying to keep two simultaneous conversations running with the guard and Randall, uncertain which was the more important. It was so difficult nowadays to gauge with certainty a man's rank or influence. He showed Randall into his room, vainly attempting to distract his attention from the layers of dust that had gathered there during months of neglect. It was bitterly cold, but the manager said nothing could be done about that until morning. Randall smiled and nodded. It did not matter in the least to him since he intended to be out of the hotel and far away by then.

As the manager was about to go, Qasemlu stopped him and spoke quietly but distinctly to him in Persian. Randall's feigned ignorance of the language at the airport had clearly convinced the guard that he could speak freely in front of him.

"Listen carefully," he said. "I will be spending the rest of the night in the corridor outside this room, just to make sure our guest does not slip away or try to contact anyone. He is not to be allowed to make any telephone calls outside the hotel or to leave messages to be passed to anyone. If he does try to give you any messages, bring them to me. Is that understood?"

The manager nodded fiercely, eager to please, his lips repeatedly mouthing *"Chashm."*

"When you go downstairs, I want you to go outside, to the front of the hotel. There should be two more guards there from the local barracks. Come back and tell me if they are not there. Otherwise, I want you to inform them that I am here, that I am staying on this floor to watch over our visitor, and that they are to remain in position outside until further orders. No one is to enter or leave the hotel without my permission. Have I made myself clear?"

"Chashm, aqa, chashm," the little man murmured over and over again as he slipped out of the doorway.

His manner changing abruptly, Qasemlu turned to Randall once more, a smile on his lips, his bearing again that of a civilian who has found himself reluctantly in military garb. Randall was not fooled for an instant. Qasemlu had served in the Army at some time, probably as a conscript. He knew how to command. And he would know how to keep a man under vigilant guard.

"I've asked him to be sure that no one disturbs you tonight," said
Qasemlu. "You must be tired, so I won't keep you up any longer. I'll
just take a chair and wait outside in the corridor until it's time for us
to go to the ministry. Don't worry about anything. I'll see you have
some rest. Good night, Mr. Byrne. And welcome to Iran."

The guard bowed slightly, then went out carrying one of the room's
two chairs. The door closed and Randall was alone. He had already
decided on his ploy for escaping from the hotel while Qasemlu had
been talking with the manager. It was already close to dawn and he
wanted to be out of the hotel before first light. Now he wasted no
time in repacking all his essential bits and pieces into the large shoulder bag he had carried on the plane. When that was finished, he took
a sheet of paper and wrote the following message in Persian:

> We have taken the Irish collaborator into our custody. He
> will be released unharmed in return for concessions from
> the present government of Iran. Failure to comply with our
> demands will result in permanent injury to our hostage and,
> if the government persists, in his death. If he dies, his peo-
> ple will hold the Iranian authorities responsible and will
> actively encourage their fellow revolutionaries throughout
> the world to sever their links with this régime. We will
> notify you of our legitimate demands tomorrow at noon.
>   The People's Marxist Front

When he had finished, Randall placed the sheet prominently in the
frame of the mirror over the dressing table. He then quietly began to
disarrange the bedclothes and the few items of furniture in the room,
creating the impression that there had been a brief but angry struggle.
This done, he took a razor from a packet in his toilet bag, drew it
quickly over the ball of his thumb, and carefully squeezed blood over
the pillow and sheets before applying a sticking plaster to the wound.
He replaced the razor in his bag and zipped it up.

To his relief, the telephone lead was just long enough to allow him
to carry the instrument into the small bathroom. Inside, he turned on
one of the washbasin taps before lifting the receiver and dialing reception. As he had expected, it took almost five minutes before anyone
answered. It was the night porter, sleepy and surly.

"*Baleh! Chi-e?*"

Speaking quickly in Persian in a low but severe voice, Randall identified himself as Qasemlu and demanded to speak to the manager. The porter knew better than to remonstrate. Two minutes later, the manager's frightened voice came on the line. Randall cut his explanations short.

"This is Qasemlu, the guard on the fourth floor. I'm speaking from the Irishman's room. I've just been in radio contact with my headquarters, and they tell me there may be trouble in the hotel from counterrevolutionaries. We have to flush them out. I want you and any of your staff who are on the premises to create a diversion. In exactly five minutes, you are to go to the lobby carrying pots, pans, anything you can find, and start making as loud a racket as you possibly can. Do you understand?"

There was silence at the other end, then the manager spoke again, his voice tight and nervous.

"But, *jenab-e ali*, you must realize that we have guests. I cannot disturb . . ."

"If you do not do as I say in precisely five minutes from now, your guests will never be disturbed again. They will be dead."

Randall replaced the receiver and returned with the telephone to the bedroom. As he had expected, the manager had not even questioned that it was Qasemlu on the other end. Persian-speaking foreign guests were a rarity even in normal times.

The minutes passed slowly, the silence intensified for Randall by his mounting expectation of the din he hoped would break out any moment. Five minutes went by without anything happening and he began to wonder what had gone wrong. Suddenly, there was a sound of rattling in the distance, and then it was as if all hell had broken loose downstairs. There were loud crashes, bangs, wild metallic thumpings, and, above them all, fierce shouts and screams. The manager had obviously told his staff to put their hearts into it. It was a matter of seconds before the noise began to have its effect. Randall could hear doors opening in the corridor outside his room, voices raised in anger or inquiry, the drumming of feet, sounds of fear and growing panic. It was obvious that the hotel contained far more guests than were listed in the register. Randall did not doubt for a moment that Qasemlu would head directly toward the source of the disturbance, leaving his own path free, but he waited to give the man time to get well away from the room.

A minute later, Randall opened his door and looked out. Here and there, frightened faces peered into the corridor. The sound of banging and shouting rose more sharply as he stepped outside. Qasemlu was, as he had expected, nowhere to be seen. No one questioned him or tried to interfere as he set off down the corridor in search of the back stairs. It hardly mattered if anyone saw him. Most of the guests would say nothing; the others would remember things confusedly. The message in his room would not fool the guards or SAVAMA for long, but it would give him a vital day in which to get under cover. That was all he needed.

There were stairs at the end of the corridor, behind an unlocked fire door. Without pausing, Randall ran down them, his feet pounding in the darkness. At the bottom, a small wooden door barred his way. It was a moment's work to push it open and step out into the alleyway at the back of the hotel, filling now with a dim gray light. Quickly, he turned to the left, heading away from the hotel toward Hafez Avenue. Near Hafez, he found a telephone kiosk and stepped inside.

He had placed all his hopes on this one call, and there was no fallback. He dialed the number and listened. A minute passed and he began to feel nervous. Just as he was starting to become genuinely worried, someone lifted the receiver and answered.

"*Baleh, ki-e?*"

"Sirus? Are you alone?"

"Yes." A pause. "Is that you, Peter?" The amazement in Rastgu's voice was obvious.

"You're getting quick, Sirus. I'm back in Tehran and I need somewhere to stay. Is the place at Darband still secure?"

"Yes, it's safe. But why have you come back? I thought I'd seen the last of you. Dammit, Randall, do you want to get me killed that badly?"

"Please, Sirus, I've forgiven you by now for the knock-out, though I admit there were times when I could have throttled you in return. I can't explain over the phone why I've returned, but you know I wouldn't be here if it weren't important. One thing I should tell you, though: I'm here freelance. I take it you understand me."

There was a short silence at the other end, then Rastgu spoke again.

"I understand, Peter. You can tell me why later. Where are you now?"

"On Hafez, corner of Naderi."

"OK, I'll pick you up in ten minutes. But listen, you bastard. This time, you're on your own if there's going to be any trouble. I have my own problems to look after here."

By the following morning, Randall had succeeded in convincing the Israeli of the seriousness of the situation. Rastgu was prepared to make available any assistance he could provide if the Americans were foolish enough to want to mess about making deals with terrorists; his own people had different views on the matter. Unchecked, the Irshadi Ismailis could wreak havoc in the Middle East, destabilizing further an already precarious political situation. Since the signature of the Camp David accord the previous year, the Israelis had been anxious to prevent any activities that might put the Arab bloc on edge, and Rastgu realized that that was only a small part of what the Irshadis were aiming to do.

For the next three days, Randall stayed at the house at Darband, preparing from memory detailed reports of what he knew about the Irshadis and their activities. These were encoded and transmitted to Jerusalem by Rastgu. On the second day, official approval came from MOSSAD headquarters to proceed with the mission. The Israelis had already been contacted by Washington during the initial investigations following the assassination attempt and were now able to compile a dossier of their own. The links revealed between the Irshadis and various neofascist groups in Germany and elsewhere caused grave concern among the Israelis and reinforced their decision to act.

On the third day, the twenty-sixth, Rastgu arrived at Darband looking flushed and a little excited.

"Peter," he said, "we've been able to get a little more information about their international links. Our people in West Germany have been able to lay their hands on material found after a raid on the headquarters of the Deutsche Aktiongruppe. These documents reveal that some of the members of the fascist group traveled to Iran between 1975 and 1978; they all spent time at a secret base offering training in small arms and explosives, unarmed combat, sabotage, and God knows what else. Four of them were ex-Bundeswehr officers who'd been in Angola, Nigeria, and other parts of Africa as mercenaries. One thing may be important, but the details aren't clear: the man in charge of this base is referred to in their files by the initials

F. R., and from some of the references we think he may be a member of the Aktiongruppe, but we can't be certain."

"A German?" asked Randall. "Are you sure?"

"We think so. Our people are still going over the material. I'll let you know as soon as we have more information."

Randall nodded, then went over to the desk and picked up one of the files he had taken from al-Shidyaq's apartment in New York and which he had brought into Iran in a secret pocket of his suitcase. From it, he took out a single sheet of paper.

"Sirus," he began. "While you were out, I went more carefully through the papers I took from al-Shidyaq in New York. I found this at the back of one of the files, tucked inside the cover. It's a letter in English written by someone in Tehran to al-Shidyaq himself. His name is Ibrahim Masoodi and he's an Ismaili who spent part of last year taking a course at Columbia: he mentions all of that in the letter. It seems that while he was there, he became friendly with al-Shidyaq and some others at the foundation and revealed that he'd once been involved with the Irshadis here in Iran. But it sounds from this as if he regretted it and left. The letter was sent with a packet of papers that he had promised to send to the foundation.

"It may be risky, but I think I should find Masoodi and have a talk with him. He's the link we've been looking for. His address is on the letter. I'd like to go to town tomorrow and see him."

"Too dangerous. It's better if I go."

"No, it's more important now that your cover isn't blown, and you can't speak to him without doing so. If anything goes wrong, he can describe you and put the authorities on to you. You can't take that risk, not now. If something happens to me, it matters less; you'll be able to continue the mission. It's better if I go."

Rastgu reluctantly agreed. His concern for his friend's safety could not be allowed to interfere with the operation or jeopardize their chances of success. He was no longer acting on his own initiative but was under orders from Jerusalem. Randall was expendable now, and there was nothing Rastgu or anyone else could do about it.

It had been a hard day for Howard Straker. He had spent the morning visiting Gorman's widow, a gesture he now regretted. Perhaps the day after Christmas had been a bad time to call. Mrs. Gorman hadn't swallowed a word of his story, and she hadn't nodded understandingly at his reference to "our boys in the Embassy." Sometimes he wondered if it were worth the sweat and blood to defend people who didn't seem to want defending. Ungrateful people like Mrs. Gorman.

In the afternoon, he had spent two hours talking with Rostoworoski. If anything, that had been worse. The old man had refused to change a word of his absurd story and, after about an hour, had simply stopped talking. Straker was still reluctant to use tougher methods on the old fool. But he disliked stubbornness almost as much as he disliked ingratitude.

He was about to leave his office when the phone rang. He let it ring and opened the door to go. It went on ringing. He swore, slammed the door, and picked up the receiver.

"Yes!"

"Mr. Straker?"

"Yes. This is Howard Straker. Who's calling?"

"This is Carl Harper, sir. You asked me to call as soon as we had a lead on Peter Randall."

Straker calmed down. He had been waiting for this call for days.

"Go ahead, Harper. I'm listening."

"Yes, sir. We've been checking all flights out of New York over the last few days. I think we've just found what we've been looking for. Someone traveling on an Irish passport under the name Sean Byrne flew on the ten o'clock British Airways flight 176 from New York to London on the night of 22 December. A passenger traveling on the same passport was on the four-thirty Iranair flight 738 to Tehran the following day. He arrived at Mehrabad at three o'clock on Monday morning. We've just received confirmation from the Irish Consulate here that a passport of that description was stolen in New York last week. It could be Randall, sir. All other passengers out of New York who transferred to Tehran flights over the next few days have been cleared. It must be him."

Straker thought quickly. It seemed to fit. If the traveler calling himself Byrne was indeed Randall, he was now in Tehran, and if they didn't track him down there, he would cause trouble, serious trouble.

"What about the girl?" asked Straker. He remembered the girl. Frequently and without pleasure.

"Nothing yet, sir. None of the female passengers on those flights check out. We're still looking. We think she may have stayed in New York."

That was logical. "Good. Keep me informed. Thank you, Harper. Call me back as soon as you have more to report."

Straker replaced the receiver, paused momentarily, then lifted it again and dialed a short number. He was answered immediately.

"This is Straker. I have an Epsilon Seven alert. Is our deep agent in Tehran still viable?"

"As of seven o'clock this morning, yes, sir."

"I want him activated immediately. Written authorization will follow. Report back to me as soon as you make contact and confirm."

42

NEW YORK CITY
26 December 1979

Christmas Day had been like any other. Fereshteh had remained in her room at the Chelsea, cut off from the world of friends and family, a stranger more than ever to festivities in which she had always taken part as an outsider. The day passed, and she woke the next morning determined to break the lethargy that had held her immobile since returning from the Iranian Consulate on Monday.

She washed and dressed, then went downstairs and out of the hotel, heading for the subway station at the corner of Twenty-third and Eighth. There she took a train north past the George Washington Bridge to 190th Street. Once outside, she followed the footpath that leads through Fort Tryon Park to the Cloisters. A rambling collection of Gothic and Romanesque buildings, most of them brought from Europe at the turn of the century, the Cloisters are the strangest of sanctuaries. Fereshteh often went there to walk in the shaded gardens or stroll through the rooms with their treasures of rare medieval art. Today the complex was more deserted than usual, and she was able to wander relatively undisturbed, alone with her thoughts.

In such a short space of time, her world had been shattered. Until last month, the worst thing that had ever happened to her was the ending of her affair with Fernwell. Now that seemed trivial and cheap, and the anxiety it had once caused her almost desirable. She longed for something to replace the fear and the numbness. Alone and frightened, she had leaned on Peter Randall. He had, after all, saved her from death and helped her find some of her own strength again during those first days of panic. But she was still afraid of him and she was not sure she trusted him. She had to fight the fear herself, otherwise she could never return to the life she had led before this all began. Even if she went to Tehran, it would not mean running away to him as her protector. She would go there to confront whatever it was that threatened her. It might destroy her, but that would be better than this endless waiting, which was sapping her more and more every day.

She ate lunch in the cafeteria in Fort Tryon Park. During the meal and afterward, as she walked back along the footpath to South Plaza, she had a sensation of being watched but saw no one gazing in her direction. She took the subway back downtown and went straight to the hotel, glancing behind her from time to time. As far as she could tell, there was no one following her. If there had been someone in the park, it had probably been a Peeping Tom.

Back in her room, she switched on the television, changing channels at random, seeking distraction. There was nothing showing but rubbish, which was exactly what she wanted. At five, there was a brief news bulletin. She watched without interest. A post-Christmas lull hung over everything. There was film of the hostages in Tehran singing carols and opening cards and presents, accompanied by pious comments from the broadcaster. The shock came toward the end, the ninth item of the bulletin.

"Dr. 'Abd al-Latif al-Shidyaq," the announcer read in his neutral, professional voice, "the director of an educational foundation attached to Columbia University was found murdered in his luxury apartment in the Dakota building on Seventy-second Street today. Police found his body tied to a chair after being alerted by the tenant of the apartment below, who found drops of blood soaking through her ceiling this morning. The police have since confirmed that the victim was drained of blood while still alive, but have refused to release details of other injuries sustained by him. It is still not clear how Dr. al-Shidyaq's assailant or assailants gained entry to his apartment. The Dakota is a security-conscious building whose tenants pay for round-the-clock protection from theft and assault. The management has issued a statement to the effect that the only way the murderer could have entered Dr. al-Shidyaq's apartment would have been at his own invitation. A preliminary homicide report estimates that the attack occurred some time late last night. We'll have more on this . . ."

Fereshteh switched off the set, her hand shaking. There had been a photograph. It fitted the description of al-Shidyaq that Randall had given her. There could be no mistake. It had taken three days, but they had got him in the end.

She crossed to the window, carefully parted the curtain, and glanced out. The light was poor, but she could just make out a figure in black on the other side of the street. She could not be sure, but he seemed to be looking toward her window. Her hand dropped the curtain and she stepped back into the room, her heart beating wildly.

It took her less than a minute to decide. She picked up the telephone and gave the operator a number in Tehran. Struggling to control herself, she listened as the operator tried to make a connection. Ordinarily, it could take an hour or more to get through. Today it was a matter of ten minutes. At last, the phone at the other end began to ring. It continued for one minute, but there was no answer. Eventually, the operator came back on the line.

"I'm sorry, but there's no answer. Do you want me to try again later? I can book a call for you."

"No. Please, it's urgent, I have to get through. Try this number instead." She read out the second number Randall had given her. Please, God, she thought, let someone be there this time.

The operator sighed audibly, then dialed the international and country codes followed by the area code for Tehran, and finally the low beeps of an Iranian ringing tone came through the earpiece. Half a minute passed, then a man's voice answered, cautious and guarded.

"Yes, who is it?"

"I want to speak to Sirus, please."

"This is Sirus. Who is calling?"

"My name is Fereshteh Ahmadi. I was given this number by Peter Randall. He said I could contact you. Is he there?"

"Yes, he's here. He said you might call. Is something wrong? Where are you? Are you still in New York?"

"Yes, I'm in New York. And, yes, something's wrong. Please, I must speak to Peter."

There was a sound of talking at the other end. Another voice came on the line.

"Hello, Fereshteh, is that you? What's happened?"

"It's al-Shidyaq. He's dead. They killed him, Peter. They killed him last night."

"Don't tell me now. Later. Are you safe?"

"Yes, but . . ."

"Have you seen anything, anybody?"

"Yes, I think so. I think I was followed. The man in black, the one without a hand. I think he's outside the hotel now, waiting. Al-Shidyaq must have found out where you were staying. He must have told them. Help me, Peter. What can I do?"

"Don't panic. Listen carefully. Pack quickly and check out at once. Don't even delay five minutes. Explain at the desk that you're being pestered by a man who's waiting outside; they'll arrange a cab to pick you up at a rear exit. Go to the airport and take the first flight to London. You can make the connection to Tehran tomorrow afternoon. Sirus will pick you up at the airport. Don't worry, you'll be all right. I'll see you in Tehran. Put down the receiver immediately in case somebody puts a trace on this call. Goodbye, Fereshteh. Take care."

The phone went dead and Fereshteh replaced the receiver. There was no time to lose and she started to pack.

She arrived at Kennedy Airport in good time for the eight o'clock TWA flight, due in Heathrow the next morning at seven-fifty local time. At the counter, she bought a through ticket to Tehran, to connect with the four-thirty Iranair flight the following afternoon. In the crowded anonymity of the vast airport lounge, she felt safe at last. An hour later, her flight was called and she made her way toward the gate. She had made it. In minutes, she would be airborne, on the first leg of her flight to Tehran.

As she passed through the gate, a figure detached itself from the crowds milling about the information desk. Molla Ahmad was still dressed in his clerical robes, and from time to time, he attracted curious stares from members of the crowd. Even in an international airport, the figure of an Iranian molla stood out, not least here in the United States, where the media had turned the Shi'i clergy into the representatives of a new and incomprehensible evil in the world. Ordinarily, there would have been hostility, perhaps even a confrontation with an overzealous patriot. But for weeks now, Molla Ahmad had moved about New York unchallenged. Those who made to confront him looked once at his face and turned aside again. His eyes held a menace that warned them off. He walked through the milling crowds at JFK and at every step the crowds parted before him.

On his left stood a row of telephones designated for international calls. He entered a booth, lifted the receiver, and dialed a long number. Traffic was light between New York and Tehran and the connection was almost immediate. He did not have long to wait for an answer. A minute later he left the booth and headed for the Lufthansa ticket desk.

"I would like to fly tomorrow on your late flight from Frankfurt to Tehran, please. I shall fly tonight to Frankfurt. Can you please book me a seat?"

The girl checked with her desk computer. Seconds later, she smiled and looked up. His face did not change and her smile faded.

"Yes, sir. I can give you a seat on the direct Lufthansa flight number 403, leaving here at nine-twenty. You'll be in Frankfurt at ten-fifty tomorrow morning. Is that all right?"

"Yes," he said. "That will be perfect."

43

TEHRAN
27 December 1979

Ibrahim Masoodi lived at 12 Dah-Metri Firuzeh, a small street off Kaj, in the western part of Yusefabad. Randall drove there in a small Volkswagen obtained for him by Rastgu. The house was easy to find, as this relatively new part of the town was well laid out. Beside the door was a set of bells with nameplates; he found Masoodi's name beside the third-floor bell, rang, and waited for someone to answer. The loudspeaker crackled and a woman's voice cautiously asked who it was. He spoke in Persian—there was no point now in pretending ignorance of the language.

"I'm a friend of 'Abd al-Latif al-Shidyaq's from New York. He gave me the name Ibrahim Masoodi and asked me to visit him while I'm in Tehran. I've got a message for him."

"You are American?" she asked.

"Yes, but I speak Persian; I teach Middle Eastern politics at Columbia University."

"You speak very good Persian for an American," she said, unable to disguise the suspicion in her voice.

"Yes," he replied, "that's because I lived here for several years until 1977. I still practice."

After a short silence, she spoke again.

"Ibrahim isn't here at the moment. I'm his wife. Maybe I could take the message."

"No, I have to see him personally. When will he be back?"

"This evening. He's at his office now."

"Could you tell me where to find his office? I don't have much time in Tehran and I had planned to see him today if possible."

"Yes, all right. He works for a firm of architects, Sherkat-e Me'mari-ye Sadra. Their office is in Kakh Street, just below Muhtasham, on the left. You can't miss it, their plate is on the door."

Randall thanked her and left. He thought he knew the place. It was at the top end of the same street in which he had lived when in Tehran. It seemed an age ago now since he had last been there. An age and a death ago.

He walked back to his Volkswagen, climbed in, and drove straight there. The office was right where he had remembered it, and once inside, he was shown to the room in which Masoodi worked. The architect was a man of about thirty, strongly built but wiry, with the drooping mustache favored by the Iranian intellectual. He welcomed Randall warmly enough. His wife had telephoned to say that he was looking for him. Randall asked if there was somewhere they could talk in private. Masoodi thought for a moment, then said, "Look, why don't we go to my *patuq*? It's just around the corner and it will be quiet at this time of day."

Most Iranian men have a *patuq*, a sort of rendezvous where they can meet their friends on a regular basis, leave and receive messages, or hold literary and other meetings. It is usually a small café, something like those in France or North Africa, with an atmosphere not unlike the English pub except that alcohol is seldom served.

It was an ideal place to meet. Seated at a quiet table, Randall told the Iranian as much as he could. He was taking an enormous risk in revealing to him the extent of his knowledge of the Irshadis, but he knew it was a risk he had to take. As he spoke, Randall watched the man's face carefully, ready for the warning signal that might impel him to his feet, ready to leave and make a run for it if Masoodi decided to turn him in. But he soon realized, now the initial shock had worn off, that the Iranian was interested in what he had to say and was already wondering how it would involve him.

"All I want," Randall concluded, "is information concerning the group. Dr. al-Shidyaq said you might help, you might know how I could find them and trace the center from which they operate."

Masoodi looked at the American sharply.

"And what then? What do you propose to do when you find them?"

Randall's answer was immediate and brief. "Destroy them," he said.

The Iranian looked at him in disbelief.

"Destroy them? Are you a fool? Do you know what you are saying?

No one can destroy them—not you, not your government, not all
your governments. They are too powerful, too clever."

"That's my problem. All I want from you is information—information and assistance."

Masoodi gazed at Randall, saying nothing. At last, he blinked his
eyes.

"Why should I help you? I have done with them. It's too dangerous; I want no more to do with it. My life is already in danger."

"Perhaps there is something I could do for you in return," said
Randall. "If you need money, I can pay you well, very well."

"I don't need your money," the architect snapped. But even as he
spoke, his thoughts were spinning with the possibilities. His voice
lowered, he spoke again.

"Can you get me out of here, out of Iran? Me, my wife? If I stay
here much longer, I'll go mad. This country has gone crazy; everything good, everything worthwhile is being destroyed. I wanted to
stay, to work for the revolution, enjoy the freedom we'd always longed
for under the Shah. But now it's worse: the mollas are everywhere,
and their henchmen, the Revolutionary Guards. Are you able to get
me out to Europe or America? Is my information worth that much to
you?"

Randall nodded. He knew that Rastgu could arrange it. "Yes," he
said, "that can be arranged. In return for information and any help
you can give. I won't ask you to take any risks."

Masoodi thought for a moment, then smiled and reached a hand
across the table. "I'll tell you what I know. I don't know whether it
will help you, but I'll tell you all I can.

"It's hard to know where to start. I was born into an Ismaili family
in Qazvin, near the old Assassin stronghold of Alamut. Our family's
said to have lived there from the time of Hasan al-Sabbah, but I don't
know whether or not that's true. When I came to Tehran University
in 1973 to study architecture, I met a few other young Ismailis there,
and we used to go around a lot together. Some of us still meet here—
it's been our *patuq* since those days. None of us knew anything about
the Irshadis, but we'd all heard rumors that there was such a group.
Then, about a year after I arrived in Tehran, one of my friends—he
was a student in the faculty of science—told me he actually belonged
to the sect, that he'd been converted four years before in Bam, which
is one of their main centers."

Randall started at the mention of Bam. That explained why Mo'ini and his colleagues had been there so long. "Is that where they have their headquarters?" he asked, his pulse racing at the thought of being so close.

"No. It used to be, but they moved it. I'll explain that in a moment. I was telling you about this friend—his name was 'Azizollah Parchamdust. When he told me about being a member, I became interested—I was curious to know just what they believed, and I was intrigued by the secretiveness that surrounded everything: he swore me to secrecy before telling me anything at all. Eventually, he took me to some of their meetings here in Tehran. Ismailis don't use a regular mosque for their prayers, just a 'meeting house,' what they call a *jama'at-khane*. The Irshadis did just the same, but they used to go along to the local mosque as well so they could pass for ordinary Muslims. You probably know all about *taqiyye*, being able to hide your real beliefs in order to avoid persecution. They were very good at it and nobody ever guessed who or what they were.

"They've got a house in south Tehran where followers who live in the city usually meet, and 'Azizollah took me there a few times. I met some of their leaders, but I never saw the so-called Imam himself. I didn't see anything to object to in the meetings I attended: as far as I could see, their beliefs didn't differ much from those I already held. They were just a lot more enthusiastic about their religion, and I liked that. Still, I wanted to pin them down about this claim that theirs was the true Imam. I wanted to know how they could justify that. So I continued going to meetings for about a year and got to know some of them quite well, but I never came much closer to what you might call the core of their beliefs.

"Well, everything changed about four years ago, in 1975. I spent the summer vacation of that year at home with my parents in Qazvin, and my friend 'Azizollah came to stay with us. We told my parents he was an ordinary Ismaili—after all, he did come from an orthodox family like ours—and I don't think they ever discovered the truth. While he was with us, though, he had a very mysterious visitor from Bam who gave him some papers to read. I don't know how I can explain it, but when he'd read them that night, he really changed. I was with him afterward, and it was as if I didn't know him. Even my parents noticed: they thought he'd had some bad news from home, except he didn't look sad—just different. Anyway, after that he started to tell me a lot of things about the sect that I'd never heard before. He told me the Imam had decided to make himself known publicly to other Ismailis and was going to summon them to join him. He gave me some letters and other writings of the Imam—they were the first I'd ever seen, and I have to admit I found them impressive.

"I went to Kerman the next summer to stay with relatives, and while I was there, I was able to go to Bam a few times, where I met some of the group's leaders and was twice introduced to the Imam in person. Even now, I think those were among the most significant experiences of my life. I'll never forget him: the way he looked at me, talked to me. He's quite old, about eighty, but very sharp and alive, and he has eyes that seem to penetrate you, to see right through you. He's frightening, I suppose, but he has an aura—as if he were divine. It was meeting him that really converted me, and I came back here in the autumn as a full member of the sect. I still kept it all quiet from my parents and friends, though I think they suspected something since I became very involved and spent a lot of time at meetings.

"Nearly three years ago, the Imam announced that the Mahdi was about to appear, and told us to start preparing to help him in the holy war that would break out after his coming. There was a lot of excitement at meetings, and we read the *Kitab al-Irshad* more and more often, finding new prophecies in it all the time. There were rumors— I've no way of confirming or disproving them—that a secret base had been established several years earlier somewhere in the desert near Kerman, and that the Imam had been training young Irshadi men in the use of weapons while building up an arsenal for their use. That was reputed to be the new headquarters; from what I heard, the Imam had moved from Bam and taken up residence there. They called it the New Alamut, and there were rumors that the Resurrection would begin in that place.

"It was also said that the Imam had recruited a group of Irshadi scientists, who had been trained on his orders in the West. They were engaged in research—some believed they were building a weapon to use in the holy war; others that they were working on protective devices so that, after the war, we could come out from shelters and take control. There was talk that a foreigner—Swedish or German, I believe—was in charge of this base."

Randall raised his head, thinking of the information he had received the day before from Rastgu. "Do you know this man's name?" he asked. "Did he have the initials 'F. R.'?"

Masoodi looked curiously at him, then shook his head. "No, I never heard his name; it was a well-guarded secret. Just that he was European, a middle-aged man with a German or Scandinavian accent. I'm sorry, I never heard more than that."

Randall paused for a moment.

"Do you know anything of a man with one hand? A molla who wears black?"

Masoodi's face went pale. He nodded.

"Yes, I know of him. He's a legend among the Irshadis. We never met, but I often heard people speak of him. They don't say much, there seems to be a mystery surrounding him. Some say he cut his hand off to prove his loyalty to the Imam. I've even heard that he had a wife and children, but that he divorced her and left his family to serve the cause. There are some who say he put her to death, that he stoned her himself because she had been unfaithful to him. He lives in Tehran, but he often travels on the Imam's behalf. That's all I know."

"It's enough for now. Please, go on with your story."

"Well, I knew something important was happening. I'd taken my degree the previous year and was already working with the Sherkat-e Sadra, the same company I'm with at present. In April '77, I was approached by one of the Tehran leaders of the sect and asked if I'd give up my job to work for the Imam; they needed a draftsman, and I was well qualified for the task. I was given no more details but was told to think about the proposal. In a way, I knew I had no choice. Then, about a fortnight later, I heard that my friend 'Azizollah, who'd been living in Kerman, had been killed. They actually announced that he'd been executed on the orders of the Imam for expressing doubts about the prophecies being made by him. It was explained that, with the arrival of the Mahdi so imminent, such doubts were a form of betrayal. Obviously, the execution and its announcement were designed to reinforce loyalty and submission to the leader.

"They had the opposite effect on me. All this talk of secret weapons, private armies, and now gratuitous executions frightened me. I was married by then, to a girl my parents had found, a second cousin from Qazvin. We were really happy together and were planning to

have a family, and I thought if I got deeper into all these crazy things
the Imam was doing and saying, I'd destroy all that. So I cut myself
off from the sect; I ignored communications, I avoided places where I
thought they might find me. They did find me in the end, though,
and I was given what amounted to a threat that I'd follow 'Azizollah
if I didn't cooperate and return to help the 'great mission.' Frankly, I
was in a state of terror for days. I knew they were totally ruthless and
that they didn't make idle threats. My life was in danger and there
seemed to be nothing I could do. Eventually, I told my wife everything that had happened, and it was she who thought of the solution.
When they came back a week later, I told them I'd prepared a full
account of all I knew about them and put copies in deposit boxes at
the Bank-e Melli, Bank-e Saderat, and a third, unnamed bank. I'd left
letters with my wife, my lawyer, and several friends, including an
inspector of police, with instructions to open them in the event of my
disappearance or sudden death; these letters in turn gave directions
and authority for the opening of the deposit boxes. Ever since then,
I've been left alone, although I think they keep an eye on me."

Randall's heart turned over. If they were watching and had seen
him with Masoodi, they were both as good as dead.

"Are they watching you now?" he asked, his voice low.

"No, I don't think so. It's not constant, just an occasional check.
They tend to make it obvious so that I should feel frightened. That's
my real reason for wanting to get out of here. How soon can you
arrange it?"

"Soon, very soon, a few days, no more. What you've told me has
been very helpful. Do you have any way of finding out more about
this secret base or the weapons they're making there? I don't want
you to take any risks yourself, but maybe you can put me onto someone else who might know."

Masoodi thought for a while, frowning, then his face cleared.

"It may not be any help, but I've just remembered a rumor I heard
recently from a friend who's a Revolutionary Guard. He knows I'm an
Ismaili, but he seems to think that if we believe in the Prophet and
the first few Imams we must be all right. Anyway, a few weeks ago, he
told me a man had been arrested and executed in Tehran who might
have been an Ismaili. He was afraid they might be starting a pogrom
against us, like the Jews and Baha'is, and he wanted to warn me. But
when I checked with other Ismailis in the city, nobody knew anything

about it and in the end I decided my friend must have been mistaken. Now it occurs to me that the man could have belonged to the Irshadis. If he did, his execution might have had something to do with their activities. Maybe the authorities know what's going on. I'll speak to my friend and see if he can find out more. He said something about books or papers having been found—there might be things you could use."

"Thanks," said Randall, "that could be useful." He already knew that SAVAMA was aware of the existence of the group, and from what Masoodi had just told him, it seemed that the Guards also knew about it. If he could find out what they knew, perhaps it would give him and Rastgu the lead they needed to go into action.

Masoodi apologized and said he had to go back to his office, but that he could meet Randall again in two days' time. They arranged a time and place and the Iranian left the café. Randall watched him go, then waited to see if anyone rose to follow him; no one did. The American went to the door, stepped out onto the pavement, and caught sight of Masoodi heading back toward his office. People passed on both sides of the street, but as far as he could see, no one was following the architect. Relieved, Randall turned and walked off in the opposite direction toward his car.

Rastgu did not arrive until late that night and Randall was seriously worried that something had happened to him. When he did arrive, he looked grim, his normally bright eyes clouded by deep anxiety.

"What's happened?" Randall asked, aware that it must be something serious. The Israeli sat down and steadied his breathing before replying.

"The Russians have invaded Afghanistan," he said, his voice scarcely under control.

"Oh my God, when?"

"This evening. We knew there'd been a massive buildup for weeks, mostly at Bagram, Shendal, and Kabul, and on Christmas Eve they flew in six thousand combat troops, so we were ready for something. They took control of Kabul earlier this evening. I was in radio contact with Jerusalem. They say the takeover was a signal to send their divisions across the border; they're moving in on Herat, Mazar-e Sharif, and the Kunduz Valley—three prongs, all unstoppable."

"You know what this could mean?" asked Randall, though he realized that the question was superfluous.

"Yes, I know. And if our friends here decide to make their next move now, God help us all."

Fereshteh arrived at two-thirty that morning and was met by Sirus at the airport as promised. She had taken the precaution of buying a length of cloth suitable for wearing as a chador, and he had difficulty at first in recognizing her from Randall's description. She seemed tired and nervous. Sirus knew from Randall the strain she had been under and he was worried. They could not afford to have her on their hands if she cracked. He would have to make alternative arrangements.

The small man who opened the door for them as Sirus and Fereshteh left the airport had no difficulty in recognizing her. Molla Ahmad had described her luggage in great detail. He tested his receiver again. The transmitter he had lodged behind the bumper of Rastgu's car was working perfectly.

44

For their second meeting, Randall and Masoodi did not choose the Iranian's *patuq*. It was risky to be seen in the same place twice together. They had agreed that there was little point in their meeting if Masoodi had nothing to report, and Randall suggested they determine on a system of signaling. At 5:00 P.M., they arrived within minutes of each other at the Bank-e Melli toward the lower end of Ferdowsi Avenue. Randall waited outside until Masoodi entered the bank, watching him carefully to check that he was not being followed, however discreetly. As far as he could tell, no one was tailing the Iranian, so Randall followed him through the massive bronze doors into the lobby, then beyond into the main banking hall. Masoodi had joined a line at the bottom end of the hall; Randall fell into the line to his right, eyes still registering the other customers, watching for signs of a tail and waiting for Masoodi to reach the till. At last, the architect arrived at the counter and in a loud voice asked to withdraw five hundred tumans. Randall reached inside his pocket, clasped his forehead as if he had forgotten something, apologized to the man behind him in the line, and hurriedly left the bank. It had been arranged that if Masoodi asked to deposit money, he had nothing to report and Randall should return the next day; if, on the other hand, he made a withdrawal, it was a sign that they should meet later at a prearranged spot. As he left the bank, Randall looked again for signs of someone watching; perhaps there was someone there in the shadows, but if so, Randall could not hope to see him.

They met five minutes later at the gate of the Turkish Embassy on the other side of Ferdowsi. It was dark, and they were able to meet and walk together unobserved. Masoodi passed a small bundle of papers to Randall.

"These," he said as they walked on slowly, "were taken from the apartment of the man I mentioned to you. From the information I've been able to obtain from my friend, it seems that the man, whose name was Mehdi Muftizadeh, was arrested on 19 November and executed at dawn the next day. The charges are unclear as usual: 'fighting against God' and being 'corrupt on the earth,' but the Revolutionary Court's report also mentions something quite unusual in such cases: *kufr*—unbelief or heresy. There's a problem with the case, though. Apparently, there was an irregularity. On 15 April, the Revolutionary Council issued an edict stating that all Revolutionary Courts were to be composed of three members, the chairman being a cleric. Generally, this ruling has been observed, but it appears that in this instance it was not. Two members of the court in question, the Yusefabad District Court, carried through the whole business without consulting the third member. The execution was supervised by Molla Mohammad Shahidi, a local cleric who preaches in the Hazrat-e Amir Mosque in Amirabad and is one of the two permanent members of the Yusefabad court. The actual sentence was delivered by Ayatollah Sayyid 'Ali Marvdashti, who lives in the south of the city and sits on a number of courts in Tehran."

"Did you say 'Marvdashti'?" Randall asked. He had heard the name before, but he could not be sure where. Had it been in connection with Nava'i?

"Yes, Marvdashti. He was a close associate of Imam Khomeini before the latter's exile in 1963. Anyway, it seems that Shahidi had obtained information about the activities of Muftizadeh. Oddly enough, the man lived only a few streets away from me at the time, although I'd never heard of him. It's not exactly clear what his activities were, but the report mentions spreading false ideas about the promised Imam, reviving the heresies of the Ismailis, and attempting to corrupt members of the Revolutionary Army. The last charge may be the most important one, but the report gives no details. It's my own feeling—and my friend agrees with me—that the two mollas were more concerned with religious issues and for some reason or other wanted to have the man tried and executed in the shortest time possible.

"The papers I've given you were taken from Muftizadeh's apartment by Revolutionary Guards sent to arrest him—my friend was one of them—but they were never referred to during the trial. Afterward, they were returned to the commander of the Guard unit who just put them straight into his files, and my friend was able to 'borrow' them without any difficulty. There was a copy of the trial report with them, so he was able to take everything relating to the case. He passed all the papers to me early this morning, and I was able to make copies at lunchtime on our office Xerox machine.

"I haven't had time to read through them in any detail. Several of them are obviously specifications for some sort of scientific apparatus, but I don't have enough science even to hazard a guess what it is. Two or three are printed letters from the Imam Hasan, which would seem to confirm that this man was an Irshadi. There's one very unusual paper—it's a letter in rather poor Persian, badly written, and signed in Roman script. You may be able to make out the name more easily than I can, but I think the signature is Felix Rascher. Does such a name mean anything to you?"

Randall was gripped by a fresh sense of excitement. The name corresponded to the initials "F. R."

"It doesn't mean anything to me as such, but I assume it's the man in charge of the secret Irshadi base. I believe he may belong to a German fascist group known as the Deutsche Aktiongruppe. What's strange, though, is that he should want to write in Persian. How bad is the writing and style?"

"It's obvious that whoever wrote it wasn't Iranian. But neither was he a beginner. It's quite legible and certainly readable. I can't make much sense of it, but that's only because I don't understand the content. It includes a lot of what seem to be English scientific terms. Rascher was asking Muftizadeh to obtain certain pieces of equipment here in Tehran."

"When was the letter dated?"

"Oh, months ago. April, I think."

Randall fingered the documents in his hand. He now had an important lead, that was obvious—but would it be enough? His steaming breath was suddenly illuminated as they moved into a patch of street lighting. He spoke to Masoodi in a low voice.

"Ibrahim, what about the house in south Tehran you told me about, the one you used to visit? Is there any chance of my getting in there? Perhaps I could find what I'm looking for, something to lead me straight to the sect headquarters."

They were in relative darkness again. Randall could not see his companion's face as he answered him. There was silence for a while, then Masoodi spoke.

"It would be difficult and probably more than a little dangerous, but I see no reason why it couldn't be attempted. You could go there by night, though I don't know how many people actually live there. I once heard something about an old molla living there with a couple of servants, but I never saw him myself. I did see the servants, though—an old man and his wife and a boy, possibly their grandson. Sometimes there were others, but those three were permanent."

"That sounds reasonably safe," Randall said. "Can you draw me a map I can use to reconnoiter and to visit the house tomorrow night."

Masoodi nodded. "I can make you a map of the area and a plan of the house—I think I can still remember the layout. Sometimes being an architect is useful. Meet me outside the City Theater tomorrow morning at ten and I'll give them both to you."

At Baharestan Square, they separated. Masoodi found a taxi to return to Yusefabad, while Randall walked back to the spot where he had left his Volkswagen. He wanted to read over the papers Masoodi had given him as soon as possible, and send copies to Jerusalem through Rastgu.

Randall met Masoodi the following morning as arranged and spent fifteen minutes discussing the plans he had drawn the night before. They were clear and detailed, and Randall was able to work out a relatively easy route. The house was situated in the heart of the bazaar district, at the center of a tangled maze of lanes and alleyways. Randall would have to familiarize himself with the way there before attempting to find it by night.

Dressed as a workman, he spent most of that afternoon walking slowly through the shadowy passages of the bazaar, checking and rechecking the path he would follow late that night. He would go alone—it would be foolish to put both Rastgu and himself at risk at such a critical juncture. Returning to Darband, he spent the evening relaxing, preparing himself for the venture he was about to undertake in the hope that it would bring him yet closer to the heart of this mystery.

He was at the Shah Mosque entrance to the bazaar at twelve. Under his jacket, he carried a fine rope ladder obtained for him by Rastgu, and in his pocket, he kept a small pistol.

Walking slowly, he set off straight down the well-lit main street, the Bazaar-e Bozorg, between rows of shuttered shops, turning left eventually on Hisam-e Lashkar and then into the smaller alleys of the district. Narrow and dark, the old cobbled lanes were deserted, like thoroughfares in a city of the dead. No one moved up or down them, no voices rang out behind the grim walls on either side, not even a dog lurked in the shadows. Instinctively, he found himself walking lightly, pressing close to the mud-brick walls, holding his breath. In the dark, strange shadows followed him. He lost his way twice, but finally found the right turning, identified the landmark he had located earlier that day—the gate of a small Sufi meeting place—and found the door of the house he sought.

The high wall, unbroken save by the heavy wooden door, stretched from ground level to the top of the second story. Like most houses built in the traditional Islamic pattern, this was designed to block out the world; it looked inward, all attention focused on the small courtyard at its heart. Once inside the courtyard, however, entry to the house proper should prove relatively easy. Checking that the alley was still deserted, he tossed one end of the ladder up onto the edge of the wall. It landed softly and the hooks engaged at once. He waited for a further minute, to be sure that no one inside had heard the ladder catch, then scaled the wall and slipped across onto the flat roof behind it. He raised the ladder slowly, gathered it in his hands, and carried it with him to the other side of the roof, overlooking the courtyard. No lights shone into the square enclosure from the house; all seemed still. Randall lowered the ladder again and climbed down slowly. Once inside the courtyard, he knew where to go. On his plan, Masoodi had marked an upstairs room which he had been told was used as an office. The stairs lay directly opposite Randall, through a passage on the far side of the house.

The door to the passage was open. Silently, Randall made his way along it, then up the narrow stairs. At the top were two rooms, on the right and left. Cautiously, he tried the handle of the door on his right; it opened and he slipped in. Closing the door behind him, he switched on a small torch and flashed its beam about the room. As Masoodi had thought, it was an office of sorts, with books and files on shelves about the walls and a desk at one side. Randall headed for the desk and began to work his way through the papers on top. He had no idea what he was looking for, but was equally certain that something of interest would turn up.

At last, under a pile of other papers of no apparent significance, he came across a letter, the handwriting of which he recognized as that of the Imam Hasan. Headed "Kerman," it was dated 25 Muharram/ 15 December.

"Sayyid 'Ali," it began, "I have returned in safety to Kerman and shall be leaving the city in a few days to go into the desert. As you know, I returned here with Izra'il, and he and I have now had time to discuss my plans further. He is in agreement with them and believes they can be carried out within the period I have suggested. The date set for the commencement of the *jihad* shall now be the Day of the Return, as was proposed. I have sent Izra'il to Tehran again to make certain preparations there. Please render him every service that lies in your power. Be assured that you shall see the Promised One and shall rejoice in his coming. The days are few now and his reappearance is near. Praise be to God, the Lord of the Worlds. Peace be upon you. Al-Imam Hasan al-Qa'im bi-amr Allah."

When he had finished reading the letter, Randall stood for a while lost in thought. He had no certain idea of what the "Day of the Return" meant, but he thought it might refer to the return of the Hidden Imam, the day of his resurrection and reappearance among men. The Irshadis might already have determined on a specific day for that event on the basis of some prophecy in their Book of Guidance, the *Kitab al-Irshad*. From the context, it seemed as if it was fairly soon. As for the Izra'il mentioned in the letter, he could not even begin to guess who it might be; all he knew was that it was the name of the angel of death.

Suddenly, quite without warning, the door opened and a figure appeared holding a kerosene lamp. It was the old molla who lived in the house. He had moved so quietly that Randall, engrossed as he had been in thought, had not heard him. Like many elderly people, the molla needed little sleep and often came here to his study during the night to read or write.

Both men froze, the molla white-bearded and white-robed, a fantastic and terrifying apparition in the weird light of the flickering lamp. Randall found his voice first.

"Don't be afraid, old man. I don't wish to harm you. Go back to

your room and I will leave without any trouble. I haven't stolen anything. Please go back."

But the old molla, shocked as he had been, was not easily cowed. In
a surprisingly loud voice that shattered the fragile silence into thousands of booming fragments, he called out, "Help! Thieves! Murder-
ers! Come quickly. A thief is in the house. Help!"

Randall dashed toward him, grappling with him, struggling to clap
his hand over the old man's screaming mouth. The molla kicked and
scratched, still shouting for help. Randall jerked back from his adversary's blows, striking his arm, and the lamp flew from the old man's
hand across the room. It smashed, spilling kerosene over the floor,
bursting into flames that rapidly spread across the carpet.

Outside, shouts and footsteps could be heard. Randall hurried to
the door. He rushed down the stairs, into the short passage, and up to
the door leading into the courtyard. Quickly, he flung the door open
and stepped outside. Almost immediately there was the loud report of
a gunshot and he flung himself back into the passage. A rough voice
shouted.

"Come out at once. You can't escape. We are Revolutionary
Guards and are well armed. Come out quietly or we'll be forced to
shoot you."

Randall crept to the doorway, keeping well inside the shadows. He
could make out the forms of two men in the courtyard, both holding
rifles pointed toward the doorway in which he stood. Silently, he drew
the automatic from his pocket and crouched in a stable firing position.

The guards had made two elementary mistakes. They were standing in the dim pool of light cast by the rapidly growing fire burning in
the room above, and they were much too close together. Randall
raised the pistol in two hands, steadied it, aimed and fired twice in
rapid succession. The guards fell almost simultaneously.

Randall dashed into the courtyard, through a second passage, and
up to the front door. A moment or two spent fiddling with the locks
and he was out in the alley. The shouting and shots had roused
neighbors, and he could hear cries of alarm on both sides. Without
pausing to think, he ran, weaving in and out of alleys, heedless of
direction. Eventually, after what seemed an eternity of running, he
came out at the southern end of the bazaar, onto Mowlavi Street.

It was a calculated risk for Randall to walk back to the north of the bazaar where he had parked his car. But he had to get away quickly before the guards cordoned off the area. Keeping to small streets, hiding in the shadows of doorways whenever vehicles came near, he made his way to the Volkswagen. There was no one around. If he could get back to Darband without being stopped, he would be safe. To be certain, he checked in his pocket. He still had the papers identifying him as Rolf Malmberg, a Swedish doctor. The Guards might just believe that a doctor would be on the road at this time of night.

As he drove through the silent streets, Randall pondered over the question that had plagued him ever since the scene in the courtyard. He could not understand what Revolutionary Guards were doing in the house. It was obvious from the letter he had found that the place was still occupied by Irshadis, and the man who had surprised him must have been the old molla Masoodi had told him about. But if that were so, how could orthodox Islamic revolutionaries be guarding the house? Had it been a bluff? Then, as if a veil had been drawn away, the answer came to him. He had seen the face of the old man before, in a photograph in the Nava'i file in Washington. He was Ayatollah Sayyid 'Ali Marvdashti, the cleric who had confirmed Nava'i's credentials for the British Embassy in Tehran, the judge who had sentenced Mehdi Muftizadeh to death. The reasons for the irregularities in the trial of Muftizadeh now seemed obvious. Marvdashti lived a double life as an Irshadi and as an orthodox cleric. Muftizadeh must have possessed papers which, if found, would have incriminated Marvdashti. After the arrest, the latter had acted quickly to secure access to the documents found in Muftizadeh's apartment and had then seen to it that Muftizadeh himself and, indeed, the whole case, were put out of the way for good. But knowledge of what must have happened served only to increase Randall's anxiety. How far had the Irshadis succeeded in infiltrating the orthodox religious establishment or, indeed, other sectors of society? What role, if any, had they played in the recent revolution? How much of Nava'i's original story had been true? Just how much power did they wield behind the scenes, and how long would it be before they began to act in support of their plans? He needed more information—and quickly.

It was five o'clock in the afternoon in Washington when Howard Straker's secure phone rang. He picked it up at once: there was only one call he was expecting on that line.

"This is Deep Operations, sir. We have Randall. He blew his cover about an hour ago when he burgled a house in Southern Tehran. Our agent has high-level contacts in the Revolutionary Guard. They're looking for him now. What do you want me to do, sir?"

"He has to be found before the Guards capture him. He mustn't talk. You will authorize our man to locate Randall and take him out immediately. He must be eliminated. Is that understood?"

"Yes, sir. I'll make contact at once."

Straker put down the phone. A tremble of unaccustomed excitement ran through him. Randall must be found and silenced. Everything depended on it. Everything.

45

TEHRAN
31 December 1979

It was long after 2:00 A.M. by the time Randall made it back to Darband. He was sure he had not been followed. The house was dark and completely silent when he entered. He switched on a light downstairs. What he saw made his blood run cold. Chairs were knocked over, a table lay on its side, a vase was smashed. Randall rushed into all the rooms on the ground floor. Nothing. He ran upstairs in a frenzy, checking each of the bedrooms, beginning with Fereshteh's. All were empty. Again and again, he called, but his shouts echoed around him and there was no answer. They were both gone.

He checked the house a second time, but found nothing. Back in the main room, he straightened the furniture, looking carefully for clues that might indicate who had been there, but there was not a trace. Rastgu and Fereshteh had been abducted. Why? And by whom? It didn't make sense. Or had whoever kidnapped them expected to find him there as well? Would they return for him? He wasn't going to wait around to find out. He had to leave the house, and quickly. The safe house in Majdiyye would do until he could organize his thoughts and make plans. Working rapidly, he gathered together the papers he and Rastgu had kept in the study. As far as he could tell, they had not been touched, but he would have to check later.

At first light, he moved outside cautiously, carrying the bag of papers in one hand and his gun in the other. There was silence, broken only by the singing of winter birds. He started the car and edged it out of the long driveway into the road. If someone were going to make a move, he was at his most vulnerable now. He tensed, ready to gun the engine into life, but the road remained empty. Turning to the left, he headed south.

He reached Majdiyye safely, parked the car in the garage, and let himself in with the key Rastgu had given him for use in an emergency. By now he was extremely hungry. The nervous energy he had used up in the course of the break-in and the mounting anxiety he had felt for his friends all that morning were now taking their toll on his strength. He knew that if he was to be of any help to them, he would have to eat and rest in order to stay alert. Just to rush off looking for them when he had no idea even where to start would be foolish and dangerous. He went into the kitchen, found various cans in the larder, and prepared himself a substantial breakfast.

When he had finished eating, he took the bag of papers into a back room and began sorting through them. Toward the bottom of the pile, he came across a report dated the previous day. It was written in Hebrew and attached to it was a longhand summary in English prepared by Rastgu. The Israeli must have received it the night before and prepared the summary while Randall was carrying out the break-in. As he read through it, Randall experienced once again the sensation he had felt while listening to al-Shidyaq give his account of the Irshadis. The report was headed "Dr. Felix Rascher":

> From several indications, including his name, supposed nationality, approximate age, and apparent technical expertise, we have provisionally identifed the author of the letter to Muftizadeh as Dr. Felix Rascher, a German scientist formerly employed at the V-2 experimental site at Peenemünde on the Baltic. Rascher was born in 1907 in Berlin and later studied physics and chemistry at the university there. He and von Braun became friends while the latter, who was five years Rascher's junior, was carrying out his doctoral research at the same university. He himself completed his doctorate before von Braun, in 1930, and, in the same year, became a member of the Nazi party. Shortly afterward, he started work for the Raketenflugtechnische Forschunginstitut, the Institute of Technical Research on Rockets, in Trauen.
>
> When von Braun and General Dornberger established Peenemünde in 1936 to replace the existing experimental stations at Reinickendorf and Kummersdorf West, Rascher and others at the institute assisted with various aspects of the V-2 experiments. In 1942, when Albert Speer took over

as Minister for Munitions and War Production, the
Peenemünde project, particularly the V-2 work on the east
side of Usedom Island, which was under the control of the
Army, was given a considerable boost. It was then that
Rascher was recruited to work full-time at the station. It is
believed that he was deeply involved in the A-9 and A-10
prototype experiments, designed to produce a multistage
rocket capable of reaching the United States.

Following the British bombing of Peenemünde in August
1943, Rascher was among the scientists transferred to the
underground V-2 factory in Kohnstein Mountain near
Nordhausen, where he worked under Albin Sawatzki. Control of the V-2 project had now been handed over to the SS,
and Rascher himself is believed to have become a ranking
officer in the SS with responsibility for supervision of the
security aspects of the scientific work at the base. He remained in constant touch with the Development Works at
Peenemünde-East, where von Braun and others were still
working.

In February 1945, when Peenemünde was threatened by
the Soviet advance, many technicians were evacuated to a
new research station in Bleicheröde, twenty kilometers from
Kohnstein, and it is understood that Rascher joined von
Braun there, probably under orders from the SS, who were
worried about the possible defection of the scientists and
needed someone of Rascher's experience to ensure adequate
surveillance. Rascher was also among the five hundred or so
V-2 scientists taken by Hans Kammler's special train to the
Oberammergau region in April, but he was not among the
prisoners taken when the American 44th Infantry Division
entered the area in May. Subsequent attempts to track him
down were unsuccessful, and it is thought he made use of
his SS privileges to flee the region and go into hiding.

The Allied authorities were particularly eager to find him,
not only because of his work on the V-2—his name was on
the list of scientists wanted by the Americans for their own
rocket projects—but because he was the brother of the notorious Dr. Sigmund Rascher, the man in charge of the
hideous "freezing experiments" and other acts of medical

sadism at Dachau. Sigmund and his wife had been arrested by the SS in May 1944, and he had been incarcerated in Dachau, where he was probably executed. But it was thought that Felix had knowledge of his brother's work, which he admired greatly. It is suspected that he may even have assisted in some technical aspects of it, and efforts were made to track him down for the famous "Doctors' Trial" after Nuremberg. He has been high on the list of wanted ex-Nazis ever since.

When he had finished reading the bizarre report, Randall sat for a long time. The terror he had felt before returned. Who were these people? How many further ramifications could there be before he tracked them down?

There was nothing in the papers that offered any clue as to what had happened to Sirus and Fereshteh. They could be anywhere, in the hands of the Irshadis or the Revolutionary Guards or SAVAMA. He would need help, and there was only one person to whom he could turn for it, someone he had promised not to involve in the matter again. But there was no choice: he would have to break his promise. He telephoned Masoodi at his office and explained that he wanted to meet him. The Iranian could not get free before lunch. At least that would give Randall a chance to sleep for a few hours.

They met at one o'clock in the Museum of Antiquities. The spacious, empty halls of the museum proved an excellent meeting place. They talked at first of the events of the night before, and Randall then told Masoodi as much as he could of the information he had received that morning. Then, as they stood beside a case of Luristan bronzes, he turned to the Iranian.

"Ibrahim," he said, "I have bad news."

The color drained from the man's face as he turned to face Randall.

"What is it? Has something happened?"

"Last night while I was away, someone came to the house in which my friends and I were living. There were two of them, a woman called Fereshteh and a man named Sirus. When I returned, they had both been taken prisoner and abducted. They may be dead, but I don't think they are. I have no clue as to who may have taken them.

I've no idea who can have discovered that we were at that address. I need your help to find them. Your friend in the Revolutionary Guards may know something, or you may be able to find out if the Irshadis have them. If you can't do that, at least you may be able to help me make my own inquiries. I'm on my own now in Tehran. I have no backup, nowhere to go. I need your help."

Masoodi looked perplexed. He shook his head.

"I am sorry to hear what has happened. But this does not concern me now. You promised not to put me directly at risk, that you would arrange for my wife and myself to leave the country."

Randall took Masoodi's arm gently.

"That's just the point, Ibrahim. The arrangements have all been made for you and your wife to leave. But they were made through my friend Sirus, with his own people. He's not Iranian, but I can't tell you more than that. Unless I find and rescue him, I have no way of getting in contact with his base, nor of finalizing the arrangements for you."

Masoodi's look of perplexity had changed to one of alarm.

"What about your own people? Can't you make contact with them?"

Randall shook his head.

"No. I can't explain, it would be too complicated. But I have no way of making contact. Please believe me. You have to help me. It's the only chance for both of us."

"It would be dangerous to ask too many questions," Masoodi said, "no matter who is responsible for their capture. I have no contact with the Irshadis, and I want none. You know that. My friend might become suspicious if I asked direct questions about suspected agents of another country. He is a good friend, but he is also a committed revolutionary."

"But if you phrased your questions carefully . . ."

"I don't know. Perhaps. I will have to think about it. Perhaps there is a way. But it will not be easy, or safe. Give me until tomorrow to think it over. I can do nothing for you until then." Randall nodded in agreement. They arranged to meet early the next day, and to avoid attracting attention, they left the museum separately, Masoodi going first. Five minutes later Randall stepped out onto the snow-covered pavement. Turning right into Qavvam al-Saltana, he headed up toward Naderi; ahead of him in the distance, sharp in the clear January air, was the snow-mantled peak of Mount Damavand, the extinct volcano that watched like a sentinel over the city.

As he was passing the Technical College opposite the junction with Furughi Street, two men whom he had noticed at the front of the museum came up behind him. The man on the right stopped him with a grip on his shoulder and a soft request to halt. Both were young men of about twenty-five, tall and dark-haired. But there the resemblance ended. The man on Randall's right was alert and intelligent, with narrow, well-defined features. He spoke with an educated Tehrani accent, politely, in a voice that seemed accustomed to command. His companion was, by way of contrast, heavy-browed, almost savage, massively built and silent. The first man spoke again.

"Mr. Byrne—or should I say, Mr. Randall?—would you please accompany us? We would like to speak with you about a certain matter that has arisen."

Randall felt his heart miss a beat as the man pronounced his real name.

"What do you want? Who are you?" he protested.

"My name is Captain Ahmad Shaybani, an officer in the Revolutionary Guards stationed at Yusefabad. I have some questions to ask. Would you please come this way?"

The man was polite, but it was clear that Randall had no choice. He did not question the credentials of the two men making the arrest. The Revolutionary Guards must have been searching hard for him since the night before, and the connection with the vanished Sean Byrne would not have been difficult to make. Whatever the case, they knew who he was and there would be little point in bluffing or trying to make an escape here in the street. He did not resist when Shaybani frisked him and removed the gun from his pocket. They set off, Randall between the two guards, their hands on his upper arms, to a van parked on the corner of Sevvom-e Esfand. They pushed him into the back, closed and locked the door, and got in the front.

As they drove off, Randall thought desperately of possible escape. There was little point in trying to get away just now. He was unarmed and even if he managed to elude his captors, he could not get far: his description would have been circulated by now to Guard units throughout the city. His best chance lay in persuading the Revolutionary Guards to trust him, to prove to them that they were really working on the same side in this affair and that the Irshadi base near

Kerman posed a threat to both their countries. If he could succeed in exposing Marvdashti, they might believe him. It mattered little what happened to him; at worst he would be shot as a spy, at best sent to join the other hostages in the American Embassy. But if the Irshadis could be stopped, his mission would be successful. The van twisted and turned quickly through a maze of streets, constantly throwing him off balance. They traveled for what seemed about half an hour.

The van stopped and the door was opened seconds later. Blinded by the bright sunlight, Randall could only see two men carrying submachine guns before he was pushed through an open doorway and along a dimly lit passage. To the right, at the end, a flight of stone steps went down at right angles to another door, which was now unlocked and opened. A push from behind sent him sprawling inside.

The room was small and poorly lit from a tiny, rather dirty window set high up near the ceiling. Raising himself to his feet, he glanced toward the far corner and was taken aback to see that he was not alone. Blinking as his eyes tried to adjust to the feeble light, he realized that his companion was Ibrahim Masoodi, who was crouching in the corner, head in hands, obviously still suffering from the shock of his arrest and confinement. He looked up as Randall was thrown into the room.

Masoodi was the first to speak.

"So they've got you too."

Randall went over and sat on the floor beside his friend.

"Yes. They found me. I thought at first it must be as a result of last night, but then I remembered that the man who arrested me said he was stationed at Yusefabad. It seems that your friend there has given us away."

"My friend?"

"Yes, your friend in the Revolutionary Guards. He must either have talked or been discovered in some way. The only thing I don't understand is how they know my real name."

"But what have Revolutionary Guards to do with this?"

"The men who arrested us were Guards from the Yusefabad unit."

Masoodi looked intently at the man beside him, then sighed and lowered his head. In a dull voice, he said, "I wish that were true. But it's not. Those men aren't Revolutionary Guards, Peter. Do I have to tell you who they really are?"

46

31 December 1979

They sat in silence in the dark cell, shivering with cold. It grew dark quickly. From time to time, they rose to their feet and stomped about the room, trying to get their circulation moving, blowing on their hands.

It must have been six or seven hours later that they heard the sound of footsteps outside. The door opened and a pale light flooded the room. Two guards stood there, carrying submachine guns. One called Masoodi's name, gesturing for him to accompany them; then the guard on the left pulled the Iranian's arms behind his back and manhandled the prisoner out of the cell. The door closed and Randall was left again in the dark and cold. His resources of physical and emotional strength were being worn away by the combined effects of cold and lack of food or drink. The unending darkness crowded in on him heavily, filling him with an unnamable dread.

Minutes went by. He heard footsteps outside the window, which was clearly just above ground level, but they stopped and all was silence again. Suddenly, a burst of machine-gun fire crashed through the stillness, leaving every nerve in Randall's body jangling. His heart thudding against his rib cage and his pulse racing, he nevertheless forced himself to sit calmly. There would be no talking his way out of this. His only chance lay in a quick dash for freedom, in using the hand-to-hand fighting techniques he had learned in Vietnam.

Time passed. Huddled in his coat, he grew drowsy and realized that, weak as he was with cold and hunger, he could do very little against his guards, but he must at least try. He had often thought of just such a situation as this when in Vietnam, and had then resolved to fight rather than be tortured or killed without resistance. Curiously, the thought of Vietnam reassured him. At last, feet sounded in the passage. The door opened abruptly and he was summoned. He raised himself painfully to his feet and shuffled across the floor. He would wait until he was outside before making a break for freedom.

The guards took him by the arms and helped him up the steps. Then, instead of turning into the passage to the left as he had expected, they went straight on down a cross corridor, halfway along which was a closed wooden door. One of the guards knocked, opened the door, and stepped in, followed by the second guard, who was still holding Randall. Once inside, he left the American in the charge of his colleague and exited, closing the door behind him. The room was sparsely but tidily furnished, with a large desk at the far end on which stood an electric lamp, the only source of illumination. On the wall behind hung a black and white portrait of Adolf Hitler. The photograph, taken by Heinrich Hoffmann, bore a personal dedication scrawled across the white shirt collar. Beside it hung a red, white, and black tasseled oblong cloth bearing a double swastika and the words "Deutschland Erwache"—the flag from a standard of the 1st SS Regiment "Julius Schreck." Behind the desk sat an old man, white-haired and dressed in an immaculate white suit. The room was warm, stifling to Randall after the freezing cold of his cell. Though the man was deeply tanned, Randall could see clearly that he was not an Iranian. The stranger gestured to a chair in front of the desk and Randall crossed the room to sit in it. The identity of the man facing him was not hard to guess. His Persian was excellent and idiomatic, evidence of long years spent in the country, but the strong traces of a German accent could be detected easily.

"Good evening, Mr. Randall. Please allow me to introduce myself. My name is Felix Rascher, though I am also known to those around me as Izra'il—the angel of death. I am sorry to have kept you waiting so long and in such uncomfortable conditions. I hope you are not too cold. But I have been extremely busy today and this is really the first free moment I have had. You and your friend Mr. Masoodi have put us to considerable inconvenience. All of this has come at a very bad time for me. I have a lot of work to do, very urgent and important work. But you did pose something of a threat to that work, and it became necessary to find you and to learn how much you and your masters in Washington know about us.

"I'm sorry about what happened to your friend Mr. Masoodi, but it was really out of my hands: a matter of religious law, over which even I have no control. I've been with these people a long time now, but I still find their ways a little strange. In some respects, they seem to me even harsher, more fanatical than my own people were. They regard apostasy as the greatest sin. To turn aside from the Imam, they say, is to turn away from God. And that is punishable by death. I do not pretend to understand, but I do not interfere.

"I don't know what will happen to your other friends. Or perhaps you have not been told. They are here as well, the man and the woman. Some of Molla Ahmad's men brought them here a few hours ago. That was how we found you, of course. Molla Ahmad had the girl followed when she arrived here from New York. Once we had an idea of how many of you were involved, a team was sent in to take you all. Unfortunately, you were not at home. I believe we now know where you were and what you were doing. In the meantime, the late Mr. Masoodi made a mistake. He told his wife they were going to leave Iran. She in her turn told her parents they were going abroad, perhaps for good, and mentioned that her husband had an American visitor. Her mother mentioned it to her sister; I don't have to tell you how efficient the family grapevine still is in this country. The sister is one of our group, of course. Many Ismaili families in Iran have at least one Irshadi member. We put two and two together and followed Masoodi to the museum today. And here you are."

So they were here in the house! Randall's mind raced. He had to gain time, keep Rascher talking, try to trick him into revealing their whereabouts. He spoke for the first time.

"What's your connection with these people, Rascher? I'll be honest. It seems somewhat insane to me that a German scientist, even a Nazi scientist, should be mixed up with a group like the Irshadis. I don't think you can be a believer, though anything's possible, I suppose. You must have your reasons. Or are you really insane?"

Rascher laughed. It was a dry laugh, sardonic and humorless.

"You seem to know a lot about me. But you are, of course, right to be surprised. My being here is the result of an unusual combination of events. Let me explain."

The German spoke for fully twenty minutes, almost nonstop. He obviously had the need to talk about himself to someone who was not Iranian or a Muslim, and presumably, the opportunity for him to do so did not arise very often. "I wonder how I can best explain it to you," he said. "Perhaps I should begin before the war.

"You will undoubtedly have heard the name of Joseph Arthur

Comte de Gobineau. Ah! I see that you have. He was, of course, one of the great French diplomats of the last century as well as a noted writer. He was a brilliant man, best known in some circles for his contribution to the theory of racial inequality and the supremacy of the Aryan peoples. He became one of the great inspirations of the later Nazi philosophy. Wagner was a staunch admirer of his and met him in 1876. By the turn of the century, there were numerous Gobineau Societies in Germany. His books were translated into German and widely read, especially the *Essai sur l'Inégalité des Races Humaines*, which we all regarded as his masterpiece. No one knows if the Führer ever read Gobineau, but it is quite possible that he did at least see part of his work while in Vienna, and there must have been copies in Wagner's library at Bayreuth.

"I myself was a member of the Gobineau Society of Berlin in the late 1920s during the years I was a student at the university there. This was some years before I joined the Nazi Party. Our Gobineau Society was made up mostly of students and professors from a variety of faculties. Many of us belonged to right-wing political groups, such as Hugenberg's German People's Party and the Stahlhelm, and a few were already Nazis. We studied most of the master's works, but concentrated above all on the *Essai*—that was the cornerstone of his thought for us. I can remember vividly the effect his theories had on me at that age: 'The racial question dominates all the other problems of history . . . the inequality of races suffices to explain the whole unfolding of the destiny of peoples.' It was exhilarating reading, especially the passages which talked of Aryan supremacy and the nobility of the German people as the finest representatives of the Aryan race. From a Frenchman too!

"But I and a number of my close friends were intrigued by another aspect of Gobineau's racial theory. He firmly believed that he would find the purest Aryans of all in the area where they had originated— Central Asia and, in particular, Iran. The very name 'Iran' means 'Land of the Aryans' and the pure Persians are among the closest to the early type of the race. In 1855 he went to Iran, where he was first secretary and then chargé d'affaires at the French Legation. After a few years, he was posted elsewhere, but in 1862 he returned, holding the post of French minister in Tehran until the following year. He then went back to France—somewhat disillusioned, because he had found the Iranians about as mongrelized as most other races, especially by the Semite Arabs. But he had seen and read about many things which intrigued and excited him. Two years after his return to Paris, in 1865, he published a book called *Religions et philosophies dans l'Asie centrale.* When my friends and I obtained copies of the German translation of this work and read it, we were filled with a new kind of enthusiasm.

"Most of the book is devoted to the history of a religious sect which had appeared in Iran not long before Gobineau's first arrival in the country. In 1844 the Babis, led by a young visionary from Shiraz, had started preaching a sort of modified, fundamentalist Shi'ism, and in 1848 this young man claimed he was the Mahdi, a sort of savior the people were waiting for. His followers multiplied very quickly and some of them took to arms. Before long, struggles had broken out with the state, and by the time Gobineau had arrived in Tehran, they had been all but wiped out. Well, of course, even though they failed, we found the whole Babi story remarkably inspiring. It was really Neitzsche's superman, this Mahdi coming to purify the world and bring a new era. Neitzsche talks of 'a particularly strong kind of man, most highly gifted in intellect and will. This man and the élite around him will become the "lords of the earth."' Later, we all saw statements of this kind as prophecies of the Führer. But the Islamic idea of the Mahdi—that too was inspiring in its way, and we were intrigued that Gobineau had devoted so much space in his book to the story of a Persian superhero."

At this point, Randall, who was growing frustrated by Rascher's lecturing, interrupted him.

"I'm sorry," he said, "but I don't see what any of this has to do with the things that have been going on here; I want to know how you came to be in Iran, how you're mixed up with these people."

Rascher nodded and then continued from where he had left off, as if nothing had been said.

"I became a Nazi in September 1930, after the Reichstag elections that raised the party to the position of the second largest in Germany. In 1931 our Auslandsorganisation in Hamburg began the work of building up small branches in the East. At first, they concentrated on the Far East, but even from the beginning, Iran was regarded as important, largely because of its strategic position. There were large numbers of Germans there at that time—the old Junkers airline concession had become the Berlin–Kabul Lufthansa service via Tehran, there was the construction of a shipyard and dry dock at Bandar Pahlavi, and, of course, the national railway network. Reza Shah was very pro-German. In 1937, while I was working in Trauen, I met some of my old Gobineau Society friends. We were all Nazis by then and enthusiastic about the expansion of the Reich. Someone mentioned our old interest in Gobineau's book about the Babis, and we got onto the possibility of spreading Nazi ideas in Iran, not only among the German population but among the natives or, at least, the more racially pure Iranians. Perhaps we could even find some surviving Babis and win their support. Three of us decided to go to Iran for this purpose, and after discussions with the Auslandsorganisation, it was agreed that we could go. Apart from the usefulness of increasing the numbers of local sympathizers, the Abwehr thought we could carry out some useful espionage work.

"We stayed in Iran for two years, mostly in Tehran and Isfahan. In 1938 I helped set up the Nazi club in Isfahan, where there were about seventy German technicians. But all the time, I was interested in following up Gobineau's ideas. I asked about the Babis and found that they had all but vanished. But at the start of 1939, I was in Kerman to meet some German engineers and, while there, was introduced to the leader of the Irshadis. The man who introduced us was a member of the Auslandsorganisation who had spent some time in Hong Kong and had become friendly with some Irshadi families there who had recommended that the party contact the Imam.

"I knew a little about Ismailis from Gobineau and was surprised to learn that they still existed in Iran. I spent several months in Kerman and became friendly with the Imam: he seemed to sympathize with many of our ideas. The concept of a universal Reich appealed to him, and he found the Führer principle most congenial."

Once again, Randall interrupted the German in mid-flow.

"So you stayed and converted him to the Nazi philosophy! I suppose you're going to tell me this is all some crazy stunt dreamed up years ago by Himmler. Do you honestly think I'll believe that?"

"No, of course not. I didn't stay in Iran, not then. With the outbreak of war in 1939, my presence in Germany became imperative; our rocket research had become extremely important. After the war, I was in hiding for some time in Germany until I was helped to escape by NERO, the Nazi Escape and Resettlement Organization. You probably know that scientists from Peenemünde and elsewhere were welcomed by the Egyptian Government, and in later years repaid the favor by working for them on a missile project with the purpose of destroying the Jewish herd that had taken control of Palestine. I spent three years in Cairo and got to know the Iranian population there. Talking with them, I realized that Iran offered unusual opportunities for our cause in the postwar period. Reza Shah had been so favorably disposed to Germany that the British and Russians invaded his country in 1941 and deposed him. Their presence was much resented— after all, Britain and Russia had been the traditional enemies of Iran since the nineteenth century. And there had been the inspiring example of Rashid Ali's pro-Nazi régime in Iraq. There were Nazi sympathizers throughout the country, although Iranian attempts at organizing a fascist movement had been inept in the extreme. But our best agent in Iran, a man of mixed parentage, called Ruhi Schneider, had succeeded in establishing small cells of pro-Nazi Iranians in different parts of the country. I discussed all of this with my NERO contacts and they agreed that if some of these cells could be reactivated, they could prove useful to the organization and to the work for the destruction of Israel. It was decided that I should go to Iran once more, and I left Cairo in 1952.

"About a month after my return to this country, I traveled to Kerman and renewed my acquaintance with the Imam Hasan. He had been horrified at the fate of Germany. Like most Muslims, he hated the Jews and had no love for the cowards who perpetrated the farce-trials at Nuremberg or for the criminals who gave Palestine to the Zionists. But he was not quite like other Muslims. He had a wider vision, something that reminded me of the Führer. He dreamed of conquering not just the Jews, but the world. His aim was to fight a *jihad*, a holy war, and to establish a sort of Islamic Reich. Of course, all of this was mixed up with the most hopeless religious mumbo jumbo—prophecies about the Mahdi, a book called the *Kitab al-Irshad*, the usual stuff. But I saw something in what he said, a hope for revenge. Not just against the Jews, but everybody who had been involved in our defeat."

"And who did that include?" burst out Randall. "Didn't the war teach you anything? Didn't you realize there was no way you could win, that we would beat you again, that we would always beat you?"

"But on the contrary, my young friend, the war had defeated our enemies as much as ourselves. And once I began to think things over here, I began to see my way to our ultimate victory.

"It was all very vague at that point, but I knew that the sect had money and the means of making a lot more. I already knew that the families in Hong Kong had been in close contact with the Nazi organization there and that they would be willing to collaborate with neo-Nazi groups in Europe to help in the sale of heroin shipped abroad by them. I discussed my ideas with a number of colleagues whom NERO had sent to Iran after me, and we agreed that we should stay and help the Imam. Over the years, we advised the sect about how to prepare for a *jihad*. I don't mean to suggest that all the ideas came from us. The Imam Hasan is a brilliant man and so are many of his followers, but we had the expertise to recommend the best ways to put his ideas into action. We began a scheme to train some of his young followers as engineers, technicians, and, later on, as scientists. In the late 1960s, we began the construction of a secret base near Kerman. At this stage, our project was extremely long-term—none of us expected to live to see it come to fruition. Our plan was to construct a number of nuclear devices which we would then have carried to various important cities —New York, Jerusalem, Moscow, London. When detonated, the result would be widespread holocaust. At the same time, we began to use part of the base as a training camp for what eventually grew to be a small army of young Irshadi men and women. We also began serious arms purchases in the early seventies and built up a large arsenal which could be used once the *jihad* began. It would come in useful if we ever had to defend the base or engage in other activities—Mecca was a case in point.

"But in the mid-seventies a number of events combined to make the Imam think we could put our plans forward by decades. At the end of the sixties, as you know, Nixon and Kissinger formulated the so-called Nixon Doctrine—arms instead of troops, for nations friendly to America to undertake their own defense. In 1971 the U.S. foreign trade balance showed a deficit—the first since 1893; there was pressure to increase arms sales to make up the balance. In May 1972, Nixon and Kissinger agreed to sell Iran any conventional weapons it wanted, and as a result, the Iranians became the largest single purchasers of American arms in the world. Nearly half of the total Pentagon arms sales in 1974 went to Iran. The Shah bought every conceivable form of conventional weapon, including jet fighters, helicopters, and air-to-surface missiles. Less well known but equally vital is the fact that, from 1973, the U.S. began to make secret shipments of uranium into Iran. The aim was to provide a stock of fissionable materials in this country for use in the event of the United States wanting to build a nuclear arsenal here. Many of the conventional weapons they sold the Iranians could be modified to take nuclear warheads without much difficulty. In 1974 a large sum of money was paid by the Imam Hasan to an Iranian general called Bayanpur. The general had partial responsibility for this store of uranium, and over a period of months, managed to extract about ten kilos of uranium 235 and thirty kilos of uranium 238 from safekeeping in a vault near Shiraz. We transferred the uranium—all of it carefully packed in small, separate containers to avoid the danger of its reaching a critical mass—to our research complex. Later that year, we were able to obtain further quantities of uranium from a source in West Germany. This batch was part of a consignment being shipped to South Africa—quite secretly, of course. From Durban, our share was diverted to members of the sect in East Africa, then through the Yemens to Bahrain and Iran."

Randall watched the old man, the horror growing within him at every new revelation. The German was garrulous and boastful, but Randall knew he would not reveal everything, that he would leave the final truths shrouded and unspoken.

"About the same time, NERO put us in contact with several of the people who had founded DRASAG, who were then setting up their operations base in Uganda. After some preliminary discussions, we came to an agreeement. DRASAG would ship us a number of rockets crated as engineering equipment. My team would then modify and refine these for our purposes. Although we had a serious problem in not being able to test-fire our rockets, visits were made by members of our team to Uganda, where DRASAG was able to test the basic missile. By now, our plan had been greatly modified. We would use our weapons to destroy all major oil installations throughout the Gulf area. We had built several nuclear devices using the uranium obtained by us. These are small devices, but quite adequate for their purpose. A nuclear device using five kilos of uranium 235 will yield an explosion of about twenty kilotons. That is enough to cause serious damage at a distance of over two kilometers.

"In 1975 the Imam Hasan quite independently began to send out letters proclaiming himself the spiritual leader of all the world's Ismailis. Then, as you know, in 1977 he started prophesying the imminent appearance of the Mahdi. I told him that this was all much too premature, that we still had numerous modifications to make before any of our rockets could reach their destinations. We had succeeded in increasing the range of the basic DRASAG rocket to about four hundred miles—but we need about six hundred miles for some of our targets.

"By now, he was convinced of the truth of the prophecies in his book and said that he had found the man who would be the future Mahdi while on pilgrimage to Mecca in the winter of 1976. He claimed that the time for the appearance of the Mahdi was at the beginning of the new Islamic century, and nothing I or anyone else could do would budge him. We pushed the range up to five hundred miles, but we needed to push it still further to reach important targets. However, the Imam had been planning things on his own, and the Iranian Revolution last year played right into his hands. He planned to destabilize the balance of fear by having President Carter assassinated in Washington the same day that the Mahdi would make his appearance in Mecca. It was his belief that once this happened, the Islamic countries would combine to attack America, whereupon we would use our nuclear rockets on a small number of chosen sites in order to escalate the situation into a full-scale nuclear conflict.

"As you know, things did not go according to plan. But that is very far from the end of the matter. The Imam believes that this Mahdi is still alive somewhere, waiting for the signal to return. International relations are extremely unstable. War could break out on a world scale at any moment, even without our intervention. But we intend to intervene. At this moment, we are preparing four rockets; one is aimed at Tehran, one at the oil refinery in Abadan, one at the city of Herat in Afghanistan, and the fourth at the American fleet assembled in the Gulf of Oman. At this moment, my team is making final tests for launchings later this month. There are still several problems to iron out, but we should be ready to go in about a week. The Imam has decided on a date and nothing on earth will stop him launching his rockets as he plans."

47

31 December 1979

Randall sat stupefied. Here he was facing an ex-Nazi who planned to destroy the world with the assistance of a Persian religious sect dreaming of the millennium. His whole world had turned upside down, and he wondered if he was perhaps under the effect of some curious drug. Maybe the stories of Hasan al-Sabbah's use of hashish were true after all. Of one thing he was sure, however. He could not be allowed to live after having heard so much.

"What's in all this for you?" he finally asked Rascher.

The Nazi frowned and looked pensively at Randall.

"That would be extremely difficult for me to explain and even harder for you to understand. You were not a German living in the Third Reich, dedicated to the Führer, fired with the vision of a new world in which an Aryan master race would at last bring order and civilization to a world in chaos and pain. You did not work incessantly, as I did, to realize your dream, to bring substance to the vision of that one lonely man who knew better than any of us the meaning of our dream and our mission. And you did not see the destruction of that vision, Germany in ruins, divided, its people slaves. When I came back here to Iran, I felt bitterness and hatred for the people who had so wantonly destroyed all that I once believed in, but I also felt the greatest possible sense of defeat, and demoralization. You can have no conception of the agonies I went through. I was powerless to strike back, helpless to take revenge. For years, I nursed such feelings, seeing no possible hope, no way in which I could serve that vision again. And then I spoke once more with the Imam Hasan and learned of his vision. I could not share it, at least not the religious elements—the coming of the Mahdi and the triumph of Islam. But because of Gobineau, I could understand it. And I saw in that vision a means of revenge, perhaps even a means of so changing things in the world that there might again be an opportunity to create a German Reich. With the Americans, British, French, and Russians all weakened beyond recovery by nuclear war, we would have only a handful of Arabs, Indians, and other trash to deal with. Does that explain my position?"

Randall felt it would be useless to argue, to try to explain that West Germany would be one of the first countries to be obliterated in a nuclear war, that no Reich could ever rise on the ruins of a world destroyed by such weapons.

"Why are you telling me all this?" he asked.

Rascher smiled.

"I don't really know. Vanity, I suppose. We old men suffer much from vanity. There is no one else I can tell, no one else I can talk to about my revenge. The others who came after me are dead now; I am alone among these people. Let us say that you are here as a representative of all those who thought they had conquered, who believed that Hitler's Reich came to an end when he took his life in that bunker beneath the Berlin chancellery."

"And now that you have told me, what do you propose to do with me?"

"I did not bring you here merely to tell you these things. That, as I say, was simply my personal vanity. There is a much more serious reason for your presence here tonight. We want to know just how much your people have learned about us—what they found out originally, and what you have been able to tell them since then. We want to find out just what action your government is planning so that, if necessary, we can persuade the Imam to put forward the date of the rocket firings."

Randall shook his head slowly.

"You must be very naïve if you think I will tell you any of that. We know a lot—more, perhaps, than you think. But I'll leave it to you to find out the hard way."

"On the contrary, my friend, it is you who is going to tell us the hard way. I assure you I had no fanciful notions about your telling us all of this of your own free will. I and some of my friends here have been busy this evening preparing for you. I should remind you that you are in Iran, a country with a most unpleasant reputation for the ingenuity of its torture chambers. There is a tradition of cruelty in this country. I am sure you have read of some of the exploits of the Il-Khanid and Safavid rulers. And you must know of Aqa Mohammad

Shah, the founder of the Qajar dynasty—one of the great sadists of history. We have learned a lot from their methods. They are crude, often involving the loss of limbs or parts of limbs, but they are extremely effective. For example"—here he picked up a long, thin metal rod from his desk—"it was common up until the last century to blind one's political rivals by puncturing the eyeballs with a red-hot wire much like this. And the recently extinguished Pahlavi dynasty made its own very special contribution to the art through its secret police, SAVAK. Behruz, the guard who is standing just behind you, was a very active member, and he has not lost his touch. I too have some tricks, learned from my brother at Dachau during the war. Being exposed to intense cold as you have been was one of his techniques. A most effective technique.

"In fact, I think we might now go on much as we have been doing. We are going to return you to your cell for the night. I regret that we have no facilities for heating the room, nor do we have any food to spare. No doubt you will find the experience sobering enough to be unusually cooperative in the morning. You may find comfort in the thought that you will not be entirely alone. Your friends Mr. Rastgu and Miss Ahmadi will not be far away. Like yourself, they have already spent several hours under rather unpleasant conditions. I am sure they will be much more helpful to us tomorrow. It is wonderful what extreme cold can do. Do you know, many of my brother's subjects would have done anything for him after a while? It was most touching, their total devotion."

Randall thought quickly. He had warmed up a great deal since entering Rascher's office and felt reasonably supple again. If he were now to be returned to his freezing cell, to spend a wretched night with the cold and the threat of further torture driving away all thought of sleep, by morning he would be past any hope of a serious escape bid. It was now or never.

As he rose, he caught the cord of the desk lamp with the toe of his right foot, sending the lamp crashing to the floor. The room was plunged into instant blackness. Having already gauged the distance, Randall threw himself across the desk, falling onto Rascher and pushing him and his chair to the ground. The guard was afraid to shoot for fear of hitting the German. Randall did not pause. Quickly, he found Rascher's chair, pulled it away from the old man as he lay groaning beside it, and hurled it toward the window, dimly visible as an area of lesser darkness. There was a great crash as the chair took the window out: Randall found Rascher and hauled him to his feet. "Out! Hurry up!" he shouted as he thrust him toward the jagged hole. Beyond the door, footsteps could be heard as more guards came running down the passage. Rascher began to struggle through the window. His moving form was just discernible to the confused guard at the back of the room, who thought it was Randall. The submachine gun rattled and Rascher fell back.

Randall had watched for the flash of the gun and pinpointed Behruz. As the guards outside reached the door, he leapt heavily at the man inside, flooring him in a rugby tackle. The door crashed open and the first guard came through, gun at the ready, sharply outlined against the square of light from the passage. Randall already held Behruz's gun in his hand; it was only a question of lifting it and firing. As the first guard fell, Randall turned the gun on the door. He fired again, sending splinters of wood flying in all directions; the two guards crowding behind the first in the corridor fell to the floor. Yet more footsteps sounded from the left. Dashing into the corridor, Randall shot at the light and, again, everything around him was dark.

Moving silently away from the advancing footsteps, Randall headed back to the vicinity of his cell. Behind him he could hear the sound of men rushing into the room he had left. A bend in the corridor took him out of their sight, and a few yards more brought him to the intersection. He paused. He had only seconds in which to find Fereshteh and Sirus. This place would soon be swarming with armed men. Stepping into the dimly lit corridor, gun at the ready, he glanced quickly to right and left. His own cell lay to the right and down the steps. As far as he knew, there were no other rooms beside it.

Suddenly, a voice called to his left.

"*Chi-e? Chi mishe?* What's going on?"

Then a man appeared out of a break in the corridor. He gasped when he saw Randall, and his hand stretched for the rifle slung over his shoulder. But the American was already aiming straight at his chest, one hand to his mouth signifying silence. The man's hand dropped and he stood nervously while Randall approached him. In the corridor Randall had just left, there were more shouts and the sound of feet pounding. Quickly, Randall grabbed the guard, pushing him into the alcove, in which a door was set.

"The key! Where is it?" Randall hissed.

The man's hand fell to his belt and he unhooked a small ring holding half a dozen keys. Fumbling, he found the right one.

"Open the door!" Randall heard the feet turn in the opposite direction, but he knew they would be back.

The door opened and Randall thrust the guard inside. Sirus Rastgu was crouched in the corner, arms clasped about his body in a vain effort to keep warm. Fereshteh was nowhere to be seen.

"Sirus!" Randall called.

The Israeli's eyes opened. He saw Randall and the guard, took in the situation at a glance, and tried to smile.

"Can you move, Sirus?" Randall asked.

"Yes . . . I think so. My body's stiff, but I'll warm up."

"Where's Fereshteh? We have to find her."

"They took her somewhere else, Peter. The molla who brought us here said she knew nothing of importance and there was no point in keeping her here. He came back about an hour ago and said he'd made other arrangements for her. She was to go with him. He didn't say where."

Randall turned to the guard, his gun leveled at his stomach, his finger touching the trigger.

"Where have they taken her?" he snapped, the tone of his voice sufficient warning that he would not ask a second time.

"I don't know, *jenab*. Molla Ahmad said he was taking the girl to Tehran, but I don't know where. There are many places in Tehran, *jenab*. By my life, I swear . . ."

"Where are we now?" Randall asked, his nervousness increasing as the sounds outside grew in volume.

"*Jenab?*"

"This house! Where is it?"

"Near Shahabad. The village is two miles away."

"Which way?"

"To the left, *jenab*. You take the road to the left."

Shahabad was just outside Tehran, to the northeast. If they could make it that far, there was just a chance. But they would have to go on foot. Any attempt at leaving in a car or van would be detected immediately. Randall moved the gun forward a fraction of an inch. As a gesture, it was sufficient.

"Is there a back way out of here?" he asked the frightened guard. The man nodded, eager to please, to see the American leave.

"Take us there. Then take us to Shahabad. Don't even think of going the wrong way. If we aren't in the village after we cover two miles, your short life will be over. Sirus, take his rifle."

The Israeli stood up, his cramped limbs an agony to move. They waited until there was a lull in the shouting outside, then cautiously went out into the passage, with Randall leading the way. The guard pointed to the left and they set off at a slow trot. The chase had drawn away to the other side of the house. Evidently, the guards thought Randall had escaped through the window of Rascher's room. The corridor led into a short passage that ended at an unpainted wooden door. The guard asked for the keys he had given to Randall and used one to turn the lock. They stepped out into a black and freezing night. To their right, loud shouts and trampling footsteps could be heard echoing. The guard pointed again and they set off straight ahead, taking care to make as little noise as possible.

As they moved off into the darkness, Randall looked back and saw lights flashing. The sound of car engines reached his ears as they roared off along the road in pursuit. He had no idea how many men had been at the house with Rascher or how soon it would be before they thought of sending patrols out into the fields.

Their eyes were now growing accustomed to the surrounding darkness, and they could make out the main features of the terrain they were crossing. All about them was silence, and Randall grew confident that their pursuers had lost them. Underneath, the ground became gradually more broken and steep. In places, the snow was deep and the ground treacherous. Rastgu fell badly twice and began to move more slowly, using the rifle from time to time as a stick. A numbing chill began to creep into Randall's bones and he hoped Rastgu could make it.

After more than an hour, Randall had begun to despair of reaching Shahabad. Either the guard was deliberately leading them astray or he was as lost as they were. Rastgu was becoming weaker by the minute and Randall did not think he could walk much further. If they were forced to stop and spend the rest of the night out of doors, the Israeli could be dead by morning. If the temperature fell any further, they would all be dead.

The light appeared suddenly. One moment nothing, then it was there, hanging golden in the darkness. Cautiously, they made their way toward it. Fifteen minutes later, they could make out the shape of a small farmer's hut.

"This is the village," whispered the Irshadi. "That's Haji Aqa's hut. I know him, he sells us yoghurt."

"Has he a van?" asked Randall.

"No, but his neighbor Ali has a Volex."

"Good. Let's wake Ali up."

They passed Haji Aqa's hut, and soon the shapes of other dwellings began to loom from out of the darkness. The "village" was little more than a collection of huts interspersed with one or two more solid, older buildings. They found Ali's hut without much difficulty and knocked gently at the door. Ali opened it a minute later, muttering and swearing, until he saw two men with guns.

There was no time to waste. "We want your van," said Randall. "Where are the keys?"

The frightened farmer reached a hand out to a hook beside the doorpost and took down a rusty length of wire holding two blackened keys. He held them out to Randall, his hand shaking.

A child's voice called from inside the hut.

"Chi-e baba? Tarsidam."

"It's nothing," Ali called gently. "Don't be frightened. Go back to sleep."

Randall took the keys, then reached into his trouser pocket and brought out a wad of notes. Only his gun had been taken from him when he had been arrested; his money had been left untouched.

"Here," he said, holding the money out to Ali. "We don't want to steal your van. But we need it badly. Take the money and buy a new one."

The farmer said nothing, but he slipped the money into his pocket and nodded. There was enough money to buy a good secondhand van, better than the one he had.

Randall turned to the Irshadi.

"I'm leaving you here with Ali. I don't think it will be worth your while trying to raise an alarm. Not till the morning anyway."

The guard seemed uncertain and ill at ease.

"Don't worry. I can't raise an alarm. I can't go back there."

"Why not?"

"They'll kill me if I go back. I should have shouted and let you

shoot me when I first saw you. They don't forgive mistakes or coward-
ice. I'll stay here with Ali until it's safe."

Randall nodded. He had to leave; Rastgu was shivering badly and
might collapse any minute. Ali looked at him, and without a word, he
slipped back inside the hut and returned a moment later holding a
fleece-lined jacket. He held it out for Rastgu to put on. The Israeli
smiled his thanks, too weak to speak. Randall shook Ali's hand, then
turned and helped Rastgu to the van.

The phone rang.

"Yes, Howard Straker."

"Deep Operations, sir. We've lost him."

"What? How?"

"We think he was snatched, sir. Our man found where he'd been, a
house in a place called Darband. There was no one there and there
were signs of a struggle. Our agent thinks the girl was there as well,
sir, and another man, unidentified."

"Who has him?"

"We don't as yet know, sir. It could be a number . . ."

"Are you telling me Randall's in the hands of the police or Guards
or SAVAMA? Is that what you're telling me?"

"It's possible, sir. On the other hand . . ."

"I don't want to know the other hand. I want to find Randall. Can
your man locate him?"

"I think so, sir."

"Don't think. Make contact and order a search. If he needs money,
tell him we'll send it. And tell him, no more mistakes."

Straker jabbed the telephone cradle and dialed briefly.

"Sir? This is Straker. Bad news, sir. They've lost Randall, he may
be in hostile hands. I need authority to initiate a cover story, sir. Yes,
sir. Thank you. I'll contact you again this evening."

48

TEHRAN/KERMAN
Tuesday, 1–Saturday, 5 January 1980

Rastgu rested throughout Tuesday at the house in Majdiyye. Food and warmth and sleep were all he needed. That evening, he told Randall what he could about the raid on the house at Darband and the capture of Fereshteh and himself. There was not much to tell. Six men had arrived in two jeeps, led by a seventh man in black, called Molla Ahmad.

"I remember him, Peter," Rastgu said. "He was the leader of the group we discovered at the *zurkhane*, the one who escaped."

"Yes, I know. Fereshteh saw him in New York. I think he was responsible for al-Shidyaq's death. Did you find out who he is? Masoodi only said he'd heard of him, that he was something of a legend in the sect. A sinister legend."

"No. He said very little. But I could see that his men were very much in awe of him. He's taciturn, but when he does speak, people listen. They took us to a house somewhere in the city and left us there all morning. I don't know where it was, we were blindfolded all the way. We drove some distance, but we could have gone the long way around to somewhere quite close. But I'm sure it was in the city; I could hear traffic. I didn't see Molla Ahmad again until he came to take us to the place near Shahabad."

"He was probably looking for me. What about Fereshteh, Sirus? What happened to her?"

All day, Randall had tried to tell himself he must forget about Fereshteh, that he must concentrate on the immediate issue of finding the main Irshadi base and destroying it. But his thoughts returned to her repeatedly. And yet somehow he could not form a clear image of her in his mind's eye. His inability to see her only worried and distracted him further. He feared that she was dead by now, and at times he feared she might be better dead.

Rastgu shook his head. "I don't know, Peter. She was with me at the house in Tehran and for about an hour at the other place. Then Molla Ahmad came to take her away again. That was the last I saw of her."

Randall wanted to say, "Let's drop everything and go after her." He felt responsible. He had rescued her in New York only to drag her more deeply into this nightmare. But he knew it was useless. He sensed that events were moving rapidly now, that things were already out of control, and that the moment of crisis would come soon— tomorrow or the next day perhaps. His presence in Tehran had been made known to the Irshadis, and Fereshteh might very well be forced to reveal what little she knew of his plans.

In his head, the phrase "Day of the Return" pounded incessantly like a drumbeat. The more he thought about it, the more certain he was that it referred to a specific date, but he had no way of determining what that date might be. And yet he was sure he subconsciously knew when it was and that it was soon, very soon. And he could not rid himself of the fear that, now he had escaped with that knowledge, they might loose their missiles ahead of schedule. He wanted to stay in Tehran to look for Fereshteh, but he knew that he had to go south, to Kerman, to locate the base where the missiles were even now being made ready. If he was still alive after that and if they had not killed her, he would find Fereshteh.

"Sirus," he said, "I don't think we have very much time left. We have to go to Kerman. Rascher told me they've been building missiles, missiles with nuclear warheads."

"I know, Peter."

"I don't understand. I only heard last night."

"Before we were kidnapped at Darband, I received another report from Jerusalem. I didn't have time to translate it for you. Our scientific staff at the Haifa Technion have made a provisional analysis of the technical papers we sent them, the ones found in Muftizadeh's apartment. They couldn't comment in detail at this stage, but they agreed that the papers were specifications and a 'shopping list' for parts that could be used to build small nuclear devices. Apparently, they're building at least two similar units—one using uranium 235, the other uranium 238. They'd be small, but very powerful—especially the 235 device. It looks as if the completed products are intended to be adapted as small nuclear warheads. Depending on a variety of factors, they could have from three to five warheads under construction, and God alone knows if they've already built others before this."

So Rascher had not been bluffing.

"That settles it," said Randall. "We leave for Kerman tomorrow."

Randall slept badly that night. His decision to leave for Kerman and so abandon Fereshteh, had triggered the nightmare once more.

He had been in Hue when the Tet offensive had been launched. The weather was cold and sunless, and rain fell ceaselessly. Randall's platoon had been one of the first to move into the Citadel. Three days later, the Vietcong were still holding out and the American casualties were rising. Toward sunset on the third day, six men had been pinned down by sniper fire near the west wall, and Randall had been put in charge of a small rescue squad that was to go in to cover their retreat.

Halfway to the wall, a grenade had landed in their rear, killing two men and badly wounding a third. The third man was Bob Riley, Randall's closest friend in the Army. When Randall got to him, he saw that Riley's right leg had been blown off above the knee. He was still conscious and screaming in terrible pain.

Up ahead, the sniper fire was growing heavier and there were shouts from the men pinned down beneath it, now within yards of them. Beside Randall, Riley lay bathed in sweat, blood pumping from his wound. His screams were becoming unbearable. Riley's hand clutched Randall's arm and his eyes, wild with fear and pain, pleaded with him. "Don't leave me, Peter," he gasped. "Take me out, please take me out." For a moment, Randall was about to lift him and drag him back to safety. But his orders had been to rescue the six men up ahead. He eased his friend's hand from his arm, untied the sweat scarf from his neck, and tied a tourniquet above his knee. He promised to return.

Circling the snipers' position, Randall's squad began to lay down a heavy covering fire. But the sun had set and a tropical night had fallen rapidly. In the poor light, it took much longer than expected to take the six men out to safety. As they moved back, Randall sprinted to the spot where he had left Riley. His friend's screams had subsided into jagged, pain-wracked sobs. He was delirious with the all-consum-

ing agony of his wound. Randall struggled back with him, under cover
of fire from their position on the wall. Five minutes later, Riley died.

They had a choice. They could travel overland to Kerman by jeep,
crossing the desert to avoid detection and possible arrest. It wasn't
just the Irshadis who would be looking for them by now. But that
would take time—two, perhaps three days, longer if they had engine
failure or other trouble. And time was the one thing they couldn't
spare.

The alternative was to fly. The trip would take an hour, getting
them to Kerman early that same morning. But if Randall was recognized at the airport, nothing could be done to save him. Rastgu told
him that the Revolutionary Guards had instituted checks on all internal flights, watching for antirégime terrorists or former SAVAK members. There was one possibility, but it involved serious risk for both of
them. Rastgu had sent his wife out to Israel two months earlier,
traveling through Turkey. But she was still included on his own passport, and her identity card had been left behind in Tehran.

They arrived at the airport at 6:00 A.M., an hour before the flight.
Randall was draped in a heavy chador, which he held tightly around
him, his eyes alone visible behind the lenses of thick glasses similar to
those worn by so many revolutionary women. On his feet, he wore a
pair of large woman's shoes belonging to Rastgu's mother-in-law, who
had left them in his apartment when she last visited. The two men
approached the guards stationed at the gate leading to the plane.
Each passenger was scrutinized, and one man was stopped and taken
away. There was a general air of nervousness; no one was quite sure
what the guards were looking for, why they might choose to stop one
person rather than another. Even the innocent were afraid: neighbors
with grudges had been known to lodge anonymous charges.

Randall and Rastgu came to the checkpoint together and presented
their identification papers. The guard beside Randall reached his
hand toward the chador, saying at the same time, "Please, let me see
your face."

The guard's mistake was to lift his hand before making the request.
Rastgu reached out angrily, pulling the man's hand aside, crying in a
loud voice.

"Shame, shame! Do you think you can lay your filthy hand on my wife? Do you think she is a common prostitute? This is an Islamic society now; has no one taught you the sanctity of the veil?"

There were murmurs of agreement behind and the guard fell back. A molla further down the line shouted at him, "The man is right. Only her husband may look at her face. Let her pass!"

And they passed through, hearts beating wildly, knowing they had come within inches of capture and certain death. Fifteen minutes later, the plane took off for Kerman.

Below them as they flew, the green forests of Mazandaran gave way rapidly to the vast brown expanse of scrub and desert of central Iran. The arid interior plateau, east of the vast spine of the Zagros Mountains, is mostly desert, dotted here and there by oases. For the most part, this is made up of a vast salt desert, divided into two regions: the Dasht-e Kavir in the north and the Dasht-e Lut in the south.

On the western edge of the desert, the plane stopped briefly at Yazd, famed for its wind towers, its deep water-storage tanks, and the broad, circular towers of silence on its outskirts. These were the towers, squat and constructed of mud brick, that had risen up in Husayn Nava'i's memory as he drove through New York on the first day of his mission in America.

As they flew on to Kerman, the landscape below looked to them more and more like photographs they had seen of the surface of the moon. To be cruising here so high above it all, encased in glass and metal, cooled by the fresh airs of the plane's ventilation system, seemed to Randall almost a blasphemy, a mockery of an ancient and terrible force.

They landed at the small airport to the west of Kerman city seventy-five minutes after their departure from Tehran. From the airport, they took a taxi to the town center, and from there walked to a house in Ahmadi Street. Early that morning, Rastgu had made contact with his agent in Kerman. Whereas Randall had been almost exclusively involved with espionage in Tehran, Rastgu's brief had been wider, encompassing Iran as a whole, and he had run small cells in no fewer than six provincial centers. His cell in Kerman consisted of only one man, a Jew from Hamadan who had been trained for a year at a desert camp in the Negev. Rastgu knew he could rely on him absolutely.

Khalil Sohbat was an intelligent man in his mid-forties who had served for nearly twenty years in the Iranian Army, rising to the rank of colonel; he now owned a carpet factory just outside Kerman. When the two agents from Tehran arrived, he welcomed them warmly and sent his wife to prepare a substantial breakfast. Both were hungry and tired; neither had slept the night before. While they ate, Rastgu introduced Randall to Sohbat, explaining a little of how they had come to be working together. After the meal, he launched into a detailed account of what they knew concerning the Irshadi group. Sohbat listened to everything he had to say in stunned silence. It was a lot for anyone to take in all at once, but Rastgu had wanted Sohbat to know as much as possible; if anything happened to Randall and him, Sohbat would have to continue the mission singlehandedly from this end. There might be no time to bring in someone new from outside.

"There are several immediate tasks facing us," said Rastgu. "The first is to establish secure communications with Israeli intelligence. A squad of commandos and a plane have been put on twenty-four-hour alert, ready to fly here as soon as we've located the base. We have to be in a position to act the moment that happens."

"How many men?" asked Sohbat.

"Ten," Rastgu replied.

"Ten? What sort of number is that? We'd need ten times that number to launch an attack."

"They don't want us to launch a full-out assault. The Iranians are as jittery as hell at the moment, with the Russians invading Afghanistan on the one side and American politicians calling on the President to order commando raids on Tehran on the other. All it needs is for a large-scale Israeli attack to be discovered and a full-scale war could be sparked off. We might actually end up doing the Irshadis a favor. The assault is to be low-key, designed for maximum effectiveness with minimum confrontation. Our task at this stage is to neutralize the missiles and get out. Unless the base is smaller than we think, in which case we just do as much damage as we can."

"How good do you think our chances are of getting out again?" asked Sohbat.

Rastgu paused before answering. "I'll leave that to you to calculate," he said at last. They all understood what he meant.

"Our second objective at this point," Rastgu continued, "is to locate the base. And that, I realize, is easier said than done. Khalil, you know this area well. Have you any ideas about a possible site? Ever heard of anything suspicious in the region?"

Sohbat thought for a moment, then went to a drawer and brought out a number of small-scale maps of the Kerman region, some of them including Bam. He laid the largest on a table and called Randall and Rastgu to his side.

"There are no very detailed maps of this area, especially for the desert stretches. But these will give us some idea of where to look. They may save valuable time. I suggest that we act on the reasonable assumption that this base is somewhere in the desert to the east of the city. The north, west, and most of the south regions are too heavily populated to keep such a place secret, and, in any case, they're very mountainous. Now if your source mentioned Kerman specifically, I think we can exclude the edge of the desert around Zahedan, Tabas, Bam, or any of the other large settlements. The whole of the central desert we can ignore for the present—most of it's unexplored, uncharted, and extraordinarily treacherous. I realize that that would be an ideal location for a secret base, but we have to think in terms of supply routes and other logistical problems. The scale of operations needed to establish anything like that in the heart of the desert would be enough in itself to ensure it stayed no secret. And they'd have to bring their supplies in by road. If they started out from Kerman, they'd have to cross the Namakzar, a salt marsh running for two hundred kilometers north to south, from below Tabasin to near Kashit, and skirting it means a long journey. I suspect the best area to search will be the stretch of desert immediately east of Kerman, from Sar-e Jangal to Pashu or Kashit. But first I suggest making enquiries about heavy transport seen in that area over the past few years. I can deal with that quite easily. I know people in the local Chamber of Commerce who'll have access to the kind of information we need."

"That's excellent," said Rastgu. "Tomorrow, Peter and I can start a search of the desert. But we'll need to rest this afternoon: we're both much too tired to operate at our best. We'll need a jeep, a good one— can you fix that? And we'll need a second one when the assault squad arrives."

Sohbat nodded. "We've got one at the factory; I can borrow it for a few days. I'll say my car's broken down. You could buy the other in town; there are two Land-Rover dealers."

"What about a transmitter?"

"You know mine's too small to reach Israel. How long will you need it for?"

"A matter of a minute or so, if all goes well. We've prearranged a code signal if the raid's on."

"In that case, we might be able to use the transmitter at the local army base. I can get us in without too much trouble."

"That sounds risky," suggested Randall.

"It is," Sohbat answered. "But there aren't many alternatives."

Randall and Rastgu began their search early the next morning. Taking turns at driving, they quartered the fringes of the desert for two days. The days were long, the desert vast, silent, and unchanging, the sky above them bright and empty. They saw nothing but sand and stone or the occasional cluster of human habitation huddled on the edge of the lonely wasteland over which they flew in endless monotonous circles. Each evening, they returned more dispirited than the day before, tired, irritated, their eyes dazzled by the glare.

"There's nothing out there," said Randall as they came back to Sohbat's on the second evening. "I think it's further down, toward Bam, their original center."

"But your document mentioned Kerman. It must be out there somewhere. Let's see if Khalil's had better luck today."

While they had been scouring the desert, Sohbat had spent his days making discreet enquiries in town. Until then, he had uncovered nothing suspicious, but that evening when they came in, they could see that he had struck lucky.

"Sirus, Peter," he said as they entered, "I think I've located it. I spoke with an old friend today, a man who runs a small transport office here in town. He says that from the late sixties on, a lot of heavy transport was hired around here by a Tehran-based company calling themselves Sherkat-e Lut. All the local haulage contractors were under the impression that the company was working on a construction project on the edge of the Namakzar, beyond a small village called Anduhgerd. But it seems nobody ever saw the actual site. The company brought in Afghan workers from Tehran; they used to get regular replacements, though no one can remember ever seeing any of the workers actually returning to the capital through Kerman. Obviously, nobody thought anything of that—it was just assumed they'd gone back to Afghanistan on the Bam road.

"Apparently, the main period of activity was from '68 to '72; after that, the construction workers stopped coming. But smaller shipments of equipment in packing cases used to go through that way till recently. Most people decided in the end that the original project had collapsed—which wouldn't have surprised anybody with the least knowledge of how these things work in this country. They supposed somebody up in Tehran was keeping it going as a tax-evasion scheme. Anyway, nobody ever bothered traveling the hundred kilometers out there to check up. I asked a few officials at the town hall about it, but nobody knew anything, of course. Quite a bit of *bakhshish* must have passed through somebody's hands."

Rastgu nodded, an ironic smile on his face. "How true. They always say the only way to hide something from officialdom in Iran is to smother it in bank notes. And from what we know, our friends have never been short of that particular kind of camouflage."

The following morning, Rastgu and Randall headed for Anduhgerd. They took the road southeast to Mahan, the mountain-ringed site of the beautiful shrine of Shah Ne'matollah Vali, the fifteenth-century mystic who founded the Ne'matollahi order of dervishes. Some miles before Mahan, they turned left onto a narrow track that would take them close to Anduhgerd. Rough and potholed though it was, the track was an important one. If they had followed it all the way, it would have taken them through Shah Dad up to Ravar and from there across the Dasht-e Lut at its narrowest point to Tabas or Ferdows, the two great oases of the Dasht-e Kavir. Fifty kilometers of bone-rattling torment later, they turned off for Anduhgerd, a tiny, drab village set in a lunar landscape, the last human outpost before the white vastness of the desert. They stopped just outside the miserable collection of dried mud houses that passed for a human settlement and asked a child to take them to the *kad-khoda*, the village headman.

The child escorted them to a large house in the center of the village. The *kad-khoda*, an old blind man called Fayz Ali Khan, sat in the company of the whitebeards, the village elders. Tea with sugar was brought and the guests given places of honor in the smoke-filled main room. Much time had to be spent in polite conversation, then in general talk of the political situation. Reassured that Randall and Rastgu were neither government tax officials nor army conscription officers, the whitebeards talked freely of the great project at the Namakzar. Here they heard a different story to that told in Kerman.

The Irshadis had been astute. They had passed themselves off as government officials and portrayed the building as a secret project financed by the Plan Organization, the department responsible for the implementation of the Shah's grandiose Five-Year Plan, which was a cornerstone of his White Revolution of the King and the People. Suspicious of officialdom and traditionally uncooperative with the central (or any other) government, the villagers ignored the comings and goings when trucks passed by three or four kilometers to the north, heading for the Namakzar. One or two of the young men had hoped for work at the site, but had been forcibly discouraged when they set out to apply for jobs there. People had seen something of the buildings which had been constructed, but reports were that there was little to see.

It was almost noon when Randall and Rastgu finally set out in the direction indicated by the villagers. They carried binoculars and planned to stop once they came within sight of any construction. Twenty kilometers further, they saw a shape in the distance which they assumed must be the site. Climbing onto the roof of the jeep, they trained their binoculars on the dark mass in front of them.

What they saw astonished them: girders, pylons, half-finished walls, oil drums, blocks of cement, iron pillars. It resembled a film set that had been abandoned by the builders when the money ran out. Vultures nested in a rusty tank. Salt had corroded the metal parts, eating into the bones of the structure. The whole thing was a sham, a mockup designed to impress villagers or a curious local official, to bolster the make-believe that a "project" was really underway here. The base, wherever it was, had been concealed by more than bank notes.

49

KERMAN
Sunday, 6–Tuesday, 8 January 1980

Next morning found Randall and Rastgu at the small airport on
Kerman's western outskirts, aboard a De Havilland DHC-6 Twin
Otter belonging to a close friend of Sohbat's. The plane was normally
used for crop spraying by the friend, Sohayl Ardekani, who owned
several large pistachio farms scattered over a wide area near Raf-
sanjan. Ardekani knew only that the two men from Tehran were
looking for signs of construction in the desert; hints had been
dropped that the affair involved one of Sohbat's business rivals. Randall was introduced as a representative of a French business company
with interests in the area.

They took off at nine-thirty, turning eastward toward Anduhgerd.
Once over the fake establishment, they began to quarter the area for
several kilometers on all sides of it. After an hour's futile flying back
and forth at varying heights, they headed north-northeast along the
strip between the Namakzar on the east and the long rim of mountains that protects Kerman from the open desert like a great rampart.
They found nothing but more desert, broken by the small villages of
Shah Dad, Shafiabad, and, at the extremity of their flight, Sar-e Jangal. They passed over several small streams that ran down from the
mountains eastward to die in the salt marshes of the Namakzar. From
time to time, they would see a line of vast holes below them, like the
tops of gopher burrowings, running across the plain. These holes,
some fifty meters apart, mark the openings of the deep access shafts
that are sunk for mile after mile into the soil to reach down to the
long underground channels known as *qanats*, which bring water from
the mountains to towns and villages and farms throughout the desert
regions of Iran. The plain of Kerman is particularly famous for the
number and extent of such *qanats*, one of which stretches for 150
miles.

At noon, they returned to the airport to refuel and have lunch. At two, they were in the air again, this time to cover the stretch from Anduhgerd to Kashit. Two hours later, their wheels bumped once more onto the tarmac of the runway as they landed for the last time that day. They had found nothing to even indicate the existence of a secret base. And every day that passed now brought them closer to the unknown deadline. They returned home that night in extremely low spirits.

Rastgu suggested that they spend the next day taking aerial photographs of the area around the decoy site. They could study these at their leisure later, with the help of magnifying lenses. Sohbat was able to obtain photographic equipment, including developing materials, at a shop in town. The equipment was far from ideal, but it would do.

On the morning of the seventh, they set off again in Ardekani's light plane, carrying cameras equipped with telephoto lenses. All morning, they droned back and forth, systematically covering the circle around the false buildings. By late afternoon, the photographs had been developed and printed. That evening, they sat in Sohbat's back room, poring over hundreds of black and white prints scattered over a low inlaid table.

Whatever tracks showed up in the immediate vicinity of the site went in all directions, petering out after several yards. They gave nothing away. Rastgu was growing certain that the site lay underneath the complex of sham buildings, and they agreed to check that possibility the next day. Randall remained skeptical—he could see that the superstructure would interfere with rocket launching, unless the entire assembly was more sophisticated than it looked, with sections that could easily be rolled or lifted away. He insisted that they keep on searching.

It was after midnight when Randall found something. He had been studying a series of photographs taken from west to east along a *qanat* toward a cultivated area dotted with small farms, several miles north of Anduhgerd, just beyond the false buildings. He held up a photograph showing several fields and a cluster of farm buildings.

"Do either of you see anything strange about this photograph?" he asked.

Both Rastgu and Sohbat peered at the glossy square, holding and turning it about beneath their magnifying glasses.

"If you mean the way the area's been neglected," Sohbat said, "yes. The fields obviously haven't been looked after for years, and most of them have dried up. Several of the buildings look as if they're falling down, and there aren't any people around. But that isn't unusual around here. A stream dries up, a *qanat* is ruined beyond repair, a landlord goes bankrupt because of some business dealings in Tehran. We could investigate, of course, but I don't think we'll find anything out of the ordinary."

"Now look at this set of photographs," said Randall. He passed over the series of shots showing the long line of the *qanat* as it swept down from the hills. Again they scrutinized the photographs, but this time neither could see anything out of the ordinary. They shrugged and passed the prints back to Randall. Sohbat said, "Sorry, but I don't see anything odd here."

"That's just the point," Randall replied. "I just wanted to be sure that you would say that. These *qanat* shafts are in perfect condition. The farming area they irrigated has clearly been neglected for quite a few years, but the *qanat's* in unusually good order. Under normal conditions, a *qanat* shaft will deteriorate quite rapidly if it isn't looked after: sand and earth will blow into it, weeds will grow around it, and it will often collapse. But not one of these shafts shows signs of this."

Randall stopped and showed the photographs around again. As the others examined them, he continued talking.

"Looking over these photographs and thinking about Sirus' suggestion about the real base being under the sham site has reminded me of something I read a long time ago. After the British bombed Peenemünde, where Dr. Rascher worked, the Germans rebuilt the Development Works for the V-2 underground, leaving the ruins on the surface as a camouflage. I'm almost certain Rascher did exactly the same thing here. But he's added a further refinement. The one flaw with Sirus' idea of an underground base was the rocket problem. I simply could not see how they could launch them. But now I think I know. It seems clear to me that some of these *qanat* shafts have been converted into launching tubes for the missiles. The rest have been kept in a good state of repair, perhaps in the hope of further expansion. The actual rocket base will be deep underground beneath the surface of the desert somewhere along the line of this *qanat*. I imagine the original stream has been channeled into pipes to provide the base's water supply. Supplies are probably flown in and lowered down a shaft designed for that purpose. The farm buildings and the false structures further down must cover other installations."

The others nodded in agreement. It was more than just plausible—it was highly probable. Rastgu turned to Sohbat.

"Khalil, I think we should try getting into the radio room at the army base tonight. Have you worked out a plan?"

Sohbat shrugged his shoulders. "It's a plan, but not much of one. It's best if I go alone, wearing my old colonel's uniform. I've made what looks like a convincing pass and signed it with the name of the present base commander; it should get me in if I go at an awkward time. What message shall I give?"

"That's simple enough. I want you to give the coordinates for a landing spot and arrange a rendezvous for tomorrow morning."

"Tomorrow morning? Before we've had a chance to reconnoiter?"

Rastgu nodded. "We've got to act as quickly as possible. They may have seen us out there on Saturday, and they'll certainly have seen the plane going over yesterday and again today. They must realize somebody's pretty interested in that area. If I were in charge and everything was ready, I'd bring forward the time of the launch to the earliest moment possible. Wouldn't you?"

It was 2:00 A.M. on Tuesday morning when Sohbat, dressed in his colonel's uniform, a heavy pistol strapped to his waist, drove up to the main gate of the Solaimani Army Base on the outskirts of Kerman. He had taken his own car, leaving both jeeps with Randall and Rastgu. Under normal circumstances, there would have been no chance whatever of his walking into the base unchallenged. But these were no longer normal circumstances, and security at Iranian military bases was probably the most ill-observed of any in the world. Following the revolution, the regular Army, Air Force and, to a lesser extent, Navy had been reduced to a state of near anarchy. The defection of large numbers of conscripts and regular soldiers during the winter of 1978–79 had left the armed forces seriously depleted. Only a handful of those who had gone absent during the revolution ever returned to barracks after things began to settle down. A great many enlisted in the Revolutionary Guards. During 1979, the revolutionary authorities carried out a wholesale purge of officers from generals to lieutenants. Discipline became lax and military efficiency and organization almost nonexistent.

The guard posted at the gate that morning was a young man, a conscript from a nearby village who had preferred to stay on in the city after the revolution. On duty from 8:00 P.M. the previous evening, he was cold and sleepy and nearing the end of his endurance. When a Colonel Sohbat appeared, bristling and authoritarian in manner, he did not even bother to ask for his pass. Officers came and went, many of them men recently promoted from the ranks, and there was little point in trying to keep a check on all of them. The uniform was enough.

The radio hut was toward the center of the compound. Sohbat paused at the door for a moment, listened, then went in quietly. Inside, he found the duty radio operator dozing, his feet perched on the table in front of him. Taking his revolver from its holster, Sohbat took hold of it by the barrel and struck the man hard on the nape of the neck; he slumped unconscious in his chair. Sohbat bent down to check that he was breathing, then lifted him out of the chair and placed him on the floor; he would be out for at least an hour—plenty of time for Sohbat to do his job and escape. He sat down at the radio set, looked at the complicated banks of dials for about thirty seconds, then switched to "transmit" and began to turn the dials he had selected. The wave band he had been given was supposed to be secure; as he spoke, he prayed it still was.

"Jericho," he began, "this is Sennacherib. Can you read me?" He repeated the call-sign three times, then switched to "receive." There was a crackle and a snarl, then a voice came faintly through his headphones.

"Sennacherib, this is Jericho. We read you. What is your pass sign?"

Sohbat switched again and read the prearranged code phrase, a verse from the Book of Jeremiah.

" 'How is the hammer of the whole earth cut asunder and broken! how is Babylon become a desolation among the nations!' "

"Understood, Sennacherib. What is your message?"

"Rendezvous as arranged 0600 today. Coordinates: Shin Qaf: Majid, Layl. Shin Lam: Yak, Yak. Bring equipment for underground passages."

"I repeat: rendezvous 0600 today. Coordinates: Shin Qaf: Majid, Layl. Shin Lam: Yak, Yak. Bring underground equipment. Good luck, Sennacherib. And thank you."

"Coordinates correct. Goodbye, Jericho."

Sohbat switched off the transmitter, removed his headphones, and placed them on the table. It was done. Now all they had to do was meet the commandos, find the way into the base, and . . . He preferred not to think of what would follow. There was a faint sound behind him and he spun in the chair reaching for his gun.

At the door stood a man dressed in the uniform of a lieutenant colonel. He was holding a gun pointed at Sohbat's head.

"I wouldn't touch that gun if I were you," he said, his hand reaching for an alarm button beside the door. A bell rang somewhere, loud and insistent. In a moment, feet would come running. "I think you ought to come along with me. Perhaps you'll be able to explain to us who Jericho is."

50

ANDUHGERD REGION
Tuesday, 8 January 1980

The Falcon 50 took off from a secret air base near the Dead Sea at 3:00 A.M. Flying at five hundred miles per hour, it moved low and fast through the night toward the east and an early dawn, hugging the landscape in order to escape radar detection. The most direct route took them over Jordan and Iraq, and the pilot knew that if his aircraft was identified invading Arab airspace, it could provoke a serious international incident. But that was the least of his worries: the first he would know about any complication would be the blip of an Iraqi MiG-25 on his tail. He wouldn't even see the missile that would take them out of the air. The ten men he was carrying chatted easily among themselves; all were nervous and keyed up for the mission, but they had learned long ago how to control and use their nerves in combat. Five of them had been on the Entebbe raid in 1976, and the others had had combat experience in the Yom Kippur War. All were volunteers, and none was under any illusions about his chances of coming back alive.

Randall and Rastgu had waited until five o'clock for Sohbat to return. His failure to arrive made them nervous. It was clear that something had happened to him, but they had no way of knowing whether or not he had been able to transmit his message first. At five, they decided to head out to the rendezvous point, each taking a jeep packed with gear for themselves. They drove through the gathering light to the rendezvous, two miles west of Anduhgerd. Shivering in the chill air of the desert, they marked out a short runway in the sand, then returned to one of the jeeps to wait, not knowing whether anyone would come.

Just before six, they heard the sound of engines. Randall trained his binoculars on the western horizon, sweeping them to find the plane. Suddenly, it appeared, a growing dot racing toward him. He jumped out and switched on the warning lights at the end of the makeshift runway; the pilot saw them, waved his wings in acknowledgment, and lowered his landing gear. One minute later, the plane touched down, throwing behind it a massive cloud of sand and stones. A door in the fuselage opened immediately and the ten commandos jumped to the ground. All were dressed in nondescript civilian clothes without labels and carried French and Belgian guns and equipment. None wore dog tags. If anything went wrong, nothing must suggest Israeli or U.S. involvement in the affair; with the exception of Randall, all could pass as Iranians. No one would allow himself to be taken alive.

The plane would stay on the landing strip as long as possible. But the pilot had orders to take off at the first signs of trouble. If forced to do so, he would return the next morning at the same time and, if it was safe, land to pick up survivors. If there were any survivors to pick up.

After stowing the equipment in the jeeps, they ate and discussed their plans. The group commander was Colonel Yitzhak Aharoni, a tough, weather-beaten man in his late thirties who spoke fluent English. He explained that he did not plan to take his men in as a suicide squad: their job was to disable the missiles badly enough to delay a launch for weeks or months. Anything more than that would have to be left to another mission, the details of which could be worked out if the present group returned with enough information.

It was after nine when they drove off at last in the direction of the construction site.

Before coming in sight of Anduhgerd, they turned off the track and headed out into the desert. When, according to Randall's calculations, they were within two miles of the abandoned farm area, they stopped and got out of the jeeps. He and Rastgu donned tattered clothing they had bought earlier from two workmen sleeping in the street near Sohbat's house. The American had grown a heavy beard over the last few days, and that morning he had darkened his face with makeup he had borrowed earlier from Sohbat's wife. Dressed in rags, their faces and hair dirtied, he and the Israeli could pass for a couple of poor peasants, although a close inspection would have revealed the truth.

They moved off on foot, leaving the other ten men to check and prepare their equipment. Before long, the huddle of low, squat buildings came into sight. A sharp wind blew from the east across the salt

flats, whipping up the gray-white dust. As they came within about
four hundred feet of the first building, a figure stepped out from the
doorway. A tall man, he was dressed in a heavy black greatcoat and
carried a powerful rifle. He shouted at them.

"Hey! You two! Where do you think you're going? You've been
told often enough to clear off from here. You know this area's out of
bounds. Now, just turn around and go back the way you came.
There's nothing for you here."

Looking sullen and dejected, the two men turned on their tracks.
As they started walking back, the man suddenly called again.

"Just a minute, come over here. I want a word with you."

Exchanging glances, they turned again and walked toward the
guard. Randall fingered the light automatic he carried in his pocket.
When they came up to the guard, he questioned them brusquely.

"Have either of you seen any strangers around here? People with a
small plane? Maybe a jeep? Yesterday or the day before?"

They shuffled, heads bowed, hands in pockets, archetypal Iranian
peasants. Randall fingered his beard, grateful for the peasant habit of
shaving only every two or three days. Their scruffy appearance was
authentic. He let Rastgu do the talking, in a surprisingly good imita-
tion of a thick Kermani accent. The guard sounded Tehrani and was
probably unable to tell a fake accent from a real one.

"No, *jenab.* Nothing. We haven't seen anyone. No planes. No
jeeps. Please, we don't mean harm."

"Are you certain? There was a plane over here yesterday and the
day before, circling, searching for something. Haven't there been people in your village asking questions?"

"No, no one. No one comes to the village. Not now, not in the
winter. Why would they come? Please, we must go back now, back to
the village."

The man nodded curtly.

"All right. Off you go. You peasants are all the same. Tight-lipped
and tightfisted. But tell the people back in your village that if we find
out they've been helping anyone poke his nose into our affairs, there'll
be trouble. Serious trouble. Understand?"

"Yes, *jenab,* we understand. God forbid we should do such a thing.
God forbid."

They turned and walked away, slowly.

Back at the jeeps, they discussed what they had found.

"Obviously, the old farm section's been kept intact as a guard post," said Randall. "It was impossible to tell if there were other guards, or how many of them there might be. I think we can assume the base is in that area, but there's no way we can approach it from any direction without being spotted well before we're even in firing range. Once we've lost the element of surprise, we've lost everything. Does anyone have any ideas?"

There was silence, broken after a while by Rastgu.

"I think I know a way. Last night, after we located the *qanats*, Sohbat told us how they maintained them. The farmers go down the shafts to carry out repairs on their own sections. They clear away any debris, shore up the sides, and so on. But the main point of the shaft is to give access to the channel itself. A man can crawl down there without any serious difficulty. There may be less room if they've introduced a pipe, but it might still be possible. To avoid any risk, we could start quite a bit further up, well out of sight of the farm area."

They talked the matter over with Colonel Aharoni. He was in agreement. It was improbable that the entire base would stretch lengthways very far. In all likelihood, only a few of the *qanat* shafts would be in use, with the rest acting as blinds. If so, the plan was feasible.

They piled into the two jeeps again and set off in a long arc to a spot two miles west along the line of the *qanat*. From here, they returned half a mile until they could barely make out the farm buildings in the distance. They selected a shaft at random and sent one of the commandos down to reconnoiter. Rope and tackle were quickly set up, and the man swung himself over the lip of the shaft before descending into the blackness beneath. Five minutes later, he reappeared.

"Everything is much as we expected, sir. The shaft and channel are intact and the water pipe's narrower than we thought. The stream was probably quite small, but the *qanat* itself seems to be large enough to allow a man or boy to crawl down it to make repairs. It'll be a tight squeeze with equipment, but not impossible—unless, of course, anyone suffers from claustrophobia."

It was a serious point. Aharoni looked around the men.

"Anyone claustrophobic? Don't pretend otherwise if you are, even mildly. We don't want someone panicking halfway along and getting stuck."

No one responded.

"All right, then, let's go. Carry everything in your rucksacks and tie them to your ankles. I'll go first and pass word back as soon as we reach our objective. I'll have to decide what to do on the spot; just wait for instructions and be ready to come out of the tunnel shooting if necessary."

One by one, they descended into the shaft. It was deep, over eighty feet, to prevent evaporation of the stream during the hot season. At the bottom, it was pitch dark. Above, Aharoni could make out stars in the sky. He oriented himself, squatted, and squeezed into the tunnel, crawling along the narrow metal pipe that ran over the floor. Using his elbows, he made rapid progress; behind, he could hear the shuffling and breathing of his small force. Randall and Rastgu were unknown factors, and their presence worried him. But he knew they might prove useful, and something told him they could be relied on. More than once, his own life had depended on his being a good judge of men, and he hoped he was not mistaken this time.

It was a long and painful crawl. Aharoni dared not switch on his flashlight, not knowing what or who lay ahead. The earth seemed to press in on all sides. Every one hundred and fifty feet or so, they crossed through a shaft, each man making use of the opportunity to stand for a minute or two, head toward the stars, stretching his aching arm and leg muscles. In silence, they crawled on. Without warning, Aharoni came to a wide-meshed metal grille set in the mouth of the tunnel as it opened onto yet another shaft. All beyond was in darkness, and he decided to risk using the flashlight.

Shining the light through the mesh, he could make out the start of the shaft ahead. This was no ordinary *qanat* shaft, however. It was somewhat wider in diameter than the others he had passed through and was covered in metal sheeting, probably steel. A little up the shaft, almost out of his range of vision, was what looked like the bottom of a small elevator. He guessed that this was a supply shaft. The floor, which was some feet lower than the tunnel he was now in, was made of concrete. The water pipe exited below the metal grid, ran vertical to the floor, and probably continued underneath it. Shining the flashlight ahead, he could make out a corridor, continuous with the *qanat* but much taller and wider; he could not tell how far it stretched. Goods and equipment were, presumably, brought down the shaft by elevator, unloaded, and wheeled down the corridor. This would certainly be the best way in.

Shearing through the mesh of the grille with wire cutters, the colonel passed word back about the nature of the area ahead, then lowered himself into the shaft. The drop to the floor of the shaft was only four or five feet. He waited at the far end until all members of the unit had debouched from the *qanat*, then started to walk down the corridor. The floor of the corridor was of concrete, the walls of the same material rising to a ceiling just high enough to allow the men to walk upright. Silent on rubber soles, they moved through the darkness.

The passage was only about one hundred feet long. At the end, Aharoni came up against a massive steel door, which was firmly locked. There was no way of knowing what was on the other side. The men decided that the space beyond was probably used for storage. A cutting torch was brought up from the rear and its operator set to work. It took ten minutes to cut out the lock section and as many seconds before the first man was through, covered from behind. Aharoni met only further darkness.

That was in itself a good sign. The door indicated that they were entering the main site area, and the darkness confirmed that it led into a storage room, presumably kept unlit while not in use. The colonel put his flashlight on at full power and shone it around him. He was standing in a central aisle of a vast store lined on all sides with shelves filled with crates, boxes, and sacks. Ahead of him was a tall metallic structure which, on closer examination, proved to be a wide shaft or chimney stretching from floor to ceiling and possibly beyond. A rough calculation of its distance from the supply shaft suggested that it was another shaft exiting above ground probably disguised as a *qanat* opening. It could well be the first of the rocket shafts he had expected to find.

On the opposite side of the shaft, the small force, now reassembled in a compact unit and carrying arms at the ready, found a heavy standard door. Their "underground equipment" included the necessary tools to deal with it. A small hand-operated drill was passed forward and a tiny hole bored in the door at eye level. Into this hole, Aharoni inserted a narrow tube equipped with a wide-angle lens, similar to the devices sold for home security but with a much longer range of vision. Through this, he could make out a lighted corridor with a second shaft some one hundred feet farther along it. He was able to distinguish two doors on his left and a third on his right. The corridor was empty. He gestured to one of the commandos who had brought lock-picking equipment and instructed him to tackle the door. It was open in thirty seconds.

Flicking off the safety catch on his automatic, Aharoni stepped into the corridor. The door closed behind him. To his left was a door marked Water and Power Supplies; from inside, the hum of an electric generator could be heard. On the wall to his right was the one thing he had hoped against all hope to find: a plan showing the layout of the site.

The diagram showed two levels, the upper level where they had entered, and a lower level accessible by elevators from above. Along the length of the site, rising through both levels to the surface, were four rocket shafts, the first of which they had in fact passed in the storeroom, the second standing over thirty yards further down the corridor. The lower level was divided lengthwise into two unequal units: a rocket assembly and storage chamber connected directly to the shafts and a main control room. The upper level was more complex. The corridor in which Aharoni now stood stretched on for about two hundred and fifty feet, with two rocket shafts running through it, one in the center, the other at the end. On the left were the water and power room, a laboratory, and quarters for the scientific staff; on the right, an extension of the storeroom, a second laboratory, and quarters designated for "the Imam and his lieutenants." Beyond the rooms on the left-hand side of the corridor was another, longer but narrower passage, flanked by five rooms: first aid and sick bay, bathroom and toilets, dormitory, guardroom, and armory. At the end of the corridor in which Aharoni stood, and running at right angles to it, was the largest room on the level, designated as a *jama'at-khaneh*, an Ismaili mosque. Behind it were two smaller dining and recreation rooms, separated by the fourth rocket shaft. Kitchens abutted onto the dining room. Beyond these, another long corridor led to a personnel shaft, corresponding to the supply shaft at the western end of the site. Four personnel elevators, four staircases, and one large goods elevator connected the two levels.

Aharoni returned to the storeroom and described to his companions the general layout of the base.

"Obviously," he said, "our primary target must be the main control

room. Once that's out of action, we can sabotage the rockets themselves. But once we've made our move, there will be guards to cope
with, and we have no way of knowing how many. Has anyone any
suggestions as to how we might eliminate the guards before attacking
the control room?"

A voice came out of the darkness. It was Rastgu.

"I think I know how it might be done. Tonight sees the start of the
celebrations for a Shi'i festival called the Return of the Head. It
commemorates the return of the head of the Imam Husayn. Now,
you say the largest room on this floor is a mosque. We know the
Irshadis to be extremely religious, and this place is the headquarters of
the sect. They're certain to celebrate this anniversary. The mosque
will probably be full for the evening prayers at sunset. How many
doors are there to it?"

"Just one, facing the rocket shaft at the end of this corridor,"
replied Aharoni.

"Excellent. That means one man could hold the mosque while
another two take out the guardroom and armory and the rest head
down to the lower level."

Expressions could not be seen in the darkness, but several individuals voiced their approval of this plan. Aharoni glanced quickly at the
luminous dial of his watch.

"It's now 2:00 P.M. Sunset is in another two hours. I would suggest
we stay here where we have a view down the corridor until then.
There may be a call to prayer, but we can't rely on that. We can't see
the door of the mosque from here, so I think we should wait until at
least ten minutes after sunset. At that point, one man can approach
the mosque and confirm whether or not prayers are being said. If so,
we act as follows." Turning on his flashlight, he drew a rough plan of
the site from memory, then went through the steps of the plan that
had formed in his mind, while one man kept constant watch through
the view hole in the door.

Rastgu turned to Randall and explained the Hebrew conversation.
The American nodded, agreeing with the plan. As he did so, something nagged at his mind, something he could not identify, but which
he knew was somehow connected with the festival that evening.

51

ANDUHGERD REGION
Tuesday, 8 January 1980

At 4:10 P.M., Avram Yerushalmi, Aharoni's second-in-command, stepped gingerly out of the storeroom, submachine gun at the ready, and padded down the corridor, keeping himself well hidden by the rocket shafts. He did not need to proceed beyond the second shaft, however, for the susurration of communal prayer drifted to him where he stood. The volume of sound suggested that large numbers were present.

One minute later, he stood, gun poised, at the door of the mosque. Rastgu and another commando had already slipped across to the guardroom and armory doors. The remainder of the unit, in two groups of four and five, under the command of Aharoni, stood ready at the head of the staircase on the north side of the base, leading down to the back of the main control room. All were armed with submachine guns and carried grenades and pistols.

The second hands of twelve watches swept along to zero hour. With perfect synchronization, the men swept into action. Yerushalmi, in an ironic parody of the seizure of the Great Mosque, kicked open the door of the *jama'at-khaneh,* fired a burst at the ceiling and screamed instructions in Arabic to the men facing him, their eyes toward Mecca. There was pandemonium as those at prayer realized what was happening and saw him waving his gun and ordering them to the back wall. Numb with shock, they retreated as ordered. The Israeli began to wonder what he would do if they tried to rush him, and what he was going to do with them when the others had finished below.

At that same instant, Rastgu and his companion slammed through the doors of the guardroom and the armory. The latter was empty, but Rastgu surprised three guards. As they saw him, they turned for their guns, but he cut them down with a rapid, sweeping burst. Dashing to the armory, he found the second man and told him to fall back along the corridor to help Yerushalmi hold the mosque. He himself snatched up some guns and ammunition and made for the stairs on his right. The sound of gunfire rose from below.

Rushing down the stairs, he almost tripped and fell over the body of one of the commandos. The passage to the control room corridor had been guarded. The bodies of two Irshadi guards lay crookedly on either side of the door. Crashing through, Rastgu almost fell onto the barrel of a gun pointed in his direction by one of the Israelis. The others stood in a helpless semicircle around a heavy steel door, while at the front, one man knelt wielding the cutting tool, burning a despairingly slow hole in the solid metal. Randall explained that the guards at the stair doors had held them long enough for others inside the control room to close the massive doors. They could not afford to waste explosives on the doors since they would need all they had to destroy the rockets. Rastgu shouted, "Use the explosives! Hurry up! I've seen more in the armory. I'll go back for some." And, taking a man to help him, he turned back up the stairs.

As he set off, loudspeakers crackled throughout the base.

"Attention! Attention! All personnel are urgently called to resist intruders. The Imam and the control room staff are safe, but the base must be defended. All who die resisting the enemy will enter Paradise tonight as martyrs. The countdown for the launching of the rocket continues. It is now zero plus three minutes."

Randall's stomach gave a sickening lurch. He understood what had been nagging him for over an hour: the "Day of the Return" referred to in Marvdashti's letter was today. It was the day of the Return of the Head, and it had started at sunset.

Hearts pounding, Rastgu and his companion ran pell-mell up the stairs and dashed into the corridor facing the armory. As they ran toward it, they could hear shouts and cries from the mosque.

The announcement had been heard by the 150 men under guard there, all of them personnel not involved in the launch. Nervous of the two machine guns pointing at them, they nevertheless began to inch forward toward the door.

"Keep back," shouted Yerushalmi, waving the gun at them. He was frightened and morally confused. If they rushed him, could he bring himself to pull the trigger? They were unarmed and were here as worshipers in a mosque. He was not the sort to fire on men without guns. But if they rushed him, they would kill him and go on to attack his companions outside. He had not understood the announcement over the speakers, but he had seen its effect on the men in the room, and he was terrified.

The loudspeakers roared again. "This is your Imam, this is your Lord. We are near, so very near to victory. Do not allow the forces of evil to cheat us of all we have worked for. Now is the moment to test your faith. I call on you all to rise up and drive back the army of Satan. I promise you the reward of eternal life."

The crowd shouted in unison and heaved. Those at the back, least exposed, began to push forward. The men at the front moved toward the door, then began to run, screaming the name of the Imam.

Yerushalmi and the commando who had joined him in the mosque opened fire. Their guns spat bullets like rain into the middle of the crowd. Men screamed. Blood gushed and bodies fell in tangled heaps, but the mob advanced inexorably. Burst upon burst of gunfire followed, accompanied by more screams, but still they could not be stopped. Using the fallen bodies of their comrades as shields, the men at the back pushed on, falling on the two commandos and finally overwhelming them.

Of the 150 men at prayer, fewer than 50 survived to rush through the door. They made for the armory as the next announcement was broadcast:

"It is now zero plus two minutes!"

As Rastgu and his companion emerged from the armory carrying boxes of explosive, they ran into the Irshadis who had escaped the carnage in the mosque.

"Quickly," shouted Rastgu. "Run for it with the boxes you have, I'll hold them off!" He dropped the boxes he was carrying, then unslung his machine gun and fired into the crowd advancing toward him. The leaders fell and the rest drew back around the bend in the corridor. It was too narrow for them to rush him as they had done the men at the mosque door.

Rastgu pursued the Irshadis to the bend but, as he rounded it, firing, two came out from the door of the mosque, where they had stopped to pick up the guns belonging to Yerushalmi and his companion. The first one shot Rastgu at close range in the head.

The commando who had been with Rastgu turned and saw him fall, then rushed for the stairs. There was no time to waste. He came on the eight remaining members of the unit at the foot of the staircase. "Rastgu's been hit," he shouted. They motioned to him to crouch as well, and seconds later there was an enormous blast as gelignite blew a hole in the door of the control room. As the roar died away, the sound of footsteps could be heard on the stairs above. Aharoni grabbed a bag of grenades from the floor beside him and rushed up the stairs, firing indiscriminately. Snatching a grenade from the bag, he pulled the pin and tossed it up into the crowd coming down. There was a blast and a flash as it landed in their midst. Aharoni ran up, snatched a second grenade and tossed it higher. The stairway was clear.

Below, Randall led his six companions to the door. They first threw in two grenades, allowed them to explode, then rushed in firing. The guards at the door had been killed by the grenades and no one inside opposed them. The seven men quartered the room, shooting down the technicians who sat around it at numerous consoles. There was no time for niceties. In the middle of the room was the central launch control chamber, built of steel with a window of reinforced glass. The remaining members of the launch team were already inside. Seated at the controls was Molla Ahmad, his black robes marking him out in the otherwise clinical whiteness of the room. All about him sat his white-jacketed acolytes, the ten members of the launching staff, busy at consoles on which lights flickered and illuminated dials moved. On the walls above them, the tick of two clocks remorselessly marked the passing of time. One of the technicians leaned forward to a microphone.

"Ignition will be in thirty seconds. Final countdown begins now. Thirty . . ."

Molla Ahmad turned toward the window of the control chamber and smiled. There was something in the nature of that smile that made Randall feel sick to the pit of his stomach.

"Twenty-eight . . ."

Randall fired round after round at the window, but the bullets merely ricocheted. Molla Ahmad was still smiling.

"Twenty-five . . ."

Aharoni came running in, his task on the stairs completed.

"Why isn't he firing? The rockets must be ready to launch! Why doesn't he press the button?"

Randall pointed to the clocks on the wall over Molla Ahmad's head.

"That's why. The first clock gives Kerman time, the second the time in Mecca. The Imam's timed it for sunset in Mecca and he won't fire a second sooner."

"Twenty-one . . ."

Aharoni rushed out again and came back carrying the box of explosives that had been carried down from the armory. He hauled it over to the door of the central chamber. Randall bent to open the box, but the Israeli pulled him away.

"There's no time to set fuses. Just leave the box there and come on."

They ran for the door, threw themselves behind it, and watched as Aharoni took a grenade from his pocket, removed the pin, tossed it toward the box, and dived behind the door again. The blast of the grenade was lost in the roar of the greater explosion as it smashed glass, bent steel, and compressed air. As the effect subsided, they rushed back into the control room. Through a haze of smoke, they could make out the battered shape of the central chamber. They clambered through the hole that the explosion had ripped through the door and part of the wall.

Inside, everything was covered in fine pieces of broken glass and the white dust of powdered cement. The staff was unconscious or dead. Molla Ahmad lay on the floor beneath the firing console, his beard and clothes spattered with blood. He was still breathing when Randall found him.

Aharoni was the first to speak.

"Let's leave this mess and go back to the armory for more explosives. We have to deal with the rockets themselves, render them useless."

They picked their way through glass fragments. As they reached the door, Randall heard a sound. Turning, he saw with horror that Molla Ahmad had staggered to his feet, as if by some superhuman effort. Leaning against the console, he stabbed with a finger of his left hand at the red button marked "Rocket One." It was sunset in Mecca.

There was a growing roar of engines outside the control room. On a console to the left was a bank of television screens. The screen marked "1" leapt into life as the rocket slowly began to lift from the shaft. On the screen, which showed the lip of the shaft lit by flood-lights, they could see the nose of the rocket rise over the edge, then its body emerge as if in slow motion. With a full-bodied roar, the rocket lifted, its engines flaming into life like the breath of the dragon in the Book of Revelation.

The molla turned and smiled, a horrible rictus twisting the blood-smeared face. He turned again to the console and raised his finger over the blue button marked "Rocket Two." Randall shot him in the heart before his finger could touch it.

Randall and his companions gazed in deepening horror at the con-sole screen. The outside camera was automatically tracking the rocket as it lifted skyward, its engines red against the black night sky. They had no way of knowing where it was headed. And they had no way of stopping it.

Flying at five thousand feet, the missile locked onto its preset course to the southeast, in the direction of the U.S. fleet in the Gulf of Oman. An Irshadi officer in the Iranian Navy stationed at Bandar Abbas, just above the Strait of Hormuz, had that morning provided up-to-the-moment data on the position of the fleet. It was picked up by the *Nimitz*'s SPS-48 3D air search equipment as it began its slow descent toward the coast beyond the Makran hills. The ship's Mark 51 detector illuminated the target as it sped toward the fleet. Seconds later, the on-board fire-control system launched a Sea Sparrow missile. The missile, carrying thirty kilos of high explosive in its warhead, locked onto the target. Lacking complex evasion circuitry, the rocket was an easy victim, and seven miles from the fleet, it was destroyed passing over Iranian territorial waters out into the open Gulf.

The television set in the control room flickered and went gray. The rocket had passed out of range. Randall turned to Aharoni, a new desperation in his voice.

"The Imam! He wasn't here in the control room! He's in the base somewhere, we have to find him."

"We've done all we can, Peter," protested the Israeli. "Let's get out of here while we can."

"No, you don't understand! As long as he's alive, they can start again. He's the heart of it all, don't you see? Even this man"—he pointed at the body of Molla Ahmad—"was only his tool. They're all his tools. If he escapes, he'll find a way to begin again. We have to find him."

Aharoni grasped what the American meant straightaway. He nodded and called his men together.

"We're going back to the upper level. I want two men to hold off anyone trying to enter this room for five minutes. After that, run for it and join us upstairs. In seven minutes, we're going to find the way out."

Two men fell back to the doors at the rear of the control room. Already they could hear the sound of feet descending the stairs, and harsh voices shouting instructions.

Randall, Aharoni, and the remaining four commandos ran to the main doors to the left of the room. Aharoni went through first, gun at the ready. The corridor outside was empty. He beckoned the others through.

"Which way?" he shouted.

"Through that door straight ahead," said Randall. "If there are elevators on the other side of the base corresponding to those on the north, they must be that way. Let's go."

The door gave onto a vast space that had obviously been used as the rocket assembly and storage area. The six men ran into the chamber, their feet raising hollow echoes in the empty, steel-girded expanse. Behind them, a submachine gun opened fire, followed by the rattle of other arms.

There was an elevator in the far wall. Randall reached it first and stabbed a button. The doors slid open. The small elevator cage was only big enough to hold three men.

"Quickly," Aharoni shouted, pointing to three of his men in turn. "You, you, and you—go to the right. There must be a second elevator. The rest, inside."

They jumped in and the doors slid closed. Randall pressed the "ascend" button, then brought his gun forward. None of them knew what they might find when the doors opened. Seconds passed as the elevator moved up slowly. It seemed an eternity.

The doors began to open, and even as they did so, Randall saw the guard, his gun pointed at them. The American fired first and the man crumpled to the ground. Randall jumped out, ready to fire again, but the corridor was empty. He could hear the sound of feet running, but they were all headed away from their direction toward the control

room on the north of the base. Aharoni and the other man followed
Randall. They waited. Thirty seconds later, there was the sound of
another elevator opening, and the three remaining commandos entered the corridor twenty yards to their right. They signaled and
moved together toward an opening in the corridor between the two
groups.

As they reached the opening, Randall glanced up at the wall. There
was a small direction indicator. As far as he could tell, the elevator in
which he and Aharoni had come up was in the south wall of the
mosque. The passage they were about to enter ran along the west wall
of the mosque, past the door through which Yerushalmi had entered
it. Facing that wall, on the other side of the passage, were the quarters
of the Imam. The door to those quarters lay on the south side, on the
far side of an opening to their left about fifty yards farther. That was
their target. It would be heavily guarded, but it must be taken.

Leaving one man to guard their rear, the others moved along the
passage in single file. The opening that led to the door of the Imam's
quarters was marked by the gray bulk of one of the rocket shafts that
projected several feet into the corridor along which they were moving.
As they came within a few yards of the turning, Aharoni whispered
rapid instructions to his men and Randall.

Just before the turning, they stopped. Randall and another man
came to the front, then dashed for the rocket shaft. There were
shouts from around the corner. Randall's companion stayed behind
the shaft while he dashed again for the wall at the other side of the
opening. Someone fired at him, but he was past and behind cover in
less than a second. A third man dashed across the short gap to join
the one behind the shaft. They now had four vantage points from
which to shoot into the passage. Their opponents could fire two ways
only.

At a signal from Aharoni, they began to fire into the passage. One
man hung back ready to move across if any of those at the shaft or far
wall were hit. The guards returned their fire, but they were badly
positioned and exposed. Three of them fell in the first exchange.
Aharoni had made a rapid count while firing around the corner. Now,
discounting the three men hit, he shouted the number across to Randall.

"Five!"

Randall shook his head. There were two others closer to him, out of Aharoni's line of vision.

"Seven!" he shouted back.

They could not afford to waste time. Four minutes had already passed. Once the sound of firing was heard from the Imam's quarters, men would come running to his assistance from every direction. Aharoni called out in the heavy silence.

"Masks!" The others followed his example and rapidly donned the light gas masks they carried by their sides. A moment later, Aharoni tossed a cylinder of CS gas around the corner into the midst of the guards. Seconds after that, he led the way into the corridor, past the choking and coughing guards. While two men disarmed and immobilized the guards, Randall, Aharoni, and the fifth man smashed open the door to the Imam's room.

The scene that met their eyes was as disconcerting as it was unexpected. Facing them, an old man dressed in white kneeled on the floor. As the battle for the base raged around him, the Imam had spread his prayer carpet on the ground and turned his face toward Mecca in prayer. The three men froze in the doorway, held there as if spellbound by the simplicity of what they saw. In the midst of violence and death, they had come upon an old man praying. He seemed neither to see nor hear them, but bowed and rose again, his lips forming words they could not distinguish. Their entry seemed an intrusion upon something holy, the desecration of a saint's retreat.

Without warning, a door at the back of the room opened. Randall raised his gun, about to fire. A figure stepped out and his finger stiffened on a trigger. Framed in the doorway, pale and wide-eyed, dressed in a black chador, Fereshteh stood gazing at him in fear and horror. He lowered the gun and moved in her direction. She started, and he realized that she could not recognize him behind the mask. In a muffled voice, he called her name, then told her who he was. She stood for a moment in disbelief, then walked slowly across the room toward him.

Outside, they could hear shouts and the sound of running feet. Fereshteh had broken the spell. Aharoni stooped and took the Imam by the arm, raising him to his feet. The old man did not try to resist. He smiled as he stood, his dark eyes unconcerned. Aharoni pushed him forward, his hand clasped firmly around his upper arm, his hand-

gun pointed straight at his head. Unmistakable in his white robes, the
Imam was now their only hope of escape.

With Aharoni in front firmly gripping the Imam, they ran from the
room. Wisps of gas still hung in the air, causing the old man and
Fereshteh to choke. Seconds later, they had left the corridor and
reentered the passage that led back to the elevators. Randall whipped
off his mask and turned to Fereshteh. She looked tired and drawn.
Her eyes were unfocused and her cheeks hollow, and he wondered
how he had ever lost the image of her face.

"Fereshteh," he asked her urgently, "which way do we go? We
have to get out." The seven minutes were up and there was no sign of
the men they had left in the control room.

She pointed along the passage.

"The stairs by the mosque. They lead to the surface."

They turned and started to run back the way they had come. There
was a shout behind them, then someone opened fire and the two men
at the rear fell. The others threw themselves to the ground, twisting
around to return their opponents' fire. But Aharoni stood his ground
and turned, forcing the Imam around with a jerk to face the guards.
Instantly, the guns fell silent. Four men stood at the north end of the
corridor, submachine guns in their hands, their eyes wide in horror.
Aharoni shouted angrily in Arabic, his gun hard against the Imam's
temple.

"We leave alive or he dies with us. It is for you to decide."

The Irshadis dropped their weapons. Randall checked the two men
who had fallen; they were both dead.

"Let's move," Aharoni called, pushing ahead with the Imam while
Randall and the remaining commando held the rear. More Irshadis
joined the four at the end of the corridor and stood helpless, re-
strained from firing by their comrades. The small remnant of the
invasion party moved along the corridor. At the opening, they rejoined the man who had been guarding their rear. The passage beyond was clear.

Running now, Aharoni almost dragging the old man with him, they
turned left and headed for the stairs. At the top of the sixth flight,
they came to a heavy metal door that could be opened by a press bar.
The door swung open and Aharoni forced the Imam out into the
open ahead of him, his grip still firm. Outside, a ring of Irshadi guards
stood waiting, guns poised ready to fire. As the Imam and Aharoni

emerged, they lowered their weapons and fell back confused. The others followed. By now, they had given up hope for the two men who had volunteered to hold the control room.

"Go back inside," Aharoni shouted at the guards, "or I blow his unholy head off!"

The combination of threat and blasphemy had its effect. Reluctantly, the men moved back to another entrance and stepped inside. As they vanished, Randall was already searching for some means of transportation. Thirty yards to their left, outside the girders and bricks of the mock factory, a large jeep stood empty. They ran toward it and jumped in, Randall at the wheel, Aharoni and the Imam in the back seat with the two surviving commandos, Fereshteh in front with Randall.

In their haste, the guards had left the key in the ignition. Randall turned it, let out the clutch, and turned in the direction of the landing strip. Even as the jeep roared off, the door leading into the base was flung open and men jumped out. They would soon be in pursuit, waiting for the moment when it might be safe to move in and rescue the Imam.

The journey back to the landing strip, a bumping, tossing flight through the dark over sand and stone and shrub, was the worst time for Randall. Throughout the attack, he had been buoyed up by the tension and the spurts of action. Now that they had come through the immediate dangers of the raid and there was a glimmer of hope, the fears and nightmares of months began to crowd back in on him. His feelings of dread were intensified by the presence of Fereshteh in the seat beside him, her eyes staring straight ahead, her hands clenched tightly on the seat for balance. He had given up any hope of seeing her again, he had resigned himself to living with the remorse he knew must come for having abandoned her. And now she was alive again, being carried down a road at the end of which lay either safety or death. When he glanced at his mirror, he could see the Imam sitting beside Aharoni, his features composed, his body swaying as they lurched from side to side, like the body of a puppet.

Familiar as he was by now with the terrain, Randall almost lost the landing strip in the dark. His headlights picked out boulders and gullies, dry bushes and flat stretches of salt, but no certain landmarks. Suddenly, there was a flash to their right, then a second. The plane was still there. They had seen their lights. Randall turned the wheel hard and the jeep careered across the sand toward the plane. He remembered another chase in the dark and how it ended. And he knew that Fereshteh would remember it as well.

Even as they tumbled out of the jeep and up the steps into the waiting Falcon, there was the sound of engines in the distance. The pilot had already positioned the plane ready for takeoff and had set up runway lights, but precious minutes were lost as his copilot lit the flares and ran back to the plane. The engines roared as he threw himself inside, the pilot pushed the throttle forward, and the plane leapt into life, hurtling down the short strip at full speed. Pushing everyone back heavily into their seats, it rose sharply, almost stalling as it climbed into the sky. At last, it flattened out and the pilot turned into the homeward path. There were no cheers. Seven of the original unit were not on board.

The plane headed westward. Beneath them, the flat expanse of desert gave way at last to the peaks of the Zagros mountains. Fereshteh spoke briefly to Randall of what had happened after Molla Ahmad took her from the house near Shahabad. She had been brought to his house in Tehran, where she was kept in confinement for several days before being brought to Kerman by road several days earlier. During that time, Molla Ahmad had scarcely spoken to her, and she had not known his purpose in keeping her alive. She suspected that she had been brought to see things with her own eyes, perhaps to be sent back to America or to the Aga Khan later as a witness to the power of the Imam. But during the launching period, she had been kept with the Imam while he prayed for the success of the mission. To see his real power, he had told her. She said little and was soon silent again. Randall knew it would be a long time before she could shake off the nightmare she had lived through in these few weeks. Perhaps she never would.

They flew on in silence. The Imam sat motionless, his eyes closed, lost in a hidden world of thought that none around him could penetrate. He was veiled to them, careless of their victory, the treasurer of a lifetime's secrets, remote and inviolable. His lips parted and his voice when he spoke was gentle, little more than a whisper, a fragile thing like a leaf in autumn; how could they think it was the voice of one who had sent men to their deaths and threatened the world with destruction?

"Qiyamatash zud miyad." His resurrection will come soon.

It was all he said. He had done with words. Without haste, he rose and leaned against the fuselage. A moment later and his hand had thrown back the handle of the emergency door. The door flew open with a sudden roar and the plane dipped sharply. Before Aharoni could stop him, the old man had thrown himself through the opening and was enveloped by the inky darkness and the cold that would kill him before he reached the ground.

The plane continued to fall while Aharoni struggled to close the gaping door. Suddenly, it gave and slammed to. Fighting with his controls, the pilot struggled to bring the little craft back to the horizontal as the mountains below rushed up to meet and crush it. At last, he regained control and the aircraft leveled out before resuming its ascent.

Peter Randall breathed again, but his heart continued to beat wildly. Had they won, or had the old man conquered after all? One missile had been launched. It would be enough if it reached its target. What, after all, could he or anyone do against the forces the Imam Hasan had unleashed? It was an ancient darkness and it bred in ancient places; it subsisted and it endured and its strength could not ultimately be broken. He and Fereshteh and men like Aharoni or Rastgu were merely lights flickering across its surface. The darkness resisted them, retreating for a while only to return, its force undiminished, its long shadows reaching out forever. Randall reached out in the darkness and held Fereshteh's hand.

EPILOGUE

World peace hung in the balance as Washington waited that day for word of further explosions. Three days before, Israeli intelligence had bypassed the CIA to make direct contact with the White House, explaining in detail what was happening. When the CIA was finally notified and asked by an angry President to explain, the Policy Committee described to him in detail the errors of judgment made by the official in charge of the matter, Howard Straker. Straker, however, had shot himself two days earlier and could not be brought to account. The committee explained that it had now taken steps to ensure that similar errors by individuals would be prevented in future. The President thanked them.

In several Western capitals, men and women waited anxiously for news. The USAF, RAF, and NATO detachments in Europe were placed on battle alert. In Europe and America, underground missile bases were put on red alert, while nuclear-armed bombers and submarines waited on the borders of Russia for orders. For a full hour that day, the world lived on borrowed time.

On 24 April 1980, eight RH-53D Sikorsky helicopters lifted off from the aircraft carrier *Nimitz* and headed northward, low over the southern coast of Iran. Several hours earlier, six C-130 Hercules transport planes had taken off from a military airfield near Cairo, flying low over the Red Sea and jamming Soviet radar installations in South Yemen and Ethiopia. They refueled on the Persian Gulf before heading across the sea, over the Iranian coast, and on into the heart of the country. On board the C-130s were ninety crew members and a further ninety commandos under Colonel Charles A. Beckwith. The commandos all belonged to the "Blue Light Squad," a special antiterrorist unit set up in 1977 at the U.S. Army base at Fort Bragg in

North Carolina. In overall command was Major General James Vaught, who was directing operations from an unspecified location in the Middle East.

The six airplanes and the helicopters—now reduced to six because of engine trouble sustained during a sandstorm—rendezvoused at a staging site near the village of Posht-e Badam, southeast of Tabas, the desert town destroyed some eighteen months earlier in one of Iran's worst earthquakes. "Desert One," as the staging site was known, had been built by the CIA shortly before the revolution. It was about three hundred miles from Tehran.

And then things began to go badly wrong. While refueling, a Sea Stallion helicopter collided with one of the C-130s, its rotors shearing through the fuel tank. The Hercules exploded. Three of its crew and five of the helicopter crew were killed. The survivors piled into the remaining planes and, leaving behind a helicopter and numerous documents, abandoned the mission. By 4:00 A.M. on Friday morning, only the charred remains of the Hercules, the Sikorskys, and the eight dead Americans remained for the Iranian forces to find.

The official version of the events at Desert One is known to everyone. President Carter, supported by various government spokesmen, publicly confessed that he had ordered a mission to rescue the hostages in Tehran which had tragically aborted. His humiliation was complete when, in November, the Americans put Ronald Reagan in the White House.

But how else could President Carter have explained the sending of a commando force into the Iranian desert—except by telling an improbable story involving a messianic sect, a plan to launch a holy war that would engulf the world, and a vision of the Apocalypse dating back to the Middle Ages and made real in the steel and uranium of nuclear-tipped missiles? Who would have believed that the operation had been launched in response to the request of an American field agent transmitted to the White House directly by Israeli intelligence? And who would have accepted that the real objective of the fatal mission lay not in far-off Tehran but less than two hundred miles from Desert One, in a secret missile base deep beneath the sands of the Dasht-e Lut, where enough uranium was still stored to arm the warheads of a dozen missiles?

On 17 September of that year, President Saddam Hussein of Iraq, addressing the Ba'athist National Assembly in Baghdad, formally declared the Algiers settlement between his country and Iran to be null and void. Five days later, fighting between the two countries broke out. The Gulf War had begun and the peace of the world again hung in the balance.

As Iraqi troops fought for control of the Shatt al-Arab waterway, a small dhow set sail from Mina Saud on the Saudi coast, just south of Kuwait. Preoccupied with the problems of controlling international shipping in the Gulf during the war, Saudi and Kuwaiti patrol boats ignored the tiny vessel as it slipped past supertankers and heavily laden merchant ships trying to avoid the Iranian coast. Light autumn winds brought it ashore outside Hisar, below Bandar Dilam. A young man dressed in white robes stepped onto the sand and the dhow returned to the sea. On a rise above the beach, a Land-Rover was waiting as arranged.

The days spent crouching in the tunnels beneath the Great Mosque had been the worst. They had been driven deeper and deeper into the subterranean passageways until, in the end, wretched and exhausted, they had been dragged out by the National Guard. All but one man had been taken, the very man they had sought above the rest. When that section of the mosque had been built, a channel had been constructed to carry water from the hills. Over the centuries, it had been repaired and rebuilt, but with the introduction of modern piping some years ago, it had now been allowed to fall into disuse. As the footsteps of the soldiers had sounded above them, making their steady approach, he had climbed into the channel seeking to lead his people out to freedom. But even as he crawled through the narrow tunnel, he had heard the sound of crashing rubble as the entrance collapsed. For more than a day, he had squeezed his emaciated body through the dark, narrow windings of the channel, never knowing when the roof might cave in and bury him alive. It had taken an immense will to fight against the suffocating panic of claustrophobia, and to keep rigid control over his muscles and his tiring brain. Several times he had collapsed from fatigue and hunger. But each time, recovering, he had crawled on, driven by a destiny he could not master.

At last he had emerged, filthy and desperately feeble, at the old entrance, over a dried-up stream. It was dark and he had been able to leave the tunnel mouth unobserved. Nearby, he had heard the tinkling of the diverted stream, and slowly and painfully, he made his way there to drink and wash. The moon rose shortly afterward, and he could determine where he was. Two miles away was a cache of food, clothing, arms, and money, one of several set up six months before in case of an emergency such as this. He made his way there slowly, a shadow beneath a gibbous moon.

Three days later, he had set off to cross again the sands of the Nafud, heading for the Gulf coast. Beardless now, and speaking in the dialect of the eastern Hasa province, he had gone by way of Riyadh, where he stayed for several months and sent some letters to "business associates" in Tehran. In late September he was in Mina Saud, making arrangements for the dhow that was to take him across to Iran.

Now, as he sat in the Land-Rover, headed for Bushehr on the first stage of the journey down the coast to Bandar Abbas where he would turn off toward Kerman, he allowed his thoughts to range once more over the plans he had conceived after his escape from Mecca. New Alamut would be rebuilt, perhaps even on the site of the original castle, high on a mountain to the north of Qazvin. There was time for rebuilding, time for all the things he had to do. Men would die, leaders and rulers above all: his assassins would be everywhere, and this time they would remain unseen and unknown until it was time for them to strike.

He had already laid his first plans. To begin with, two men must die: President Sadat, whose willingness to negotiate with the Israelis threatened to stabilize the conditions in the Middle East; and the new Pope, John Paul, whose international activities as a peacemaker could hold in check for some time those very forces the Mahdi wished to see unleashed. Men had already been chosen and orders given; when the moment was ripe, his emissaries would make their presence known.

In the west, behind him, the sun was setting, shrouded and invisible behind a great pall of dense black smoke belching skyward from the broken and burning oil refineries of Abadan and Khorramshahr. The war was still young, but already it had caused irrevocable damage to the region. He turned to look at the holocaust, smiling and confident. It was a sign from God, a divine token sent to assure him that, this time, he would fill the earth and the heavens and all that lay between them with fire and blood. And there would be no end to his dominion.